Praise for The Crown Conspiracy

The Crown Conspiracy took me on a breath-stealing, heart-stopping adventure through castles, Venice, and the Alps. Connie Mann's terrific novel is chock-full of fascinating layers of romance and intrigue amid a backdrop of art forgery that segues into a treasure hunt. Highly recommended!

COLLEEN COBLE, *USA Today* bestselling author

The story grips you with the first words and doesn't let go until the last page. I highly recommend this exciting thriller!

CARRIE STUART PARKS, Christy Award–winning author of *Fallout*

This novel will take you deep into a world of dangerous deception and a high-stakes conspiracy, where one woman must decide how far she will go to protect those she loves. The fast-paced action left me breathless!

DIANN MILLS, bestselling author of *Facing the Enemy*

Mann spins an intriguing action adventure with the kind of twists and turns that take the reader on an exciting ride. A delightful read.

RACHEL HAUCK, *New York Times* bestselling author

Consider me officially hooked! Connie Mann had me on the edge of my seat with her latest heart-pounding romantic suspense, *The Crown Conspiracy*! From page one, her clever blend of intrigue and action kept me glued to the page. I fell in love with Robin Hood art thief Sophie and investigator Mac (swoon!), watching the sparks fly between these two as they unearthed decades-old secrets while trying to stay alive. A riveting, rich story—I can't wait for their next adventure.

SUSAN MAY WARREN, *USA Today* bestselling and RITA Award–winning author

A SPERANZA TEAM NOVEL

Tyndale House Publishers
Carol Stream, Illinois

CONNIE MANN

A SPERANZA TEAM NOVEL

THE CROWN CONSPIRACY

Visit Tyndale online at tyndale.com.

Visit Connie Mann's website at conniemann.com.

Tyndale and Tyndale's quill logo are registered trademarks of Tyndale House Ministries.

The Crown Conspiracy

Designed by Sarah Susan Richardson

The Crown Conspiracy is a work of fiction. Where real people, events, establishments, organizations, or locales appear, they are used fictitiously. All other elements of the novel are drawn from the author's imagination.

For information about special discounts for bulk purchases, please contact Tyndale House Publishers at csresponse@tyndale.com, or call 1-855-277-9400.

Library of Congress Cataloging-in-Publication Data

A catalog record for this book is available from the Library of Congress.

ISBN 978-1-4964-8738-4 (HC)

ISBN 978-1-4964-8739-1 (SC)

Printed in the United States of America

30	29	28	27	26	25	24
7	6	5	4	3	2	1

For every woman who has dreamed of being part
of a team that could change the world.
May we be brave enough to build a Speranza Team of our own—
and have the courage to step out together and make a difference.

Hope is an anchor for the soul.

PROLOGUE

She ran down the quiet streets, her fine leather slippers making no sound on the worn cobblestones. She skidded past another alley and risked a quick look over her shoulder. At this time of night, most everyone in the coastal village would be safely tucked into their beds. No footsteps fell behind her, but the unmistakable certainty she was being followed forced her to make haste. Her breath rasped in the frosty air as she hurried on, feeling time tick away with every heartbeat. The darkness of the new moon helped to hide her, but it also meant she was out of time.

The ship would sail with the tide.

A block away from the smithy, she stopped and pulled the heavy boots she'd been carrying over her slippers. She tugged her cap lower and secured the square of rough fabric hiding her face, then wiped a sweaty palm over the trousers and shirt she'd taken from one of the young stable hands.

When she reached the blacksmith's forge, she swung the heavy wooden door open, cringing at the squeak of rusty hinges. The

1

smithy glanced up as she slipped into the courtyard, his work-weary eyes narrowed, swarthy skin glistening with sweat, then stuck the metal rod back into the glowing coals.

"Come back tomorrow." He pulled the metal out and set it on the anvil, where it pulsed with heat and light. His hammer rang against the glowing iron circle at the end, flattening it.

She kept her voice pitched low, raspy. "My master needs them now. I can't return without them."

He held the glowing round emblem up with tongs, the two-inch circle displaying an anchor with a feather superimposed across its center. Her breath caught. It was exactly right.

"I need time to finish the others."

"There is no more time," she hissed. As if to underscore her words, running footsteps and clanking weapons sounded outside. They made no attempt at stealth or silence.

The smithy's face paled in the light of the forge. "Go. Now."

He plunged the emblem into a bucket of water, where the iron hissed and sputtered. Quickly, he grabbed another metal rod and stuck it into the fire, eyes darting from it to the door and back again as he pretended he was hard at work.

Her heart pounded, eyes focused on the bucket. She couldn't leave without the emblem. Too many lives depended on it.

The footsteps stopped outside the gate. "Open up!"

She leaped toward the bucket and plunged her hand inside, closing her fist around the metal. The searing pain dropped her to her knees, but she bit back an agonized cry and struggled to her feet.

She had to get to the ship.

She spun and raced across the courtyard, then grabbed the handle of a small door set in the opposite wall with her uninjured hand.

Locked.

The gate burst open and armed men charged in.

Frantic, she looked up and spotted a window high on the wall. She clambered up several storage crates, flung the shutter open, and swung a leg over the sill.

"There!" someone shouted, pointing upward.

She was too high, but she had no choice, so she swung her other leg over and dropped to the ground. She lost her footing as she fell and slid on her palms. A groan escaped as her burned flesh was torn away and the emblem rolled into the filthy gutter.

One of the soldiers poked his gun through the opening above. She scrambled to her feet and scooped the metal circle into her mangled palm as the ground exploded with gunfire around her.

Blood pounded in her ears and kept pace in her palm as she raced toward the docks. She yanked the square of cloth off her face and wrapped her hand, trying to stanch the flow of blood. She wouldn't leave such an easy trail for them to follow.

She turned down a dark alley and skidded to a halt. Dead end. She'd turned too soon. The voices behind her got louder, so she flattened herself into a shadowed doorway until they ran past. Breath heaving, she peeked out the alley and circled around a different way, cursing her own foolishness. She didn't have time for mistakes.

Once she reached the waterfront, the lanterns along the gangplank tempted her to run headlong in that direction. But that way lay certain death.

Instead, she took a sharp left and hurried to the very last row of slips, where the young stable hand whose clothes she'd borrowed waited at the oars of a rowboat. "Ready, mistress?" he whispered.

"No titles, no names," she reminded him. He nodded, Adam's apple bobbing as he glanced behind him.

She followed his gaze, saw the men rounding the corner toward the docks. "Hurry."

He leaned on the oars and she moved in front of him, grabbing the second set. When she put her injured hand on the oar, she swayed as another wave of dizziness hit, but she couldn't give up now. Too many lives were at stake.

"I can do it," he whispered, when a whimper escaped her throat.

She nodded but set her hands on the oars anyway, pulling with all her strength. They had to move fast.

They slipped through the water, hidden in the shadows of the other vessels, and made their way to the port side of the cargo ship, which faced the open water and wasn't visible from shore.

A stiff breeze blew off the water tonight, and it smacked the rowboat into the wooden side of the ship with a loud thump. They glanced at each other, frozen, then let out a little sigh of relief as a rope ladder descended from the darkness above.

Seconds later, someone started climbing down toward them. The stable boy kept the rowboat steady while she helped the trembling teenage girl aboard. "Crouch down and don't make a sound," she hissed when gratitude and fear tumbled from the girl's lips.

After what was probably less than ten minutes, but felt like four days, all six young women were aboard. The rope ladder disappeared back aboard ship, and she and the boy pushed off from the side and rowed back the way they had come. They moved as fast as they dared, as quietly as they could.

Sweat ran down her neck and her hand kept slipping off the oar, blood soaking through the makeshift bandage. The pain made her eyes tear and stomach roil. She gritted her teeth. She could pass out later.

A quick look over her shoulder at the ship they just left showed the armed men marching up the gangplank, lanterns and weapons held aloft. The wind carried the sound of raised voices. The captain stood at the rail trying to placate them, making calming gestures, voice firm and unruffled. Seconds later, a muffled scream rang out, then more cries of pain and an ominous splash. One of the girls in the rowboat let out a terrified squeak, and another quickly silenced her with a palm over her mouth.

Her uncle had discovered her plan. Retribution would be swift and deadly.

She and the boy rowed with all their might, the extra weight adding precious minutes to the return trip. Minutes they didn't have.

As they neared the last row of slips, she whispered, "Keep going." The boy nodded, young face pale with terror and determination.

They pulled up in the shallow water just past the dock, and she scrambled over the side into frigid, waist-deep water. He joined her and they helped the girls to shore. They shivered in the cold air, their breath making puffy clouds in front of them.

She moved to the oldest of the girls, slipped the emblem from her trouser pocket, and wiped the blood off with her shirt. She handed it over, folding the girl's hands around it. "Stick to the woods and go up into the hills. You will see the monastery. Wait until dark tomorrow and make your way there. Show this to the sisters. They will help you."

The girl looked at the emblem, then back up. "What does it mean?"

"*Speranza.*" Hope.

The girl threw her arms around her and sobbed.

She pulled the arms away, turned to the group. "You must hurry. Go. And don't look back."

The oldest girl kissed the emblem and closed her fist around it, then took off running, the other girls hurrying to keep up.

"We must go, mistress," her stable hand whispered, shivering.

She turned, looked behind her. The ship was on fire, flames shooting into the sky. "You must flee as well, before they find you."

He straightened his narrow shoulders, jaw set. "I stay with you."

"No! If you want to help me, run! As fast and as far as you can." She gave him a shove in the same direction as the girls.

The sounds of pursuit grew louder, the night growing brighter from the raging fire. He glanced past her shoulder, finally gave a reluctant nod, and disappeared into the cover of the trees.

She took off in the opposite direction, toward town, the only way she knew to save them.

They caught her as she tried to slip into the shadows of the cathedral on the square.

Arms grabbed her roughly from behind, spun her around, and shoved her against the stone walls of the church. "Where are the girls?" The voice was a deep, menacing growl. His grip tightened until she feared her bones would break. "Where are they?" he shouted.

She raised her chin and held her silence. First fists, then clubs beat her until she collapsed on the hallowed ground, looking up at the inky blackness above. As her vision dimmed and her life-blood slipped away, she glanced over at the emblem burned into her palm, and the whisper of a smile spread on her lips. The girls would be safe.

Speranza.

1

Sophie Williams paced the darkened living room of her third-floor Munich apartment, listening to an icy December rain pounding on the slate roof, the swish of water as the occasional car drove by, the irregular beat of her heart. In the hour before dawn, the last of the tourists had finally staggered off to nearby hotels. Most locals hadn't started the new day yet.

But not everyone slept.

With the tip of one finger, she parted the aged curtains again, slowly, just far enough to study the quiet street below.

She waited. Watched.

There.

The glowing tip of a cigarette flickered in the doorway of the apartment building across the street, two doors down.

She'd spotted him earlier, farther down the block. Dismissed him as someone stepping outside for a late-night smoke.

She'd been wrong.

The realization that she'd been followed jolted her, like the unexpected blaring of a security alarm whose trigger she'd missed.

He was getting closer. Braver.

She calculated how much time she had. Would he act before she had a chance to herself?

Not if she could help it. She stepped back, sifting through possibilities. Whatever his agenda, she knew her next play. She had to protect the painting. For Lise's sake.

She hurried to her studio.

The portrait lay face up on the desk, exactly as she'd left it.

A sound from the street had her heart beating triple time, but no bullet shattered the antique glass window. No one forced their way in at gunpoint.

Yet.

She grabbed the roll of brown paper and expertly wrapped the painting with the speed of long practice, the swish of paper the only noise.

Within ten minutes, she'd stepped into the Boho artist persona she used when she came and went from her apartment. Shoulder-length curly red wig, ripped jeans and a flowing blouse, cowboy boots, and a battered beret. *Ensure people only see what you want them to see* was one of her mantras.

She slipped a lined raincoat on, grabbed her favorite leather tote, and tucked several disguises and toiletries inside, then secreted her best tools of the trade in the false bottom. She opened her wallet and sighed. She'd spent the last of her cash at the coffee shop yesterday. She raided the emergency stash inside her hollowed-out copy of *Robin Hood*, giving it a pat before she tucked it back on the shelf. If she had a patron saint, it was Robin.

She slid her knife into her boot and tucked her umbrella under one arm.

"Come on, Lise. Where are you?" Sophie muttered when another call to her friend's phone went straight to voice mail.

Was she too late?

On her way out the door, she kissed her fingers and pressed them to the small portrait hanging there, as always.

She whispered a prayer for courage, grabbed the wrapped

painting, then strolled toward her favorite café as if she didn't have a care in the world.

The rain had let up, so she heard his footsteps behind her, keeping pace but not getting too close. She began to sweat in her rain jacket.

Would they try to grab her right off the street?

She'd find out soon enough. She kept walking.

A quick peek in a shop window confirmed he was gaining on her. She quickened her pace, then gave up all pretense of stealth and darted through an alley and sprinted across two lanes of traffic on the always-busy main thoroughfare.

Breaks squealed. Drivers honked, but she didn't slow, zigzagging around them. Breath heaving, she hurried three more blocks before she chanced a glance over her shoulder and allowed herself a quick sigh of relief when she didn't see him.

She turned back around and collided with a man who stepped from a darkened doorway wearing a 5:00 shadow at 7:00 a.m. He grabbed her arm and jabbed a gun against her side, his body hiding her from passersby.

Hired thug, no doubt. She clutched the painting in one hand, trying to maneuver her umbrella into position with the other. Perhaps she had one last surprise in store for him.

A ball cap hid his face, but his low growl was clear as day.

"Scream and you die right here."

2

"*Zeitung*, Frau Bauernstein?" The driver handed her a copy of *Der Spiegel* over the back of the seat. They'd been inching their way up the mansion's curving driveway behind a long line of high-end vehicles, the slow drag of cars more drawn out than the old Frau at her building's drag of her morning *Zigarette*.

"*Danke Shön.*" Sophie Williams closed a gloved hand around the newspaper. One glance at the headline reflected in the lamps along the drive and she muttered an unladylike word. When the driver's eyes widened in the rearview mirror, she carefully smoothed her features as she scanned the article. Maybe, just maybe, Lise had a point when she'd urged Sophie to lie low.

Interpol Steps Up Search for Elusive Robin Hood Art Thief

Sophie couldn't believe their client had gushed her excitement over the return of her mother's beloved painting to an investigative reporter, of all people. Especially after Sophie had stressed—over and over and over again—the need for confidentiality. What happened to German stoicism and closed-mouth discretion?

Jaw clenched, she smoothed out the pages she'd unconsciously crumpled and laid the paper on the leather seat beside her. She wasn't a thief. Thieves stole things for their own gain. She replaced previously stolen artwork with expertly forged copies and returned the originals to their rightful owners. Why didn't people—especially law enforcement—understand the difference? She wasn't committing crimes. She was righting wrongs.

The burner phone she carried on retrieval nights buzzed with an incoming text from Lise's burner phone. **Don't worry about bringing the gift to the party tonight. Just come early and we'll get it later.**

Which was code for: abort the mission. Sophie's jaw firmed. **Thanks, but I have to run an errand first. I'll see you later, as planned.**

When her phone immediately buzzed again, Sophie turned off the ringer and tucked it into her iPad case. She wouldn't let Lise's worry change her mind. True, the timing of the article was decidedly inconvenient, but it was too late to turn back now. Sophie had given her word to retrieve the Limbergers' painting, which meant it had to be tonight. It was not only the perfect opportunity; it might be her *only* opportunity.

When their Mercedes finally arrived under a massive portico, the driver opened the rear door and Sophie placed her gloved hand in his as she stepped out, all grace and elegance. She averted her gaze from the reporters' strobing flashes as she smoothed the skirt of her floor-length designer gown over her Mary Janes. Not her preferred footwear for a ball, but oh-so-practical for tonight.

Shoulders back, she cleared her mind and became Edith Bauernstein, a sixty-year-old wealthy society matron. As she strode up the walkway to the Flasks' elegant three-story mansion, Sophie tightened her faux mink stole against the chill and feigned impatience at the snaking line at security. Foot tapping, she scanned the mansion, noting the lights glittering from all fourteen windows. Ground lighting illuminated several paths, and she cataloged the exact location of every entrance and exit.

When it was her turn, she handed the tuxedoed doorman her invitation, her chin jutted at a haughty angle. He studied her a moment before scanning the list on his clipboard. A little shiver of excitement slid down her spine, and she fought a smile. Call her crazy, but she loved this part: the adrenaline rush, the glitz and glamour, but mostly she loved tiptoeing along the razor's edge of discovery and coming out the other side with a grin and a bow.

She raised an eyebrow as he flipped pages, then glanced behind her before meeting her gaze. "Is Herr Bauernstein not accompanying you tonight, Frau Bauernstein?"

Sophie tightened her grip on her wrap and patted her stylish gray wig, the emerald on her gloved finger flashing green fire. "Sadly—" she threw her voice just a bit—"Herr Bauernstein isn't feeling well this evening." Which might be true. Her research confirmed the Bauernsteins were on a monthlong cruise somewhere in the Mediterranean. "We've never missed the annual auction, so he insisted I come without him. It's such a worthy cause."

She widened her eyes behind cat's-eye glasses and glanced nervously at the crowd visible through the wide front doors. She leaned in slightly and confided, "But after forty years of marriage, I'm not quite sure how to navigate this without Herr Bauernstein at my side."

The doorman's guarded expression softened instantly. "I'm sure you'll be quite all right." He hesitated, then pointed to an iPad nestled in an oversized, bedazzled leather cover dangling from her wrist. The fake emeralds and diamonds she'd glued along the edges were quite eye-catching, if she did say so herself. "I apologize, but I must check your bag while you step through security. A mere formality, you understand, but necessary in these times."

"Of course." Sophie handed it over and ignored the little trip in her heartbeat as he opened the leather cover, checked that the iPad was turned on, then opened the zippered compartment and pawed through her toiletry bag, glanced at the phone.

She walked through the metal detector, breathing easier when he handed everything back with a smile. She slid the leather straps over her arm, patted the case. "I've finally learned to operate this newfangled contraption and quite like the ease with which bids can be made." She put a smile in her voice. "And I do love the camera feature. The tiny buttons on my old digital were a trial."

"Technology is certainly making life easier."

You have no idea.

"Do you still require a paper catalog?" He took one from the stack beside him.

She patted the case again and winked. "I have it safely downloaded right here."

He murmured, "Enjoy your evening," and was greeting the next guest before she'd finished speaking.

Hurdle number one, check. She strolled into the grand entry and pretended she didn't notice the incredible multilevel chandelier sparkling like a thousand jewels above her.

Her pace deliberate, she entered the ballroom, then paused and carefully studied the white table linens and elegant centerpieces, taking note of the evergreen boughs and poinsettias surrounding multiple floating candles. If she were unexpectedly forced to make inane chitchat, the decor always provided a handy fallback. Which she definitely preferred over deadly-boring discussions of the weather. When she played a part, she played it exactly right.

She wandered the room, examining the auction items displayed on long tables around the perimeter. Paintings stood on easels, while expensive jewelry and artifacts glittered behind locked glass cases. "Beautiful, isn't it?" She stepped up behind an older woman and pointed a gloved hand toward the painting Lise had donated.

The tiny birdlike matron, who looked to be in her nineties, nodded, though it was a wonder she could lift her head, what with the spectacular emerald-and-diamond choker circling her neck. She grinned and hitched her chin toward the painting entitled *Daydreaming*. "If all goes well, this lovely lady will be coming home with me tonight."

She winked, surprising a laugh out of Sophie. The voluptuous, mostly naked Renaissance woman reclining on a settee with a sultry look in her eye seemed at odds with this lady's regal, buttoned-up appearance.

"Good luck." Sophie smiled.

As the woman wandered away, Sophie pulled out her iPad and almost whistled at the most recent bid on *Daydreaming*. With that many zeroes, the woman would most certainly win the bid. Which was very good for *Neue Anfänge*, "New Beginnings," the local non-profit Lise helped to run that would benefit from tonight's auction. Sophie took several pictures of the painting before moving to the next, all while surreptitiously studying the ballroom. It didn't take long to locate the four security guards on duty. Since Lise's Fortier Art Gallery was also one of the evening's sponsors, no one had batted an eye at Lise's questions about event security.

Twenty minutes later, Sophie tucked her iPad over her arm and marched toward the sweeping staircase that led to the gallery over-looking the ballroom.

If you look like you know where you're going, nobody will question your presence.

———

Brody "Mac" McKenzie leaned a shoulder against one of the many columns that dotted the ballroom floor, analyzing the crowd, lazy smile on display. He was here at his mother's request, the plus-one of a German socialite whose father and Mac's late father had become friends back when Dad was stationed at the German embassy. Elke had pecked his cheek after they walked in, said she'd see him later, and disappeared into the crowd.

When she was ready to leave, she'd seek him out. In the mean-time, he raised his champagne glass in response to various smol-dering glances sent his way, but he pretended not to notice the seductive invitations behind the smiles.

Would the so-called Robin Hood thief strike tonight?

It seemed the sort of event conducive to his or her work, and the idea of someone returning stolen artwork to its rightful own-ers intrigued him. It was the exact opposite of his usual cases.

Apparently, it intrigued Interpol as well, since his contact there had offered a hefty finder's fee for information that led to the capture of the elusive thief. Given the exorbitant cost of his mother's experimental cancer treatments, Mac figured this was the perfect place to start looking.

As the crowd swelled, he shifted positions, his gaze on the activity surrounding the auction items. He spotted two society matrons chatting, one significantly older than the other. Were they mother and daughter? Both dripped with jewels and were impeccably dressed. The younger one pointed to a painting, and Mac's attention was snared by her old-fashioned elbow-length gloves and the graceful way she gestured, emeralds flashing on her fingers. She tucked the fur stole tighter around her shoulders, then suddenly threw her head back and laughed at something the older woman said.

That laugh tugged at something deep inside him, as though he'd heard it before. Or maybe it reminded him of someone, though he couldn't for the life of him think who. He would have shrugged off the weird sense of déjà vu, had she not blasted her companion with another blinding smile and teasing wink before she turned away.

He set his glass on a passing waiter's tray and straightened the line of his black tuxedo jacket as he followed her toward the grand staircase in the corner. He wanted to hear that laugh again, see if his memory conjured up why it seemed so familiar.

He quietly slipped behind her as she started up the carpeted stairs. When she lifted her skirts so she wouldn't trip, his eyes widened. He was at the perfect angle to catch a brief look.

Those shapely calves weren't typical for a woman in her sixties. Neither was the colorful tattoo above her ankle that looked like a . . . lizard? Though he supposed the sturdy-looking, low-heeled shoes might be worn under a designer ball gown.

His investigator's instincts twitched, and he hid a smile as he followed her at a discreet distance.

His evening had just gotten a lot more interesting.

Sophie hurried up the stairs, eager to make the switch, then caught herself and grimaced. She couldn't break character in even the smallest detail. She slowed her pace and reached for the banister, pausing every few steps as though to catch her breath.

A shiver of awareness slid down her back, and she glanced over her shoulder. The few people heading up behind her didn't seem to be paying her the slightest attention, but that didn't quiet the instinct that said she was being watched.

Once she reached the gallery, she took a few minutes to study the guests crowding the ballroom below, but nobody stood out. She'd just have to be more careful than usual. She noted the guards' positions around the perimeter, then turned and wandered the long corridor, studying the various family portraits lining the walls. She smiled and nodded to several couples who appeared to be doing the same.

It took only seconds to locate the security guard patrolling this area. If his bulky frame hadn't given it away, the shoulder holster ruining the line of his suit jacket would have. Watching him from the corner of her eye, she meandered to the last room on the right, gripped the doorknob with her gloved hand, and let the door swing closed behind her.

She shook her head as she studied the gold fixtures and marble countertops. Only the ultrawealthy would install a multiseat bathroom in a private home. A quick peek under the stall doors confirmed she was alone. She removed the lid from the trash can, grabbed the trash bag, and retrieved the duplicate picture frame, screwdriver, and mounting brackets hidden below it. She let out a small sigh of relief. Lise had come through, as always.

Once she'd set the trash bin to rights, Sophie went into one of the stalls and used the drop-down handbag shelf as a makeshift worktable. With quick, sure movements, she pulled out her iPad and removed the painting hidden inside the oversize cover. These custom-made evening gloves had cost the earth, but they were worth every penny. She slid the canvas inside the frame and used the screwdriver to secure the mounting brackets.

She wrapped the screwdriver in hand towels and hid it in the trash can, then fluffed her gray wig and walked out of the room, holding the iPad in front of her, the painting hidden behind it, both tucked against her chest. A quick check over the gallery railing showed the guard heading downstairs, right on schedule.

Which meant she had less than five minutes. She turned from the gallery and strolled back down the long hallway where the family's portraits and personal artwork adorned the walls.

Plenty of time.

When the woman entered what appeared to be a powder room, Mac ducked into a handy alcove where he could watch for her without being seen. He casually perused the artwork covering every available wall, surprised at the caliber of some of the paintings. There were some museum-quality pieces, yet several hung between what appeared to be flea-market finds and cheap knockoffs. Interesting.

He quickly turned his back when she stepped into the hallway, pretending intense interest in a lovely landscape. He waited, expecting her to return to the party downstairs. When she headed deeper into the mansion instead, a little kick of excitement pricked him as he followed.

Had he found Robin Hood?

Sophie's heart rate picked up speed as she wandered toward her target. This was where all her planning and preparation came together. She opened the cover of the iPad and pretended to take photos of various paintings that lined the walls, her back always to the security cameras. Lise had assured her there were no motion sensors. Just cameras.

Child's play.

When she finally reached the painting she sought, Sophie pushed her glasses farther up her nose and leaned closer, holding the iPad up until it almost touched the frame, murmuring her praises of the composition, use of color. She backed up, fumbled a bit for effect, and took fake pictures from a different angle, inching ever closer.

Finally, she moved all the way in, completely blocking the painting from view, and in a lightning-quick maneuver she'd spent hours perfecting, she slid the painting off the wall and replaced it with the one she'd been holding behind her iPad.

Then she casually walked back to the restroom. She ducked into a stall and quickly slid the painting inside the leather cover, zipped it into place, then slid the iPad in beside it.

A piercing shriek sounded from outside.

Not good. Sophie raced out of the room, eyes wide. "What's happening?"

Ahead of her, an older couple seemed equally bewildered, hurrying toward the stairs. She caught up to them in two long strides. "Do you know what's going on?"

"I don't know," the gentleman shouted, his hand on the woman's elbow. "Some kind of alarm."

"Oh, my ears," the woman cried, clapping her hands over them.

"Turn off your hearing aids," he yelled.

Sophie took the woman's other elbow and kept her head down as though watching her feet.

As the three of them hurried down the stairs, all four security guards passed them, rushing in the opposite direction, shouting into their radios.

They were halfway down when the alarm finally stopped shrieking, and everyone in the vicinity let out a collective sigh of relief.

A smooth male voice came through the speakers on the raised platform in the corner of the ballroom below. "Ladies and gentlemen, all is well. It was a false alarm. Kindly help yourselves to more hors d'oeuvres and join us on the dance floor." He nodded to the band leader, who raised his baton. The familiar strains of a waltz filled the room.

Sophie and her companions continued their descent. Another half dozen steps and they'd reach the ballroom floor and one of the handy French doors that led to the outside.

As her foot touched the last tread, a firm hand wrapped around her upper arm and a deep masculine voice murmured, "May I have the honor of this dance?"

Sophie froze at the steel under the whiskey-smooth voice but kept her bland smile in place as she glanced over her shoulder. All the breath backed up in her lungs, and it took every ounce of her acting skills not to react.

Under normal circumstances, being approached by an incredibly handsome blue-eyed, black-haired, tuxedo-clad man would have tempted her to step closer, certainly flirt a little. Instead, the questions and sharp intelligence in his eyes froze every brain cell for crucial seconds, and she barely kept from stammering like an idiot.

Stay in character. He can't possibly know who you are.

Sophie forced a flirty smile. "Why, young man, you certainly know how to charm an old lady."

He grinned, showing off the deep dimple in his chin. "Not old, wise. And beautiful. Shall we?"

Don't look in his eyes. Just play your part. It's fine. "You remind me of Herr Bauernstein, with your gallantry."

"A compliment, to be sure." He bowed. "Mac McKenzie, at your service." Dozens of couples were already moving in time to the music as he led her onto the dance floor, then turned and held out his hand, clear challenge in his gaze. "Frau Bauernstein?"

Sophie kept her gaze on his chin and nodded as she placed her hand in his much larger one. Through the thin gloves, she felt the ridges on his palm, calluses that said he did more than sit at a desk. She wouldn't risk looking into those blue eyes, afraid of giving herself away, supremely conscious of her own colored contacts.

Without a word, he put his other hand at her waist and spun them into the waltz, his easy grace proving he'd done this many,

many times before. She gripped his shoulder, so tempted to get swept into the fantasy, just for a few minutes. Instead, she kept her mind on her steps lest she trip over her gown. Every time he inched her closer, she eased back, keeping a respectable distance between them. The way her heart was pounding, she worried he could hear it—or feel it—through the padding.

It took the rest of her concentration to will her muscles to relax, gliding in time to the music, pretending she danced with handsome men in swanky ballrooms every single weekend. When the waltz neared its conclusion and he hadn't tossed out a single accusation, she let out a small sigh of relief.

He leaned close and whispered in her ear, "One has to wonder why a rich matron has the legs of a thirty-year-old and is wearing such practical footwear under her ball gown."

Her heart slammed against her rib cage. At least he wasn't asking why he'd seen her in the vicinity where the alarm had gone off. Or was that merely a ruse and he was undercover security?

She schooled her features into a haughty expression and looked down her nose at him, which was hard since he towered over her. "Herr McKenzie, didn't your mother teach you it's incredibly rude to peek under ball gowns?"

He quirked a brow, shot her a cheeky grin. "She taught me curiosity, among other things." He twirled her out and back, eyes steady on her face all the way.

Sophie's mind raced as she collided with his chest, and he held her close. Even if he suspected she wasn't who she said . . . Scratch that. Even if he knew for sure she wasn't who she *said*, he had no way of knowing who she *was*.

Play the part.

She arched a brow. "Never underestimate the value of regular exercise, young man. Or the lengths a woman of a certain age will go to for comfort. I have suffered enough pinched toes for three lifetimes."

Mac threw his head back and laughed, attracting several admiring glances, but his knowing smile sent a shiver down her spine.

When he drew her another inch closer, Sophie eased another step back, ignoring how good he smelled. Or the way the sound of his voice touched something deep inside her. Too much was at stake.

When the waltz finally, mercifully ended, she nodded once. "Thank you for a lovely dance, young man. Now if you'll excuse me." She slipped from his grasp and started to turn away.

He stepped into her path, and she froze, ready to run. He leaned over to whisper, "I don't know what you're up to . . . madam. But I intend to find out."

His threat echoed in her ears as Sophie turned and melted into the crowd. She wove her way across the room, then ducked behind a column to see if he was behind her. Fifteen minutes and two long hallways later, she slipped out a side door.

She casually meandered down a brick walkway, then stepped through a wrought-iron gate to the sidewalk and wandered down the street. At the end of the block, she eased into the shadows of a building and looked back the way she'd come. Not two minutes later, Mac stepped out the mansion's front door, spotlighted by one of the many lanterns. Hands on his slim hips, he scanned the area, taking his time, studying each bush and shrub as though it wasn't pitch black beyond the lights. When he glanced toward her hiding place, he suddenly went very still, as though he could see her in the gloom.

Sophie's heart hammered in her ears as she waited, plastered against a rough brick wall. Finally, one side of his mouth quirked up in a grin and he shot her a two-fingered salute before he turned and walked back into the ballroom.

Relieved, she started to slide down the wall but stiffened her legs just in time. The dress cost too much to ruin over a man. Especially a gorgeous, suspicious, aggravating man. She took a deep breath, then another, before she stepped from her hiding place.

She glanced at her watch and picked up her pace. She had another stop to make before she headed back to Lise's gallery.

3

FORTIER ART GALLERY—MUNICH

After 10:00 p.m., the art gallery was still thronged with people when Sophie slipped down the hall from Lise's office, her art gallery manager persona in place, the designer gown carefully hidden in the back of the closet. She'd pulled her crushed blonde hair into a low ponytail, popped out the colored contacts, and added dangling earrings. Once she slipped into a light-blue blazer, pencil skirt, and sky-high heels, she looked the part exactly. "I'm sorry I'm late, Frau Fortier," she murmured as she stepped up behind her friend.

Lise spun around, hazel eyes flashing with annoyance before relief flooded in. "Oh, thank—"

At Sophie's warning look, Lise caught herself and smiled, leaning up to kiss first one cheek, then the other. "I was getting worried you wouldn't be able to make tonight's showing."

"Nothing could keep me away," Sophie said with a wink and a grin, snagging a glass of wine from a passing waiter. Details would come later. Right now, they each had a role to play. "That dress is fabulous, by the way."

22

Lise never hesitated to use her charm and striking good looks to get people to open their wallets, both to buy artwork and to support Neue Anfänge. She'd kicked things up a notch tonight. Her short blonde bob was slicked back, and her slim figure was draped in a shimmery, knee-length aquamarine dress designed to draw attention.

"I found it at my favorite boutique last week." Lise swallowed hard and furiously blinked back sudden tears. "I should have been visiting *Mutti*."

"Don't do that to yourself, Lise. You had no way of knowing what would happen."

When Lise's mother, who resided at an assisted-living facility in Austria, had begged her to come visit, Lise had put her off due to the gallery opening. The next day, her mother had died of a heart attack while boarding a train for Munich. Presumably to see Lise. The private burial, with only Lise and Sophie in attendance, had been yesterday.

Sophie studied her friend's slumped shoulders and the dark circles under her eyes that makeup couldn't hide. "I should have rescheduled. You need time to grieve."

"I wouldn't have let you." Lise nodded toward the two artists posing together while a magazine photographer snapped photo after photo. "They've been waiting so long for this night. I couldn't disappoint them."

Sophie glanced around the crowded gallery, the harpist playing in the background, black-clothed catering staff circling with drinks. The two artists Lise had debuted definitely looked over-the-moon excited and were flying high on champagne and success. The young woman, who had a spectacularly bold, impressionistic style, was now chatting with several gallery regulars. The young man, with his shy, awkward demeanor, was causing quite a stir among the ladies since his Renaissance-style paintings were decidedly risqué. The one Lise had purchased and donated to the Flasks' auction tonight had garnered similar attention.

"I appreciate you looking out for me, Soph, but there's no need."

Lise patted Sophie's cheek like she was a child. "Someday, when you finally let me show your work, I won't let anything stop me then either."

Sophie jerked her chin away and narrowed her eyes. "Nice try. I told you, I don't show—"

The bell on the front door jangled merrily.

"I'm not giving up, you know. You're too talented." Lise arched an eyebrow, then searched her eyes. "Everything went well?"

Sophie checked to be sure no one was close enough to overhear. "It was fine. An unexpected alarm went off after the switch, but I don't expect a problem."

Lise studied her. "And?"

"And what?" Her face heated at the memory of Mac McKenzie scanning her from head to toe.

"You're hiding something."

This was what happened when you'd been friends forever. "I'm just tired." Which was true, if not the whole story. After she'd wound her way around the city to the clients' home, 95 percent sure he hadn't followed, she'd carefully disabled the security system and returned the painting to its place of honor on their living room wall. From there, she'd taken another roundabout route back here to change into the clothes she'd stashed in the office earlier. Constant vigilance and the inevitable adrenaline crash afterward had sapped her energy.

Lise studied her a moment longer. "Well, I'm glad you're here. Let's go chat with some happy artists."

If for one split second Sophie longed to be one of them, she didn't let herself think about it. She had far more important work to do. Like tonight. She'd righted another wrong, balanced the scales. Painting was something she did for other people.

They circled the room, gratified by the many SOLD signs affixed to the paintings. "You need to eat something," Sophie said when they reached the hors d'oeuvres table in the back room. She shoved a plate filled with cheese and crackers in Lise's direction.

Suddenly, Henri burst into the room, half hidden behind the

large, wrapped painting he was carrying. "This just came for you, *mon ami*. Special delivery." The thin forty-year-old man had worked for Lise for years, his mercurial personality a constant source of frustration and amusement. He propped the painting up on the sideboard, grinning like a kid at Christmas, just as he did whenever they got a new acquisition. "This came with it." He handed Lise a manila envelope.

She glanced at it, paled slightly at the name of the law firm, and then slid her finger under the flap. She pulled out a long silver chain with a medallion on it, and her eyes filled with tears. Lise slipped it over her head and ran her fingers over the round disk. "It was my mother's."

Sophie stepped closer, studied the simple design. Inside the circle was an anchor, with a feather embossed diagonally across it. "It's lovely."

Lise pulled out a typewritten letter next, the color draining from her face as she read. Slowly, she slid a second envelope from the larger one, her name handwritten on the outside. From the way her hands trembled, Sophie guessed it was from her mother.

Lise took a deep breath and slid the smaller envelope into a hidden pocket of her dress. "I'll look at this later." Then she pushed the lawyer's letter into the sideboard drawer and raised her chin.

"Open it, open it." Henri nodded toward the painting, vibrating with anticipation.

"We have other things to do tonight, Henri," Lise said firmly, reaching for the painting. "We'll put it in the safe and look at it tomorr—"

The words slipped from her mouth just as Henri, impatient as ever, ripped the brown paper from the 30 x 25-inch frame. As he parted the edges, he froze, dumbstruck. "It can't be," he whispered, pulling the rest of the paper away.

Lise gasped and Sophie's jaw dropped open in shock. No, it couldn't be. But it was.

Behind them, Geoff, the young artist, chose that moment to thrust his head through the swinging double doors. "Li—"

He stopped midword when he spotted the painting. "Whoa. Is that . . . ?" Geoff turned, his normal bass voice pitched high, and called out for Althea, the other debut artist.

Behind him, more heads appeared. Excited whispers rose in a chorus of disbelief. Sophie turned to see people rushing farther into the room to get a better view, all with their cell phones out, snapping pictures. She stepped between them and the painting, trying to block their view. "No pictures. Please. No pictures. You must leave now."

A flash went off and Sophie looked up to see the reporter they'd invited to the opening taking photo after photo. "Please, sir." She started in his direction. He snapped several more pictures of the painting, then spun and took one of her. He shot her a triumphant grin and disappeared.

Lise finally shook herself out of her shock, and the two of them herded the guests back into the other room. But the damage had been done.

There could be no going back.

"I'm sorry, I'm sorry," Henri muttered, dogging Lise's heels like a puppy who'd just peed on the rug.

She stopped, held up a hand. "Enough. Start quietly moving our guests toward the exit, hmm?"

Sophie waited until he was gone before she stepped in front of Lise, gripped both her hands. "Are you all right?"

Lise nodded once, sharply. She held herself so stiffly, Sophie worried she'd snap in half. "I will be fine. Please. Help Henri."

"Of course." Sophie squeezed her hands, then released them. "Everything will be fine." But they both knew it was a lie. This painting would put the gallery front and center of the art world. Possibly the entire world. The chaos had only begun.

The very last thing they needed was people scrutinizing them. As understatements went, it didn't even come close to addressing the depth of this catastrophe.

Where on earth had Lise's mother gotten the painting?

Sophie and Henri deflected the endless questions, asked people not to post the photos—which would never happen—and thanked them for coming. The genie was well and truly out of the bottle. They couldn't put it back.

After she locked the gallery door behind the last guest, Sophie turned to find Henri wringing his hands. "I am so sorry. Truly. You know how excited I get when a new painting comes in. I didn't think. I just—" He shrugged. "I got caught up in the moment." Despite his apologetic demeanor, excitement and curiosity danced in his eyes. "But who sent it? Why send it here?"

Sophie couldn't scold him, since he was asking the same questions she was. The same ones the reporter and every single person here tonight would be asking.

Why had Irmgard's lawyer sent Lise the missing portrait of the Princess of Neuhansberg and her husband and two children, painted almost forty years ago?

It was one of three paintings that had disappeared after the beloved princess and her children died in a car accident. Could it be the real thing? Why did Irmgard have it?

"We don't know yet, Henri, but Lise will figure it out. Thank you for your help with the opening. Go on home."

His excitement dimmed a little as he realized he was being dismissed. "I'll just go say good night to Lise—"

Sophie held up a hand. "I'll tell her. Go on, now."

He hesitated. "I'll see you tomorrow?"

"Lise will be in touch about when we're reopening."

He nodded, tucked his chin, and left. But as Sophie closed the door behind him, she saw him pull out his cell phone.

With a sigh, she returned to the back room and studied Lise, who paced in front of the painting, the remnants of the brown paper balled in her fists.

"Everything is locked up. I sent Henri home."

Lise turned to her, expression dazed, face devoid of color.

"I'm assuming the painting came from your mother. Did she say how she obtained it?"

Just as Lise opened her mouth to respond, her cell phone rang. She pulled it from the pocket of her dress and checked the caller ID. "What is it, Nadine?" As she listened, her earlier pallor vanished, pushed aside by spots of high color. "They're throwing them out right now?" She muttered a curse. "I'll be right there."

Lise hung up and started for the door. "Nadine just got a panicked call. Some men are destroying the small women's homeless camp by the Isar River. She said the last time they showed up, two of the women disappeared."

"Disappeared? What does that mean? Where did they go?"

"I don't know. But I need to find out."

"I'll come with you."

"No. I need something else from you." Lise pointed to the painting. "Before the jackals from the media have time to descend, take this home. Copy it, as quickly as you can. And then we'll hide the original somewhere safe." She spun toward the stairs.

Sophie gripped Lise's arm, swallowed hard. "I can't. Not this painting. I work in oils. This is acrylic." Asking her to copy a Rainier? And these subjects? No. She didn't have the skills or the talent.

Lise turned back, gripped her by the shoulders. "Yes, you can. You have copied Renoir and Matisse, and nobody could spot the difference. You can do this. You must."

Sophie glanced over at the painting of Princess Johanna and her family. "She died before my time," she said reverently. "But I feel like I knew her. It's hard to explain, but learning about her death in school felt like someone close to me died."

The princess's death had rocked not just her home country, but the whole world. Gone was the glamour and mystery of their beloved princess in one tragic, horrible afternoon of twisted metal and burning fire.

Long before her death, her name was on everyone's lips and her photo was in every paper and graced the covers of countless magazines. Her hat of choice made headlines as often as her charitable work and her forward-thinking politics. And then when the twins were born, well, she became iconic, the perfect combination of all things female: princess, mother, wife, and outspoken world-changer in one beautiful, delightful package.

"Which makes you the exact right person to do this. You have to, Soph. We can't risk it disappearing again without a trace. I need you to keep it safe while you copy it. I'll work on safeguarding the original tomorrow. But right now, take the delivery van to your place. I'll take your car and lose anyone watching us before I head to the camp. Okay?"

Lise turned away, and Sophie stopped her with a hand on her arm. "Tomorrow, I expect you to tell me exactly how your mother got hold of this portrait." Sophie couldn't protect Lise—or the gallery—without knowing the whole story.

Lise raised an eyebrow at Sophie's tone, one she'd never used with her, and nodded. "I will. But I don't have time to deal with that tonight."

When Sophie prepared to leave the gallery a while later, she carefully studied the alley before she slipped out the back door. She didn't see anyone, but the instincts that made her excellent at what she did told her she was definitely being watched.

4

Lise gripped the steering wheel of Sophie's nondescript sedan as she sped across the city, trying to formulate a plan of some kind. Sophie was the creative one, who could improvise on the fly and always had a Mary Poppins–style satchel filled with useful things. Lise only claimed a handful of self-defense classes and her wits, and right now, her brain felt stuffed with cotton.

As she neared the park where the small group of homeless women and children had been camping at night, she turned off her headlights and glided to a stop at the curb, surprised to find everything quiet.

Quite a few of the women camped here were refugees from Middle Eastern countries, so she grabbed a headscarf and tucked it into place as she buttoned her thrift store jacket against the cold. She'd changed into her oldest jeans and ratty tennis shoes before she came so she'd blend in better. Sophie wasn't the only one who could go undercover. Or the only one trying to right wrongs.

On the phone, Nadine had said Amalia was the one who called

her. The young mother and her little boy were favorites among the staff at Neue Anfänge. Hopefully, she could tell Lise what was really going on.

Lise cut across the grass to where twenty or so women stood in a tight knot under a tree, whispering furiously, babies in arms and small children tucked around their knees. They reminded her of early settlers circling the wagons for protection.

"Guten Abend," she said as she approached.

"Lise!" Amalia broke from the group and hurried over, one-year-old Samuel clinging to her. "Thank you for coming." She motioned for Lise to step away from the group.

"What's happening? Nadine said some men were destroying the camp."

"They were. And then the *Polizei* drove by, and they left our tents and scattered." She rubbed Sam's head. "But I think they'll be back." She paused. "One of the new girls is missing."

Lise's heart pounded, but she kept her voice calm. "Are you sure? Did she maybe just move on?"

Amalia shook her head adamantly. "No. She had just told me yesterday how glad she was to have found us. Protection in numbers, new friends." She paused again. "She disappeared. Just like the other two."

Lise's mind kicked into high gear. This was one of several encampments around the city, and public opinion was pretty vocal about getting them off the streets. Without some sort of proof the women were in danger, it was unlikely the police would get involved. So she'd have to find proof. "Can you stay with one of the other women for a few hours? I'll set up in your tent."

"If they come back? How will you stop them?"

"I'm not sure yet, but I'll figure it out. You and Sam need to get some sleep."

Three hours later, Lise had a rough plan in place, but her patience was gone. *Come on, you cretins. Make your move.*

She clenched her teeth to keep them from chattering, despite the tattered blanket wrapped around her shoulders. A peek through the tent flap showed clouds flitting across the crescent moon. Would they still come back tonight?

Amalia and the others had set up under one of the highway overpasses inside the Englischer Garten near the Isar River, which flowed down from the Alps in Tyrol and eventually converged with the Danube farther south. What kind of lowlife tossed people out of their makeshift beds and then had the nerve to confiscate their meager supplies?

But it was Amalia's certainty that women were going missing that fired Lise's blood. Not while she was alive to stop it.

Lise peeked at her watch, eyes blurry. It was almost three in the morning, and the events of the past week were taking their toll.

She snapped fully awake when she heard male voices shouting in rapid-fire German. "Up. Everybody up. Let's go. Get out here. Now!"

She wanted to march out of her tent and demand answers. Instead, she shuffled out with the others, blinking against the harsh lantern beams aimed her way. "What's happening? Why do we have to leave?" she asked one of the men. She tightened her grip on the cell phone in her pocket. The fact they were wearing identical ski masks made her stomach cramp. Even if she managed to snap a few photos, it wouldn't help.

He gripped her arm and shoved her in the direction the others were being herded. "No questions. Just get moving."

"Wait. I just need to get my things—"

He stepped in front of her and made a show of putting his hand on the weapon at his hip. "Keep. Moving."

"Or what? You'll shoot me? What is wrong with you?"

His gaze sharpened and she bit her lip, wishing she'd kept her mouth shut.

They stared each other down for a few seconds before Lise nodded, joining the line of women walking away from their shelters.

Ahead of her, Amalia tried to comfort a crying Sam as she walked.

Lise stepped up beside her. "Let me carry him for you," she whispered.

Sam immediately shrieked at being separated from his mother, but Lise cooed and rocked him and breathed a sigh of relief as he slipped back into sleep. She'd already drawn way too much attention to herself.

"Why are they doing this?" Amalia whispered.

"I don't know." But her heart rate kicked up when she spotted two men, one on either side of the line of women, giving each one a thorough once-over that made bile rise in her throat. Their eyes stopped on Amalia, then some sort of signal passed between them.

"You need to take Sam and slip into those trees," Lise whispered urgently, handing the child back.

Amalia's eyes went dark and wide. "They have evil in mind. I feel it too. But I can't run very fast. Please, keep Sam with you. Protect him."

"No time for arguments. I'll create a diversion. Hide in the trees. I'll find you."

She squeezed Amalia's arm and then launched into an acting routine Sophie would envy. Arms flailing, she flung herself to the ground, crying out as she landed. "My leg. Ow! Oh, my leg. I think it's broken."

Several women gathered around, offering reassurance, helping her to her feet. She made a great show of collapsing back to the ground the minute they pulled her upright.

The same masked man shoved his way through the crowd and propped his hands on his hips.

"I fell! I think my leg is broken," Lise wailed, cupping her knee.

"I'm done with you." He hauled her to her feet, grip tight on her arm. "Go on."

He gave her a shove and Lise stumbled as she hobbled away from the others. Two men were tossing tents and belongings into the back of a van, but they didn't single out any of the other women like they had Amalia. Thank God.

She limped away from camp until she was out of sight, then

sprinted toward the trees, approaching from the other direction. "Amalia? Where are you?"

The forest was eerily calm. No animals rustled, which meant they were in wait-and-watch mode. "Amalia?"

"I knew you were up to something."

She spun around. The man had his arm around Amalia's throat, while she had her hand over Sam's mouth to keep him from screaming. He writhed and struggled to get free.

"Let her go." Lise needed the man's attention on her, not Amalia. "Who are you?"

"Just a woman trying to help a friend." She stepped closer.

"You should have left well enough alone." He pulled out his weapon and aimed it at her. "Let's go. Both of you."

Tears slid down Amalia's cheeks. Lise sent her a reassuring smile as she stepped up beside them, then spun and punched the man in the throat with everything she had. While he gasped and sputtered, she pulled back and slammed the heel of her hand into his nose. Blood spurted and he loosened his grip, the gun sliding from his grasp.

She scooped it up, kicked him in the groin for good measure, then turned to Amalia. "Run!"

Lise sprinted into the woods, away from Amalia and Sam, the man hot on her heels.

Every sense on high alert, Sophie slipped out the back door of the gallery, tucked the painting into the delivery van, and drove the quiet streets of Munich for forty-five minutes, one eye firmly on the rearview mirror. She finally decided it was safe to head to her flat a mere three minutes from the gallery.

She pulled up to the back door and snuck the painting upstairs to her apartment. Then she moved the van several blocks over, locked the doors, and walked back.

Once inside, Sophie changed into her paint-splattered Joan Jett

T-shirt, circa 1981 when Bernadette Rainier painted the portrait, and her well-worn jeans with holes in the knees. She propped two easels side by side—on one, she set the princess's portrait, called *Today*. Then she stretched some of the old canvas she kept for forgeries onto a new frame and set it beside the original. The better to fool those with a discerning eye.

She was always nervous when she started, but somehow this famous painting, done by an incredibly talented artist Sophie greatly admired—coupled with Lise's connection to it—inspired a whole other level of anxiety.

"You have copied Renoir and Matisse. You can do this."

Lise was right. Usually a forgery was discovered because of things that shouldn't be there rather than things that were. So she checked online catalogs of Ms. Rainier's work and studied the back of the paintings first, inspecting the frames, their construction, how the canvas was secured inside the frame, comparing everything to the portrait she had. Little things like the wrong fasteners had landed more than one forger in jail.

Several articles confirmed Ms. Rainier had used mineral-spirit acrylic paints, a newer version of the original Magna paints that were mixed with turpentine. Acrylics dried faster than oils, which was a huge help given the time crunch. Also, MSA paints could be manipulated a little more freely than today's more common—and fast-drying—water-based acrylics.

Luckily, Sophie had the necessary acrylics on hand, as she sometimes used this particular medium for her own dabbling. But she had to mix the colors just right, as acrylics could dry darker than what you expected.

Next, she studied the portrait itself. She needed to know how heavily Ms. Rainier loaded the brush. Did she favor a specific direction for her brushstrokes? How much blending did she do? How much layering? Could Sophie replicate Ms. Rainier's preferred color palette?

Sophie got out a magnifying glass and studied the royal portrait until she could answer those questions precisely.

Even though most forgers copied an artist's style, not an actual painting, she did it on the regular for the gallery. With the insurance company's blessing, she copied priceless artwork so clients could display their "old masters" while the original was kept in a climate-controlled vault elsewhere. Personally, that made no sense to her, as art should be enjoyed, but there you go.

Expert forgeries were also Robin Hood's stock-in-trade. Replacing stolen artwork with an exact copy was how she returned the originals to their rightful owners.

She set the blank canvas aside, pulled out one of her smaller do-over canvases, and set it on the easel. She found another portrait by Ms. Rainier and carefully studied it. She always did a practice run before she copied the actual work.

To set the mood, Sophie turned on music by Ella Fitzgerald, Bernadette Rainier's favorite jazz singer.

Only then did Sophie select her brushes, grab her palette, and begin mixing the colors she wanted. Eyes closed, breathing deliberately slow, she let herself become Bernadette.

Her shoulders gradually relaxed as she painted the background wash, then moved on to outlining the shape of the head, the ears, the slope of the nose. She took her time, letting instinct and the photo on her iPad guide her strokes.

Three hours later, she stepped back and smiled at her practice painting. "Well, look at you, Mr. Clooney."

She'd not only re-created George Clooney's likeness, but she'd done it in a way that exactly mirrored Bernadette's portrait, down to the last detail. She checked a few things, dabbed a bit more paint here, made a tiny adjustment there, and then stopped herself from futzing further. If she kept on, she could ruin the whole thing in the last five minutes by letting her perfectionism run amok.

Just as she was cleaning her brushes, her cell phone rang. She wiped her hands on a rag, then grabbed the phone. "Geez, Lise. You gotta give me more time than this to—"

"Come get us, Soph. Quick."

Lise was clearly out of breath, and a baby was crying in the background, a frantic female voice crooning, trying to calm him down.

"Tell me where." As Lise rattled off an address, Sophie was running for her apartment door, grabbing keys and a jacket as she ran. She shoved her feet into boots and locked the door behind her. "Be there in ten minutes."

5

Lise dodged and weaved around the trees, glad she'd walked these woods many times over the years. Though normally, the urban park was a quiet place to clear her head.

The man crashed through the underbrush in hot pursuit, cursing all the while. She smirked. It wasn't hard to figure out where he was.

One ear cocked to his location, Lise led him exactly where she wanted him to go. One minute he was running and the next there was a loud thud, followed by a cry of pain and a whole spate of curses, in both German and English. He'd found the old half-buried drainage ditch.

Without slowing down, she ran back to where she'd last seen Amalia. She found the young woman crouched behind a tree, rocking Sam to keep him quiet, her whole body shaking.

"It's okay. Let's go."

"Where is the man?"

"I slowed him down, but he'll call in reinforcements. We need to hurry."

Lise carried Sam as they hurried to the opposite side of the park, crossed the street, then stepped into the shadowed corner of a building.

They heard the sound of running feet heading toward them.

Lise grabbed Amalia and shoved her behind a trash bin. She snatched off her headscarf, shoved it into her pack, and replaced it with a fisherman's cap. She pulled out a whiskey bottle, then curled up in the doorway like a drunk, the bottle propped in the crook of her arm, her back to the street.

The men ran by.

Sam let out a quiet whimper that changed to an all-out shriek faster than Lise would have thought possible.

Shouts sounded and the pounding feet turned back in their direction. "They're back here!"

"Oh, dear God, help!" She leaped up, fists clenched, ready to fight them off. "Get ready."

When headlights appeared, barreling toward them from the opposite direction, she breathed a quick sigh of relief and reached back for Amalia. "When I say run, hop in the back of the van and duck down as far as you can."

Sophie made it there in eight minutes, the van's almost-bald tires squealing as she lurched around a corner and slid to the curb. Lise opened the sliding door, hurried an obviously terrified woman and screaming child inside, then slammed the door and hopped into the passenger seat. "Go! Go!" She whipped off her fisherman's cap and reached behind the seat and tossed the young woman a paint-splattered tarp they kept in the back. "Hide under this, against the back wall."

The woman did as she was told, and a minute later, blessed quiet filled the van.

"We've got company." Sophie glanced in her rearview mirror as a white van raced up behind them. "Hang on." She hit the gas.

Tires squealing, Sophie led them around the city, darting down narrow alleys and through quiet streets. "Lucky for us I know these roads like the back of my hand."

Lise looked into the passenger mirror. "I haven't seen them the last couple turns."

"I know, but let's make sure." On a tree-lined street on the outskirts of the city, Sophie backed the van up a long driveway, tucking them next to the large home.

"What if you wake someone?" Lise whispered.

Sophie raised a brow, grinned. "The Bauernsteins are on a Mediterranean cruise, last I heard."

Lise just shook her head and let out a sigh as they watched the road. One minute, two went by. Just when they thought they were clear, the white van approached, creeping down the street. The passenger window rolled down, and Sophie swallowed hard as she spotted the barrel of a gun.

Lise saw it too, and they exchanged a glance before Sophie hit the gas. "It's gonna get dicey. Hang on!"

They burst onto the street. Grass and shrubs alongside the road exploded from gunfire as they careened past the van, racing in the opposite direction. Sam started screaming again and Amalia tried to comfort him, while Lise kept an eye on their pursuers and Sophie drove like a madwoman, all too aware that their lives depended on her skill.

6

Like everyone else in the world, Mac was riveted to the mystery unfolding on his television screen the next morning. He turned up the volume as he sat at the breakfast bar in his functional Munich apartment, sipping coffee and munching Frosted Flakes. His place had all the charm of a 1980s-era hotel room, but it was close to his office and had a comfortable bed. In the ten years since he started his own business, he'd still traveled back and forth between here and the States too often to want something permanent.

He grabbed the TV remote, not surprised that the lead story on every channel was the same. The reappearance of the missing portrait of Princess Johanna, Prince Benedikt and their twins after forty years meant all the old questions surrounding the princess's fiery car accident were rehashed at length. Was the crash that killed the beloved royal and her year-old children really an accident? Or had someone tampered with the car, as speculation at the time indicated? The news outlets had hunted up all the old photos, including the graphic ones of the burned car, which really didn't need to be shown while people were eating their breakfast cereal, did they? He set his bowl aside and reached for more coffee.

The princess had been a vocal advocate for having Neuhansberg's laws of succession changed to allow women to inherit the throne—and all the power that went with it—by eliminating the male-only language. At the time of her death, there was a vote by Parliament scheduled for the following week. It was postponed, but on the first anniversary of her death, Prince Benedikt had the law changed in honor of her memory.

Mac did a quick online search for the value of the portraits and his eyes widened. He hadn't expected that. Despite the fact that Bernadette Rainier, the highly sought-after portrait artist who'd painted them, had retired, he suspected the princess's ongoing popularity, especially her vocal support for women's rights, was what really jacked up the price.

Even now, on the anniversary of her death, his mother got weepy as though a dear friend had just died. He'd never quite understood her emotional connection to a wealthy woman half a world away she'd never met, but his mother said he didn't have to. Princess Johanna represented hope for women. She was part of the wave of the future, and her death felt like women everywhere had lost a friend—and a champion for equal rights.

Flash forward to the present, and in a surprising move only a week ago, Prince Benedikt had decided to hand the reins over to his brother's son, Hereditary Prince Felix, at a coronation ceremony on his beloved Johanna's birthday in less than a week's time. Speculation about Prince Benedikt's health had been running alongside concerns about Felix's fitness for the job due to his irresponsible reputation. Add in speculation about the timing of the portrait's reappearance and the media was having a field day.

The questions surrounding the princess's death had always piqued Mac's interest. What had really happened? Out of habit, he grabbed a yellow legal pad to jot down a few notes, then pushed it aside.

He had more immediate concerns to worry about this morning. He'd gotten back from another assignment late last night, and an e-mail from his mother's doctor, marked *URGENT*, had been waiting when he opened his laptop this morning.

He scrubbed a hand down his face. His art-investigation firm made good money, so taking care of his mother since his father's fatal heart attack four years ago had not been a hardship, even with the ongoing cancer treatments. Until now. The cost of this new experimental treatment, which her doctor deemed her "last, best hope," had a staggering number of zeros attached.

Where on earth was he going to get that kind of money in time to make a difference?

He tapped his pencil on the legal pad, trying to come up with some ideas. When his cell phone rang, he picked it up and laughed when he glanced at the caller ID. "His Supreme Highness, Prince Benedikt of Neuhansberg." What kind of game was this at—he checked his diver's watch—six thirty in the morning? He muted the television. "McKenzie."

"His Supreme Highness Prince Benedikt would like to speak with you, in person. Kindly present yourself at Hans Schloss, the royal residence in Neuhansberg, at ten o'clock."

"Right. Who is this and what game are you playing?"

"This is not a game," the man said stiffly. "My name is Alfred, Prince Benedikt's personal assistant. As I said, the prince requests your presence this morning."

Mac glanced at the television, still running old footage of the princess, including a poignant shot of the castle staff lining the road as her casket passed by. Another picture flashed on the screen, identifying Alfred as the man standing beside the famed missing portraits. Mac sat up straighter. Maybe it wasn't a prank after all.

"Why does the prince want to speak with me?"

"I am not privy to that information."

Mac calculated the distance in his head. "I can't get there that fast." It would take almost four hours to make the drive. "Make it eleven o'clock, just to be safe."

There was an indignant sniff. "The prince does not adjust his schedule for others. See that you arrive promptly, Herr McKenzie."

Click.

7

Mac sat there a moment, then laughed and shook his head. Either someone was playing an elaborate hoax or he really had just been summoned by royalty. Neuhansberg was a teeny little speck on the map, right next to Liechtenstein, but royalty was royalty. His eyes were drawn to the television screen. If this summons was legit, dollars to donuts, as his father used to say, it had to do with the portrait.

Which meant he just might have found the solution to his financial dilemma.

He grabbed a quick shower, pulled on an immaculately tailored suit and power tie, slipped his Glock into his shoulder holster, and hopped into his late-model Mercedes. Appearances mattered for someone who excelled at "discreet private investigations," which his business card claimed he did.

Traffic getting out of Munich wasn't too bad at that hour of the morning, and he hit the gas once he got on the B2. Still, it was 10:20 when he pulled up in front of the castle and a guard directed him to drive over the honest-to-goodness drawbridge. He reluctantly locked his gun and the combat knife he wore in his boot into the safe under his seat and exited his vehicle, expression bland as he smoothed his tie and headed toward the massive wooden doors.

Not a hoax, then.

He presented his card to another uniformed guard, who eyed him up and down. "Are you armed, Herr McKenzie?"

"I am not." He held out his arms as the guard patted him down, then indicated he step inside. There was no X-ray scanner in sight, so he figured the public didn't get invited here often. Though he made note of every strategically placed security camera.

"You're late," the same voice he'd heard on the phone earlier scolded as a thin man with a pinched face stepped from a doorway.

"You must be Alfred." The man ignored Mac's outstretched hand, so he made a show of checking his watch, though he knew exactly what time it was. "I'm early for eleven o'clock," he quipped, then grinned, just to be annoying.

The man stiffened and stared back, unblinking. Clearly not someone with a sense of humor.

"Are you going to tell me what I'm doing here?"

"Prince Benedikt will tell you everything he wishes you to know." Alfred waved a hand toward another door off the foyer and headed in that direction.

Mac stepped inside the reception room and suppressed a whistle at the opulence surrounding him. "This will do."

Alfred muttered something about "uneducated commoners," and Mac waited to laugh until the door closed behind the older man. Playing the "uneducated commoner" often served its purpose. He scanned the room. Given that the royal family was one of the wealthiest in the world, this place was a museum all its own, with gilt everywhere, gorgeous artwork by famous names littering the walls, and fancy, uncomfortable furniture grouped in intimidating clumps. He folded his six-foot-four-inch frame into a little chair and hoped it would support his weight.

Then he waited. And waited. And waited some more.

The fancy grandfather clock chimed eleven. He was done waiting. He had his hand on the doorknob when a panel in the wall opposite opened, and two men entered laughing. For a moment he thought it was Prince Benedikt, but then the man's face registered. This was the prince's younger brother, Prince Moritz, and his son, Felix. The moment they spotted Mac, they went silent as the grave. Mac felt about as welcome as a circus clown at a funeral.

"Who are you?" the young prince demanded.

Yup. Nailed it.

Mac extended his hand. "Mac McKenzie." He did not offer any more than that.

When both men ignored his hand, Mac wondered if he'd missed an important bit of protocol or if the men were just living up to the lifestyles of the rich and terrible.

"What are you doing here?" Felix's eyes narrowed, and he crossed his arms over his chest. He and his father were dressed as though they were headed for the tennis courts.

"I have an appointment with His Supreme Highness Prince Benedikt."

"Why?"

Mac let the silence stretch while he studied Hereditary Prince Felix, who was about his own midthirties. Everything about him, from his clothes to his attitude, exemplified the supreme confidence of someone born to immense wealth who, unfortunately, fit the stereotype of condescending rich kid to a tee. Mac grinned and shrugged one shoulder. "I'm not sure. I'm waiting for the prince to tell me."

As if on cue, another hidden door opened and Prince Benedikt walked in, hand extended, his silver hair slicked back. He was taller than the dour Alfred, who trailed him. "Thank you so much for coming, Herr McKenzie." He indicated his brother and nephew, who both wore scowls. "I see you've met the rest of my family."

"What's he doing here?" Felix demanded.

Prince Benedikt raised an eyebrow. "That is between myself and Herr McKenzie. May I remind you that you are not the prince . . . yet."

Mac found the play of emotions on Felix's face telling. His

eyes blazed, then flashed with something close to terror before he assumed a blank mask and bowed to Prince Benedikt. "My apologies, Uncle. I meant only to protect you."

"This is about the painting, isn't it?" Prince Moritz demanded. "I told you I have someone who can—"

Prince Benedikt held up a hand. "Please do not let me keep you from your tennis match. Herr McKenzie and I have business to discuss."

Father and son exchanged glances, then marched out of the room, clearly unhappy about being summarily dismissed.

Once the door closed behind them, the prince turned to Alfred. "Kindly obtain refreshments for us, would you?" The tone was polite, but the command obvious.

Alfred didn't look any happier at being dismissed than the other two. He nodded stiffly and marched out of the room.

Prince Benedikt let out a sigh. "Please, have a seat."

Mac sat back down and crossed one ankle over his knee, as much to keep his balance as anything else, and studied the man sitting across from him, who drummed his fingers on the arm of the chair. Prince Benedikt was nearing seventy and the dark circles under his eyes, as well as the way his clothes hung off his lean frame, lent credence to the spate of health issues the news media had been squabbling over for the last few months, like a pack of dogs wanting to pick a bone clean.

When the silence lengthened, Mac asked, "What can I do for you, sir?" On the drive, he'd asked Siri to read him whatever she could find online about Prince Benedikt and the royal family. Mac always wanted to know what he was walking into. Would Benedikt correct him, tell him to refer to him as Your Supreme Highness? The prince didn't appear to have noticed the slip in protocol. He seemed distracted, nervous.

"Alfred, my assistant, has researched some of your previous cases. Some for very high-profile clients. You have a reputation for being discreet, especially when it comes to art and art authentication."

Mac raised an eyebrow. Neither his client list nor the details of his cases was public knowledge. Apparently, there was more to Alfred than met the eye. "I wouldn't get far as an investigator if I wasn't."

Again, the silence stretched while the prince seemed to decide how much to tell him. Mac waited patiently. In his experience, this kind of waffling was standard operating procedure for clients. They were about to pay a great deal of money to have you dig up all their secrets. Or uncover information they really didn't want to know. That kind of vulnerability was always rather disconcerting.

"You've seen the news coverage, about the painting?" the prince finally asked, meeting Mac's eyes directly for the first time.

"I have."

"I want that painting."

That wasn't what he'd expected. "You don't need me for that, Your Highness. Since it was delivered to an art gallery in Munich, simply call them and have it shipped to you. It is obviously yours."

"There's more to it than that."

Of course there is. Mac eased back in his chair, trying to look relaxed on his uncomfortable perch.

"You've read that I'm turning over the reins to Hereditary Prince Felix next week?"

"I read that, yes." Which to Mac's mind was a terrible idea. Their brief encounter had confirmed Felix's entitled attitude. Which went right along with his reputation as a spendthrift and a womanizer, neither of which boded well for the country's future. "May I ask why your brother, Prince Moritz, isn't going to succeed you?" Generally, that's how things went, if the heir didn't have any living children, as in Prince Benedikt's case.

"My brother has never had any interest in leadership and I've been unable to convince him otherwise, though I have tried. He prefers to live out the rest of his life without the pressure and responsibility." The prince sighed. "I can't say I disagree with him."

Mac would bet his Mercedes there was far more to it, but he kept silent.

"My wife, Princess Johanna—God rest her soul—had convinced

me it was time to change our tradition, to bring it into the modern world by allowing the firstborn to inherit the title, whether male or female." He glanced at Mac. "You probably also heard her idea was met with some, shall we say, resistance."

The man was also a master at understatement. "I heard that as well."

The prince paused for a moment and cleared his throat. "My beloved Johanna and little Katharina and Werner died just before Parliament was set to make the change. I had it ratified on the one-year anniversary of their deaths." Suddenly, the dimness in his eyes abated and a fire lit them. The look he shot Mac could have melted steel. "The timing of the accident has always bothered me."

Now they were getting closer to the real reason for this visit. "How can I be of assistance?" Mac had learned early to make sure clients spelled out exactly what they wanted from him. No ambiguity.

"I want to know where the painting has been. Who had it all these years? How did they get it? Is it authentic, or is this merely a copy?"

Still not the real reason. He waited some more. The silence lengthened, interrupted only by the magnificent grandfather clock ticking in the corner.

"I want you to find out if the car accident was really an accident."

Bingo. A jolt of anticipation shot up Mac's spine. He'd been right. Sinking his investigative teeth into a forty-year-old mystery piqued his interest in ways nothing had for a long while. Still . . . "I'm an art investigator, Your Highness, not a criminal investigator."

The prince waved that away. "The basics are the same. And you're discreet. That's worth a great deal."

"I will do my absolute best. First, I'll need everything you have on—"

"That's only step one," the prince interrupted. "I want you to find the other two paintings as well."

Mac's eyebrows shot to his hairline. "There are three of them?" How had he missed that?

The prince nodded and outlined, step-by-step, exactly what he wanted. *No more ambiguity.* When Mac exited the castle thirty minutes later, his mind was spinning.

Between his commitment to Interpol and the deal he'd just struck with Prince Benedikt, he was about to walk a tightrope unlike any he'd ever tiptoed across before.

Uneasiness slid through him as he climbed into his car. He opened the lockbox under his seat and returned his weapon to its holster, tucked his knife back in his boot.

If he succeeded, he'd have the money needed for his mother's treatments.

But one wrong step and he could lose everything that mattered to him too.

8

The pounding on her front door jolted Sophie awake. She glanced at the late-afternoon sun slanting across the sofa, where she'd collapsed several hours ago, and shoved her hair off her face as she sat up.

A fist pounded again, and she leaped to her feet, suddenly wide awake.

Had the police found her? Mac? Whoever was after Amalia?

She didn't move toward the peephole, lest the creaking floorboards give away that she was home.

The pounding stopped and her cell phone buzzed from her studio. She tiptoed down the hall, carefully avoiding another squeaky spot, and picked up her phone. Then sighed with relief at the caller ID. "Are you outside my apartment?"

"Yes. Open the door already." At her friend's annoyed tone, she deliberately took her time walking back through her apartment and undoing the locks.

Lise pushed inside, shoved a bakery bag into her hands. "Where is it?" she demanded as she headed for the studio.

"Hello to you too," Sophie drawled as she shut and locked the door.

Bleary-eyed after working all night, she detoured to the kitchen to make a cup of coffee, letting the smell of the freshly ground beans start to wake her up. Cup in one hand, one of the croissants from the bakery in the other, Sophie wandered to her studio, propped a shoulder against the doorframe. Lise studied the side-by-side paintings of Princess Johanna and her family.

"Is Amalia safe?"

Lise looked over her shoulder and smiled as she carefully stepped around the portable heater and the fan Sophie had set up to dry the paint faster. "Yes. After we dropped her and the baby off at one of our temporary shelters last night, Nadine started making calls." Lise's passion for her work with Neue Anfänge was the reason she'd handed the reins of the gallery over to Sophie and Henri to begin with. Nadine wouldn't admit she was getting older, but Lise was gradually assuming more and more of the day-to-day running of the charity. And satisfying her own drive to make amends for the sins of her past. "Nadine is helping her find a permanent situation."

"You still think Amalia was targeted specifically?"

At that, Lise spun to face her, jaw tight. "I do. And I'm going to figure out who they are, who's paying them."

"Any word on the other three women?"

"Not yet." Lise took a calming breath, then pointed at the paintings. "These are amazing. Absolutely incredible, Soph. Your talent never ceases to amaze me."

Lise stepped over to another easel. "Well, hello. Who is this gorgeous hunk of manhood?"

When she'd finished the copy earlier, Sophie had still been too wired to sleep, so she'd dabbed some paint on another of her smaller, do-over canvases, hoping to exorcise the twitchy feeling that hummed under her skin. She rolled her shoulders. Obviously, it hadn't worked. "He was at the auction last night."

"He clearly caught your attention." Lise raised an eyebrow and leaned closer to the painting. "Wow, he's quite the stunner. You've captured every detail perfectly."

"He grabbed me, pulled me onto the dance floor, asked questions."

"What kind of questions?" She studied the man's square jawline, her face inches from the painting.

"The kind that make even me nervous."

Lise stopped her examination, spun toward her. "Tell me everything."

As Sophie described their encounter, Lise's eyes grew wider. "So you don't know if he saw you make the switch?"

"I can't be sure." She took another sip of coffee, tried to keep her hands steady. "But what if he did?"

Lise cocked her head and studied her with an intensity that made Sophie squirm. They'd never had a close call before. Sophie was usually a ghost at these events. An apparition that seemed to flit in and out of reality.

Finally, Lise nodded. "I think we're fine. I called Louise Flask earlier and apologized again for missing the event, then asked about last night's commotion." Lise put that last bit in air quotes. "According to her, video footage at check-in confirmed Frau Bauernstein was closest to the painting when the alarm went off, but security was unable to locate her for questioning. The Flasks confirmed nothing was stolen. All their artwork was exactly where it was supposed to be. Still, the police went to the Bauernstein residence, where a sleepy housekeeper informed them the couple was away on a cruise."

"The Mediterranean. I hear it's lovely this time of year."

Lise rolled her eyes. "You are incorrigible." She paused. "You got it done, right?"

Sophie shot her a grin. "Don't I always? Frau Limberger's favorite painting is back in its rightful place in their living room."

"Which means we'll get the extra bonus for retrieving it before the party. Neue Anfänge will get to buy more blankets and food."

Sophie raised her cup in a toast. "A good night's work then."

The painting had been taken from the Limbergers' apartment several months ago while they were out of town. When Herr Limberger spotted it hanging in the upper gallery at the Flask mansion, he'd contacted Robin Hood Retrieval through their secure e-mail. They were very selective and never, ever took on a commission unless Lise's extensive research confirmed the painting or other artifact had, in fact, been stolen from its rightful owner.

"I'm guessing the media has lost its collective mind speculating about Princess Johanna's portrait."

Lise snorted. "Understatement of the millennium. They've been camped out in front of the gallery all night, and the phone won't stop ringing. It's as exhausting as Henri's apologies." She quirked a wry smile, then sobered. "I called Herr Dengler, Mutti's lawyer, this morning and we're doing a joint news conference in—" she checked her watch—"two hours."

"Won't the royal family want it back?"

"Prince Benedikt's people already called Herr Dengler. He told the prince's people he has proof it belonged to Mutti."

Sophie's eyes widened. "Princess Johanna gave it to your mother?"

"I don't know. Herr Dengler was annoyingly vague over the phone. Said we needed to talk in person. In the meantime, I'm going to run the original to the bank before they close and make sure it's safely in their vault for the time being. You bring the copy to the gallery. Our vault should be enough to keep it secure. I'll tell the media the painting will *not* be on public display after all and has been secured at an undisclosed location. We don't have the capacity to handle the crowds."

"This will definitely bring out the crazies too."

"It already has. There's actually an online group saying the crash was a cover-up for an alien abduction." Lise twirled her fingers round her ears. "We had a line of people two blocks long outside the gallery this morning, and there are flowers and a makeshift shrine by the front door. It's like she died all over again." She shook her head. "I get it, I really do. But I had to call the police to clear the street."

"You're sure you weren't followed by any reporters?"

"I hope not. Took me forever to sneak out of the gallery and then wind my way around the city before I came here." She yawned. "I'm sorry I woke you. I couldn't wait another minute to see the portrait. Now I need to get to the bank."

Sophie noted that the dark circles under her eyes were deeper than before. "You need to get some rest too. But before you go, can you look at one more thing?" She picked up the original portrait and set it on her worktable, face down. "Check out the back."

Lise squinted to read the tiny lettering that bordered the bottom of the frame. Done with a fine-tip brush, the words were barely visible.

Just like St. Irmgard and St. Agnes, I believe in God even when He is silent.

"Does this phrase mean anything to you?" Sophie asked.

Lise looked up, a frown creasing her brow. "No. Is it something the princess said? Or maybe the artist painted those words on the frame?"

"Either one is possible. But what does it mean?"

"No idea. Another mystery in the tragic life of Princess Johanna." Lise glanced at her watch, then reached for the heavy butcher paper. "I have to go, or Henri will talk to the media 'to be helpful' before I get there." She rolled her eyes, then cupped Sophie's cheek. "It's all going to be fine. And stop worrying."

"Yes, Mother." Sophie grinned as she expertly wrapped the original painting, then padded it with the down comforter from her bed and handed it to Lise. "I'll bring the copy while you're busy doing the news conference. Be careful."

"You too." Lise checked the hallway in both directions before she hurried out of the apartment, the portrait buried in the thick fabric. Once Sophie locked the door behind her, she watched from her window until Lise drove away. Then she went back to her studio and reread the words she'd copied onto the back of the forged painting, an exact match to the original.

What did the phrase mean? Lise's mother's name was Irmgard. How was she connected to the portrait?

A chill slid down her spine, a sense of foreboding Sophie couldn't put a name to. But was it connected to Princess Johanna or the handsome man with the sexy grin seducing her from her almost-finished painting?

She picked up her brush and added a few more strokes to the line of his jaw, a few creases around his eyes. She stepped back. Now it was done.

But she was absolutely certain the trouble had just begun.

9

Even though the temps were in the low eighties today, Bernadette Rainier wrapped her cardigan a little tighter around her shoulders. She stood on the deck of her fifties-era adobe house, ten miles from the outskirts of town, and watched the plume of dust get closer and closer as a vehicle headed in her direction.

It wasn't Yolanda, the heavyset nurse who came to annoy and nag her every day about one thing or another. She drove an aging maroon Buick and showed up at 2:00 p.m. like clockwork. She was from South Carolina and clucked with disapproval over Bernadette's eating habits, the cigars she refused to give up, and the medicines she forgot to take. The reprimands somehow sounded gentler in her Southern drawl.

Bernadette huffed out a breath, tossed her white braid over her shoulder. How was she supposed to remember them all? There were so many these days, and she was so tired.

She'd been painting quite a bit recently, trying to stay ahead of the bone-deep knowledge that time was running out. She wasn't kidding herself. The sheer volume of different pills she was required to choke down every day made it abundantly clear that they were experimenting. Nobody knew what in blazes was wrong with her. She snorted and took another sip of Dr Pepper. She was old, that's what was wrong with her. And everything was starting to hurt. At eighty-seven, she'd had a good run.

But she wasn't ready to go quite yet. She glanced down at her paint-stained fingers. She wanted to finish a couple of paintings first. She'd been in her studio all night working on them. To get them ready in time.

She squinted up at the noonday sun. Ready in time for what? And why couldn't she remember?

As the cloud of dust got closer, a little tingle of uneasiness slid over her skin. It wasn't Yolanda. Not Earl, either, whose red pickup was more rust than paint. He wasn't due to take care of what little landscaping she had out here for another few days. Right?

The warning dug deeper as the shiny silver SUV started up the winding path to her house. Not somebody who had gotten lost then. They were headed here.

She picked up the shotgun that leaned against the adobe wall and aimed it at the pretty young thing who climbed out of the SUV.

The woman, more of a girl really, yelped in surprise and shot her hands up in the air. "Please don't shoot. I'm Gina Dodge with the *Phoenix Sun Times*. I just want to talk to you."

Bernadette didn't lower the shotgun. "Why?"

Little Miss Dodge leaned against the side of the vehicle so she didn't lose her balance in her ridiculous heels. Not exactly the right kind of footwear for Bernadette's dirt and gravel drive. "Why do I want to interview you?"

"If you'd done your homework, Miss Dodge, you'd know I don't do interviews."

The girl smiled broadly. "I know. You're kind of a recluse, which is really cool and—" When Bernadette snorted, she added, "And is totally fine. But I thought . . . okay, I really, really hoped that you'd be willing to talk to me about the painting."

"What painting?" The one she'd been working on last night? She had been painting, right? Why was everything so fuzzy?

"The portrait you did of Princess Johanna, Prince Benedikt, and their kids years ago. The one titled *Today*."

"So? That painting was destroyed decades ago in a barn fire on the royal estate. Why talk about it now?"

Ms. Dodge fairly danced with excitement, eyes shining. "That's what everyone thought. But they were wrong." Her voiced dropped to barely a whisper. "The portrait showed up last night at a gallery in Munich."

Bernadette slowly lowered her weapon. Her mouth hung open like a puppet's, so she snapped it closed. "Where has it been all these years?"

"That's what everyone is trying to figure out. I wanted to ask you a few questions—"

Bernadette's voice was hard. "You're wasting your time. I don't know where it's been."

Ms. Dodge picked her way across the dusty drive, wobbling in her heels, blonde curls escaping her tidy bun, sweat stains appearing under the arms of her suit jacket. "That's fine. I just wanted to talk to you about what it was like back then, spending time with the royal family, getting to know them. Sort of a look back."

Bernadette studied her a moment. So much young optimism and enthusiasm, she was fairly vibrating with it. Bernadette wished she had a thimbleful of it, just enough to get through the days without dozing off in the middle of things. This whole aging bit annoyed the ever-living snot out of her.

She nodded toward her modest adobe home. "Come on in out of the heat then. You'll have heatstroke out here in that getup. And for goodness' sake, leave the shoes outside."

Out of the corner of her eye she saw Gina raise a hand in a tiny victory gesture but pretended she didn't see it. If the girl thought Bernadette was going to impart some new information, she was in for a shock. But it was a way to pass the time until Yolanda came again. And maybe the young thing's energy was catching?

Wait.

Was Yolanda coming today? Or had she already been here?

She shook her head to clear the cobwebs and led the girl inside.

"Oh my goodness. Your home is amazing." Gina stared at the paintings that lined every available inch of wall space. She made a slow circuit of the room, exclaiming over the bold colors in the high desert landscapes, the softer shades of green in the redwood forest.

Bernadette took a seat in her favorite Mission style rocker and waited.

"These are all landscapes," Gina said over her shoulder. "Where are the portraits?"

"Hanging on the walls of the people's homes who commissioned them."

A flush stole over Gina's cheeks. "You didn't keep any of them?"

"They weren't for me. They were commissions, so no, I didn't keep them."

Gina perched on the sofa across from Bernadette's chair and pulled a pad of paper and a pen from an enormous purse. Then she set her phone on the table, looked up. "May I record this?"

"Absolutely not."

Her eyes widened. "Oh. Okay." She tucked the phone back in her bag. "We'll do it old-school then."

Bernadette held out her hand, waggled her fingers. "Give me the phone."

"What?"

"I'll hang onto it until we're done." To her credit, the younger woman didn't ask if she knew how to use it, just handed it over. Bernadette checked the bar at the top to see if any apps were open, then set it under one of the sofa cushions in case she was wrong.

"I'll give you fifteen minutes. Ask your questions."

"Was Princess Johanna as wonderful as people said she was?"

Bernadette smiled at that. How could she not? "She was a beautiful person, inside and out. She loved her family, but she was also passionate about her country and about using her position to make changes."

"You mean like trying to change the lineage thing?"

"Yes, like the lineage thing. I'm surprised Prince Benedikt went ahead with the plans to have it changed after they died. Felix will inherit the title regardless, since the twins died in the crash, but I still didn't expect the prince to go through with it."

Pen poised over her notebook, Gina fairly vibrated with excitement. "Can you tell me what you talked about as you were painting? How did you get the job, by the way?"

"I'd met Johanna when she and the prince were in London and I was there for a charity event. Several of my pieces were up for auction and the princess commented on them. Several weeks later, she contacted me through her personal secretary." Bernadette smiled. "The rest, as they say, is history."

"And working with her? What was that like? How was she as a mother?"

Bernadette let her mind drift back, to the sound of laughter in the nursery, and later, the way the twins tumbled about in the thick grass of the gardens outside. "We spent time in the royal residence, but we also went outside to the gardens. I took pictures and also did dozens of sketches of all of them before I found a composition that she and I both liked."

"The portrait was her idea?"

"Most definitely. Prince Benedikt was doing it to humor her because he loved her very much. Later, she asked me to do a series of three portraits."

Gina leaned closer. "The other two haven't been found yet. Do you think they survived the fire too?"

Fire? What fire? Bernadette blinked rapidly, heart pounding, then went to the kitchen for another Dr Pepper to buy time. These fuzzy moments, when the world seemed blanketed in a white fluffy cloud and the line between past and present, memory and fairy tale faded into the mist, were increasingly terrifying. What was happening? Was she losing her mind?

She came back into the room, handed a can to Gina. "I can't tell you anything about a fire."

"Can you tell me any little stories about those days? About what happened or what you said? Anything that makes the princess come to life for my readers."

What an odd thing to say. Why not just call Johanna and ask her all these questions yourself? A memory burst into her mind and she blurted, "The princess was afraid."

"Afraid? Of what?"

"That she might die. That's why she wanted the paintings done. There were people who didn't want things to change. Who didn't want women in power, for any reason."

"What did she say?"

"She said that if she died, I should take care of her children."

Gina gasped and Bernadette realized what she'd said and shook her head. That wasn't right. "No, not me. Ilse. She told Ilse to take care of the children and protect the paintings."

"Who's Ilse?"

"Her personal secretary." *Yes, that's what Johanna said. Right?*

Gina's eyes were round as saucers. "The princess told her secretary to take care of her children? When? While you were doing the sketches?"

Bernadette struggled to see past the wisps of clouds, the thick layer of cotton that lay over all the memories, making them hard to recall. "No, I think that came later, along with the code." Her eyes snapped open. "But I know she talked about the treasure. That I know for sure."

Gina scribbled like a madwoman, then paused, pen over paper. "I'm sorry, I'm trying to follow what you're saying. The princess hid the paintings, along with some kind of code that led to a treasure?"

Bernadette shook her head. "No. The code doesn't have anything to do with the legend. But no one can find the treasure without it."

"Yoo-hoo! Miss Rainier!" Yolanda pushed her dark head through the front door without even knocking, as always. She said it was in case Bernadette was asleep. She was just nosy, that's all.

Gina stood, held out a hand. "I'm Gina Dodge with the *Phoenix Sun Times*."

"Ms. Rainier does not give interviews."

"So she said. But we were having a nice talk anyway."

She hated when people talked about her like she wasn't there. "I'm old. Not invisible. Yet."

"Ms. Rainier was telling me about painting the portraits for Princess Johanna and her family years ago."

Yolanda propped her hands on her ample hips and harrumphed. "Then I suggest you do your homework, young lady, and take everything you hear with a grain of salt. Some of those old memories have gotten a little scrambled over time. You understand what I'm saying?"

"She's saying my mind is like Swiss cheese."

Yolanda walked over and laid a gentle hand on Bernadette's arm. "Maybe like baby Swiss, but you're all right, Ms. Rainier. You're doing just fine."

The two kept talking and maybe they asked another question or two, but the cloud got heavier and the sounds of the world became even more muffled.

As Gina left, Bernadette heard Yolanda say, "If you're a smart woman, and I get the feeling you are, you won't print a word of what Ms. Rainier said until you confirm that from another source. She gets confused."

10

When Sophie left the apartment a while later, she wasn't Mrs. Bauernstein, the rich society matron she'd been last night. This time she was Genevieve, a young, rich socialite. Her sleek brown bob skimmed her shoulders, and she wore a colorful scarf tucked under her chin and Sophia Loren sunglasses. A stylish white coat hid a thin layer of padding around her middle, and tall black boots hid her calves from prying eyes. She shook her head. She wouldn't let Mac McKenzie distract her. Not now.

Lise had called to say she'd made it to the bank with plenty of time. She'd also hired extra security in case some overeager fan got the crazy idea to try to break into the gallery and steal the painting. Between the guard and the cameras trained on their vault, they figured the copy should be safe enough.

On the advice of the gallery's insurance agent, Lise also hired a car to bring Sophie and the copy to the gallery. They'd timed it so while Lise and Irmgard's lawyer, plus several members of local law enforcement, held everyone's attention out front, Sophie's driver

64

would go around back and provide coverage while she slipped in the back door.

At least, that had been the plan.

Before she left her apartment, Sophie built another frame, mimicking the original's gilding with quick-drying paint. She added a few nicks in all the right places to match the other. This kind of work was always, always about the details.

She'd used her hair dryer to be sure the paint was dry, then had taken her George Clooney painting and set it into the frame, with her copy behind it, hidden from view.

As they wended their roundabout way through Munich, Sophie studied the uniformed driver. He was average height, with an accent that suggested an Eastern European heritage. He also wore a weapon in a shoulder holster. Not something they'd requested. Was that SOP for the agency, or did someone have another agenda in play?

She reached a hand into her pocket and fingered the knife she'd slipped in at the last second. She'd learned to trust her instincts. And right now, they were screaming at her to pay attention. She didn't know if the threat would come from the driver or someone else, but she'd be ready.

As the black Mercedes sedan approached the gallery, the chaos closed in around her. Amidst the milling crush of reporters and cameramen, news vans, and what looked like thousands of fans holding flowers and candles spilling onto the street, the driver couldn't even turn onto the block. The half dozen police officers didn't seem to be making any headway in holding them back.

"Stay focused. Stay in the moment." Her late father's words reverberated in her memory as she scanned the crowd.

"We will need to take the next cross street, madam," the driver said.

"Yes, thank you." She waited until he'd made the turn before she said, "Actually, let's go around to the back entrance. It will be less crowded." Sophie deliberately hadn't given him too many details ahead of time. Just in case.

"Of course, madam," he murmured.

She watched his expression in the rearview mirror, the way his jaw tightened the tiniest bit. As he turned down the narrow alley behind the gallery, the noise and pulsing energy lessened and she exhaled a slow breath. But her relief was short-lived.

"Over here! Over here!" A female reporter sprinted toward them in five-inch heels, her cameraman right behind her.

Unfortunately, she wasn't alone. Several more news vans lined the narrow alley, and reporters hurried toward the car, microphones in hand.

The only good thing was that if the driver had planned anything, he'd have a hard time carrying it out with so many cameras pointed at them.

Sophie tightened her grip on the painting. "Please get as close to the back door as possible." She pulled out her cell phone and dialed Lise. "I'm in the back."

"I'll send the security guard to the door. Wait until he gets there before you get out of the car. How bad is the crowd out there?"

Sophie's pulse skittered as more reporters and fans rushed toward them from both directions. "Tell him to hurry. It's getting deep out here."

"On it. Two minutes." The line went dead.

Sophie flicked her gaze between the back door, the driver, and the pushing, shoving crowd. She slid the knife from her coat pocket. When people started rocking the car, the driver let out a low growl. He looked into the rearview mirror, expression fierce. "Shall I put a stop to this?"

"Not yet. As soon as the back door opens, I'll slip out."

He dipped his head in acknowledgment, then reached for his weapon.

———

Mac watched the black sedan slip down the alley. His hunch had paid off. If he owned the gallery and someone had just delivered a long-lost royal portrait, anything important he had to do would be handled in the back, while the reporters and fans thronged the front.

Who was coming to the gallery? He scanned the area from his location in the shadowed entrance of a building across the way. No police escort back here, so they were attempting to fly under the official radar. Interesting.

He shifted to get a better view as reporters surrounded the car. When the back door opened a crack and the driver stepped out of the car, Mac headed that way before his feet had even decided to move.

The driver held the rear door open, blocking the crowd with his body. A woman stepped out, dressed like Sophia Loren, complete with scarf and huge glasses. She held a wrapped painting in front of her and turned toward the gallery's back door.

When a gun appeared in the driver's hand, seemingly trained on the woman and not the crowd, Mac put on a burst of speed.

Before he got halfway across the street, the woman pivoted left and knocked the gun from the driver's hand with her tote. As it clattered to the ground, she used her shoulder to shove past the driver and sprinted for the back door.

Two seconds later, she disappeared inside the building.

The driver scooped up his weapon, hopped in the car, and sped out of the alley, scattering reporters in his wake.

Mac hurried back to his vehicle. Who was she? And what had she brought to the gallery?

He would have expected them to try to get the painting of the princess *out* of the building. It was already inside, wasn't it?

He retrieved his phone and looked up the gallery again, pulling up the photos of the staff. He'd spotted Lise Fortier out front preparing for the press conference. And clearly, this hadn't been Henri Marchant, the assistant. Even in disguise, his build was all wrong.

That left Sophie Williams, the gallery manager. He studied the photo, then used her name to do a larger search. More images popped up, from gallery openings and events all over the city since she'd become manager several years ago.

The thirtyish blonde had a buttoned-up business style, usually pictured wearing blazers and silk tops paired with pencil skirts and sky-high heels, her hair clipped in a low ponytail. He kept reading her bio, surprised to learn she was American. Interesting.

So who just slipped into the gallery looking like Sophia Loren? Ms. Williams? And if so, why did she remind him so much of the sixtyish matron he'd seen at the Flasks' mansion the other night?

Far more importantly, what had she brought *to* the gallery?

Oh no you don't. One glimpse at the intent look in the driver's eyes and Sophie had slung her tote bag with enough force to send his gun flying. Heart pounding, she spun in a tight circle, breaking his grip on her arm. While he bent to retrieve his weapon, the back door of the gallery opened a crack, and she leaped toward it.

The uniformed security guard yanked her into the building. He slammed the door shut behind her and turned the dead bolt seconds before fists thumped on the door and reporters shouted questions.

She leaned against the wall for a moment and took several deep breaths to steady her thudding heart.

"Are you all right, miss?" The guard was in his forties, fit and trim, looking completely at home with the weapon on his hip.

She heard tires squeal as the driver sped away.

Had he been trying to protect her and she misread the situation? Or was he trying to steal the painting? She'd think about that later. *Play the part.*

She calmly headed to the worktable and set the painting down. "I'm fine." She sent him a smile. "Thank you for your help."

"You appeared to have the situation well in hand."

Sophie undid the scarf and tucked it and her sunglasses into her tote. "As did you." She fluffed her wig, then picked up the painting and headed toward the vault.

It wasn't until after it was safely locked away and the security guard had whisked Lise inside after the press conference that Sophie dropped her guard enough to stop pacing.

"Wow, that was insane." Lise sank into her desk chair and heaved out a breath.

"Where's your lawyer?" Sophie asked.

"He had another appointment so he couldn't stay." Lise didn't look up, rooting around in the drawer for her handbag.

Sophie glanced at the security guard hovering in the doorway. "Would you give us a minute?"

He nodded and retreated, quietly closing the door behind him.

"You promised me an explanation." Sophie folded her arms over her chest, leaned a hip against the desk.

Lise glanced up, set her purse on her lap and started digging through it. Without a word, she pulled out her cell phone and dialed.

"Hey!" Lise had never, ever been rude to her like this. Sophie opened her mouth to say more but shut it when Lise held up one finger. It was trembling.

"Nadine? I'm finished here. Yes, it was as much a nightmare as we expected. I'll be there in twenty minutes, maybe longer with the crush outside." She stood, slung her bag over her shoulder and started for the door.

Sophie stepped in her path. "I understand there's a lot going on, but I need an explanation, Lise. Where did your mother get the portrait? What did the letter say?"

Lise finally met her eyes, her own shadowed. She clearly hadn't slept any more than Sophie had. "I don't know. I, ah, haven't been able to bring myself to read it yet. Right now, I need to get to work. You locked our copy of the portrait in the vault?"

"Yes, but what about—?"

Lise came around the desk, gave her a quick peck on each cheek, her voice choked. "We'll talk more later. I promise. I'll call you."

Without another word, she slipped out of the office. Sophie peeked through the blinds as the guard assisted her into an Uber.

Once the car disappeared from view, Sophie headed straight for the sideboard in the back room. Normally, she would never do such a thing, but these were not normal circumstances. With a quick peek to be sure Henri wasn't nearby, she opened the drawer where Lise had put the letter from the lawyer.

It wasn't there.

"Tell me you have the painting." It was not a question.

Laszlo Deak gripped the steering wheel and forced his fury deep, so far down inside that it wouldn't show in his voice. He understood the power of words, that one wrong response, even a wrong tone, could destroy what was left of his family, and he wouldn't take that risk. He'd debated ignoring the call, but that would only have made things worse. "Not yet, ah, sir. I didn't expect her to—"

"You didn't expect. It's your job to expect. This should have been child's play. All you had to do was take the painting from the woman and bring it to me."

He swallowed hard. "Sir, I'm not sure she had the painting."

The silence grew ominous, and his hands started to shake.

"Why wouldn't she?" The question was asked softly, quietly, but his stomach clenched anyway.

"Because logic would indicate the painting was already in the gallery and being smuggled out. Not the other way around."

More silence. Laszlo took another shallow breath, wished he'd kept his logic to himself. But it made sense.

"Have I asked you to think?"

"No, sir," he answered immediately.

"Then get me that painting. Today."

"Yes, sir. Of course."

"Do I need to explain what happens to people who make excuses? Or worse, what happens to the family of those who fail me?"

His heart hammered in his chest and sweat rolled down the side of his face, but he was frozen, too scared and too angry to wipe it away. He squeezed his eyes closed, but that just brought the picture of his son's terrified face to mind. And his mother's. "I will have it today," he promised.

"Don't contact me until you do."

The line went dead.

Laszlo reached into his pocket and pulled out the picture of his family from happier times, before his articles condemning the Hungarian government's increasing shift toward totalitarianism got his wife killed, before his son and his mother were taken hostage when he answered an ad for an artwork researcher. He would not lose what was left of his family to his own foolishness, his need to be right, to speak up.

He started the engine, pulled back onto the road, and headed back toward the gallery.

Ten-year-old Mozes was the light of his life. For him, Laszlo would keep his mouth shut and do whatever he had to do.

No matter what.

11

Lise had always found clarity and comfort in work, but tonight it wasn't helping. She'd been sitting in front of the computer in her office at Neue Anfänge for over an hour, but the missing persons reports blurred in front of her eyes, and all she could hear was her mother's voice begging her to come see her as soon as possible. Why hadn't she gone?

She dropped her head in her hands, fingering the medallion around her neck. Because she'd been busy with the gallery opening. Even though she'd told Mutti she'd come right after that, her mother clearly had things to say. Irmgard had barely been able to walk, but she'd managed to get herself to the train station and had purchased a ticket to Munich before she collapsed and died.

Lise swallowed hard before she pulled the envelope with her mother's letter from her pocket, held it with fingers that trembled.

"How did things go at the press conference?"

Nadine stood in the doorway, arms crossed over her tan suit jacket, gray hair scraped into its usual severe bun at the nape of her neck.

Lise shoved the letter back in her pocket and indicated the straight-backed guest chair. The furnishings in their aging building were a comfortable mishmash of antiques and donated furniture. Any cash donations went to helping their clients, not to decor. "It went as well as could be expected, I suppose. Have you seen the coverage?"

Nadine sank down, ankles crossed, hands folded in her lap, and speared her with sharp gray eyes. At sixty-seven, her body showed signs of slowing down a bit, but the woman inside who'd single-handedly started a nonprofit to help women and then run it for forty years wasn't giving ground easily. "Who hasn't? Princess Johanna is all anyone is talking about." She leaned forward slightly, voice brisk. "Take a few days off to deal with all this."

"Absolutely not. We hired an extra security guard, and Sophie and Henri will be fine. This should all die down in a couple of days. I have far more important things to do here."

"Our work is always important, no question." Her voice softened a hair. "But Irmgard was your mother. You haven't taken a moment to grieve."

Lise ignored the hitch in her chest, where waves of grief and regret stole her breath. "I'll grieve later, when I know for sure the women are safe. Besides, she was your friend too."

"She was, for many years. And I'll be forever grateful that she sent you to me and Neue Anfänge." Nadine studied her for a long moment, her eyes drawn to the medallion Lise rubbed between her fingers. "Do you know why Irmgard sent you the painting?"

Another whisper of foreboding slid over Lise's skin, and she looked away. Why did everyone keep asking her that? "Not yet." Herr Dengler had said the letter would explain things, but some sixth sense told her that whatever it said, it would forever alter her relationship with her mother. Lise hadn't been able to face it.

"Are you?"

Lise's head snapped up. Nadine's expression said she'd asked the question more than once.

"I'm sorry, am I what?"

"Are you going out to the encampments again tonight?"

"Not tonight. According to Amalia, it was a few days between raids. I've been scouring missing persons reports, but none of the three women match the descriptions she gave me."

"Is it possible they just took off since no one saw them being taken? Sadly, it's not uncommon."

"You're right. But the way those men were eyeing Amalia makes me think there's a definite agenda at play here."

"We'll need more than that to get the Polizei involved."

"I'm working on that." Lise checked her watch, then shut down her computer. "I want to check in with Amalia and Sam before I head home. I'll see you in the morning."

Nadine rose. "Your mother was proud of you, Lise. Always. And so am I. Get some rest. And if you need some time off, just let me know."

Lise swallowed the knot of guilt threatening to choke her and nodded. "I won't. But thanks."

After the press conference, the crowd outside the gallery subsided, but only slightly. Sophie played eighties rock through her earbuds to block out the noise.

When Joshua, one of the other security guards, knocked on her office door sometime later, she yelped in surprise.

"Pardon me, miss. I thought you would want to know many of the reporters left to check out whatever is going on with the sirens." He waved a hand toward the windows, where more blared.

"While I don't wish tragedy on anyone, I hope it gives us a little breathing room."

"Would you like my replacement to pick up dinner for you on his way in?"

Sophie glanced at her phone, surprised to see it was almost nine o'clock. "No, I'm fine. Thank you for asking, though. Maybe check with Henri?"

When he slipped from the room, Sophie scrolled through her phone. There were no messages from Lise. No calls either. Strange. She'd told Sophie she'd be in touch. She sent a text: **All good by you?**

She went back to poring over all the information she could find about Princess Johanna and especially the portraits, but she didn't feel like she made any headway. Not without knowing why Lise's mother had sent her the portrait. Or where she got it.

By ten o'clock, she left Lise a voice mail. "I know how you get with your volunteer work, but with everything that's going on, send up a flare and let me know you're okay."

After she locked up her files, Sophie double-checked the vault and all the security cameras.

"Good night, Henri." He was in the back room, dusting. "Go on home. There is nothing more to be done here tonight."

He turned, eyes still alight with anguish. "I just want to finish up—"

"You are done doing penance, Henri. Nobody is angry with you. Truly."

"If only I hadn't—"

She held up a hand. "None of us could have predicted this. Let's just move on, okay? Please. Go home."

He nodded but still wouldn't meet her eyes. "As soon as I'm done here, I'll be on my way."

Sophie slipped into the coat, scarf, and sunglasses she'd worn earlier, minus the wig this time, as it gave her a headache. She confirmed that the Uber she'd ordered was outside and then asked Joshua to walk her out.

As soon as he cracked the back door open, the remaining reporters started shouting questions. She kept her head down as Joshua held the door, using his body as a visual shield as she slipped inside the Uber.

The moment the door closed, Sophie said, "You'll have to hurry or they'll block us in."

The driver glanced in the rearview mirror and hit the gas with enough force to push her against the seat. He careened down the alley, grinning like he'd been waiting for someone to say that his whole life.

When he took the corner on two wheels, Sophie gripped the seat back. "You might want to slow down a bit, or we'll draw even more attention."

"Of course, my apologies." He slowed their pace the tiniest bit. Sophie wanted to laugh at his pout.

She turned to look out the back window and sighed. Several of the news vans were hot on their heels. What did they think she could tell them?

Another look back and she said, "Turn left at the next intersection. Then a quick right. Let's see if we can shake them."

The driver's grin returned as he squealed around the next corner just as the light turned red.

She had him lead them on a merry chase through the city, her anxiety leveling a bit more as one news vehicle after another dropped out of the strange caravan. There was still one car, though, that he hadn't been able to shake. The nondescript Fiat had been keeping pace without a problem, no matter what the driver did.

Whoever this was, she didn't want them to know where she lived. "I'm sorry. I need to go somewhere else instead. Is that a problem?"

"That is probably wise, miss. I don't have another fare right now. Where would you like to go?"

She rattled off another address, and he zipped around the next corner with enough speed she worried about whiplash. She looked over her shoulder, sighing when the Fiat sped straight through the intersection.

As the driver wound his way back across the city, Sophie kept watch out the back window.

"I think we lost him," the driver said.

"Nice driving. Thank you."

He grinned, showing a missing front tooth, and sped through yet another yellow light, careening around the next corner.

When he brought the car to a rocking stop at the address she'd given him, Sophie added a generous tip. "That's if you don't mention to anyone where you dropped me off."

"Of course. Shall I wait until you get inside?"

"That won't be necessary, but thank you." She smiled her gratitude and hurried into the building.

When she walked into the lobby, the young man at the check-in desk smiled politely. "May I help you?"

Sophie stopped to remove the scarf and sunglasses, and his eyes widened with recognition. "Ah, Ms. Williams. Good evening."

"Good evening, Andre." Normally, she stopped to chitchat, but not tonight. She felt like her skin was going to burst with all the pent-up energy and anxiety squirming below the surface. If she wanted to work it out, she'd best get moving. The studio would close in just over an hour.

Ten minutes later, she'd changed into her white fencing uniform and entered one of the bright, airy salons. The studio occupied the second floor of a building from the 1700s, with high ceilings and tall windows, the polished wood floors gleaming beneath her feet.

The studio was quiet this late in the evening, except for two men dueling in the far corner. Sophie chose her weapon and began her warm-up routine, running through a series of lunges and whipping her foil through the air.

This was when she felt closest to her parents. During her childhood, their jobs kept them away more than home, but when they returned, the three of them fenced. It was the one thing they did together, the only time she didn't feel like a third wheel, on the outside looking in.

She'd have preferred a sparring partner to work through her pent-up emotions tonight, but she could practice alone. She'd certainly done it enough after they died when she was sixteen.

But even then, no matter how many lunges she did or how tired her arm got from whipping her foil through the air, nothing exorcised her fury that they'd lied to her. Not once, but her entire life. Everything she believed had been a lie.

With Lise's help, she'd eventually worked through the anger and betrayal—mostly—but trust was still a whole other issue.

She was midlunge when a male voice said, "I am in need of a partner. Would you be willing to do me the honor?"

Sophie turned and found a tall, well-built man standing behind her, much too close given that she'd not heard him approach. His face was hidden behind the mask, as hers was. He held his foil in one hand and bowed from the waist. Despite the gallant gesture, tension vibrated off him in waves.

A flicker of unease passed over her skin. They were the only ones in the room. The other gentlemen had left. "Are you a regular member? I don't recall seeing you here before."

"I just transferred from a facility across town." He raised his saber. "Shall we?"

"Stay focused. Stay present." Her father's voice echoed in her mind.

She placed her dominant foot forward, back leg sideways, and raised her weapon. "En garde."

They crossed swords and began the dance. Sometimes when she practiced against men, they held back so as not to overpower her. This man gave no quarter, parrying with speed and strength. They moved across the floor together, advancing and retreating, lunging and blocking, the balance of power shifting easily between them. Sweat beaded on her brow and dripped behind her mesh mask. He was good. There was no question.

"How long have you been fencing, miss?"

Sophie avoided his lunge and spun out of reach to push him back again with a series of advances. "Since I was twelve. It's good stress relief."

"It is that. It's also a test of strength and skill."

He deftly backed her toward the wall, but she wouldn't let him trap her that easily. She spun, avoided his blade, then advanced again.

She thought she caught a grin behind his mask and realized she was grinning too. She hadn't enjoyed a session this much in a very long time.

Just as she had him on the retreat, a bead of sweat dripped into her eye and she blinked it away. That one second of inattention was all the opening he needed.

He lunged forward and before she could react, he had her pinned against the wall with the tip of his blunted foil. "Do you surrender?"

"This match, perhaps. But I'll best you next time."

He tilted his blade toward the floor, leaned closer, and whispered, "Never underestimate your opponent, Fräulein."

The tendril of alarm that slid down her back had nothing to do with the husky timbre of his voice. The blue eyes boring into hers belonged to none other than Mac McKenzie.

She whipped her sword up and those eyes widened as she pressed the blunted tip under his chin. "You might remember the same, sir."

Before he had a chance to question her further, Sophie turned and hurried into the women's changing room. She locked the door behind her and sagged against it.

Had he followed her here? And more importantly, had he started to connect the dots?

12

Mac was grinning like a fool as he changed back into his street clothes. Sophie had surprised him with her strength and speed, to say nothing of her determination. But none of that would hold up against a bullet.

He'd almost lost her on the way here. He gave her driver credit. He'd maneuvered like this was a street race and he was desperate to win. Mac wouldn't lose her again. He didn't know how yet, but Ms. Sophie Williams was intricately connected to whatever was going on.

He'd left a voice mail earlier for Lise Fortier's lawyer, not really surprised that he hadn't gotten a call back. The clip of the press conference showed Dengler insisting that the portrait was authentic and the legal property of Ms. Fortier, who would display it at some future date.

Neither Mac nor Prince Benedikt was willing to take the lawyer's word for anything related to the portrait.

Mac had to get his hands on that painting.

He was already back in his car when Sophie hurried out of the studio and into another Uber, her cell phone pressed to her ear.

Henri waited to make his move until the new guard went outside for a cigarette. The man wasn't supposed to leave the building or smoke on the job, but that worked to Henri's advantage. He figured he had six minutes, probably five, but he wouldn't need that much time.

He slipped down the hall to the large vault hidden behind a bifold closet door in Lise's office. Keeping his face out of camera range, he took the can of spray paint he'd bought earlier and sprayed the camera. At the last second, he remembered the newly installed second camera and sprayed that too, then hurried to the safe. Lise had given him the combination six months ago, and he'd fairly burst with pride at the responsibility. Even now, he couldn't believe what he was about to do. The idea of stealing artwork was abhorrent to him. He loved art, all of it. Paintings, sculptures, classical and modern works, and everything in between. He still couldn't believe his good fortune to work here, surrounded by all this beauty.

But he was desperate. The portrait of Princess Johanna was the answer to his prayers. It was both his salvation and his ticket to hell.

He, like everyone, had loved the princess and he fervently wished it could be displayed for all to see, even if he couldn't keep the portrait for himself. But self-preservation demanded otherwise.

His fingers shook as he spun the dial. Right, left, back the other way two more times. When it finally clicked open, he swallowed hard. There could be no going back now. Sweat slid down the back of his neck and pooled under his arms.

With a trembling, gloved hand, he opened the heavy door and reached in for the portrait Sophie had locked away earlier. He unwrapped the brown paper, turned the frame over, and removed the decoy painting of George Clooney, then set it inside the safe. Once he reassembled everything, he stood back and looked his fill of the portrait, carefully brushing aside tears of joy. Realizing he'd lost track of time, he quickly rewrapped it, closed and locked the safe, and peeked out the blinds. The tip of the guard's cigarette glowed red in the dark.

Henri waited.

The guard stubbed it out, then started his circuit around the outside of the building, checking windows and doors.

Before he lost his nerve, Henri grabbed the painting and hurried to the back door. He eased it open, checked the alley, then slipped outside, the scent of rain heavy in the air.

He hadn't gone more than ten meters when he heard a whisper of sound behind him.

He froze. Turned.

Too late.

The shadow morphed into human form, and something metal collided with his head in a sickening thud. Pain exploded through him, and shock held him in place for one suspended moment.

"My princess," he murmured as he staggered and fell to the ground, making sure he landed on his side to protect the painting. He couldn't let anything happen to it.

The dark shadow hovered over him and tugged the frame from his grasp. *No. No, no, no!* Henri tried to stop him, tried to hold tight, but his fingers wouldn't cooperate, and it slid from his grasp. He tried to scream, to call for help, but his voice wouldn't work either. *My princess.*

Footsteps receded into the night and with them, the last of Henri's hope.

The painting was gone. He couldn't let someone take it. He had to get it back.

Even as the pain grew to unbearable levels and his limbs began to go numb, he whimpered and tried to climb to his feet.

He fell back down and soon the darkness outside crept inside. It slid over his vision until everything, including the pain, slowly, gradually, disappeared.

13

Lise was still smiling after her visit with Amalia and Sam. She'd been rocking him when he accidentally kicked her purse and dumped everything onto the floor, giggling with delight. But it was Amalia's growing concern over the three missing women that had Lise scouring the streets tonight.

She pulled to the curb where another group of women and children huddled under a bridge, doing their best to stay warm. She'd met several before, when Neue Anfänge distributed food, homemade soup, and coffee from their portable kitchen.

She murmured encouragement here, patted a back there, smiled at a child, and handed out blankets at every stop.

Everywhere she went, Lise asked the same question: "Have you seen them take any women? Has anyone disappeared?"

The responses were always the same. Shrugs. Averted eyes. Fear. But nothing concrete to help her figure out what was going on.

She drove until she found another small encampment, but everyone there was tucked into their makeshift shelters. She stayed in her car and kept watch, not wanting to disturb them.

When her head started bobbing like one of those dashboard dogs, she turned on the small battery-powered lantern she'd brought with her.

She'd been a coward long enough.

With a deep breath for courage, she slowly pulled out the crumpled letter from her mother. Just looking at Mutti's handwriting brought a wash of grief. Lise didn't want to know what it said.

But she needed to know. She smoothed the wrinkles out of the envelope and removed the sheet of paper.

My dearest Lise,
    As I write this, I know my time is growing short, but I have much to tell you and want to get the words out before I lose my courage yet again. You have been the greatest treasure of my life, and I cherish every moment we have spent together. I decided you won't read these words until after I'm gone because, selfishly, I want to die knowing your love for me is secure and that you will mourn me as the mother you loved, regardless of what comes next.

Lise swiped the tears from her cheeks and shoved the letter back into the envelope, then tucked it into her pocket, her fears about the letter's contents confirmed. She wasn't ready to read the rest. Not tonight. Maybe never.

She turned off the lantern and was about to head home when the familiar white van pulled up to the curb, no lights, sliding to a stop in the shadows beyond the streetlights.

Every sense on high alert, she turned off the dome light and slipped from her car, keeping to the trees as she approached.

"Let's go. Everybody out. Come on. Hurry up."

Sleepy women milled around, trying to get their bearings. Children cried at being rousted from a deep sleep.

Just as they'd done last time, they herded the line of women between two of the men. Ski masks covered their faces, like last time, so she couldn't tell if these were the same men. But her blood ran cold when they nodded at a pretty young woman no more than seventeen or eighteen.

She reached for her cell phone, determined to take pictures despite the masks. Maybe they could still identify them somehow. Where was her phone? A quick search of her pockets yielded nothing, but as she looked up, the men grabbed the girl and shoved her into the back of the van.

"Oh, heck no!" Lise spun around and raced back to her car, desperate to follow them.

By the time she sped away from the curb, the van had disappeared from view, so she floored it to the next intersection.

There! Brake lights blinked on as the van barreled around another corner, a block away.

She had to get closer. Foot pressed to the gas pedal, she rooted around in her bag with her free hand, still searching for her cell phone. She had to get help.

Where was it? Frustration built as the van careened through the streets, no match for her little car. She tried to make out a license plate, but the glimpse she caught under a streetlight told her it had been covered with mud.

She'd just have to ram the back of the van, try to run it off the road. It was the only thing she could think of to get the girl back.

The van screeched through the next intersection, ignoring the red light. Lise stomped the gas pedal to the floor to keep up when a garbage truck pulled out from the cross street.

Both feet on the brakes, she swerved right and missed broadsiding him by inches. With the wheel gripped in both hands, the vehicle's back end fishtailed, then she sped through the intersection.

On the other side, everything was quiet. Where had they gone? There was no sign of the van, no taillights. Nothing.

She circled the block several times, searching in all directions, but the van had disappeared.

Tears of frustration and fury clogging her throat, Lise pulled to the curb, turned on the dome light, and dug through her purse, upending it on the passenger seat. Her phone was gone.

Now what? She looked around the deserted street. She was in a familiar part of Munich. Where could she find a phone? In the distance, the lights of an all-night mini-mart shone like an oasis in the desert, and she muttered her thanks. They still had pay phones, didn't they?

She grabbed coins from the cup holder, scrambled out of the car, and ran toward the lights. Fool that she was, she didn't know Nadine's number from memory, but she knew Sophie's. She'd let her know what had happened, then go straight to the Polizei and file a report.

The old-fashioned pay phone stood in a dark corner. She didn't have a Telekom card, but she should have enough coins for a short call.

She put the receiver to her ear and dialed. "Sophie! Come get—"

The telltale click of a cocking gun sounded behind her as a revolver pressed against her temple.

"Hang up the phone. Now."

━━━━━━

Sophie huddled into her jacket, but the bone-deep cold had nothing to do with the predawn temperature. She stood in the alley behind the gallery and swallowed hard. The *Kriminalpolizei* detective standing beside her crouched down and pulled back the sheet. Bile rose in her throat.

"Yes, that's Henri Marchant." He looked anguished, even in death. *What were you thinking, Henri? We trusted you.*

She'd seen the video footage, and it clearly showed him spray-painting the security camera before he'd whipped toward the newly installed additional camera and sprayed that too. He must have taken her copy of *Today* out of the gallery's vault after that. But he'd known it was a copy, hadn't he? Was he planning to sell it as the original? Did he need money? It didn't make sense.

Yet.

"Ms. Williams, please come inside," the detective said. "We can talk out of the cold."

Sophie nodded and followed him inside the gallery. Once they were seated in her office, he asked how she liked her coffee and went to fetch some. While he was gone, she pulled out her cell phone and tried to call Lise, but it went straight to voice mail. Again. Just as it had the last four times she'd called.

Anxiety hummed under her skin. She sent another text: **We have an emergency. Call me.**

"Have you been able to reach Frau Fortier yet?" The detective set a cup on her desk and took the seat across from her.

"No. And that's very unlike her."

"Did she give any indication of her plans this evening? A date, perhaps?"

Sophie shook her head. "Not that I know of. She left here to go to her charity work, said she'd call me later, but I haven't heard from her."

He sipped his coffee, sharp eyes never leaving her face. "She works with Neue Anfänge, correct?"

Sophie hid her annoyance, as he'd already asked her that. And what did Lise's work have to do with Henri's death?

As though he could follow her train of thought, Detective von Binden asked, "How long has Henri worked for the Fortier Gallery?"

Sophie had to smile. "A long time. Lise hired him years ago, and he absolutely loved his job. He was like a kid in a candy store every time we got a new shipment of artwork in. He loved art. So this—" she waved a hand—"makes no sense. Why would he steal the portrait?"

The detective's eyebrows shot to his hairline. "Why indeed? Half the population of Munich would like to get their hands on that painting, Ms. Williams."

Sophie opened her mouth to tell him it was a copy, not the original, but snapped it shut just in time. She wouldn't divulge that until she'd talked with Lise, possibly the estate lawyer too. For now, the fewer people who knew, the better. "I understand what you're saying, but he had to have known he wouldn't get away with it. He's one of only three people who have the combination to the safe."

. "Would it surprise you to learn Henri Marchant had a gambling problem?"

Her mouth dropped open in shock, and she shook her head. "I had no idea. He was always impeccably dressed, courteous, an art lover, as I said. We never talked much about personal matters."

"What about Frau Fortier?"

"What about her?"

"Did she have any financial problems we should know about?"

Sophie bristled. "If you've checked Henri's financials, then you've checked hers and know the answer yourself. The gallery does quite well and she works for Neue Anfänge, though she donates much of her time. And her mother left her the priceless painting."

"Her mother also left considerable medical debts."

"Which Lise will take care of," Sophie shot back. "Where are you going with this?"

Before he could respond, Sophie's cell phone rang, and she pounced on it. "Lise? Where are you?"

"Sophie! Come get—" Her voice was cut off, then a male voice growled, "Hang up the phone. Now."

"Lise! Lise!" Sophie leaped from her chair.

The line went dead.

She tried to call back, but the phone just rang and rang.

"What's happened?" the detective demanded, and she jumped. She'd forgotten he was there.

"Lise asked me to come get her, but some man told her to hang up the phone. I need to figure out where she called from, how to get there."

"Give me the number."

Sophie stopped by the door, tote bag in hand. "What?"

"I'll get the address. Give me the number and we'll both go."

She read it to him and raced from the room.

When she opened the door to her car, he stopped her with a hand on her arm. "We'll take my car. It'll be faster."

14

When Sophie and Detective von Binden arrived at the all-night gas station and mini-mart, Sophie leaped from the car and ran toward the phone.

The detective caught up to her and stopped her before she could touch the receiver. "We need to dust for prints."

"And you'll find Lise's," Sophie snapped.

"And if we're lucky, also whoever told her to hang up." He turned and surveyed the dimly lit lot. "No security cameras. Of course." He speared her with a shrewd look. "What would Ms. Fortier have been doing at a place like this in the middle of the night? This is a long way from the gallery."

Sophie tossed up her hands. "I don't know. I don't know why she wouldn't have just called me on her cell phone either." She checked again and there were still no messages from Lise. "I've been trying to reach her all evening."

"So perhaps she lost her cell phone or it malfunctioned. Hence the need for a Telekom phone."

Anxiety raced under Sophie's skin. "But where's her car? Why didn't she drive here?"

"Another of the many unanswered questions tonight." The detective pulled out his cell phone and walked several paces away, issuing orders. She heard him describe Lise's car and then tuned him out.

Instead, she pulled up the map feature on her phone, looked up their current address, and zoomed out to see what might have brought Lise to this part of town. Her eyes widened and she dialed Nadine, Lise's boss at Neue Anfänge.

Nadine's gruff voice demanded, "What's wrong?"

"Hi, Nadine, I'm so sorry to bother you this early in the morning. Did you see Lise last night?"

There was rustling, as though she was getting out of bed. "Yes, she was at the office. Why? What's happened?"

Sophie startled when Detective von Binden stepped up beside her so he could hear her conversation. She took a step away. "We're not sure yet. Was she going to the encampments?" Sophie's map showed one of the makeshift homeless camps was less than half a mile away.

"No, she said she was tired. She was planning to stop by to see Amalia, but that was it. Isn't she home?"

Sophie wanted to smack her own forehead. "I'll check there next." After she promised to keep Nadine updated, Sophie turned to the detective. "I need to check Lise's apartment. Make sure this isn't all for nothing."

"She lives above the gallery, no?" At Sophie's nod, he dialed his phone again and asked one of the officers to knock on the door. If she didn't answer, they were to break in and make sure Ms. Fortier was all right.

Sophie shoved her hands on her hips. "You can't just break into her apartment!"

"Do you have a key?"

"Of course."

"Then we'll head back." He told his officers to hold off breaking down the door until they arrived, then ignored Sophie's demand that they leave right now. Instead, he paced beside his car until one of his colleagues pulled up and he handed the scene over to him.

Sophie's gut churned as they raced back to the gallery. *Please let her be there, safely asleep.* But Sophie was a realist. Nothing about tonight suggested her friend would be asleep upstairs while a murder investigation commenced in the alley below. Especially after that phone call.

When Sophie unlocked the apartment door several minutes later, her fears were confirmed.

Lise's bed was made. There was no sign of her purse, cell phone, or anything to indicate she'd come home last night.

The good news was that there wasn't a body either.

She walked back into Lise's bedroom and dialed her friend's phone again, left another message. "Lise. Call me. Please. I need to know you're safe."

She spotted something peeking out of the drawer of the bedside table. With a quick glance over her shoulder to be sure the detective wasn't sneaking up behind her, she pulled the drawer open and found the envelope from the lawyer. A quick check inside revealed the lawyer's cover letter but not the letter from Irmgard to Lise.

Sophie tucked it in her tote, then rejoined the detective in the living room.

"Detective, sir! Down here!" one of the crime scene techs shouted from below. The detective spun and hurried back downstairs.

Sophie clutched her phone as she followed. *Where are you, Lise?*

He raced through the city streets, sure that every car behind him was a police vehicle that would pull him over and arrest him at any second. He still couldn't believe fate had handed him such an amazing opportunity. He'd gone to the gallery to scope it out, see if he could figure out a way to gain access to the safe and the portrait, when Henri Marchant, whom he'd met at the recent gallery opening, came sneaking out the back door with the painting in his hands. Well, he'd assumed it was the painting. But what else could it be? It was the right size and shape, and Henri had definitely been in an all-fired hurry to get to his car.

He still wasn't sure why he'd grabbed the tire iron from the trunk of his car before he got out, but it had seemed good to have a weapon in case the other man was reluctant to give up his prize.

Another glance in his rearview and he slowed his pace. It would be foolish to come this far and then get caught for something as idiotic as speeding.

He hoped Henri was all right. He really hadn't meant to hit him quite as hard as he had. He'd simply gotten carried away in the moment. Maybe he should go back and check. Or call in an anonymous tip.

As his home came into view, he pushed such foolishness aside. He had to stay focused on the goal. There was nothing to connect him to what happened. He'd kept his hat pulled low in case there were security cameras, which he assumed there would be. He'd worn gloves, so he wouldn't leave fingerprints. And he'd taken the tire iron with him when he left.

Once the garage door slid closed behind him, he took the tire iron out of the trunk and set it in the utility sink, where he used bleach to remove all traces of blood. He swallowed hard at the bit of hair stuck to the shaft, but he wouldn't let himself think about that. Once the rod and sink were completely clean, his hands stung from the bleach, but that would ensure there was no trace evidence on him either.

He went to the trunk and studied the dark spot in the carpet. Thinking quickly, he reached across the console and took out his thermos. He always filled it before he went to work and kept it at his desk, but he hadn't finished all of the coffee that day.

He quickly dumped the dregs over the bloodstains, then used bleach to scrub the area until the carpet had white spots where it had been. Everyone would believe a coffee stain, right? If you didn't get the cream out, it would stink.

He glanced down. What about his shoes? He slipped them off,

his stomach churning at the blood caught in the treads. Had he left shoe prints? He couldn't be sure, so he scoured the soles of the shoes with more bleach, tucked them into a trash bag, then stepped outside and slipped the bag into his neighbor's trash can.

Satisfied, he sanitized his hands one more time, then reached into the trunk and took out the portrait. He carefully unwrapped the brown paper hiding it and hurried into the dining room. He took down the landscape that hung on the wall and replaced it with Princess Johanna's portrait.

He walked down the hall and slipped into his wife's room. Anna was dozing in the hospital bed and stirred as he entered. A tired smile curved her sunken cheeks. "You're back. I miss you when you're not here."

Guilt sliced through him. He hated, absolutely hated, watching this vibrant woman, his best friend and soulmate, waste away from the leukemia eating her from the inside out. So he hid at work. They needed the money, of course, but he couldn't bear to spend his days in a deathbed vigil.

He sank into the chair at her bedside and gently clasped her hand. "I have a surprise for you." He smiled and tucked the scarf more securely over her bald head. "Can you get into the chair? Or shall I carry you?"

A spark of interest lit her eyes. "Where are we going?"

"Just to the dining room."

The spark dimmed. "I'm not hungry."

He stroked her hand, swallowed hard. "I know, *liebchen*. I'm not going to force-feed you. I want to show you something. A present."

She struggled to sit up and his grin widened. She couldn't resist the idea of a present. "Put me in the chair."

With one careful swoop, he lifted her from the bed, trying to ignore how light she was. He wouldn't spoil this moment thinking about all she'd lost, not just in weight, but in time. He had to stay positive, had to look ahead. And part of that meant fulfilling her heart's desire.

He settled her in the wheelchair, tucked a soft blanket over her knees and another around her shoulders. He crouched down to smile at her. "Are you ready?"

Her eyes twinkled the way they used to when they first fell in love so many years ago, and he swallowed hard as he stood. *Think about today. Now.*

When they reached the archway that led to the dining room, he said, "Close your eyes."

Once he confirmed she'd obeyed, he wheeled her in front of the painting. "You can open your eyes now."

He stood by the painting so he could see her reaction. First came wide-eyed shock, then disbelief, then the tears he'd expected.

"No! It can't be." She tried to get closer but couldn't manage the wheels. He hurried over and positioned the chair where she wanted it.

She turned her wet eyes toward him. "Where did you get this? Oh, liebchen, I've wanted this for so long. Johanna is so beautiful in this portrait. She looks just like she did when we were girls together."

"You have always been far more beautiful, my love, cousin or no cousin."

"Second cousin."

He raised an eyebrow. "You're still the most beautiful woman in the world."

She studied the portrait in silence for several long minutes, drinking in every detail. He could almost see the memories washing over her in the sudden smiles, the quick spurt of tears.

Finally, she turned to him, her gaze troubled now. "But I didn't think it was for sale. How did you get it?"

He leaned down and placed a kiss on her brow, thanking his lucky stars that she'd never been one to watch much of the news. She'd been fascinated by the discovery of the portrait, but that was the extent of it. He'd be extra careful she didn't start tuning in now. "Gifts are not to be questioned. They are meant to be enjoyed. And you are enjoying this, no?"

She reached out and took his hand, kissed the back of it. "More than you will ever know." She wrinkled her nose. "Why do your hands smell like bleach?"

He regaled her with the tale of the spilled coffee and made her laugh. But even the few minutes in the chair took their toll and she began to slump, as though she didn't have the strength to stay upright any longer.

"Will you hang it in my room? I want to be able to look at it all the time."

"Of course." He wheeled her down the hallway, tucked her under the covers, and then fetched a hammer and nails and hung the portrait on the wall opposite her bed.

Once he'd finished, she sent him a tired smile and drifted off to sleep.

He slipped out of the room and retreated to his study. He poured a shot of whiskey and turned on the news, choking on his drink when a solemn-faced young man reported a death outside the Fortier Gallery. The deceased was not identified yet, pending notification of next of kin.

Stomach churning, he raced into the bathroom and retched until there was nothing left. Except the truth. He'd killed a man.

His hands shook as he studied his face in the mirror. There was obviously nothing he could do about that now. He just had to go on as though nothing had happened.

Step one would be to make sure the nursing staff he'd hired didn't put two and two together.

But the news hadn't mentioned the portrait. There was no reason to connect him to the crime. Right?

He spent the rest of the night pacing his study, running scenarios through his mind. He'd tell the household staff he'd purchased an inexpensive copy—which were cropping up all over the Internet—but to keep that news from his wife since she'd longed for a portrait of her cousin for years. Yes, that should work.

When a rainstorm moved through the area and no police pounded on his door, he decided he was safe. As least for now.

And even if he wasn't, he'd granted his wife her dying wish. That was all that mattered.

15

Laszlo's cell phone rang again, and he jumped, eyeing it like he would a coiled snake. Nausea roiled in his stomach and sweat broke out on his skin, despite the cold, predawn air. He couldn't admit he'd failed again, not if he had a prayer of keeping his son and his mother alive. He'd seen what the man did to those who didn't do what he told them to. And their families.

Laszlo squeezed his eyes shut, but he couldn't block out the horror of what he'd been forced to watch. Or the smell of the blood. Bile rose in his throat, and he brought his focus sharply back to the present.

When he'd arrived at the gallery earlier, he'd spotted what looked like Henri Marchant—one of the employees, according to his research—dead on the ground and a security guard with a cell phone to his ear. There was nothing Laszlo could do at that point, certainly not with hordes of police converging on the scene, so he'd quietly driven away before they arrived.

But now, he slowly eased his car back into the alley and parked in the shadows. There was still plenty of police activity at this early hour, and a driving rain helped camouflage his car.

He pulled out the picture of Mozes and took several calming breaths to steady himself. This was who he had to worry about.

Which meant he had to buy time while he figured out who had snatched the painting before he arrived. And then figure out how to get it back. Frustration swamped him, and he rammed a hand through his hair, then shoved the gun he'd been given back under the seat. His father had made sure he knew how to use it, but he was a history professor and a sometimes freelance writer. He wasn't a thief. Or a hired killer.

To save his family, he would be both, if necessary. He'd spent years studying the movements of people throughout history, so finding the painting couldn't be that hard. Certainly no harder than the proof of corruption in Hungary's government he'd uncovered.

He squeezed his eyes closed as memories of his burning house—payback—scorched his eyelids. He determined to harness his anger over Gitta's death as a way to sharpen his focus. Once he had the painting and had secured his family's freedom, he'd figure out how to free others being held captive by this monster. He would give them a voice, make sure their stories were heard, make sure their captor never hurt anyone again. Ever.

Memories of that other man's desperate pleading, of his anguish, rang in his ears and Laszlo shook his head, trying to dislodge the sounds, settle his queasy stomach. He couldn't focus on that right now. He had to think clearly. Follow the facts, one at a time.

When his phone rang again, he turned the ringer off and dove into the history of Neuhansberg's royal family.

As the minutes ticked by, he scoured the Internet, compiling details and obscure facts while he waited and watched.

When he couldn't sit still another minute, he climbed out of his car.

When the rain started, the police erected a pop-up tent over the crime scene, with Detective von Binden cursing under his breath all the while. He and Sophie ducked under the canopy, where a crime scene technician held up a plastic bag with a scrap of brown paper inside. "We found this clutched in the deceased's fingers."

Detective von Binden leaned closer and glanced up sharply as Sophie crowded in to see as well. "This is an active crime scene, Fräulein Williams."

"And Henri is—was—my coworker and someone I considered a friend. I deserve to know what's going on."

He turned those sharp eyes on her. "Do you recognize the paper?"

Sophie managed not to roll her eyes, barely. "Yes, as I'm sure you do. That's what we wrap paintings in for transport."

The detective took her by the elbow and steered her toward the building. "Let's go check the safe, make sure everything else is still where it's supposed to be. Which we should have done earlier."

Sophie stopped short, planted her hands on her hips. "I thought we were trying to find Lise."

He waved a hand. "After you, Fräulein."

Sophie marched ahead of him. The man was like a burr under her saddle, an expression Lise taught her during one Christmas break at a horse ranch when her horse suddenly started bucking for no apparent reason.

"Herr Marchant knew the combination to the safe?"

"Yes. We gave it to him about six months ago."

"Why?"

Sophie stopped in front of the safe. "Why did we give it to him?" At his nod she said, "It was just easier. Lise was spending more and more time at Neue Anfänge so we wanted someone besides the two of us to have access."

Sophie spun the dial, angling her body so the detective couldn't see.

The lock clicked open, and the detective stepped closer. "Is anything missing besides the portrait of Princess Johanna and her family?"

Sophie quickly flipped through the pieces stored inside the large safe. "No, just that one piece." She went to close the safe, but he blocked the movement with his arm.

"I'd like to get a few pictures of what's inside the safe."

"I don't think so, Detective." She tried to nudge his arm aside, but he didn't move. "What's in here is confidential. Some are pieces we safeguard for clients. There is an expectation of privacy I intend to maintain."

"And this is a murder investigation."

At the word *murder*, she had to stop and take a deep breath. "If word of what's in here gets out, it could severely damage the gallery's reputation. Some collectors are obsessive about their privacy. They don't want anyone to know exactly what pieces they have."

He raised a brow. "I'll do my best to keep that information confidential."

Which didn't mean doodley-squat. But her hands were tied. She stepped back while he took pictures.

"Frau Fortier has had some money issues lately too."

Sophie's head snapped up. "What?"

"We dug a little deeper and found she'd cashed in some stocks she's held for many years. Were there issues at the gallery? In her personal life?"

"No, she—" Sophie stopped as though she'd run headlong into a brick wall. "Wait. You think Lise—what? Murdered Henri and stole her own painting?"

He propped his hands on his hips, expression implacable. "Until I have reason to believe otherwise, it's a possibility I have to consider since she's conveniently missing and can't account for her whereabouts. She could take the insurance payout, sell the painting quietly . . ."

Sophie was pretty sure flames were shooting out the top of her head. "You're wrong, Detective. Dead wrong, as it were. There is no way Lise killed Henri. She would have absolutely no reason to."

"Except for a painting worth millions."

Sophie met his gaze without blinking. She wouldn't tell him the truth about the stolen painting. Not if keeping that secret would protect Lise in some way.

He narrowed his eyes. "Do you know where she is?"

"Would I be standing here wasting time with you if I did?"

The silence lengthened while they stared each other down. "If you have any shred of proof about your friend's innocence, now is the time to speak up, Fräulein Williams."

She stood, took out her keys. "What are you doing to find Lise, Detective?"

"Everything we can. We've put out an alert on her and her vehicle and are checking security cameras in the area."

Which meant he had zilch. "If there's nothing else, Detective, I think I'll head home. I'm exhausted."

"I can send one of my men to make sure you get home safely."

"That won't be necessary."

He nodded, but when she got in her car, a policeman followed her all the way home and didn't leave until she turned on a light in her apartment.

Don't worry, Lise. I'll find you.

16

Mac had barely fallen asleep when his phone buzzed. He bolted upright, mind instantly awake. He'd set several notifications to let him know whenever anything related to the royal family, the portrait, the gallery and anyone who worked there, or any other search criteria he could think of was mentioned either on the news or on the police scanners in several nearby countries.

This came from the local police. The address given was for the Fortier Gallery and indicated a detective with the Kriminalpolizei had requested the medical examiner and a crime scene investigation team.

Mac's hands were clumsy as he hastily pulled on clothes. Had Sophie gone back to the gallery while he was gone and been killed?

He nuked some cold coffee and poured it into a thermos, grabbed his laptop, and headed that way. Once there, he parked in the alley where he could keep watch without being seen. The driving rain helped, though it must be making the investigators crazy. Worry hummed under his skin. Even with the zoom on his camera, he couldn't get a close enough look at the body to know if it was a man or a woman. He released a sigh when Sophie finally emerged through the back door and climbed into her car. A police car followed, so he did the same.

Since the authorities would have an officer posted outside the gallery overnight, sneaking in to grab the painting wasn't an option.

The officer left once she reached her apartment, but Mac stayed.

He pulled out his laptop and spent the next few hours going over every scrap of information he could find about Princess Johanna's death, but considering the media storm, there weren't actually many new details, just a lot of rehashing of what happened years ago. According to a source at the royal family's home, it had been a sunny day and the princess wanted to take the children on a picnic. She'd asked the cook to pack pretty little teacups and saucers, tea sandwiches, and scones.

Her trusted secretary, Ilse, offered to drive, but the princess preferred to do that herself. In their initial interview, Prince Benedikt had told Mac he'd agreed and then told Ilse to follow a few minutes after they left, just in case. There had been some unrest in the wake of the unveiling of the portraits, and the prince was feeling extra cautious. There were those who opposed changing the line of succession, and he had warned Johanna to be careful.

When Ilse came around the corner twenty minutes later, she found the princess's car wrapped around a tree.

According to the police report, Ilse was questioned later and said that the car was engulfed in flames when she arrived. Distraught, she'd driven back to the palace to tell the prince. Sobbing, she'd claimed there was no way she could get close to the car.

Mac sat back in his seat. Had Ilse somehow been involved? To what end? She'd retired shortly after the princess's funeral, and no one had ever heard from her again. He ran a search, but absolutely nothing turned up to tell him where the woman had been for the past forty years.

He waded through several dozen more articles rehashing the princess's death, then googled Prince Benedikt's plan to change the rules of succession. Now he was getting somewhere. The opposition had been adamant and incredibly vocal. One high-ranking member of Parliament stopped just short of calling it treason.

Mac spent the next half hour researching Walter Starling, who would be near eighty now, but didn't turn up anything suspicious. By all accounts, he was well regarded by all who knew him. Still, could Starling have been involved in the princess's death?

Another article caught his eye. Prince Benedikt had hired extra guards after Johanna's death and one of them claimed he'd caught three teenage girls trying to scale the castle wall in search of a keepsake of their beloved Princess.

"Those girls are living proof of why changing the laws makes absolutely no sense," the guard said. "Putting emotional women in authority? Whoever came up with such idiocy? Ah, no offense to Prince Benedikt. Men rule countries. Women make babies."

Mac rolled his eyes and almost stopped reading, but the reporter's next question had him sitting up straighter. "Has anyone else tried to get inside Neuhansberg Castle to make off with a souvenir of Princess Johanna?"

"It, ah, looks that way, though, ah, we can't be sure. I ran into a masked figure trying to escape, but when I gave chase, the intruder leaped over the wall and landed outside the castle walls."

"What did they steal?"

"They, ah, disappeared into the woods before we got there. But it looked like maybe it was a map. Tied up with some kind of round emblem."

Interesting. Mac drummed his fingers on the armrest. Was this when the paintings disappeared?

It was nearly dawn and his legs had gone numb. As he shifted and stretched, he caught the flicker of a cigarette in the doorway of a building down the street. He scrubbed a hand over his face. He was really losing it if he was just noticing this guy now.

He tucked his laptop behind his seat, sucked down the last cold dregs of his coffee, and kept his gaze on the watcher.

Once she reached her apartment, Sophie paced, frustrated. She didn't have any better ideas than Detective von Binden on where to look for Lise.

Her brain buzzed with exhaustion, but she'd never sleep, so she wandered into her tiny kitchen and made coffee, hoping the slow, step-by-step routine of the French press would steady her. She couldn't believe the detective seriously suspected Lise of killing Henri. Or perhaps she could, from his perspective.

But she knew Lise.

Sophie curled up on her living room sofa, sipping slowly, determined to organize the thoughts galloping through her mind.

One shouted louder than all the rest.

Why hadn't Lise told her what had been worrying her? She'd been acting strange lately. Sophie had attributed it to the grief of Irmgard's sudden death, but looking back, it felt like more than that. Maybe something else from Lise's past. Sophie knew her friend was doing everything she could to make up for the way she and her late husband had sometimes disregarded provenance when the gallery was foundering. Robin Hood's first projects had been restitution, an effort to make things right.

She'd thought she and Lise told each other everything, were like family.

Apparently not.

Unbidden, images of her childhood, of the way her parents had stopped talking whenever she entered a room, skittered through her brain. Of course, she hadn't known they were CIA agents, and she was a kid, but still. Why wouldn't anyone trust her with the important things, the things that really mattered?

She shot to her feet and marched into the kitchen, annoyed with herself. Hadn't Lise reached out to her tonight when she was in trouble?

Bottom line, in order to find Lise, Sophie had to figure out who was after her. Which meant she had to think like her. Follow the logical steps.

Had Lise seen who killed Henri? Had she tried to intervene? Which would be totally like her.

Or what if someone kidnapped Lise before Henri's death because they wanted the painting? But Sophie had gotten no ransom demand. If she had, she would have given the kidnappers whatever they wanted for Lise's safe return.

Wait. Suppose someone killed Henri thinking he had the real portrait? They'd think they were home free now. Portrait secured.

But the call from Lise came *after* Henri was killed. Sophie wasn't naive enough to think others weren't after the portrait too.

If Lise could call again, she would. If she couldn't, how would Sophie find her?

The only thing that made sense was that someone had taken her captive to force her to hand over the portrait.

Except Lise had taken the original to the bank, and Sophie didn't believe for a New York minute that her friend would give it up, not after her dying mother sent it to her.

Sophie paced her apartment, back and forth, trying and discarding various scenarios before she went into her studio and booted up her laptop.

She pulled up all the recent articles she could find on the portraits, including the interview with Bernadette Rainier that mentioned clues, a legend, and a treasure. A quick scroll through her phone and she pulled up the photo she'd taken of the back of the portrait.

Just like St. Irmgard and St. Agnes, I believe in God even when He is silent.

There were a total of three portraits; that much was fact. If Ms. Rainier was to be believed, the three were tied together somehow and hidden, and whoever found them would get some kind of treasure.

It made sense that whoever had Lise knew about the portraits and wanted to get their hands on the treasure.

Which meant that to save her best friend's life, Sophie had to find the other two portraits.

17

Sophie paced the darkened living room of her third-floor Munich apartment, listening to the rain pounding on the slate roof, the swish of water as the occasional car drove by, the irregular beat of her heart. In the hour before dawn, the tourists had finally staggered off to their hotels. Most locals hadn't started the new day yet.

But not everyone slept.

With the tip of one finger, she parted the aged curtains again, slowly, just far enough to study the quiet street below.

She waited. Watched.

There.

The glowing tip of a cigarette flickered in the doorway of the building across the street, two doors down.

She'd spotted him earlier. Dismissed him as someone out for a late-night smoke.

She'd been wrong.

The realization that she'd been followed jolted her instincts like the unexpected blare of a security alarm whose trigger she'd missed.

He was getting closer. Braver.

She calculated how much time she had. Would he act before she had a chance to herself?

Not if she could help it. She stepped back, sifting through possibilities. Whatever his agenda, she knew her next play.

For Lise's sake, she had to get her hands on those portraits.

But how? Where should she start looking? She studied the picture on her phone, rereading the quote on the back of the painting over and over. She hurried to her laptop and typed *St. Irmgard St. Agnes* into the search engine.

When the results popped up, she let out a whoosh of relief. There was a St. Agnes Church in Cologne. Also, St. Irmgard's relics were interred at Cologne Cathedral. Sophie doubted the painting would be hidden in a sarcophagus, so logic said the second painting should be somewhere in St. Agnes Church.

A sound from the street had her heart beating triple time, but no bullet shattered the antique glass window. No one forced their way in at gunpoint.

Yet.

She picked up the painting of Mac, snapped pictures of the front and back, then put it in the frame and wrapped it in brown paper with the speed of long practice. She tied it with string for good measure and then peeked out the window again.

He'd gotten closer still.

Within ten minutes, she'd stepped into the Boho artist persona she used when she came and went from her apartment. Shoulder-length curly red wig, ripped jeans and a flowing blouse, cowboy boots and a battered beret. *Ensure people only see what you want them to see* was one of her mantras.

She slipped a lined raincoat on, grabbed her favorite leather tote, and tucked several disguises and toiletries inside, then secreted her favorite tools of the trade in the false bottom. She opened her wallet and sighed. She'd spent the last of her cash at the coffee shop yesterday. She raided the emergency stash inside her hollowed-out copy of *Robin Hood*, then patted the book before she tucked it back on the shelf. If she had a patron saint, it was Robin.

She slipped her knife into her boot and tucked her umbrella under one arm.

"Come on, Lise. Where are you?" she muttered when another call to her friend's phone went straight to voice mail.

Was she too late?

Despite the anxiety pushing her, she paused briefly beside the door, kissed her fingers, then pressed them to the small portrait hanging there, as always.

She'd painted her family as she wished they'd been: her parents standing on either side of her, fencing masks tucked into the crooks of their arms, smiling at her, swords crossed like the Three Musketeers.

All for one and one for all.

Except they hadn't been. Her parents had been a team of two, with Sophie forever on the outside, trying to break in.

Wrapped painting in hand, she pulled the door closed behind her, effectively shutting out the memory. No time for ancient history.

Still, her father's voice echoed in her memory. *"Love you, kid. Go be awesome."*

As a child, she'd rolled her eyes every time he said it.

Now, she whispered, "Love you, too, Dad," added a prayer for courage, then strolled toward her favorite café as if she didn't have a care in the world.

The rain had let up so she heard his footsteps behind her, keeping pace, but not getting too close. She began to sweat in her rain jacket.

Would they try to grab her right off the street?

She'd find out soon enough. She kept walking.

A glance in a shop window confirmed he was gaining on her, so she quickened her pace, then gave up all pretense of stealth and darted through an alley and sprinted across two lanes of traffic on the busy thoroughfare.

Brakes squealed. Drivers honked, but she didn't slow, zigzagging around the cars.

When the light in Sophie Williams's apartment winked out, Mac sat up straighter and stuck the key in the ignition.

He sensed rather than saw the doorway watcher stub out his cigarette and get ready as well.

Nobody would grab her off the street if Mac was around to prevent it.

It took a split second to realize the red-haired artist was actually Sophie. She casually walked out the door and started down the block as though she didn't have a care in the world, a painting clutched in her hands, her tote slung over one shoulder.

What was she thinking?

In that second, he knew. She'd set herself up as bait.

But for whom?

He started the car and eased forward, lights off, one eye on her and the other on the man following her.

18

Don't look back. Sophie fought the urge to glance over her shoulder, but she didn't have to, as the man obviously didn't know the first thing about stealth pursuit. He lumbered down the street, making no attempt to be quiet or hide the fact he was following her.

He was getting closer, so she picked up her pace slightly, scanning the street in front of her, searching for an escape route. One quick peek into a storefront window's reflection showed him reaching into his pocket.

She didn't wait to see if he drew a gun; she just took off running, the painting clutched to her chest.

The city bus was almost on top of her when she darted in front of it and sprinted down the opposite sidewalk, her boots sliding on the slick surface, while the driver laid on the horn.

She darted around the corner and into an alley, not surprised to hear his footsteps on the cobblestones behind her.

A quick left at the mouth of the alley and she sped down the next street. This busy thoroughfare had more traffic, which meant more places to hide.

She dodged delivery drivers unloading goods, pedestrians intent on getting to work, and risked another glance over her shoulder.

He was not giving up.

She skirted a flower vendor's display and darted around the next corner, hurrying down another side street.

As she passed a narrow alley between buildings, he stepped from the shadows and grabbed her.

She pivoted to run, but his hand clamped down on her left arm and a gun jabbed her side.

A five-o'clock shadow darkened his jaw and his breath reeked. "Scream and you die right here."

Sophie jabbed her elbow back to try to dislodge his grip, but he held tight. She shifted the painting to her left arm, gripped the handle of her tote with her right, and swung it for all she was worth.

It made a satisfying thump as it collided with his head. Unfortunately, he didn't go down, but he stumbled back a few steps, which was all the opening she needed.

His grip loosened and she took off running again, painting in her left hand, tote bag in her right.

A black Mercedes pulled up to the curb, tires squealing. The passenger door swung open. "Get in!"

Sophie missed a step. She leaned down to see Mac McKenzie behind the wheel.

"Argue later. Get in."

She glanced over her shoulder. The man sprinted toward her.

Rock. Hard place.

In one quick move, she shoved the painting in the backseat, slid into the front, and yanked the door closed.

The man reached out and gripped the door handle just as Mac hit the gas. He tumbled into the street as Mac roared away.

Sophie's heart was speeding like a runaway train and adrenaline had her panting.

"Buckle up," he said, swerving in and out of traffic.

That's all he had to say? But she didn't argue, just clicked the belt into place, eyes on the side mirror studying her pursuer, trying to figure out if she'd ever seen him before. She hadn't.

After half a block, Mac turned the corner and the man disappeared from view.

She expected him to slow down, but he kept a brisk pace, weaving in and out of cars and buses, wending his way to another part of the city.

"Head toward Leopoldstrasse," she said.

"Any particular reason?"

"I want to check on something."

When he merely raised a brow, Sophie added, "Indulge me. Please."

"Your wish is my command."

She couldn't help it. One corner of her mouth curled up in a smile. The man had an uncanny ability to keep her off-balance.

Several minutes later, he cruised past the bank whose vault the gallery used to store paintings. It had occurred to Sophie that maybe Lise had taken the copy from Henri and taken it to the bank. But that didn't make sense either. The bank wasn't open during the night.

"Turn left here."

He did, and she scanned the cars parked on their side of the street. "Right turn."

Her instructions had him driving the streets surrounding the bank in a grid pattern.

"Are you going to tell me what we're searching for?"

"I'll know it when I see it."

Several minutes later, she pointed. "Stop." Lise's nondescript tan Fiat was parked at the curb. She hurried over to it and cupped her hands around the window. The fresh flowers in the little vase attached to the dashboard confirmed this was Lise's car. What had she been doing here in the middle of the night? Had she been meeting someone?

Sophie scanned the sidewalk but didn't see any security cameras pointed at this mostly residential street.

She pulled out her phone, checked the GPS to see how far they were from the pay phone her friend called from earlier.

There was a pop and the glass in the car window shattered. Another pop and the concrete around her feet exploded.

Tires squealed.

"Get in!" Mac shouted.

A bullet pinged off the bumper of Lise's car.

Sophie crouched between vehicles and leaped into Mac's Mercedes, and he took off again before she even had the door shut. She managed to close it, then leaned back against the seat and tried to catch her breath.

"Somebody is clearly not happy with you. Care to share?"

She debated how much to say. Who even was this man? "That was my boss's car. She didn't come home last night, and I haven't been able to reach her." She called her friend again and left another voice mail message. "Call me, Lise. Please."

Mac wove around the city, saying nothing.

"She called me from a pay phone near here last night. A male voice told her to hang up the phone."

"You think someone kidnapped her?"

"I'm not sure what to think. But it's the only thing that makes sense. Although Detective von Binden thinks maybe she murdered a gallery employee last night too." She snorted.

"This is about Princess Johanna's portrait." It wasn't a question.

"I can't think what else it could be."

"What will you do now?"

Good question. Finally, she said, "Working on it."

Several minutes later he pulled up in front of a little café and turned off the engine. "Why don't we start with coffee."

Sophie turned to look at him. "Not that I don't appreciate you showing up and playing knight in shining armor on my behalf, but what were you doing outside my apartment before dawn?" She narrowed her eyes. "Or are you after the portrait too?"

Instead of answering, he asked his own questions. "Should you be carting it around like this?" He studied her. "Or are you using it as bait?"

"You let me worry about that."

"Let me see what all the fuss is about." He turned and reached behind the seat.

She gripped his arm. "I'd rather you didn't."

He raised a brow. "I just want to see it."

Their eyes met, clashed, before he calmly shook her off and reached for the painting. Within seconds, he had the paper off, and she could swear his jaw dropped before he pulled himself together. "Wow. This is not what I expected."

No, she supposed it wasn't. Embarrassed heat raced over Sophie's cheeks, and she twisted her hands in her lap.

He seemed to catalogue every brushstroke, every nuance of his own face on the canvas he held. He finally looked at her, his eyes the dark blue of the sea at night. "You painted this? When?"

Sophie almost said, "The night of the gala," but clamped her lips shut just in time. She was Mrs. Bauernstein that night. She opened her mouth, closed it again. Finally, she said, "I paint when I can't sleep." Which was true.

"You are incredibly talented." One corner of his mouth curled up in a roguish grin. "Kept you awake, did I?"

She snorted. "Don't flatter yourself. I paint lots of annoying people."

He put both hands over his heart. "You wound me, Sophie. Your tongue is even sharper than your sword."

The reference to their fencing match sent a wash of heat to her very core, but she ignored it. Especially when his glance slid from the painting to her tote bag and back again. The heat from moments ago froze into solid blocks of ice. Without thinking, she'd tossed her iPad, still in its bedazzled cover, into her tote. She wanted to pound her head against the dashboard in frustration. She was an idiot. And Mac wasn't stupid.

"Now that my heart has decided it won't actually leap out of my chest, let's grab some coffee and you can explain how you happened to be in the right place at the right time this morning?"

Before he could stop her, she slipped the portrait from his grasp and rewrapped it. Painting under her arm, she slung her tote over her shoulder and headed for the coffee shop.

He stepped up beside her. "You can leave the painting in the car."

"No thanks. I'd rather keep it with me."

He stopped. "What game are you playing, Ms. Williams?"

She kept walking. "I could ask you the same thing, Mr. McKenzie." She'd googled his name, of course, and the fact he was a high-dollar art investigator did nothing to settle her nerves.

He nodded and mumbled, "Touché" as he held the door for her.

By unspoken agreement, they took a table by the window so they could see his car and anyone who approached on the street.

Sophie heard the rumble of a train and almost smiled. They were only a few blocks from the München Hauptbahnhof, the city's main train station. Perfect.

After they ordered, she pulled out her cell phone and dialed Lise yet again. It rang once, twice, three times. Just before it rolled to voice mail, a female voice asked, "Sophie?"

"Lise! Where are you? Oh, thank God."

"I'm sorry. This isn't Lise. This is Amalia."

"Amalia? But . . . what are you doing with Lise's phone? Is she with you? What's wrong?"

"No, she isn't with me. I'm sorry."

"Why do you have her phone? What's going on?"

Amalia let out a long sigh. "She stopped by the shelter last night to see me. Lise was holding Sam and he kicked her purse off the bed, and everything fell out. It must have slid under the bed. I just woke up and heard it buzzing."

"I've been calling all night."

"I'm sorry. I didn't hear it."

Sophie took a deep breath. "Please stop apologizing. You did nothing wrong. I'm glad you picked up. Did Lise happen to mention where she was going after she left you?"

"She didn't say. Just told me not to worry." The young woman sighed again. "But I do. Is she okay?"

Sophie debated what to say. "I hope so. I've been worried because she hasn't been answering her cell phone." She tried to put a smile in her voice. "Now I know why."

"Will you let me know when you hear from her?"

"Of course. Now try not to worry. I'll be in touch." She hung up the phone, then dialed Detective von Binden. "*Guten Morgen.* This is Sophie Williams."

"What can I do for you, Fräulein Williams?" His voice sounded tired, but she didn't get the sense she'd woken him from a sound sleep.

"I just wanted to let you know that I found Lise's car. It's parked along Herzogstrasse, near the Indian restaurant halfway down the block, but when I walked around it, someone started shooting, so I got out of there fast."

"Did you see the shooter?"

"No. I just ducked and ran."

"I'd like you to come down to the stat—"

"Sorry. You're breaking up. Gotta go." She hung up, put the phone in her pocket, where it immediately started ringing again. She sipped her coffee as though she didn't hear it.

"You going to get that?"

"Nope. Bad connection." She finished her croissant and wiped her mouth with her napkin. "Let me run to the restroom and then I'll have you drop me off at home, if it's not too much trouble." She stood and gathered the painting and her tote bag.

"Leave that here. I'll watch it."

"Given all that's happened, color me paranoid." She winked. "I'll be back."

She walked to the back of the café and down the dimly lit hallway. She bypassed the restrooms and kept walking, apologizing to the surprised staff as she hurried through the kitchen and out the back door to the alley.

Once there, she took a moment to get her bearings, then headed to the train station.

19

THE ALPS—SOUTH OF MUNICH

He rose on Sunday morning and went through his usual routine. Coffee, a light breakfast, and the morning paper in the breakfast room, followed by a brisk three-kilometer walk. Once he'd showered and dressed, he climbed into his car as though he were headed out for a leisurely drive.

Instead of turning left at the end of the long driveway, he turned right. Hands tight on the steering wheel, he wound his way through the mountains, memories assaulting him with every bend in the winding road. He'd never expected to take this road again.

Never thought he'd need to.

Anger churned just below the surface, but he buried it deep. He unclenched his jaw, loosened his white-knuckled grip on the wheel. The media's renewed frenzy over Johanna's death left him no choice. Why couldn't they leave the past alone? The princess was dead and gone, going on forty years now. He shook his head. Hard to believe. Some days, it seemed as though it had all happened yesterday.

But the press swarmed like vultures, pecking at all the details of the car accident, digging, always digging, for some tidy morsel they'd missed before. Still, no matter how much they exposed, it was never enough to satisfy the public's ravenous appetites where royalty was concerned, even minor royalty.

He couldn't risk the old man following through on his threat. Which he still couldn't believe he'd had the gall to make. Certainly not now.

When the low stone wall surrounding the farm came into view, he relaxed slightly, leaning back against the leather seat, just a man out for a drive to see an old friend. He hated the necessity of what he was about to do, but it couldn't be avoided. He slipped on his leather gloves, then stepped from the car, buttoning his coat as he went.

He walked onto the porch of the stone cottage and knocked on the heavy wooden door. When the door opened, rheumy blue eyes blinked up at him from beneath a low cap, the flash of fear quickly disguised. "Well, now, can't say as I'm surprised to see you, but you could've just mailed the money."

"I paid you plenty to destroy that car years ago."

The whiskered chin came up. "So you did. But I decided a bit of insurance wouldn't be amiss. Got some medical expenses coming up and my grandson is heading to college, so a little extra cash would go a long way."

His hands clenched at his sides. "How dare you try to blackmail me."

"Think of it as a form of insurance, a way to guarantee that certain facts never come to light."

"How do I know you're not bluffing?"

The man studied him a moment, then harrumphed and stepped onto the porch. "Come have a look then."

The man had seemed taller forty years ago, though he supposed he had changed too. The old man's heavy jacket seemed to hang on his frame as he marched across the yard toward the barn. He passed it and several other outbuildings, until he came to the farthest shed in the back. He pulled out a key ring and undid the rusty padlock, then struggled to open the door. He was huffing and puffing by the time he worked it over the dirt that had collected in the doorway over the years.

"Still not willing to lend a hand, are you?" the farmer muttered, shooting an annoyed glance his way.

Irritation spiked at the man's tone, but he didn't respond, simply bided his time.

Once the door was open, he followed the farmer into the dim interior and waited until he pulled on the chain and a bare bulb flickered to life. Gnarled fingers tugged on the dusty tarp and pulled it back.

Another rush of memories shot through him, but he pushed them back. The mangled car looked exactly as it had when he'd carefully diverted it during the transport from the crime scene all those years ago.

"Satisfied?" the farmer said.

He nodded once, then waited while the farmer repositioned the tarp, turned off the light, and secured the padlock.

They started back toward the house. "That barn is new."

"Added it about five years ago."

"May I see it?"

The old man raised an eyebrow and simply led him through a small side door.

Once the door closed behind them, he stepped up behind the old man and clapped his hands over his nose and mouth, cutting off his air.

The farmer was stronger than he looked, and it was all he could do to hang on as the man thrashed and struggled like a landed fish. But he didn't let go. He held on tight and waited.

And waited.

After the man stopped struggling, he waited some more. Just to make absolutely sure.

The old man didn't move. Then he shifted the man in his grip and smashed the back of his head against one of the support beams. He let him slide to the floor, as though he'd had a heart attack and lost his balance.

Satisfied, he walked out of the barn and climbed back into his car and started for home.

His stomach roiled, but he squelched the urge to retch. He'd done what he needed to do. Same as always.

His secret was safe.

———

What was it about women and restrooms? They went in there and it was like they fell into a time warp. Mac checked his watch for the third time, dropped some bills on the table, and headed down the hallway. He thought he had lost whoever had been shooting at them, but it wasn't smart to stay in one place too long. He knocked on the door. "Sophie?"

The door swung open.

"It's about ti—"

A businesswoman in a tailored suit glared at him as she stepped out.

"Excuse me, is there anyone else in there? I'm looking for my, ah, girlfriend."

"There is not. But if there were, she will not be your girlfriend for long if you hound her every step." She sniffed and stepped around him.

Mac turned and spotted the doorway to the kitchen. He stepped inside. "Did anyone see a woman come through here in the last few minutes?"

"This is not a public area, sir," a man said.

"I understand. But I'm looking for a friend."

The man eyed him up and down. "People do not usually sneak out the back door to avoid friends."

Mac nodded and hurried out to his car. Where would she have gone? A train whistle sounded. Of course.

He aimed straight for the train station, searching for Sophie and trying to find a parking spot at the same time. Pedestrians clogged the sidewalk, surging toward the station doors like salmon being funneled in an ever-narrowing stream. He thought he spotted her ahead of him, but it was impossible to be sure. He couldn't lose her now.

He double-parked half a block from the main entrance, punched his hazard lights on, and sprinted back the way he'd come, ignoring the traffic policeman's indignant shout and shrill whistle. With any luck, Mac would get back before they towed his car.

As he threaded his way through the crowd, he searched for either the red curls or her blonde hair, scanning, always scanning as he went down the escalator. Once there, he hopped over the turnstile when he caught a glimpse of her beret-covered red curls rounding the corner several yards ahead of him.

"Hey! You can't do that!" someone shouted, and he picked up his pace.

When she glanced over her shoulder, relief flooded him. There was no way she'd get away now, not toting that painting.

The train pulled up to the station and the doors slid open. He lost sight of her for a moment amidst the people milling around, a steady stream disembarking while others surged onto the train.

There! He plowed through the crowd, desperate to board before the doors closed. Above the noise, the recording announced the train was ready to depart.

He had one foot on the train when a hand closed over his arm and yanked him back. A policeman stepped in front of him. "Sir, you'll need to come with me."

Mac looked past him, huffing out a frustrated breath as the doors closed and the train started moving. He scanned the crowded car and his eyes locked with Sophie's. She stood among the press of bodies, a flicker of apology in her eyes, the painting clutched to her chest as she disappeared from sight.

20

When Munich's skyline faded into the distance, Sophie finally drew a deep breath and settled into her seat, the painting wedged between her knees. Her last glimpse of Mac should have filled her with relief, but the worry in his deep-blue eyes gave her pause.

Not that it would change a thing. She was going to find Lise. Period. Which meant she had to get her hands on those paintings before anyone else did.

How did Mac fit into all this? She'd never believed in coincidence, so his popping up in her life right now was obviously deliberate. Had someone hired him to find the paintings? Or worse, did he suspect she was Robin Hood?

Either possibility made her blood run cold, and she forced herself to think logically. If he was an undercover cop of some kind, he could have hauled her off for questioning earlier. Instead, he'd offered help. Which made her think the paintings were his goal.

Her hands still trembled at how close one of the bullets had come to hitting her instead of Lise's car. If she hadn't ducked at just the right moment . . . She'd never, ever admit it to him, but there had been something nice about having a partner of sorts when the bullets started flying.

Leaving him and his unknown agenda behind was the smart thing to do. Since she'd come to Germany years ago, she had trusted no one but Lise. No need to change that now. She'd be fine on her own.

Her cell phone rang. The quick spark of hope died when she saw the caller ID. "Have you heard from Lise?"

"No," Nadine said. "I was calling to ask you the same question."

Sophie put a hand on her stomach, where anxiety sloshed the coffee she'd sucked down earlier. "Nothing. But I do know she doesn't have her cell phone, so no need to keep calling it." She relayed her earlier conversation with Amalia.

"Maybe she changed her mind and went to check on the encampments anyway," Nadine said.

"Was there another raid?"

"Not that I've heard, but Lise has a better relationship with the young women than I do. I spend most of my days behind a desk."

The conductor announced the next stop.

"Where are you?" Nadine asked.

"I'm on a train to Cologne."

"Cologne? But why?"

"I think that's where the next painting is."

"Painting? Why does that matter? I don't understand. We have to find Lise."

"I believe the paintings are why she's missing."

"Sophie, dear, you're wrong. This is all my fault. She's been trying to figure out who is behind these raids, trying to collect evidence that women are disappearing. I think she must have uncovered proof, and someone discovered her last night."

Sophie's heart stuttered at the possibility. Was Nadine right? Was she headed in the absolute wrong direction?

No, her gut said this was the way to go. Every single time she'd made the wrong decision, it had been because she ignored that little voice. She wouldn't make that mistake this time. The stakes were too high.

"I disagree on the reasons, but we both want to find Lise and bring her home safely. So how about this: You keep following the trail of the encampment raids and I'll follow the paintings."

Sophie could hear the other woman drumming her fingers. "There is someone I can call . . . Promise me you'll be careful, Sophie. I worry that you'll be next, the way you go haring off all by yourself."

She grinned. "I hare off by myself all the time." Then she sobered. "But I do appreciate the concern, Nadine. I'll be careful. Trust me."

"I expect regular updates. And if I don't hear from you, I'll hound you like a bear after a beehive. Got it?"

"Yes, ma'am. I'll keep you posted."

For all her gruffness and starch, Nadine had a huge heart and a determination that could put military commanders to shame. If Lise was somewhere in Munich, Nadine would find her.

And if it turned out she wasn't in the city or that she was being held somewhere in connection to the paintings, Sophie would find them and use them to get her back.

All she had to do was solve the teensy little problem of deciphering the "code" on the back of the painting and actually locating it.

AN ISLAND OFF THE COAST OF SPAIN

The Mediterranean Sea was calm this Sunday morning, palm fronds murmuring in the slight breeze. But Willa Campos felt the anxiety in the air. Or maybe it lived inside her. She'd waited too long.

A coffee mug in each hand, she pushed a button hidden in the wall and a door slid open, revealing a secret room built into the back of her small house on a private island just off the coast of Spain.

Once Scoop saw her lights on, she expected him to show up too. Longtime friends and sometimes more, she and the former Special Ops leader owned the only two houses on the island, which meant Willa didn't have to worry about waking the neighbors or people peeking over the back fence, asking questions she didn't want to answer.

She desperately hoped they weren't too late.

She sat at her computer and booted up the bank of monitors that filled one wall. She opened the secure video link and called Picasso in their underground New York office.

"Good morning," Willa said, raising her coffee mug in greeting. "Sorry to get you out of bed so early."

Picasso muttered a distracted, "Good morning," typing furiously on one of the multiple keyboards surrounding her semi-circular desk. She was wearing her usual long-sleeved blouse and long pants, a ball cap hiding the worst of the scars that covered her face and much of her body. Willa had been delighted to hire her as part of the team, with her amazing computer skills. And Picasso admitted she liked having a job that kept her hidden from public view while putting her skills to good use.

From one of the screens, Camille's face appeared. She raised a cup of coffee in salute to Picasso. "Morning, sugar." She checked her old-fashioned wristwatch. "Actually, it's not anywhere near morning there, is it? Willa tossed you out of your comfy bed again, didn't she?" Beyond Camille's Munich balcony, traffic made it hard to hear her.

Willa held up her mug. "Good morning to you too. There was no tossing, by the way. She offered. How you doing, Camille?"

"It's too noisy out here. Hang on." Camille stood with the kind of grace Willa would always envy. Her slender, six-foot height, along with the sculpted cheekbones, gorgeous olive skin, pouty lips, and huge brown eyes could have made her a fortune if she'd gone into modeling. Which she threatened to do regularly. "What's happening?"

"You're not working today, are you?" Willa asked. Camille took on freelance photography work between assignments, and she was talented. Her camera also provided great cover and let her move around Europe without anyone questioning her presence.

"Nothing I can't change. Why?"

Another face popped onto the wall of screens. "What couldn't wait an hour?" Hank grumbled. Even at just past 8:00 a.m. in

Germany, she had a smear of grease on her cheek. "I have a cranky rotor shaft waiting for me."

"Morning, Hank." Willa indicated her cheek and the other woman took a swipe at it with a crumpled rag, which only made things worse. Hank's short dark hair was hidden under a ball cap, and she wore coveralls over a tall, slender frame. "Appreciate you heading over there to give it a look-see. Can you fix her?"

Hank snorted. "Please. Child's play. But why the rush?"

Willa had sent her to a small town in Germany two days ago to purchase a chopper for the team. Just in case.

Now she wished she'd done that sooner.

Another face appeared on the screens and Mercy appeared, clothed in her nun's habit, out of breath. "Sorry. Got your message in the middle of morning prayers and couldn't get away."

"No problem," Willa said. "Sorry to interrupt."

Mercy was part of the Sisters of Mercy, a medical order, and lived in Paris, working in medical clinics for the poor. Unless she was needed elsewhere. "What's up?"

"Thanks for being here, all of you. We have a situation that could use our help. And given the phone call I just received, it appears I waited too long before calling you."

Hank rolled her eyes. "Tell us what's going on before you start blaming yourself for who knows what."

Willa smiled. "Thank you. I just got off the phone with Nadine Langwasser of Neue Anfänge, aka 'New Beginnings,' a charity based in Munich that helps women and children, especially homeless ones. Lise Fortier, originally from Austria, is her publicity and fundraising chairman—and right-hand woman, as it were. She's gone missing. Problem is, we can't pinpoint exactly why, which will make finding her more difficult." Willa outlined what Nadine had told her about the raids on the encampments.

Camille shook her head. "Somebody oughtta horsewhip those thugs, tossing women and children out of their tents in the middle of the night."

"It's possible it's worse than that, I'm afraid. Lise was convinced that at least three women had disappeared after the raids."

"Say what?" Shock and anger filled Camille's voice.

"Oh, dear Jesus." Mercy made the sign of the cross.

"Do we know where they're taking them? Any clues?" Hank asked.

"Actually, Nadine doesn't know if they've been taken or left on their own. Lise was trying to find proof."

"And maybe she did and that's why she's missing," Hank offered.

"Exactly. That's part of what we need to find out."

"And the other part?" Mercy asked.

"You all have seen the news coverage about the portrait of Princess Johanna of Neuhansberg showing up at a Munich gallery all these years after it disappeared?"

There were nods all around.

"What's the connection?" Hank asked.

"Lise Fortier also happens—" she made air quotes—"to own the art gallery. The painting is said to have come from Lise's mother, who left it to her. She just passed away last week."

"That all seems a wee bit coincidental, doesn't it?" Camille drawled.

"The painting is all over the news, worldwide, and last night a gallery employee was murdered. Speculation is that he got killed trying to steal the painting."

"Holy Moses!" Mercy exclaimed, then muttered, "Sorry, Father," before she made the sign of the cross again.

"This just keeps getting better," Hank mumbled.

"There's more." Willa nodded to Picasso, who pulled up several news articles so everyone could see them. "According to Bernadette Rainier, the artist who painted them, the set of three paintings have some kind of code that will lead to a treasure of some kind. But Ms. Rainier is in her late eighties and her nurse is quoted as saying she gets confused sometimes."

"If that won't bring out the crazies and the treasure hunters like ants at a picnic, I don't know what will." Camille shook her head, dark curls dancing.

"So, is this Lise person missing because of the homeless situation or because of the painting?"

Willa smiled at Hank like a teacher whose brightest student just aced a test. "That's the big question we need to find the answer to."

"Where do we start?" Hank asked. "The chopper won't be ready to fly for at least another day."

"Picasso, put up that picture of Sophie, would you?" When the picture appeared, Willa continued, "This is Lise's best friend and gallery manager. Sophie is ten years younger than Lise's thirty-nine, but they've been best friends for years. From what Nadine said, Sophie believes Lise's disappearance has everything to do with the paintings, and she's determined to find the other two. She's on a train right now, headed to Cologne."

Camille checked her watch. "What time is she due in?"

21

The swaying motion of the train lulled Sophie into dozing between stations and then jolting awake every time the conductor announced the next stop. By the time she stepped onto the bustling platform in Cologne, she was so tired she'd be worthless to anyone if she didn't get a few hours' sleep.

She opened a travel app on her phone and instantly closed it again, then turned off the GPS and the phone itself. That wouldn't stop anyone determined to find her.

But if she ditched it, Lise couldn't call her.

She got the name of an out-of-the-way youth hostel at one of the tourist information booths between the train station and Cologne Cathedral, then purchased a burner phone with a decent camera along the way. The fact that she was dressed like the proverbial starving artist meant no one at the hostel gave her—or the painting—a second look.

She avoided the ancient-looking elevator and walked up three flights, breathing a sigh of relief when she locked the door behind her. It wasn't much, but it was exactly what she needed. Double bed that didn't sag too badly in the middle, small dresser, one chair.

After she washed up in the communal bathroom down the hall, she peered around the old-fashioned window shade and studied the narrow side street below. Satisfied that no one had followed her, she kicked off her cowboy boots, tucked her knife under her pillow, and instantly fell asleep.

"She's actually pretty good with a brush."

The voice penetrated her fuzzy brain, but Sophie held herself perfectly still as she oriented herself. She was lying on her side, facing the door. Where was she? Right. Youth hostel. Cologne. Trying to find Lise.

"You might as well stop playing possum, Sophie," the same female voice said. "We know you're awake."

Definitely American. Southern, from the hint of her drawl.

Sophie closed her hand around the hilt of her knife and then rolled from the bed, landing beside it in a crouch, weapon at the ready.

A strikingly tall, beautiful woman stood by the window, studying the painting of Mac. "You painted this?"

"Who are you? And why are you in my room?" Sophie's eyes landed on the other woman, who sat in the straight-backed chair. Small and compact, she wore a traditional nun's habit, of all things, that framed wide brown eyes set in a brown face.

"I am Sister Mercy and this is Camille."

"What are you doing in my room?" Sophie repeated, louder this time. She felt a bit like Alice in Wonderland. Or maybe Dorothy in Oz. She definitely wasn't in Kansas anymore. And none of this made sense.

Camille set the painting down. "Easy. We're here to help."

Suspicion raised the hairs on the back of Sophie's neck. "You followed me."

Camille lifted one shoulder. "Even with the GPS off, people can be tracked. If you know how."

"And you know how?"

Camille laughed. "Oh no. I don't have a clue. But I know some-one who does."

Sophie glanced from one to the other. "What makes you think I need some kind of help?"

This time the nun answered. "Your friend Lise is missing. We're here to help you find her."

Shock tensed every muscle in Sophie's body. "Who are you and how do you know that?"

The two exchanged glances. "Nadine is worried about you," Sister Mercy said.

"And she thinks you're searching in the wrong direction." Camille propped her hands on her slim hips.

Sophie tilted her head toward the door. "Then by all means, go look in whatever direction you and Nadine think is the right one."

"Just because we think you're wrong doesn't mean we won't help," Camille said.

"Your friend is in danger, Sophie," the nun said.

"Let's suppose you're right about any of this—what can you two possibly do to help?"

Camille raised one perfectly groomed eyebrow. "You, of all people, know looks can be deceiving."

Sophie tried to hide her reaction. How much did they know about her? Or about Lise? What did they really want? And why had Nadine talked to them?

Sophie moved to the door and held it open. "Thanks for drop-ping by. But I have things to do."

Camille shrugged. "Have it your way. But let us know if you change your mind." She stepped into the hall.

Sister Mercy put her palms together in a gesture of prayer and followed Camille out the door. Sophie closed and locked it behind them and listened until their footsteps descended the creaky wooden stairs.

She went to the tiny window and peered around the shade, tap-ping an impatient finger on the windowsill until they reappeared on the street below and started walking in the direction of the train station. The tiny sister had a slight limp.

Once they disappeared from sight, Sophie sank onto the bed and pulled out her burner phone. Who were these women? What did they want?

She was bursting with the need to confront Nadine and demand answers, but her call went straight to voice mail.

———

Mac spent a frustrating hour in a cramped office inside the terminal with the Munich police, trying to explain why he was chasing someone through the station without official knowledge or permission. He finally resorted to dropping Eloise Cuvier's name, insisting the Interpol agent would vouch for him. They'd gone out a few times, but Mac eased away when she tried to take things further. He hoped she didn't carry a grudge.

The officer reluctantly called her, straightening as he listened to whatever she said. Finally, he handed Mac the phone. "She wants to speak with you, Herr McKenzie."

"If this is your version of keeping a low profile, we need to talk, Mac."

"Now why did I know you were going to say that?" He kept his voice light as he glanced at the officer, who sat behind the desk of his small office, arms crossed over his chest, eyes narrowed as he openly eavesdropped.

"Any news on our person of interest?"

"Working on it," Mac said.

"We want Robin Hood, asap, so if you're still interested in that nice consulting fee we discussed, you'll have to work harder. I am counting on you, Mac."

"And so you should. When have I ever let you down?" he teased. When she snorted, he added, "Well, not recently. Relax. I've got this. I was trying not to lose sight of our person of interest when I accidentally leaped over a turnstile or two."

"Accidentally?"

"Adrenaline and all that. You know how it is."

She harrumphed. "Is this a solid lead?"

Mac smiled at the officer. "Absolutely. I don't plan to let, ah, them get far." He'd almost said *her* but caught himself in time. "Just out of curiosity, why's Interpol so interested if items are being returned to their rightful owners? Seems like a waste of time."

"I don't like being bested," she muttered.

He grinned. Eloise was nothing if not competitive and Robin Hood had scooped her. More than once. But as long as she kept paying him, he'd keep looking. "If you could please get me out of here, that would be great."

"You are enjoying this entirely too much," she groused.

"What good is a job if you don't enjoy doing it?" He turned to the officer and winked. The man's scowl deepened, especially after Mac handed the phone back to him and Eloise told the officer in no uncertain terms to quit interfering and let Mac go.

Mac was still grinning as he left the office and headed for the ticket booth. "One ticket to Cologne, please."

22

"Just like St. Irmgard and St. Agnes, I believe in God even when He is silent."

Sophie paced her room, repeating the phrase over and over, hoping some new clue or idea would jump out at her. She pulled up the pictures of the painting on her regular phone and used her burner phone to take pictures of the pictures. Not the best quality, obviously, but she needed the photos. Since those women had tracked her old phone, she had to get rid of it, but before she ditched it, she copied Nadine's and Lise's numbers into the burner phone and texted Nadine and Amalia the new number.

Her research hadn't turned up a St. Irmgard's church in Cologne, but there was a St. Agnes. She was gambling that the painting was somewhere inside, but what if the saints' names had nothing to do with churches and she was in the wrong city altogether?

Lack of sleep was making her brain fuzzy. She stopped pacing and took a deep breath. The only way to know was to check. Her stomach rumbled, reminding her that she was hungry, so she made the bed and set the painting of Mac against the headboard. If anyone came looking for it, they wouldn't have to trash her room to find it.

She quickly braided her hair and tucked it under a black wig, then used the tiny mirror over the dresser to pop in brown contact lenses. She pulled on her cowboy boots, smoothed out the long sweater and leggings that made movement easy, then slipped her scarf over her head and tied it under her chin. She tucked her metal-detector-friendly polymer knife in the sheath at her ankle, some cash in her pocket, then scattered a handful of lemon drops on the floor behind the door. She took a quick picture with her phone, then slipped on her Sophia Loren sunglasses and left the room.

Her city map said it was an easy ten-minute walk to St. Agnes Church from her hostel, so she headed north on foot, stopping at a heavenly smelling *Bakerei* for a pastry and coffee. At a busy intersection, she dropped her old phone into the coat pocket of a well-dressed businessman and kept walking.

According to the brochure she held, St. Agnes was located on Neusser Platz (Neustadt-Nord) smack in the heart of the Agnesviertel, or St. Agnes quarter. As she walked, Sophie took pictures of the lovely houses on both sides of the street with her burner phone. Not only was she a sucker for great architecture, it kept her tourist cover in place.

She regularly glanced in shop windows but didn't see any signs of a tail. Which didn't settle her nerves at all. Just because she didn't see them didn't mean they weren't there.

Once the church came into view, her tourist's surprise was completely genuine and she gaped. The church was so much bigger than she'd expected, and the clock tower did, in fact, look like a chess piece, just as Google had said. She'd read that St. Agnes was the second biggest church in Cologne, right after the more famous Cologne Cathedral, but while the cathedral was medieval Gothic, St. Agnes was neo-Gothic, consecrated in the early 1900s. Practically brand-new, as cathedrals went.

It wasn't crowded at this time of day, so she followed a family of tourists in and sat in the back pew to look around first. During her travels with Lise, she'd learned to take a moment to absorb the feel of a church. Some were beautiful and filled with incredible artwork and statuary but gave off an empty, lifeless vibe, a mere museum to faith. Others, like this one, felt like a church. She could almost hear the whispered prayers of those who had come before her echoing through time.

Had they been disappointed too, when their prayers went unanswered? All these years after her parents' deaths, she was still angry that God hadn't intervened, that He hadn't kept them safe. They were doing important work, for crying out loud, making the world better, safer. Shouldn't that have counted for something? Gained them extra protection?

Apparently not.

Her throat closed. And now Lise was missing. *Please, God, help me find her.* But in case He was busy with more important things, she'd move heaven and earth to find her friend and keep her safe, on her own.

She scanned the nave again, then froze as quiet footsteps sounded on the stone floor behind her, stopping just behind her pew. She breathed another quick prayer as she waited, bending forward so her knife was in reach.

Seconds ticked by, then the footsteps slowly moved away, toward the left side of the cathedral. Sophie eased out of the pew and glanced that way, half expecting to see Mac. But this guy was shorter and leaner, his face hidden under a gray hoodie.

The unmistakable impression that he was stalking her kept her senses on high alert as she started a careful circuit of the church, making sure she knew where the man was at all times. The church was built in the shape of a cross, as most were, with two naves flanking either side of the main sanctuary.

She stayed along the right side, studying the beautiful stained-glass windows. Unfortunately, none of them shed any light on her search. Neither did the paintings along the walls, depicting the fourteen stations of the cross. They were moving and beautifully done, but they didn't help. None of them were the right size for a painting of the princess to be hidden behind, which was the assumption she was working under.

As she made her way around the cathedral, her watcher kept pace on the opposite side, stopping when she stopped and moving again as she did. Once she completed the circuit, she had exhausted all the possibilities, so she asked the young woman at the entrance if there was a basement.

"*Das ist alles,*" the young woman said with a shrug. *This is all there is.*

Sophie thanked her and slipped out the door, heading left and ducking behind some thick foliage.

It didn't take long before the watcher stepped outside. Dressed in jeans and the gray hoodie, he didn't look terribly intimidating at first glance. Then she spotted the wicked-looking knife gripped in his hand, the careful way he studied every inch of the surrounding area.

Sophie held her breath and didn't let it out again until the man headed down the walkway, still scanning, took a right at the corner, and disappeared from view.

She waited five more minutes before she backed out of the shrubbery. The gardener yelped in surprise when she bumped into him.

"*Entschuldigung,*" she muttered and hurried in the opposite direction.

This obviously wasn't the right church. As she walked, Sophie typed *St. Irmgard* into Google, instead of *St. Agnes*. Though there wasn't a St. Irmgard's church, Saint Irmgardis's sarcophagus rested in the St. Agnes Chapel. Which was inside Cologne Cathedral.

Bingo.

She hoped.

Thirty minutes later, Sophie turned a corner and the entire Cologne Cathedral came into view. She stopped dead on the sidewalk and gawked. *Holy moly.* Known as the Kölner Dom, or just the

Dom, the sheer size of it boggled the mind. She'd seen pictures, of course, but they didn't even come close to doing justice to its size. Her research said the whole thing took 632 years to build, from the time it was started in 1248 until it was finished in 1880. *Crazy.*

Focus, girl. You are not a tourist.

Though she was pretending to be one. She purchased a guidebook from a street vendor and flipped through it, getting a feel for the place before she went inside. Larger than a football field, it could easily hold twenty thousand people.

Any other day, Sophie would have spent hours roaming around, taking in the magnificent structure, gawking at the beautiful stained glass, but sadly, she didn't have time for that today. The church would close before long.

She paid the extra fee to get into the treasury in the basement but made a careful circuit of the main floor first. She studied the stained-glass windows that, along with most of the statues, had been carefully crated and packed during World War II. They survived, thanks to the forethought of Max Loosen, the cathedral vicar at the time.

Guidebook in one hand, burner phone in the other, she again sank onto a rear pew and breathed in the atmosphere. Definitely a house of worship. She scanned the groups and families milling about but didn't spot her watcher anywhere.

But that didn't mean he wasn't lurking nearby.

She rose and casually made her way to the Chapel of St. Agnes, hands a bit tingly as adrenaline hummed through her. All her senses went on high alert, just like when she moved in to retrieve a painting.

She found the chapel, stepped inside, and stopped dead. St. Irmgardis's small sarcophagus stood by itself on a raised platform, surrounded by a chain-link fence. There was no way she'd be able to get to it. She moved around the chapel reading inscriptions, waiting for a young family to leave so she could get closer. But the stark reality was that no matter how much she wished it, no paintings were here. Nothing behind the fence was even close to the right size to hide a portrait of the princess.

Had she been wrong again?

"Just like St. Irmgard and St. Agnes, I believe in God even when He is silent."

She turned in a slow circle, making absolutely sure, but there was nothing here. Another dead end.

Frustrated, she walked back to the main part of the cathedral and slipped into another pew, studying the artwork, the stained glass, the statues again. What had she missed?

Beside her a tour guide stopped next to a pair of tablets embedded in the wall and started talking about their historical significance. On them were carved the instructions worked out by Archbishop Engelbert II (1262–67) under which Jews were permitted to reside in Cologne.

But that wasn't the part that made Sophie's ears perk up. During World War II, the Dom was bombed several times, but it stood firm and was used as a navigational marker for planes flying overhead.

According to the guide, Jewish families had hidden in the basement to escape Hitler's Nazis. After the war, a poem was found scrawled on the basement wall, supposedly written by a child.

As the guide read the poem, Sophie's eyes filled. What would it be like to be a child, hiding in a dank basement, terrified?

. . . and I believe in God
even when He is silent.
I believe through any trial
there is always a way.

Her heart pounded as the words washed over her. *"I believe in God, even when He is silent."* If a young child had that kind of faith, could she trust God—?

"Wait! That's it!" She flinched as her outburst echoed through the cathedral and everyone in the nearby group turned toward her. "Sorry, so sorry," she mumbled. "It's beautiful. I got a little excited."

Clutching her guidebook, she slipped out of the pew and crossed the huge room to get in line to see the treasury in the basement.

She had no idea how she'd access the location where the words had been written on the wall, but that had to be where the painting was hidden.

Or somewhere near there.

The line moved slowly enough that she caught herself fidgeting. Finally, she inched her way down the stairs and oohed and aahed at the treasures along with everyone else. But her mind wasn't on gold and priceless works of art.

One quick spin around the room told her this wasn't the place. She slipped up beside an unsmiling armed security guard near the entrance. "Excuse me." Eyes wide, she sent him her best damsel-in-distress smile. "I heard about the poem the child wrote on the walls down here during World War II, and I wondered if you could tell me where it is."

He was shaking his head before she stopped speaking. "I'm sorry, but that area is not part of the treasury."

"Oh, I was so hoping it was." She sighed with disappointment, adding a sad little pout. "My grandmother couldn't come with me. She's in her nineties, but she so loves that poem and wanted me to take a picture of it for her." Sophie had never met either set of grandparents, but she liked to think if she had, her grandmother would have loved the poem.

"I'm sorry. I can't help you." His eyes now held a glimmer of sympathy.

"Not even a quick peek?" She leaned closer. "No one would have to know. And you'd be doing a kind deed for an old lady."

He frowned, looked away. When he sighed in resignation, Sophie squelched the urge to raise her fist in triumph. He glanced her way, and she hid her smile.

Turning to the radio on his shoulder, he muttered something in German and then said, "When my relief gets here, I'll take you. Five minutes. No more."

Her smile could have lit up the whole basement. "Thank you so much. Five minutes is all I need. You've made me—" she cleared her throat— "my grandmother so happy."

Another guard arrived, there was a quick spate of muttered German she couldn't catch, and then he whisked her past the velvet rope, down a long hallway, and through an invisible door in the back wall.

The difference between this section and where the treasury was kept was striking. No gilt or spotlights. This looked like the creepy basement of every horror movie ever made. Never mind that it was in a church. Dim fluorescent bulbs shed weak light on the boxes, statues, and odds and ends haphazardly piled here and there in what was obviously a storage area.

Suddenly Claus, according to his name tag, stopped and switched on the flashlight he carried on his utility belt. "Here we are." He shined it over the writing on the wall, then glanced uneasily in both directions. "Take your pictures, but do it quickly, please."

Sophie stepped over to the childish writing on the wall and swallowed back the tears that clogged her throat. Quickly pulling herself together, she snapped picture after picture.

She looked to the right of the flashlight beam and barely stifled a gasp. There, mounted beside the poem, was a framed magazine article recounting what happened down here.

But it wasn't the article that caught her attention. It was the frame.

It was exactly the right size.

A quick peek right and left didn't turn up any handy statuary that could be used as a weapon. Not that she wanted to hurt the guard. She just needed a distraction. She could throw her knife, but she might need that to get the painting out of the frame.

Peering farther into the shadows, she smiled. There stood a medieval suit of armor, complete with a sword.

"Oh my goodness. I love knights!" she squealed as she ran that way.

"Miss, what are you doing? We have to go!" He hurried after her.

Sophie reached the knight, yanked the sword from his grip, and almost dropped it on the stone floor. Dang, it was heavier than she'd expected. No matter.

She used two hands to grip the hilt and spun around. She under-estimated her reach and neatly sliced through the guard's uniform sleeve.

He yelped and grabbed his arm. "What are you doing?"

She pointed the sword at his chest. "Tell your coworker you'll be a few more minutes."

When he hesitated, she poked his chest, lightly.

He reached out for the sword and cursed when she pulled it back and his hand came away bloody.

"You cut me!"

Sophie's stomach flipped as it always did at the sight of blood, so she kept her eyes on his face. "You grabbed the blade, Claus. Not smart."

He swore again, face pale, then clicked his radio. *"Es wird noch einige minuten dauern."*

Sophie nodded, then indicated a large trunk several feet away. "Now you're going to climb in there."

"I will not. This is madness."

Sophie raised a brow and leaned forward just enough that the sword tip pierced his uniform shirt.

"Ja. Okay. Just don't kill me."

"I have no intention of killing you, Claus. Not as long as you do what I say." When he moved in front of the trunk, she said, "Put your radio, flashlight, and cell phone on the floor, then kick them to me."

Eyes narrowed, he did as instructed.

"Now climb inside the trunk and close the lid. And don't try anything stupid."

"You will not get away with whatever you are planning."

She smiled. "Oh, I'm pretty sure I will."

Once the lid closed over his furious expression, Sophie shoved the sword through the clasp, effectively locking Claus inside.

At least temporarily.

She tossed his cell phone and radio into another trunk, scooped up his flashlight, then grabbed the framed article off the wall and took off at a dead run.

The basement was a maze of narrow corridors, dead ends, and small rooms and former offices.

She ran down one hallway, then stopped short after it ended abruptly. She retraced her steps and paused to listen. The guard was creating a racket, but she didn't have time to go back and gag him. She'd just have to hope his coworker didn't come looking for him too quickly.

After a second wrong turn, Sophie slipped into a small dusty storage room and closed the door behind her. She set Claus's flashlight on a box, then slipped her knife from the sheath inside her boot. Her hands were a little twitchy from the adrenaline, so she took a few deep breaths and then carefully slipped the magazine article from the frame.

Her breath whooshed out in relief as she peeled the pages away.

Underneath was *Tomorrow*, the second portrait by Bernadette Rainier. This one depicted a seated Princess Johanna with young Werner leaning against her knee, while Katharina sat in her lap. All three wore the ducal hats, as the crown was called in Neuhansberg. But it was the artist's gall in depicting females wearing them that had kicked up the big ruckus, as though females should be allowed to inherit the throne and rule.

Her head snapped up at a shout, followed by the sound of running feet.

She pulled out her phone and snapped several pictures of the portrait. Then she turned it over and snapped several more of the back. Sure enough, there was another inscription:

Venice is like eating an entire box of chocolate liqueurs in one go.

Well, that seemed easy enough. Next stop, Venice. But first, she had to get out of here.

She eased the door open and listened. More shouts, more running feet. Apparently Claus's coworker had gotten tired of waiting for him to return to work.

Knife in her right hand and the unwieldy painting tucked against her left side, Sophie slipped out the door and hurried down the corridor. She stopped at the end and looked right, then left.

She hurried down another hallway, searching for an exit sign. One would think they'd have lots of them, but apparently that wasn't a thing in the 1200s. Or the 1800s. Surely today's fire codes would require them?

Another dead end had her huffing out her frustration. She spun around to go back the way she'd come and a woman stepped in front of her, a cleaning cart beside her. She appeared to be in her late fifties, with short graying curls. She lifted a finger to her lips, then indicated the large trash can mounted on the cart.

What the heck?

The woman nodded to the trash can again. *Hurry up.*

Sophie hesitated. Could she trust her?

Did she have a choice?

More footsteps pounded down the hallways.

With a nod of thanks, Sophie climbed into the trash can. It was a tight squeeze with the painting, but she contorted her body to avoid crushing the portrait. The woman slapped the lid in place and put the cart into motion, humming under her breath.

Not two minutes later a male voice called, "Halt!"

The cart stopped. *"Ja, was ist los?"* the woman asked.

"Wier suchen eine dame."

"Ich hab sie nicht gesehen." I haven't seen her.

The footsteps receded. The woman patted the side of the can and kept walking, still humming.

After several more twists and turns, the cart stopped, and the lid opened. The woman nodded at Sophie as she slowly stood and looked around. The woman pointed and there, finally, was an illuminated exit sign.

Sophie clambered out of the can and reached for the painting. "Thank you so much."

"Sei vorsicht." Be careful. She hitched her chin toward the painting.

Sophie nodded her understanding, then carefully worked her way toward the door in little sprints, stopping to listen between every corridor.

She was several yards from the exit sign and freedom when a man stepped into her path from a side corridor, his gun aimed at her chest.

23

Sophie might not have recognized the Glock he pointed at her chest, but the gray hoodie said it was the same man who'd followed her at St. Agnes.

"Just hand over the painting and no one gets hurt."

His accent declared he hailed from somewhere in Eastern Europe, and the way he held the gun said he knew how to use it. But his words seemed robotic, like he was reading from a script.

She noticed a flicker of movement behind him and tried to keep him talking. "What do you want with it, if you don't mind me asking?"

"It's not for me," he muttered.

Sophie studied his face, surprised when he met her gaze. Even in the dim lighting, she read the mix of abject terror overlaid with absolute determination. A deadly combination.

Never let them see you sweat. She quirked an eyebrow. "Looks like we have a problem then, because I need it too."

Whoever was behind him slipped closer to where they stood, but she kept her eyes on the gunman's face.

"Since I have the gun, I win. Please don't make this harder than it needs to be."

Hadn't she just said something similar to Claus?

"I don't want to hurt you, but I will if you don't hand over the painting. Right. Now." He put his finger on the trigger, aimed at center mass.

"Well, hey there, handsome." Camille, one of the women who had broken into Sophie's room this morning, stepped out from behind some boxes. She wore impossibly high heels and a wide smile. The man glanced over his shoulder, and the gun wavered as she sashayed toward them.

"Get out of here. This doesn't concern you." His voice rose at the end as Camille kept walking toward him. Sophie hid a grin. If she swiveled those hips any more, she was going to hurt herself.

Camille walked up behind the man and ran one long fingernail along the nape of his neck. "Aw, come now, sugar. Let's not do this."

He spun toward her, leading with his gun.

At that moment, Sister Mercy stepped into view, holding what looked like a rope in her hands. In a quick snap worthy of a rodeo star, she cracked it like a bullwhip and knocked the gun right out of the man's hands.

"Run!" Camille shouted as she grabbed one of the man's hands and twisted it up behind him. Mercy grabbed the gun and they had the man trussed up like a prize heifer at a roping competition faster than Sophie could blink.

Still shocked over their sudden appearance, she grabbed the painting, muttered, "Thanks!" and took off.

———

Keep going. Almost there.

Adrenaline buzzed under her skin as Sophie raced toward the exit sign, which shimmered like a mirage on the horizon. She wanted to run straight toward it, but her instincts urged caution. She heard the guards behind her, searching, moving ever closer.

Just a couple more yards and she'd be home free.

She had one hand on the bar that would open the door when an arm snaked around her neck, cutting off her breath.

"Don't yell. Just let go of the painting."

Since she couldn't breathe, yelling wasn't an option. Everything in her rebelled as the man tried to wrestle the portrait out of her grasp.

She reached up and used all her strength to loosen his hold, squirming frantically, trying to punch his neck, but none of the self-defense moves she tried made a difference. His grip kept tightening until her vision went hazy and her strength seeped away. She silently cried out as the painting slipped from her grasp and she started sliding toward the floor.

"Hey, what are you doing?"

The voice seemed to come from far away, but she'd heard it before. Suddenly her assailant let go and she dropped to the ground, her head bouncing on the cold stone floor. She groaned at the impact.

Above her, the two men fought. Sophie rolled away and slowly sat up, sucking in great gulps of air, taking inventory. She touched the back of her head, not surprised to find a smear of blood on her fingers. But at least her vision wasn't blurry, so she didn't think she had a concussion. She climbed to her feet and waited for a wave of dizziness to pass.

Beside her, Mac punched the guy in the jaw. The man bounced off some shelves and came back swinging. As they hammered each other, she searched the area and spotted the painting leaning up against a wooden crate.

She eased her way around them.

More blows and grunts of pain were exchanged behind her, followed by the crash of things breaking, but she ignored it all. She focused on getting her hands on the portrait and making a quick exit, stage left.

She picked it up and just as she turned to slip away, a hand snaked out and spun her around.

"Not so fast. That goes with me."

Mac was breathing hard and a bruise was already forming on his cheek. His blue button-down shirt had a rip in one sleeve.

She leaned around him to see how her assailant had fared. He was sprawled on his stomach, not moving. "Is he dead?"

"No, but he'll have the mother of all headaches when he wakes up."

The man groaned and started moving, trying to stand.

Mac held out a hand. "The painting, if you please."

She clutched it to her chest. "No."

The footsteps and shouts were getting closer. "I don't have time to debate this, Sophie."

She studied his hard expression. "Why do you want it?"

He shrugged. "It's for a client."

She'd been right, but that didn't make her feel better. "And you get a commission or finder's fee or something?"

"Or something. It's what I do." He made a *gimme* motion when the sound of footsteps rushing in their direction grew even louder. They were down to seconds. "Now."

Desperate, Sophie bent over and came up with the knife in her hand. "This painting is mine."

He took one look at the knife and reached for her. "You don't want to do this, Sophie."

"Don't I?" She sidestepped his grasp, aiming for his arm, intending to slow him down, but he grabbed her wrist in one smooth move and sent the knife flying over her head.

With a low growl of fury, she leaped onto his back and wrapped her hands around his neck, only then realizing she'd let go of the painting. The miserable wretch shook her off like she weighed nothing and spun her sideways into a shelf laden with pottery. Everything shattered as the shelves collapsed.

She scrambled to her feet, desperate to reclaim the painting, but before she could locate it through the cloud of dust, Mac nabbed it and rushed out the door. The moment he ran through, alarms started screeching.

Sophie snatched up her knife and raced after him.

24

Sophie ran out the back door and straight into a group of people crowded around a tour guide. She walked several paces with them, then stepped out the other side to find Mac. He'd vanished. She spun in a circle, stunned, as she'd expected his height to make him easy to spot. No such luck.

A glance over her shoulder showed not only security guards, but also various police officers now methodically searching the crowd. She had to hide. She crossed the street and purchased a Cologne Cathedral windbreaker and a pair of cheap sunglasses before she slipped into a small café. She went straight to the restroom in the back, slipped off her wig and coat, stashed them in the shopping bag, then popped the lenses out of the sunglasses before she slipped them on. She sat at a table by the window and sipped her coffee while eyeing the commotion outside.

Mac had been after the painting all along. Disappointment washed over her, followed by disgust at her own naiveté. She'd been a fool to believe, for even one second, that he'd merely been trying to help her. She knew better than to take people at face value.

Trust, but verify.

She'd ignored one of her own mottos, and look where that had gotten her.

She had to get that painting back. But how?

Fifteen minutes later, she'd dialed her anger back enough to think, but she still hadn't come up with a viable plan. She decided to focus on something else for a while as her subconscious went to work.

She pulled out her phone and studied the inscription on the back of the second painting again.

Venice is like eating an entire box of chocolate liqueurs in one go.

Her head snapped up as the two chairs opposite her scraped the hardwood floor. Camille and Sister Mercy sat down.

"Are you all right?" the nun asked.

Camille propped her chin on her fist and studied Sophie a moment, then leaned forward. "Are you sure you don't want our help?" She raised an eyebrow and waited.

"Look, I really appreciated your help earlier. Truly. And that thing you did with your belt, Sister Merc—"

"Just Mercy." The nun's eyes twinkled as she shrugged. "My father's family had a cattle ranch on the island of Coron, in the Philippines, so I learned to handle a bullwhip at a young age."

"Shame about the painting. And the hot guy." Camille hitched her chin toward the window, and Sophie looked up to see Mac tuck the painting into the trunk of his car, which was now parked directly across the street, as though he were taunting her. She leaped to her feet, ready to fight him for it in broad daylight, if that's what it took.

Sister Mercy put a hand on her arm to stop her as a dark-haired woman in a severely tailored suit approached him and got right in his face.

"She's not happy," Camille said. The woman's body language suggested Mac was on the receiving end of a stern lecture.

"I know that woman. Where have I seen her?" Mercy squinted, muttered a curse, then quickly made the sign of the cross and murmured, "Sorry, Father." She drummed her fingers on the wooden tabletop, then her eyes widened. "That's Eloise Cuvier. Interpol."

"Interesting. Who's the hunk?" Camille asked.

"Mac McKenzie," Sophie said.

"Do you know him?"

"We've met a few times. He helped me out of a couple jams."

"And then he stole the painting from you. The rat."

"He said it's for a client."

Camille and Mercy exchanged glances.

"Wonder which member of the royal family hired him," Camille said.

Mercy leaned forward. "Look, Sophie. We're here to help."

A waitress appeared and asked the newcomers if they wanted anything. Camille ordered coffee, Mercy requested tea, then they waited quietly until the waitress returned with a carafe, tea bags, and thick mugs.

Camille folded her arms, and without thinking, Sophie reached out and grabbed her wrist. Camille whipped her hands free, leaning back out of reach.

Sophie raised both hands, palms up. "Sorry. I didn't mean to grab you." She pointed to the inside of Camille's wrist and the tattoo there. "You have the same symbol."

"Same as who?" Mercy raised an eyebrow.

"My friend Lise's mother gave her one, on a chain." She glanced from one to the other. "What does it mean? Who are you?"

Camille looked around the quiet café. "Not here."

Mercy pulled a cell phone from a hidden pocket in her habit. "If you give me your number, I'll text you the address."

Sophie met her eyes, said nothing.

Camille smiled. "You're learning. Okay, how about this?" She scribbled an address on a napkin and handed it to Sophie. "Meet us here tonight at six and we'll explain. It's on the rooftop, so take the elevator all the way up."

They pushed their chairs back and stood. Mercy said, "Take the risk," then dropped several bills on the table as they walked out.

﹉﹉﹉

After they left, the waitress approached their table. She kept staring at Sophie's neck. "Are you all right, miss?"

"Why do you ask?"

The young woman blushed scarlet, then indicated Sophie's neck. "It looks painful."

Crud. She knew better than to be memorable in any way. "I'm fine. Thank you."

As soon as the waitress turned away, Sophie dropped some euros on the table and walked out, hoping to catch up to the women, but they were gone.

Too tired, suddenly, to walk back to her hostel, she caught a cab instead.

She climbed the stairs, then slowly opened the door, not really surprised that all the candy she'd strewn about had been pushed into a straight line when someone opened the door.

At least they hadn't trashed the room. The painting of Mac mocked her from where she'd left it earlier.

Who'd been in here? Mac? Or one of the men who'd tried to take the painting from her in the cathedral basement?

She glanced into the tiny mirror and winced. No wonder the waitress was concerned. Her throat looked red and angry and exactly like someone had tried to choke her.

Nothing a scarf couldn't hide.

She went back to Mac's website, looking for a client list, not really surprised when that info was carefully glossed over. Had he been hired by the royal family, as Camille guessed? She scrolled through several more pages, and the hair on the back of her neck stood straight up.

He had degrees in art history and business, but he specialized in authenticating artwork, especially paintings.

25

Mac's phone rang not five minutes after he pulled away from the Dom. He had it connected to the car's Bluetooth, so he hit the Accept button without taking his eyes off the road. Or checking the caller ID. "McKenzie."

"Why were you talking with Eloise Cuvier of Interpol?" Prince Benedikt demanded.

Mac's hands tightened around the wheel. The fact the prince didn't trust him wasn't that surprising. He was more annoyed with himself for not spotting the tail. Whoever the prince had hired had wasted no time in reporting back.

"I've crossed paths with her on a number of occasions."

"You didn't give her the painting, did you?"

"I did not." Though she'd made no secret of the fact she expected him to hand it over.

"Did you tell her you have it?"

"I told her I was looking for it, same as half the treasure hunters in the world." Which was true, as far as it went.

The silence lengthened as Mac threaded his way down the

crowded boulevard toward his hotel, Sophie's furious expression when he'd taken the painting jabbing at his conscience. He liked her spunk and determination, but she was in way over her head. He'd actually done her a favor by taking the painting. It would get her out of the game and keep her safe.

He cringed inwardly as his internal lie detector screamed foul.

Finally, the prince asked, "Which painting did you find today?"

"It depicts Princess Johanna and both children and is called *Tomorrow*. Werner is standing next to her and Katharina is on her lap."

"Is it authentic?"

Mac stifled a snort just in time. "I will need considerable time in a lab before I can make such a determination."

The prince ignored that. "I still can't believe the portraits survived the fire. Where did you find the painting?"

"Hidden in the basement of the Kölner Dom in Cologne."

"Why would someone hide it there?"

"I don't know that either."

"What *do* you know, Mr. McKenzie?"

Again, Mac took a breath before he answered. "I know that the first painting was sent to an art gallery in Munich and subsequently stolen. Whoever stole it may have murdered a gallery employee in his or her quest to obtain it. I followed another interested party to Cologne where she retrieved the second painting from the basement of the cathedral."

"Who is this woman? What's her connection?"

"I will let you know as soon as I have more information." He wasn't ready to reveal Sophie's identity to anyone. Not yet. Especially not to whoever the prince had hired to follow him.

"If you want that bonus, you will not only find the third painting—and authenticate all three—but you will provide me with all the information I hired you to find. By coronation day. Am I making myself clear?"

He opened his mouth to make some smart-alecky response, then closed it. He needed the money the prince was offering.

Finally, he said, "I'll be in touch."

He hung up before he said something he'd have to apologize for later.

―――――――

Sophie absolutely wasn't going to the meeting. But at five thirty that evening, she stopped pacing and muttered, "Who am I kidding?" She spread the candy on the floor again, then carefully closed the door behind her. She wore a short red wig under a ball cap, jeans with holes in the knees, a bandana around her neck, and a battered T-shirt advertising the Rolling Stones. Chunky black boots, where she hid her knife, and a black leather jacket completed the outfit she'd scored at a used clothing store.

She punched the address into her GPS, figuring if they were somehow tracking her new burner phone, then they'd know she was coming.

Too restless to sit in a cab, she walked to dispel her nervous energy. The women seemed to know Nadine. That had to count for something, didn't it? She dialed Lise's boss again, and again got her voice mail. "Call me, Nadine. I met some women who claim to know you."

By the time Sophie reached the apartment building, Nadine still hadn't called back. Sophie debated turning around, but her gut said go, and even if it hadn't, her curiosity would have overruled it.

She rode an ancient elevator to the roof of the brick apartment building, eyes scanning, hand on her knife. Just in case.

"Welcome," Mercy said, as soon as the doors opened. She indicated a chair at the small table she and Camille shared. It was cold up here, but a freestanding gas heater beside the table pumped out heat. Sophie rubbed her hands together as she sat.

Camille closed her laptop and leaned back in her chair. "What made you decide to come? Did Nadine vouch for us?"

"I decided to hear what you had to say and make my own decision."

Camille arched a brow. "Didn't call you back yet, huh?"

Sophie hitched her chin and met her gaze head-on. "You said if I came, you'd tell me what I want to know. Start talking."

"She's feisty anyway. That's a good thing."

Mercy sent Camille a chiding look before she turned to Sophie. "I like the red hair. It suits you." She paused as though choosing her words carefully. "How did you come by your love of disguises?"

Sophie narrowed her eyes at their good-cop/bad-cop role-playing. If they knew Nadine, they would have already checked into Sophie's background. "Here and there." She shrugged. "It's handy if you want to remain unnoticed."

"It can be useful in what we do," Mercy said.

"Which is what, exactly?"

"Let's talk while we eat." Mercy went over to a cooler, where she removed several covered plates and set one in front of each of them. "I hope you like traditional sauerbraten, with spätzle noodles and red cabbage."

Camille went to a different cooler and returned with wineglasses and a bottle of Riesling. "Can I pour you a glass?"

Sophie nodded, sipped. She wanted to tap her foot impatiently during the whole food ritual, but it was delicious, she was starving, and she had a part to play. Tonight she was "casually curious."

Camille's phone rang and she grimaced. "Excuse me a moment." She stepped away. "Why aren't you in class?" A pause. "We've been over this, Cass. You can't skip school every time Uncle Marcel comes to town and wants you to go exploring with him." Another pause. "I don't care that there are only a few more months of school. You belong in class. Hang out with Marcel after school." A pause. "Yes, I'll call him, and no, you can't go on a river cruise with him this week. I need to go. I love you, baby."

She returned to the table. "Sorry about that. Teenagers are a challenge at the best of times. And my cousin is . . . not helping."

"How old is your . . . daughter? Son?"

Camille's proud smile said she loved her child, frustration or no. "Daughter. Cass is eighteen, going on twelve, and my charming scoundrel of a cousin, who is like a brother to me, is just as bad."

She shook her head and picked up her fork. "They keep me on my toes."

"Sounds like," Sophie said. "Tell me who you are."

Camille ignored her and kept eating.

When Mercy handed out thick slices of layered chocolate *Schwartzwalder kirschtorte*, Sophie pushed her chair back. This whole buddy-buddy, "let's eat together" thing was wearing thin. Her internal sensors were elevating toward alarm level. "Enough already. Start talking or I'm out of here."

In answer, Camille calmly pulled up the sleeve of her sweater, displaying her tattoo. "You asked about this earlier. How long ago did your friend Lise get her emblem?"

"The other day. Lise got a letter from her late mother by way of her lawyer and inside was a necklace with that symbol on it."

"Lise is your boss?" Mercy asked.

Sophie smiled. "She is. She's also been my best friend for a very long time."

"You think she went missing because of the paintings?" Camille asked.

She narrowed her eyes. "Yes. Why do *you* think she went missing?"

"We think it may be because of her work with Nadine at the nonprofit. Our guess is someone is rousting the homeless as a cover to make pretty young women disappear. We think Lise got too close and someone isn't happy about it."

Camille's words made Sophie's gut clench. "Do you know where she is?"

Mercy's voice was utterly confident. "If we did, she'd already be free."

Sophie hitched her chin toward Camille's tattoo. "You haven't told me what that means."

"If we tell you, we have to swear you to secrecy first."

Sophie grinned. "Sounds very James Bond, all cloak-and-dagger." Her smile disappeared as she looked from one to the other. They were dead serious.

"We know it sounds absurd, but the truth is, if we trust the wrong people, women will die."

The silence lengthened as Sophie tried to absorb the ramifications of that statement.

Finally, Camille said, "Maybe this will help. Do you have a picture of the first painting with you?"

"In the cloud, yes." Sophie took a few moments and downloaded what she wanted onto her burner phone, then turned it so they could see it.

Camille used her fingers to enlarge Princess Johanna's face, then turned the phone back to Sophie. "What do you see?"

Sophie's eyes widened. She zoomed in further, then slumped back in her chair. In the portrait, Princess Johanna wore the anchor and feather emblem in the center of the pearl choker around her neck. "Tell me what it means."

"Do you swear, on Lise's life, to keep it a secret?" Mercy asked.

Sophie's heart skipped a beat. "Yes."

Camille tapped her tattoo. "The anchor and feather is the symbol of Speranza, which means *hope*. Since the Middle Ages, women have been helping women under its banner, passing the responsibility to offer aid from generation to generation."

"Is there a club you join? Like, I don't know, a secret society for women, like the Freemasons?"

"Not in the traditional sense. There are no meetings or dues or uniforms. It's just women helping women, especially when someone is in trouble because she's trying to do some good in the world. It's really simple: if you see the symbol, you offer help."

Sophie's mind spun, trying to take it all in. "That's why Nadine called you. She's part of it."

Mercy nodded. "Yes. But at the same time, Lise is also connected to the princess, who was also part of Speranza."

Did she believe their story about a secret society of women helping each other? It sounded unbelievable. And like something she very much wanted to be a part of.

If it was true.

She looked from one earnest face to the other, then said, "Lise's mother died recently, and when the painting arrived, it was delivered by her attorney's firm. There was a letter from the attorney with it, and another one from her mother, Irmgard, to Lise. Along with the medallion, which, based on what you're saying, tells me Irmgard was also Speranza."

Sophie chewed the inside of her lip. "I didn't read the letter from Irmgard, of course, but after Lise disappeared, I found the one from the lawyer. It basically said there was more Lise had to do before the coronation and to be very careful. Based on that and Bernadette Rainier's interview saying there were three paintings, which I confirmed online, I figure she was supposed to find all three paintings for some reason."

"How did you know to look for the second one at the Dom?" Camille asked.

Sophie wanted to tell them everything. But could they be trusted? For Lise's sake, she'd tell them *almost* everything.

Trust, but verify.

She pulled out her phone and showed them the photos she'd downloaded earlier, of the inscription on the back of the first painting.

Camille read it out loud. "'Just like St. Irmgard and St. Agnes, I believe in God even when He is silent.'"

Mercy cocked her head in Sophie's direction. "It's a powerful statement of faith, isn't it? Trusting God even when He doesn't explain, when we don't understand."

"You have no idea." Sophie didn't realize she'd spoken aloud until Camille's eyebrows shot to her hairline.

The silence stretched, then Mercy asked, "What does it mean? And where was this written?"

"It's inscribed on the back of the first painting, the one delivered to Lise. I first thought the second painting was in St. Agnes Church, but it wasn't. Then I learned that St. Irmgard's sarcophagus was in the Dom, in St. Agnes Chapel. But that wasn't right either." Sophie paused and took a sip of her wine. "I overheard a tour guide talking about how Jewish families hid in the cathedral's basement during World War II and that supposedly a child had written a poem on the wall. When she read it to the group, I realized that's the second part of the inscription. 'I believe in God even when He is silent.' I headed for the basement."

"Where was the painting?" Camille asked.

Sophie smiled, knowing she looked a wee bit smug, but she couldn't help it. "I didn't find the painting, per se. I found the frame. I noticed that they'd hung a framed copy of a magazine article beside that section of wall. It was the right size to hide one of the royal portraits. I, ah, distracted the guard and took off with it."

"How can you be sure the painting was behind the article?" Mercy looked skeptical.

"I stopped in a small storage room and made sure."

"But people were following you. At least two, from what we saw today," Mercy said.

"Three, if you count the hunk," Camille added.

"The sneaky hunk," Sophie corrected.

"Do you know who they were?" Mercy asked.

"I saw the one in St. Agnes Church. It's possible he followed me from Munich. I'm pretty sure Mac did too."

"And the other one?"

"No idea."

"Since Bernadette Rainier told a reporter about a treasure of some kind, every treasure hunter in the world will be trying to find the paintings. And right now, the starting place is the gallery in Munich and anyone connected to it. Namely, you and Lise," Mercy said.

Sophie couldn't argue with that. "Hopefully, the fact that I'm not in Munich anymore will buy me some time."

Camille propped her chin in her hand. "Let's suppose you're right and we're wrong and this is all about the paintings. How will that help you find Lise?"

It was the million-dollar question. "I don't know. Yet. But my gut says Lise was trying to do whatever her mother asked in that letter and got snatched by someone. If I find the paintings, either they'll lead me to Lise or I'll find a way to use them to buy her freedom."

They listened to the muted sound of traffic far below until finally Mercy said what they were all thinking. "We don't have the one you found today."

Sophie barely heard her, her attention snagged by something about the second portrait that bothered her. She pulled up the picture of the portrait again and zoomed in on Katharina. She studied her face, then Werner's face, then the princess's. Slowly, inch by inch, she zoomed in on each of the children, trying to figure out what her subconscious had registered.

When she found it, the hair on her arms stood straight up. She set the phone down, leaned back, and rubbed her hands on her arms.

"You just went pale," Mercy said. "What did you see?"

Camille also leaned closer, concern in her brown eyes.

Sophie's heart raced. Could she risk telling them? Yes. If it meant saving her best friend, she'd risk everything, including her life.

"Do you have a way to enlarge this photo?" Sophie nodded to Camille's laptop.

"E-mail it to me and let's see what we can do."

Several minutes later the three of them were huddled around the laptop as Sophie zoomed in on a spot on Katharina's sturdy little leg, just above the ankle. The closer she tried to get, the grainier the image became.

"It's still not clear enough." Sophie huffed out a frustrated breath.

Camille and Mercy exchanged a look.

"This still falls under the confidentiality part of what we've told you, okay?"

Sophie looked from one to the other. "Okay."

"Even though Speranza isn't formally organized," Mercy began, "Camille and I are part of a frontline team, if you will, that spearheads rescues and assistance around the world. I want to send this picture to Picasso, our technical whiz, to see if she can enlarge it further." She cocked her head. "What are we looking for?"

"Go ahead and send it, and let's see if we can get a closer look first."

They cleared the dishes and Sophie wandered to the edge of the roof and peered out over the city, amazed again at the cathedral and its size and influence, so many generations later.

Not fifteen minutes later, Camille's laptop chimed and they crowded around.

When Sophie zeroed in on the enlargement, she stumbled into the nearest chair and sat down with a thump, her mind struggling to accept what her eyes were telling her. The ramifications were huge. And impossible.

Her fingers trembled slightly as she pulled out her phone, logged into her cloud account, and scrolled through her photos. The picture she was looking for was taken last New Year's Eve at the gallery. Henri had snapped a picture of her and Lise in their party finery, facing each other, each holding a champagne glass up in a toast. For fun, they'd both kicked up their heels in a flirty little pose.

Sophie downloaded the photo and once again zoomed in as far as she could. Her hands trembled as she held her phone up beside Camille's laptop, so both images were side by side.

Mercy whispered, "Sweet Mary, mother of God!" and made the sign of the cross.

Camille's eyes widened and she swallowed hard. "Well now. That changes everything, doesn't it?"

26

Sophie gazed at each woman in turn. "Now it's my turn to demand confidentiality. No one can know about this."

"No one except the rest of our team. It's more important than ever that we keep Lise safe."

Mercy added, "And that we find her before the transfer of power in three days. Felix has no business taking over the throne."

"This must be the 'additional things' Irmgard wanted Lise to do before the coronation ceremony. Which means finding the paintings matters more than ever," Sophie said.

"Let me call Willa, who heads the team, and we'll get the ball rolling. We don't have much time," Camille said.

Sophie's mind spun. Had Lise read Irmgard's letter? Did she know the truth yet?

So many unanswered questions, but again and again, Sophie came back to the same thing: find the paintings. Somehow, someway, they were the key to getting her friend back alive.

Irmgard had a reason for the letter she wrote and the things she wanted Lise to do. Sophie believed absolutely that Irmgard was trying to protect her daughter. Since she couldn't anymore, Sophie would pick up the torch and finish it for her. She'd make it right.

When Camille hung up, Sophie said, "We need to get the second painting back from Mac, then find the third one."

"You don't happen to know where he's staying, do you?" Camille asked.

When Sophie shook her head, Camille picked up her phone again. "Hey, Picasso, sorry to bother you, but I need you to check some security cameras for me." She described Mac's Mercedes and gave the time he left the cathedral and which direction he was heading. "We need to know where he went from there. We're assuming a hotel, but we're not sure."

Twenty minutes later, they had the information they needed and were headed there.

When Mac returned to his seventh-floor hotel room, his brain was running a hundred miles an hour. He grabbed a bottle of water and sucked it down, then paced the room, trying to sort facts, assumptions, and theories into some sort of logical pattern, but none of the pieces seemed to fit. There was obviously more going on than what Prince Benedikt was saying, and that annoyed him. Mac expected it, as clients always hid things or lied for one reason or another, but that didn't mean he had to like it. Flying blind had never been his favorite mode of transportation. He didn't like being tailed either. He'd have to be more careful.

He sat at the small table and booted up his laptop. Since the painting's arrival at the Munich gallery was what unleashed the current firestorm, he decided to dig deeper there. He spent a bit of time looking over Henri Marchant's background, then moved on to Lise Fortier. It didn't take long to confirm that she'd been a do-gooder long before she became a gallery owner. She'd been all over the world trying to help the less fortunate, especially women and children, as articles and photos of her on the Internet attributed.

When she and her late husband purchased the gallery, it was on the brink of bankruptcy, but they had turned it around. Not long after his death, Sophie Williams entered the scene. Mac found one piece that said the two had been friends since the summer Lise was Sophie's camp counselor, more than fifteen years earlier.

Where was Lise now? There was no mention of her in the media since the press conference the day after the painting was delivered.

Had she been kidnapped? Was she in seclusion and simply avoiding the media? It would make sense following the recent death of her mother. He also checked missing persons, just in case, but didn't find anyone listed who matched her description.

For whatever reason, Sophie was handling the paintings. He assumed she knew more than what Bernadette Rainier had revealed, since Sophie was looking for the painting in Cologne.

He stood and stretched, then walked to the window and stared out over the city skyline as darkness fell. At the press conference, Lise Fortier had said the painting was left to her by her late mother and she would have more to say in a few days.

Mac returned to his laptop. Who was her mother? He ran several searches, including on Lise's social media platform. Her mother was never mentioned, by name or otherwise. Which wasn't uncommon. Lots of people avoided naming family members to protect their privacy.

He didn't find an obituary either. Not in Germany or any of the surrounding countries.

He scrolled through Lise's online photos again, looking for an older woman who appeared more than once. It took a while, but he finally found her. At least he was 90 percent positive it was her. In every photo she wore a hat and sunglasses or a scarf, and she never looked directly at the camera. She was usually half hidden at the outer edges of the frame or obscured by a potted plant, there but not center stage.

Using a skill set he'd never admit to publicly, he dug deeper and tracked Lise's travel over the past year.

Now they were getting somewhere. Every month like clockwork, she'd flown to Zurich, then rented a car and driven to a small town in Switzerland. Using the map feature, he discovered the tiny town's single biggest employer was an exclusive assisted-living facility. Several small pensions catered to family and friends who came to visit.

He picked up his phone. "Hello, I'm hoping you can help me. I'm trying to get in touch with Lise Fortier. She was coming to visit her mother and I said I'd accompany her, but I can't get through on her cell. Is she there yet?"

The woman sucked in a breath. "Sir, you must be mistaken. Frau Scholz is no longer with us."

"But Lise said her mother loved it there. Why did she move her somewhere else?"

"You misunderstand. Frau Scholz passed away last week." There was a beat of silence. "I'm sorry, sir. I've already said too much." She hung up.

Now that he had her last name, a little more digging into the facility's records told him her first name was Irmgard. He found Lise's birth certificate, which listed Irmgard as her mother and her father as unknown. And that was it. Nothing showed up online, not unusual before social media, and none of his usual searches and databases spit out anything helpful. Irmgard was a dead end.

He hated feeling like he was missing something, so he reread Bernadette Rainier's interview, but no clues jumped out at him. He pulled up several photos of her artwork and studied them closely before he turned his focus to the painting *Tomorrow*. He held it up to the light and studied Ms. Rainier's brushstrokes, the way she used bold colors and minute details to bring the royal family to blazing life. Everything matched what he'd seen online. Of course, he'd need to study the painting more closely, run some tests in his lab, but he was 99 percent certain this was no forgery. Her skill with acrylics was incredible. It was no wonder people had lost their minds over these paintings. They were spectacular.

His stomach rumbled, reminding him he hadn't eaten dinner. He slipped a jacket over his T-shirt, his feet into loafers, and his

Glock into his shoulder holster before he secured the painting. He didn't want to draw attention to it by storing it in the hotel safe—provided it would even fit—so he improvised. He picked it up to hide it in the closet when something on the back caught his eye. He brought the portrait back into the room and held it under the light in order to read the barely-there writing on the back of the frame.

Venice is like eating an entire box of chocolate liqueurs in one go.

What did that mean? And why was it written on the back of the royal portrait?

Someone knocked on the door to his room.

He laid the painting on the closet shelf and arranged the spare blanket and pillow over it so no one would know it was there. Unless they were specifically searching for it.

Whoever it was knocked again, louder.

He slid the closet door partially closed, then glanced out the peephole before he swung the door open. "What are you doing here?"

27

Sophie stepped forward and used both palms to shove Mac backward. She'd caught him off guard or that would never have worked. He backed up half a step, then planted his feet and crossed his arms over his chest.

"What do you want, Sophie?"

She waved her arms in the air, in full drama-queen mode. "What do you think I want? Where's the painting?" She tried to shove past him, but he shifted his weight to block the doorway.

"Don't do this, Sophie. You're not going to win."

She narrowed her eyes at his infuriatingly calm superiority. Then she smiled, all Cheshire cat. When she spoke, her voice was low and husky. "Really? Because I'm not so sure."

A flicker of unease flashed in his gaze as she stepped closer and ran a finger down his cheek. He tilted his head back slightly but didn't move away, blue eyes searching hers, trying to anticipate her next move.

She took another step closer until she could feel his breath on her cheek and hear his heart beating. Scratch that, the loud thumping was her own. Without giving herself time to change her mind, she closed the final distance between them and laid her lips on his, sliding her right hand around the back of his neck.

He froze for a moment, then his lips softened against hers. She suddenly wanted to lose herself in the taste and feel of him, but now was not the time.

She placed a line of small kisses along his jaw until he captured her mouth again and deepened the kiss.

In one smooth move, she slipped her left hand under his jacket and yanked the gun from his holster. As he reached for her, she crouched low and slid the gun out into the hallway.

He grabbed her arm, pulled her up, and tried to spin her up against him, but she kicked out backward and knocked him off-balance just enough to slip out the door.

Once in the hall, she scooped up the gun and took off at a dead run, Mac hot on her heels.

He closed in fast and caught her after she rounded the corner of the hallway. One second she was sprinting down the industrial carpet and the next he had her pinned flat against the wall. It took almost no effort for him to wrest the gun from her grip and tuck it back into his shoulder holster. The annoying man wasn't even breathing hard.

He stayed just far enough out of reach to keep his holster protected. "What the heck, Sophie? What was that about?"

She cocked a brow, sent him a half smile, and shrugged. "I hadn't decided yet if I was actually going to shoot you."

"Why does it matter so much for you to get the painting?"

Sophie studied his sincere expression, debated telling him about Lise. *Don't be stupid, Soph.* The man had taken the painting from her. He wasn't trustworthy, never mind the way his kisses made her weak in the knees.

"It belongs to my family."

He cocked his head. "You and Ms. Fortier aren't family."

"Not by blood, but in every way that matters. The paintings, all of them, belong to her."

"I think Prince Benedikt would argue that. He's been pretty vocal about the paintings belonging to him."

"Give it back."

"I can't. I have an obligation to my client."

The silence lengthened as they stared each other down.

"This is all about money for you, never mind what's right or wrong." Oddly disappointed once again, she stepped away from the wall, surprised when he let her go.

He looked like he wanted to argue, then shook his head. "Be careful, Sophie. The next person you encounter might not let you off that easy."

Without a word, she walked to the bank of elevators and pressed the Down button. She stepped in, and as the doors closed, she glanced up and their eyes met, held.

Neither one looked away.

⸻

Once at street level, Sophie walked around the corner and two blocks south before she hailed a taxi. She had the driver let her out three blocks before her destination and went the rest of the way on foot.

When she reached the fourth-floor furnished apartment Camille and Mercy had rented, Sophie tapped on the door.

Camille looked through the peephole, then opened the door and scanned the hallway before she pulled Sophie inside.

"You got it?" Sophie shed her coat.

Mercy rose from her seat at the small, round table and indicated the painting lying there. "Of course."

"No thanks to you," Camille scolded. "What were you thinking, kissing the man like that?"

Sophie shrugged off the memory of Mac's lips on hers and shot the women a cheeky grin. "It worked, didn't it?"

"Trying to grab his weapon was too risky," Mercy chided. "You were supposed to wait for us to pull the fire alarm."

"Sometimes you have to improvise. Relax. It all worked out."

Camille and Mercy had been in the stairwell, ready to activate the alarm and snatch the painting once Sophie and Mac left the room.

She moved to the table and looked at the painting again, studied the faces. The birthmark. Then she turned it over. "Have you looked at the back of it yet?"

Both women shook their heads. They crowded around and Mercy read the inscription aloud.

> *"Venice is like eating an entire box of chocolate liqueurs in one go."*

"Okay, our next stop is Venice. But where in Venice?" Camille asked.

Mercy pulled her cell phone from the pocket of her jeans, tapped the screen.

"Why no habit today?" Sophie asked.

"Same reason for your disguises. I didn't want to be memorable in any way."

Camille had a press badge around her neck, but she'd set her camera on the side table, beside the one Mercy had been carrying.

"The quote is actually by Truman Capote," Mercy said, looking up from her phone. "He was an American novelist and screenwriter. He wrote *Breakfast at Tiffany's*."

"Did he live in Venice? Could it be in his house?" Sophie asked.

Mercy tapped a few more keys. "He visited, I think. But he didn't live there, not that I can tell. I'll have Picasso dig deeper."

"How about chocolate factories?" Camille suggested.

Several seconds passed. Mercy shook her head. "Not a lot of those. But the Caffè Florian has been serving hot chocolate since it opened in 1720."

Sophie mumbled, "Wow," through a yawn, then glanced at the clock. "I'm beat. I'm heading back to my hostel for some shuteye." She picked up the painting. The other two women exchanged glances. "What?"

"We think you should leave the painting with us. Nobody knows who we are, so we're not targets. When Willa gets here in the morning, she'll stash it somewhere safe."

Anxiety slithered down Sophie's back, raising gooseflesh. She'd trusted them with the truth about Lise. Was she ready to trust them with one of the paintings? If she didn't and someone took it from her, then what? At least two people besides Mac had been following her. Their logic made sense. But still . . . "Where will you hide it tonight?"

Mercy started for the small back bedroom. "Come see." Inside a tiny closet, Mercy lifted the shelf along one side, then opened the hidden door behind it. "The painting will fit. We already checked."

"How did you know this was here?"

"The owner is also Speranza."

"Can you trust her?"

"Our whole network is based on trust, Sophie," Mercy said. "It has to be. Otherwise, it wouldn't work." Then she grinned. "But we're not stupid either. We subscribe to the Russian proverb *doveryai no proveryai*: trust, but verify."

Sophie relaxed, slightly, at hearing one of Lise's favorite sayings, and her own personal motto, quoted back to her. "Willa will let me know where the painting is?"

"Of course."

Sophie studied Mercy's sincere expression a moment longer, then slowly nodded.

Once she slipped the painting into the hidden compartment, Sophie said good night and headed for the door before she changed her mind.

"Be careful," Camille said. "The hunk is not going to be happy when he realizes the painting is gone."

Sophie swallowed hard. She didn't think he'd physically hurt her, but her heart might be another matter entirely.

She patted her tote bag and indicated the knife in her boot. "I'll be ready."

28

He was sitting on her bed, hands stacked behind his head, when she opened the door to her room at the hostel.

Her first thought was that he looked like a panther, all long and lean and deceptively casual. Her second was that under the relaxed pose, he was furious. And her third was profound gratitude that she'd left the painting with Mercy and Camille.

She closed the door, careful to keep him in her line of sight. "Hello, Mac. Didn't expect to see you again tonight."

He arched a brow. "Didn't you?"

Sophie shrugged, slid her tote off her shoulder, and froze. Her bedazzled iPad sat on the chair, half buried under a sweatshirt. *Crud.* Her worry for Lise had made her careless. Would he remember where he'd seen it before?

She kept her eyes on him as she slid her jacket off, folded it, and placed it on the chair over the iPad. She unwound the scarf from around her neck, added it to the pile.

"How is your throat?" His intent gaze focused on her neck, then moved to her face. Was the concern genuine?

She shrugged. "It could have been worse."

"What's really going on here, Sophie?"

"I could ask you the same question. I've been assuming you're working for the prince, but I also saw you with an Interpol agent." It was risky, letting him know she'd seen him. But she had to know.

"Eloise and I have crossed paths before."

Which told her exactly nothing. She folded her arms, leaned back against the door, and waited.

He rose from the bed and was suddenly standing much too close in the tiny room. "Where's the painting?"

She had to tilt her head back to see his face, but she wouldn't let on how much his proximity affected her. She arched a brow. "You know I'm not going to tell you that."

His hands came up and she froze. They settled lightly on her face, and he rubbed his thumbs gently over her cheeks. "You are playing a very dangerous game, Sophie. I won't always be there to protect you."

"Protect me? You stole the painting from me!"

"Who were those women you were with earlier?"

His voice was a low purr, drawing her in, but she steeled herself against him. "You know I'm not telling you that either."

Frustration crossed his chiseled features a split second before his lips came down on hers. The annoyance was there in his kiss, and she gave it back, measure for measure. Until somehow, the irritation was gone, and the kiss became something else entirely.

They were both breathing hard when he pulled away and yanked the door open. He looked over his shoulder. "Be careful, Sophie. You don't want me as an enemy."

When his phone buzzed with a call from a number he never wanted to hear from again, it took every ounce of his hard-won self-discipline to keep his face expressionless.

He set his drink on the coaster with great care and rose from the table. "Gentlemen, if you'll excuse me a moment. I need to take this call."

He stepped outside the exclusive restaurant, far enough from the hovering staff so as not to be overheard. It was time to regain the upper hand. "Why are you calling me? I've fulfilled my part of the bargain."

The electronically altered voice made a tsking sound. "You would do well to remember that you are not in charge. The client was very pleased. So pleased, in fact, that he wants another, larger shipment. By tomorrow."

He turned toward the neatly clipped hedge, wiped sudden sweat from his forehead, but kept his voice cool. "I agreed to facilitate one shipment. We're done here."

A pause followed. "You agreed to buy my silence. We're done when I say we're done."

He tugged on his shirt collar, felt the noose tightening around his neck.

"I need another secure location. By tonight."

"That is not possible," he stated calmly, trying to keep the desperation from his voice. "With everything going on, I'll need a few days to make arrangements."

"You have until tonight." There was another pause. "It's your choice, of course. But you know the consequences of refusal. I'm quite certain the media—and law enforcement—would be very interested in some of your more . . . unusual hobbies . . . and their consequences."

In the ensuing silence, he pictured everything he'd worked for going up in flames. Frustrated, he ripped a hunk out of the hedge and threw it aside before he noticed a gardener watching him. He turned his back and muttered, "I will text you a location. By tonight."

"Excellent."

The line went dead.

By 3:00 a.m., Nadine was exhausted, discouraged, and wishing she'd had the heater fixed in her aging little sedan. But there were always more pressing needs at Neue Anfänge, and she'd just never gotten around to it. She climbed into the car and leaned her head against the back of the seat. The dampness of the cold night had settled into her bones, and her feet hurt from walking through every encampment she could find.

Even though she'd shown Lise's picture everywhere and confirmed she'd been all over the city last night, no one had seen her since.

Nadine rubbed her hands down her arms, trying to keep her teeth from chattering. Right now she was feeling every one of her sixty-seven years. For all her effort, she'd gotten nowhere and still had absolutely no idea where else to look for Lise.

She raised her glance heavenward. "I'm sorry, Irmgard. But I am not giving up, my dear friend. I will find your girl and bring her home."

While she debated where to look next, a white van pulled up to the curb, lights off, which had her grabbing her camera and zooming in to get a better view. Four masked men climbed out. Two started shouting for everyone to leave their tents and then funneled them between the other two men. As Nadine watched, one nodded to the other and suddenly they'd separated a teenage girl from the crowd, walked her around the van and out of view of the others at knifepoint, then quickly bound and gagged her and tossed her into the back of the van.

Nadine was halfway to the vehicle before she'd made a conscious decision. She had to save the girl. She waited for the men to go back to join their cohorts, then rushed from the cover of the trees and slipped inside the van. The teen was trying to scream behind her gag.

"Shhh, I'm here to help," she soothed as she scrambled to loosen the ropes around her wrists. Why hadn't she brought a knife?

From outside, there was the sudden scream of a siren. Relief flooded her, but it was short-lived. The back door of the van swung open and they tossed in another young woman, then two of the men hopped in after her and slammed the door just as the driver peeled away from the curb, sending Nadine tumbling.

He took the next turn on two wheels and everyone slid to one side. For a split second, a streetlight illuminated the interior of the van.

"Who the heck are you?" one of the men demanded.

"Toss her out," the other man suggested, and Nadine's blood ran cold.

She stayed silent but worried they could hear the thundering of her heart.

"Tie her up and gag her," the driver said. "We'll decide what to do with her later."

The van swung around another corner, and Nadine's worry climbed higher still when her cell phone slid from her pocket and bounced against one of the men. He snatched it up, then grinned as he opened the door a crack and tossed it out onto the street. Then he bound and gagged her.

They made another stop and before long, two more teen girls were tossed in the back. This time the driver sped out of town, the elevation rising as they collected more bruises with every zigzagging turn.

Nadine's heart filled with dread when the vehicle finally stopped, and they were hauled out by men waving guns around. But she stood tall.

Come what may, she had to find a way to save these girls. And hopefully, find Lise too.

———

Laszlo huddled in a shadowy doorway across the street from the woman's hostel. He shivered under his hoodie and clutched a cup of coffee in hands that shook. His phone had rung too many times today. All from the same number. He hadn't answered. How could he? If he said he'd failed again, his son was as good as dead.

He swallowed the lump of emotion that clogged his throat. He couldn't give up. Not until he had the painting. He'd followed the woman, Sophie, all over Cologne but she hadn't had the painting since she left the Dom. He'd been ready to give up when the black-haired guy who had been following her showed up at the hostel a little while ago.

The outer door opened, and he appeared. Tall and confident, he walked like someone who'd been in the military. But was he still? Or worse, Interpol? He had the look of a cop about him.

Didn't matter. The man didn't have the painting with him either. Then who had it?

The phone in Laszlo's pocket started ringing again. He wanted to throw it in the nearest trash bin, but he didn't dare. He'd just decided to grab an hour or two of sleep when two men appeared from around the corner. They headed directly toward the hostel's front door.

The light over the door illuminated their faces, and his heart almost stopped. They weren't after the woman.

They were here for him. He'd seen them before. When they showed up, death inevitably followed.

The cup fell from suddenly nerveless fingers and coffee splattered over his boots and pant legs.

He was out of time.

Laszlo turned and ran. They must have traced his cell phone. But he couldn't toss it. For his son's sake, he couldn't.

Heart pounding and lungs burning from the effort, he ran until he reached the train station. He bought a ticket, a ball cap, and a newspaper, then boarded the next train. He didn't check to see where it was going until after it pulled away from the station.

His hands shook as he took out his phone. He had to find that painting. But who had it? And how was he going to find them?

29

Sophie checked out of her room at the hostel and took an Uber to the small municipal airport as instructed. Had she well and truly lost her mind? She hadn't trusted anyone but Lise for more years than she could count. And despite what Camille and Mercy thought, Sophie knew her friend would have contacted her if she could.

Wouldn't she? Old fears and insecurities reared their ugly heads, and she pushed them aside. She could trust Lise. Her gut said she could trust the two women as well, enough that she'd even managed a few hours of sleep. Their help with the photo had certainly been spot-on.

As the driver raced down mostly empty streets at this hour of the morning, Sophie checked her reflection under the guise of taking a selfie. She'd gone punk today. Short, spiked pink hair, temporary tattoos covering the fading red marks on her neck, nose piercing, tattered tank and torn jeans, ratty Converse sneakers.

She didn't think even Mac would recognize her. An unsettling wash of emotions swamped her at the thought of him, but she ignored it. She had more important things to worry about.

The driver pulled up to a small, sad-looking hangar where a lone helicopter sat on cracked concrete. A mechanic in blue coveralls had his head inside the cockpit and was cussing a blue streak. In multiple languages.

Sophie paid the driver and waited until he left before she approached the bird. Her stomach flip-flopped. She didn't mind flying. In nice, big commercial jets with comfy seats. The clear bubble that surrounded the two seats in this thing didn't even have doors. She swallowed hard.

"Hello?"

The head snapped up, banged the steering thing, and more cussing ensued before the mechanic backed out, straightened, and turned.

"You're a woman," Sophie blurted out.

She was tall and slender, her short dark hair under a ball cap. Her sharp gray eyes didn't miss a thing as she gave Sophie a critical once-over.

"And you look twelve." The mechanic wiped her hands on a greasy rag. "You must be Sophie."

"And you are?"

"Hank. Give me a minute to clean up and we'll get out of here." She hitched her chin toward the hangar. "Restroom and vending machine are in there."

The text early that morning from Camille had been short on details, simply telling Sophie that the "package" was safe and to be at the airport on time. She eyed the chopper that looked like it was held together with duct tape and baling wire and wished she'd asked a few more questions.

Ten minutes later, as Sophie buckled her seat belt and slipped on the noise-canceling headphones Hank handed her, she couldn't help asking, "You know how to fly this thing?"

"Since you were playing in a sandbox. You look a little green. You ever been in one of these babies before?"

Sophie shook her head.

Hank's laugh sounded a wee bit too excited. "Well, hang on,

girl, 'cause you're in for an adventure." In less time than Sophie expected, the big bird left the ground. Sophie looked out at the ground rushing away beyond the open door and squeezed her eyes shut, hands locked on the armrests in a death grip.

"Open your eyes, Sophie. Don't chicken out now."

Her eyes snapped open to find Hank grinning at her.

"Look around you. This is what it's like to be a bird, flying above it all."

Sophie chanced a peek and ignored the way her stomach turned over when she glanced at the open doorway. Instead, she looked out farther, seeing the towns and hamlets below, the ribbons of roadway connecting one to the other.

She'd just started to relax when things changed again. Solid ground gave way to water rushing by below them. Hank leaned forward and pointed in front of them. "That's Venice."

Sophie studied the speck of land in the distance. "How long before we get there?"

"We're not going to Venice. Not directly."

"Then where are we going?"

Hank pointed to a spot halfway between their location and the island.

Sophie strained to see but couldn't figure out what she was talking about. "There's nothing out here but water and a boat."

"Exactly. We're going to the boat."

Her stomach did another turn, adding a half twist this time. "How is that going to work?"

"You'll see. Trust me."

The chopper swooped down toward the water, Sophie clutched the armrests tighter, and Hank laughed.

Mac had never believed in coincidence. But he did believe in being thorough. When he'd returned to his hotel room the night before, frustration still spurting through his veins over Sophie's stubbornness—and the fact that she'd pulled a fast one and gotten the painting from him—he'd booted up his laptop and done some more digging into everyone connected with the Fortier Gallery.

Despite the countdown clock ticking away in his head, worry for Sophie bubbled under his skin like an itch he couldn't reach. Did she not understand the danger she was in? Who was she working with? Who did she have steal the painting from his room while she'd distracted him in the hallway? The two women he'd spotted earlier?

Those questions kept him up most of the night and had him at her door at barely seven thirty the next morning. Again. "Sophie, open up. We need to talk."

No answer and no sound indicating anyone was in the room. He knocked again. Still nothing.

After a quick look in both directions, he pulled out a slender case, extracted the tools he needed, and made short work of the flimsy lock. He slipped inside and quietly closed the door behind him.

She was gone.

The bed was neatly made, and there was no trace she'd ever been here.

Except one. She'd propped the portrait of him against the headboard with a note that read: *For Mac.*

Irritation that she'd so easily outsmarted him gave way to admiration as he studied the painting anew. She really was incredibly talented.

If she were here, she'd laugh at his predictability. Unbidden, the memory of her laughing at something he said morphed into the profile of Mrs. Bauernstein, the matron he'd met at the fundraiser what seemed like a lifetime ago. Same throaty laugh, head thrown back. He stopped, searched his memory for additional confirmation. The sparkling iPad. She'd covered it with her leather jacket last night when she returned to her room. The truth slapped him, hard.

Sophie Williams was Robin Hood.

She was who Eloise was paying him to find.

He locked the door behind him and tucked the painting in the trunk of his car. He'd have to decide what to do about Sophie later. Right now, he had a hunch to follow up on.

He wasn't far out of the city when his cell phone rang. His gut tightened at the caller ID. "Hi, Mom. Couldn't sleep?" It was the middle of the night in the States.

"I'll sleep when I'm dead," she quipped, but he heard the exhaustion in her voice. The latest chemo cocktail they'd given her not only messed with her sleep, it threw every system out of whack.

"Not funny, Mom. Not funny."

"Actually, sometimes, it needs to be. Humor helps."

He grimaced at the subtle chiding. She was right, but even the possibility that she might not survive was something he refused to consider. Jokingly or otherwise. He forced a light tone. "Well then, did you need something besides my sparkling repartee to keep you company in the middle of the night?"

She yawned. "I've just been thinking about the princess again. I've seen news of the painting all over, of course, and just wondered how things were on your end."

"I'm bringing you a surprise next time I come visit." His mother would love the portrait Sophie had painted.

"Ooh, you know I love surprises, especially happy ones. Will you give me a hint?"

"That would kind of ruin the whole surprise thing, wouldn't it?"

"Just a tiny one."

"It's a painting, but not one of the ones everyone is chasing," he hurried to add.

"Hmm. What's the subject matter?"

He snorted. "Nice try. That's all you get. I'll bring it with me. You're going to love it."

She huffed out a disappointed breath. "Fine, I'll wait until you get here. Now tell me about the investigation." So much for diversionary tactics. His mother could be like a dog with a bone.

"I'm checking out a hunch this morning."

She chuckled. "You and your hunches." She paused. "They've saved your life more than once. I hope you're being careful."

Not the direction he wanted this conversation to go. "Did you get the pictures I sent you?"

"Yes. The hotel is lovely. And the view from your room is spectacular. It makes me feel like I'm in Cologne again."

Which was the whole point.

"Did you get to the Dom? It's my favorite place in the city. Incredibly peaceful, despite its size."

"I did. And it's as beautiful as ever."

"Even though I have cancer, I haven't lost my mind. I know every art thief and treasure hunter is looking for those paintings right now. You're staying safe?"

He smiled. "Yes, Mom. I'm staying safe."

"I can see you rolling your eyes from here, you know."

"You do remember I've been taking care of myself for a while now?"

"Not as well as I'd like," she shot back, which made him laugh.

"Would it help if I said I'm stopping right now to buy yards of bubble wrap to fashion a suit out of?"

This time she laughed, as he'd meant her to.

"Make it bulletproof instead and I'll sleep better at night."

He sobered. "I'm always careful. You know that. Try to get some rest. I'm heading into the country this morning and will send you more pictures for when you wake up."

"You're a good son." Her voice sounded drowsy.

"And you're an amazing mom. Rest. I've gotta go."

He hung up and took several deep breaths. He couldn't lose her. The doctors had exhausted all the traditional treatments, but the cancer wouldn't stop. If this experimental new treatment with its astronomical price tag her insurance wouldn't cover was the only option, he'd get that money.

Which meant he had to find the answers the prince wanted, in barely three days' time.

When he arrived at the farm halfway between Neuhansberg and Zurich, the place showed no signs of life. The short article he'd discovered in the local paper last night said the farmer had been widowed years ago and his children had moved away. But it was the casual mention that he'd spent several years on staff at Neuhansberg Castle around the time of the princess's death that had brought Mac here. He'd rewatched the footage of the princess's funeral procession and found the man amongst the castle staff lining the road.

His death might have no connection to the paintings, but Mac couldn't assume it didn't either. Investigations usually required chasing down endless leads before you found enough pieces of the puzzle that a picture started to emerge.

There was no crime scene tape since his death had been deemed from natural causes. According to the reporter, the police speculated the man had been out in his barn when he had a heart attack, hit his head on a support post, and died. He'd been found when a neighbor came to return some tools.

Mac knocked on the door of the farmhouse, though the place had a deserted air about it. He glanced through the sheers on the front window, but there was no sign of movement inside.

He went to the barn first, tried to picture the scene. But still, something nagged at the back of his mind. He wandered over to a nearby smaller, older outbuilding. It was padlocked.

A quick circuit around the outside and he discovered a grimy window in the back wall.

Inside, what looked like the shape of a vehicle lay covered by a tarp.

His mind raced, pieces shifting, fitting together. He used his elbow to break the glass, then shimmied through the narrow opening and landed on the dirt floor inside.

He pulled back the tarp and stopped, letting the horror of the past wash over him. He shuddered as he studied the crumpled, burned-out hulk of a car. Unless he'd completely missed his guess, he'd just found Princess Johanna's missing vehicle.

30

The knot in Sophie's stomach tightened as the boat in the distance grew from a mere speck on the horizon to something the size of a child's toy.

Hank sent her a glance, laughter in her eyes. "If you don't loosen your grip, you'll yank those armrests out, and that's going to tick me off. I've spent too much time getting this bird back in the air."

That did not reassure. It wasn't the fear of flying that made Sophie's heart race. It was the fear of crashing. Like her parents. She squeezed her eyes shut as memories yanked her back to when she was sixteen.

It had been barely 8:00 a.m. on a Thursday morning when Sophie heard a noise by the front door. Thinking her parents had come back early from their consulting job, she swung the door open and stopped short. Two somber-faced, dark-suited men stood on the front steps. One held out an official badge of some kind. "Sophie Williams?"

Before she could respond, her nanny stepped in front of her, easing Sophie behind her. "Who are you?" Helen demanded.

"CIA," the older of the two men said. "May we come in?"

When Helen gasped and went pale, Sophie's heart started thumping. Something was wrong.

The men sat on the sofa and faced her across the coffee table. "Miss Williams, we're very sorry to inform you that your parents have passed away."

Sophie froze, then snorted. "I think you're at the wrong house. My folks are teaching a seminar, for a client. They'll be back in a few days."

The older man cleared his throat. "Sadly, they won't. They were working for us."

She rubbed her chest over her suddenly pounding heart. This had to be some kind of bad joke. "Doing what?"

"Unfortunately, we can't say. It's classified." The younger man's tone was kind but firm.

"Oh, please. You're lying. You're saying they were what, like, spies?" She searched their eyes, looking for the punch line of some cruel joke. "Why would you say something like that? Get out of my house."

"Your parents were heroes, Miss Williams, and they served their country with honor. Their work and dedication saved countless lives over the years and kept our country safe."

Their somber expressions opened a deep pool of fear. Could they be telling the truth? "If you expect me to believe this, then tell me how they di–died." She lifted her chin. "And don't tell me it's classified. I deserve to know."

The men exchanged glances before the younger one said, "They were on a mission when the helicopter they were in abruptly left the air."

Sophie felt like she was free-falling. *"Abruptly left the air"?* She gripped the sofa cushions, tried to anchor herself. "What does that—?"

The older one raised his hand like a traffic cop. "We've already said more than we should." They stood. "You have the thanks of a grateful nation. We're very sorry for your loss."

On his way out, the younger man whispered to Helen, "I'd recommend closed caskets for the funeral."

At that, Sophie raced into the hall bath and retched until nothing was left in her stomach. They weren't lying. Her head buzzed and her skin tingled. She raced upstairs and crawled onto her bed. She wrapped her arms around her knees, rocking back and forth, trying to contain the anger, disbelief, and grief churning inside her. This couldn't be happening.

Her parents were gone. Dead in a helicopter crash. Because they were spies, not consultants.

They'd lied to her. Her whole life had been a lie.

This was why she'd always felt like an outsider. They had a whole other life separate from her. She'd never been part of their circle.

Now she never would be.

Emotions and random thoughts raced through her, a chaotic, incomprehensible mix that overwhelmed her senses. *God, how could You let this happen? Where were You?*

She couldn't stop rocking, couldn't think, couldn't speak. She kept rocking until Lise showed up late that night, straight off a plane from Germany. She wrapped Sophie in her arms and held tight.

The tears she'd held inside burst free. "How could they have lied to me my whole life?"

"They loved you, Soph. They wanted to protect you."

All of it poured out in anguished sobs she couldn't stop. A long time later, after she'd exhausted her tears, her father's voice floated through her mind. *"Love you, kiddo. Go be awesome."*

Sophie wiped fresh tears, looked up at Lise. "What happens now?"

"We'll figure it out. Together."

And they had. As Sophie gradually worked her way through her anger and grief and unanswered questions, her former camp counselor became her best friend, her mentor, and her family, the one person she trusted implicitly.

Sophie pulled herself back to the present, took several deep breaths, and forced each finger from the armrest. Now it was her turn. She wouldn't fail Lise now.

When the chopper reached the boat, which still looked like a bathtub toy, Hank hovered just to the right of it. A man stood at the helm on the upper deck, fighting to hold the vessel steady in the wash from the rotors.

A woman climbed into the inflatable dinghy behind the boat and started the motor. She untied it and sent Hank a thumbs-up.

Hank dropped the chopper even closer to the water. "Go ahead and unbuckle, then climb out onto the skids. As soon as Willa's under you, just let go and hop into the dinghy."

"You have got to be kidding me."

"I hear you disarmed a security guard with a rusty sword. This should be a walk in the park for you."

Sophie looked down. Willa waved impatiently as the dinghy bobbed in the waves.

"Don't make me push you," Hank warned.

"You wouldn't!"

Hank merely raised a brow.

Sophie's heart pounded in time to the rotors, and she feared she was going to be sick. *Focus, girl. You can do this. For Lise.*

She pulled off her headset, zipped her tote before she slung it over her shoulder, then gripped the sides of the open cockpit with all her strength. She turned and faced Hank, then slowly, gradually, inched her left foot down until it rested on the skid. Then her right.

Hank lowered the chopper another couple feet. Sophie glanced down as Willa positioned the dinghy directly below her.

"Jump, Sophie! Now!" Willa shouted.

Sophie eyed the distance, waited until the inflatable started up the crest of a wave, and jumped.

Mac took pictures of the car from every angle, then pulled out the gloves he'd tucked in his pocket. He leaned into the window openings before lying on the floor and photographing the under-carriage. He wasn't sure what he was searching for, exactly, but once word got out, he'd never get another chance to poke around.

He studied the car, tried to picture the scene. By all appearances, it looked like exactly what it was: the result of a car hitting a tree and bursting into flames.

So why had someone gone to such lengths to hide it? It certainly lent credence to the conspiracy theory being rehashed in the worldwide media.

Prince Benedikt would want to know immediately. He'd also want answers, and right now Mac had none.

His phone rang. He pulled it out of his pocket, glanced at Eloise's number, and let it go to voice mail. He wasn't ready to notify her just yet.

Ten minutes later, his Mercedes bumped down the dirt driveway of a neighboring farm. He parked in front of a small stone cottage and was greeted by a black-and-white dog, tail wagging, yipping happily. Mac let the dog sniff his hand, then gave him a good scratch behind the ears.

An older gentleman wearing a cap and ratty sweater trudged over from the barn, the scent of manure clinging to his rubber boots.

"Guten Morgen," Mac said. "Are you the gentleman who found your neighbor and called the police?"

The farmer pushed his hat back and narrowed his eyes. "Ja. What do you want? Are you a reporter?"

Mac held up both hands, palms out. "Oh no. Nothing like that. I'm a private investigator and I think what happened might be connected to a case I'm working, but I'm not sure. Could you tell me what you saw when you arrived at your neighbor's house?"

"I already told the police everything I know. Several times."

"I understand. I won't take much of your time. But it might help me solve a murder." Which could be a stretch, but Mac didn't think so. There were too many loose ends.

"A murder? Hans hit his head. He had a bad heart. He wasn't murdered."

"Can you think of anyone who might want him dead?"

The man's eyes widened. "No. Absolutely not. He kept to himself; his children moved away years ago. After his wife died, he hardly ever left the farm."

"Can you tell me exactly what you saw when you found him? I know it's difficult."

The man scrubbed a hand over his face. "I went over to return some tools I'd borrowed. He wasn't in the house and the barn door was closed, which seemed strange, so I went inside to look for him."

"Did he usually keep the door open?"

"I'd never seen it closed during the day. When I went inside, I found him lying near one of the support posts." He paused, cleared his throat. "He was already gone."

Mac asked the question carefully. "Can you tell me what convinced you?"

The old man's eyes flashed. "Because he had no pulse, and he wasn't breathing. Because the back of his head was all smashed in. And because of his throat."

Mac nodded, kept his tone matter-of-fact. "Was he lying face up or down?"

"Up, but I could see the trail of blood from the post to his, ah, to where he was lying."

"What did you mean about his throat?"

"He must not have been able to breathe, because his throat was all red and scratched up, like he'd been trying to get air." He shook his head. "I wish I'd come by sooner. Maybe I could have saved him. The look on his face . . ." He looked away, swiped a hand over his cheeks.

Mac gave him a moment, then asked, "Based on what you saw when you got there, what would you say happened?"

"He had a heart attack and couldn't breathe and was clawing at his throat, stumbled and hit his head, and fell." He swallowed visibly. "And then he died."

"Did the red marks go all the way around his throat? Or were they just in one place?"

"Why does it matter?"

"It might not."

The farmer took off his cap, rammed a hand through his thinning hair. "Seemed like it went all the way around, like a collar."

"Was your friend a large man? How much did he weigh?"

"He'd always been a skinny guy. We joked about him being like a bantam rooster."

"How tall was he?"

The farmer held up a hand. "Couple inches shorter than me, for sure."

Mac stuck out his hand. "Thank you for taking the time to talk to me. I'm concerned your friend didn't have a heart attack. For your own safety, please don't mention our conversation to anyone. I think somebody went to a lot of trouble to make this death appear to be from natural causes."

The man's eyes widened in horror. "But why?"

"I'm not sure. Yet." He pulled out a business card. "Please call me if anyone asks about your friend. And be careful."

Once Mac got back to the main road, he picked up his phone to call the prince, then set it down again. Not yet.

He repeated the message on the back of the second painting: *"Venice is like eating an entire box of chocolate liqueurs in one go."*

A picture was slowly emerging, and the ramifications would have far-reaching consequences.

But first, he had to figure out where in Venice Sophie would go to look for the third painting.

31

Nadine came awake with a jolt as a metal gate clanked somewhere nearby. She shivered, her back against a cold stone wall, her backside and legs numb from sleeping in a sitting position.

The metal cot she was sitting on had no mattress or bedding, and there was a five-gallon bucket in the corner, presumably her toilet. Several women cried softly nearby.

As her eyes adjusted to the dimly lit cell, horror washed over her. They were being held in an honest-to-goodness dungeon, with rusty chains still bolted to the stone walls. At least she wasn't attached to the manacle at the other end.

She wasn't sure if it was day or night, but her rumbling stomach told her it was probably morning. After they left the city last night, they'd headed south, into the Alps. She guessed several hours passed before the trucks drove into what appeared to be a narrow tunnel, deep enough into the earth that her ears popped from the pressure.

She pushed to a standing position, flexing her hands and using the rock wall for balance as blood flow returned to her extremities.

Where were the other girls? She shuffled to the iron bars across the front of her cell and counted at least four cells surrounding hers, all empty. She couldn't see into the others. The lanterns mounted on the walls didn't cast much light.

"Hello?" she called quietly. "Anybody there?"

"I'm here," a small female voice answered from the gloom. Then another. And another. And one more. Nadine's breath whooshed out in relief. All four teens from last night were accounted for.

"Lise?" she called. No response.

"Where are we?" one of the girls asked.

"I think we're in some sort of underground prison," Nadine said.

"What do they want with us?"

"I don't know." Though she could guess, and the knowledge made her furious.

A gate screeched on rusty hinges, and then a male voice barked, "Back away from the bars if you want food."

Nadine backed up a step as one of the masked men from the van opened a slot in the middle of the bars and passed a rusty metal tray inside the cell. Once she took it, he locked the slot and moved to the next.

From farther away she heard another male voice. "Come and get it, pretty thing. Get a little closer and I'll let you have dessert too." His laugh sent a shiver over her skin.

"No thank you," a small voice answered.

"I wasn't asking. Now *get* over here!"

"Leave her alone!" Nadine shouted, gripping the bars.

The thug appeared and reached through the bars, yanking her forward. He slammed her forehead against the bars, then shoved her backward. She yelped as she landed hard in a mildewed puddle.

"Keep your mouth shut, old hag, or you won't last the day."

He disappeared and she hauled herself to her feet as he kept taunting the girls.

"Stay away from the bars, girls," she ordered hoarsely, her neck throbbing, then scuttled back out of reach when he reappeared, eyes narrowed behind the mask.

"You won't get away with this, you know. People are looking for us."

The thug laughed—a low, ugly sound—as he turned away. "Nobody's looking for them. They're nothing."

Everything inside Nadine rebelled at the sad truth of that statement.

Another man, taller than the others and with mean eyes, who Nadine figured was in charge, stepped into view, arms folded across his chest. "He's right. They're invisible. And expendable." He looked her up and down. "But somebody might miss you. And that presents a problem."

His intent stare made her heart pound, but Nadine held her ground.

She waited until she was sure they were gone before she called, "Stay strong, ladies. I'm Nadine and I'll do everything I can to get us out of here."

"How?" one of the girls cried. "We're in a freaking dungeon."

"As long as there is life, there is hope." And because Nadine didn't know what else to do, she started singing. Lullabies, hymns, folk tunes. Anything to help them feel less alone.

As she sang, her mind raced. Where was Lise? And how was Nadine going to save these girls?

32

Soaked and queasy, Sophie needed three tries to grab the boarding ladder and scramble from the bobbing inflatable into the boat. She flopped onto a built-in bench, panting, while Willa tied the dinghy to the back of the vessel and climbed the ladder with an ease that made Sophie jealous. She'd never been on anything larger than a canoe. She'd tried paddling the summer she met Lise and had capsized immediately. Both times.

The boat rolled with the swells, and Sophie tried to ignore the way her stomach flipped in tandem.

"Welcome aboard, Sophie. I'm Willa Campos." The fortyish woman held out a hand, smiling. Sophie returned the handshake, studied the other woman. Her silver hair was cropped close, highlighting high cheekbones and piercing blue eyes, her compact figure encased in capris and a soft T-shirt with tennis shoes. She looked ready to tackle anything, and Sophie felt like an awkward preteen by comparison.

Willa opened a sliding door. "Let's get comfortable while we get acquainted."

The light-filled salon was paneled in polished teak, with comfortable furniture covered in buttery leather. Whatever Sophie had expected, it wasn't this.

Willa caught her gaping. "The *Nodo D'amore*, or 'Love Knot,' belongs to an old friend of mine who is letting us borrow her."

"Boats are female, I take it?"

Willa smiled. "Aye. They are."

Sophie nodded at the Speranza medallion Willa wore around her neck. "How long have you been part of it?"

"Most of my life. My mother told me when I was just a girl, though I think she'd planned to wait a few more years." Her eyes twinkled. "When we met Princess Johanna, I spotted her medallion. Since my mother had one, too, I immediately started asking questions in a very loud voice, as only a curious eight-year-old can do." She grinned. "I was quickly shushed with the promise of more information later."

So Willa was somewhat older than she looked. "Is Lise part of it?" Sophie asked.

"Not that I know of. Why?"

"Her late mother was. She sent Lise a medallion after her death."

"Interesting." Willa nodded.

"There isn't a master membership list somewhere?"

"There isn't anything about us. Anywhere. And we intend to keep it that way." Willa paused. "Camille and Mercy already explained this to you."

Sophie shrugged, watching Willa carefully. "Just double-checking my information."

The other woman raised an eyebrow. "Trust, but verify?"

Sophie couldn't help smiling. "Something like that. Nadine is part of it?"

"Yes, from what she said when she called."

"So how does it work? Someone calls you and then you send out a spotlight with the medallion, kind of like a Bat-Signal to the women of the world?"

Willa threw her head back and laughed. "I like you, Sophie. It would be great if it were really that easy." She paused. "We have a number and a secure e-mail. Women, and occasionally men, call and ask for our help. Sometimes we hear about situations on the news. We almost always get help from local women along the way."

"How do you get the word out?"

"Word of mouth, mostly. Social media is a wonderful tool too."

Sophie's eyes widened. "Seriously?"

"Our tech wizard is amazing."

"I take it Nadine hasn't been able to find any information about Lise from her end."

"Actually, we haven't been able to reach Nadine since last night."

Uneasiness slid down Sophie's spine. She grabbed her cell phone and dialed Nadine's number, waiting through several rings. "It went right to voice mail." She dialed Lise's phone number next and it was picked up on the first ring.

"Lise? Is that you?"

"Amalia, hi. No, it's Sophie."

"Oh. I was hoping . . ." Her voice trailed off. "Have you heard from Nadine? Nobody knows where she is."

Sophie heard the panic in the young mother's voice. "Take a breath, Amalia, and tell me what happened."

"It's like what happened to Lise. Nadine stopped by the shelter last night. She borrowed a headscarf and said she was going to the camps to question the women, see if anyone had seen or heard from Lise. But there was another raid." Amalia swallowed hard. "No one has seen her since. I heard that they took several women too."

"We will find her, Amalia. We'll find all of them. Do me a favor and keep Lise's phone with you at all times. This number is a burner phone. If you hear anything, please contact me, day or night."

"You sound like Nadine." Her breath hitched. "She said the same thing to me last night."

"She's right and so am I. We won't stop until we find them."

Footsteps sounded on the circular staircase, and the man Sophie had seen at the helm joined them. Sophie's first thought was *military*. He was dressed casually, but he had the same erect bearing and ever-alert eyes that characterized Mac.

He held out a hand. "You must be Sophie."

"And you are?"

"Scoop."

She grinned. "Are you a reporter or something?"

He and Willa exchanged glances and something about the intimacy of the look spoke volumes.

"It's a long story. Welcome aboard."

Willa motioned them to the table, then opened her laptop and turned it to face them. "Mercy sent the quote from the back of the second painting to Picasso and she did some digging."

"Picasso is your tech wizard, right?" Sophie asked.

"Yes. What she can do with a computer is pure art. She confirmed Truman Capote said it, but he didn't own any property in Venice. So Picasso compiled a list of all the chocolatiers that would have been here during the 1960s when Capote spent time in Italy. Since it's not a long list, she added hot chocolate and pastry shops too."

"Great. That gives me a starting place." Sophie pushed up from the table. "If you'll send me the list, I'd appreciate it if someone could drop me off in the city so I can start checking them out."

Willa and Scoop exchanged another look before Willa turned to her, eyes serious. "You're not alone anymore, Sophie. We're going together." She picked up her phone. "First, let me update Camille, Hank, and Mercy. I sent them back to Munich to look for Nadine."

Sophie's mind raced. They'd gone to a lot of trouble, but she wasn't into this whole teamwork thing. At least not the way Willa described it. Sophie was used to planning with Lise, sure, but she always executed the actual retrieval by herself. It was cleaner and easier to rely on her own wits and improvise as needed.

"I'm not going to get in your way, you know."

Sophie turned, met Willa's calm gaze. "I'm not used to anyone following me around."

"Oh, I won't be following. That's not how we operate. Scoop

will stay with the boat to keep an eye on things while we head into the city."

Unsure how to say no, Sophie followed Willa up to the bridge, then leaned on the railing as Venice came into view. Despite the rising water levels threatening the ancient city, it was one of Sophie's favorite places. Normally, she didn't have time to enjoy it. The few times she'd been here, it was in the dead of night to retrieve a painting. Now, her head swiveled back and forth as she tried to take it all in.

They approached the Grand Canal, filled with boats of every size and shape ferrying people and goods hither and yon. In the distance, St. Mark's Basilica filled one side of the square with its beautiful domes, while the impressive bell tower stood sentinel on the other. Artists had set up their easels along the seawall. Sophie's fingers itched for a sketchbook. Or better yet, for time to sit and paint alongside them.

"Ready?" Willa asked.

Sophie reluctantly turned her back on the artists and followed Willa to the dinghy. While Willa steered them up and down the narrow side channels, Sophie studied the beautiful old buildings up close.

They quickly developed a rhythm. At each chocolate shop, Willa pulled the small craft to the seawall while Sophie went into the shop, eyeing the walls for either the actual portrait—admittedly a long shot—or a painting of the right size and shape that might be hiding the portrait. She'd buy a treat and head back outside.

After the fourth stop, Sophie came back with a chocolate-filled pastry and handed it to Willa before she climbed into the boat. "Your turn."

Willa bit into the pastry and sighed. "Oh, man. This is even better than the last one."

Sophie took a deep breath as she scanned the buildings on either side. There was something incredibly beautiful about Venice. The architecture, water lapping at the seawall. Even the damp scent of decay had an appeal all its own. "At this rate, we'll both be wide as a barn."

"Totally worth it," Willa mumbled, wiping chocolate from her lips. "Nothing?"

"Nothing new, anyway." The familiar twinge of unease slid over the back of her neck. Sophie yanked down the Venice ball cap she'd purchased earlier and scanned the narrow side canal and the row houses lining it. "We still have company."

Willa lifted the camera around her neck and used it to conduct her own scan. A moment of silence, then, "Left side, green doorway."

"Got him. And if I'm not mistaken, Gray Hoodie Guy from St. Agnes is just behind me."

Willa aimed the camera over Sophie's shoulder and snapped a few pictures, then took a few more in either direction, just a wide-eyed tourist taking it all in. "He's heading our way." She set the camera down, pull-started the motor, and turned the inflatable in the opposite direction.

Sophie looked over her shoulder as they picked up speed.

Hoodie Guy started running, his weapon visible under his windbreaker.

33

MUNICH, GERMANY

"Open the curtains so I can see it better. Yes, that's it. Isn't it beautiful?"

Bright sunlight streamed in through the bedroom curtains and landed on the painting. As soon as Vera's eyes adjusted to the light, she gasped. "Is that . . . ?"

"It is," Anna whispered. "I miss her so much."

The nurse's eyebrows climbed to her hairline. "You knew Princess Johanna?"

Despite her sunken eyes and the way her skin hung on her thin frame, Anna's eyes glowed with happy memories. "We were cousins and we used to play together as children. How I've missed her. We were like sisters."

"But—but where did you get the painting?" She'd seen it on the news last night. Everyone in the entire world, it seemed, had seen the painting. But what was it doing here?

"Heiko gave it to me. He knows how much I miss her. He

204

wanted me to have it. It makes me feel like she's right here with me."

Had her client's husband stolen it? She'd also heard about the man who was murdered while supposedly trying to steal the painting from the gallery. Her heart pounded. Had her employer killed the man to get it?

Vera paused, took a deep breath. She was letting her imagination run away with her. Maybe this was a copy. Surely thousands were printed at the time the princess died. Vera hadn't even been born then, but she'd heard about the tragedy. It seemed everyone had.

She stepped closer to the painting, gingerly touched the paint. It was textured, not smooth, as she'd expect from a print. Though she was no art expert, by any means.

"What are you doing? Don't get the oils from your skin on it!" Anna's bark held more strength than Vera had ever heard in her voice. The nurses had been comparing notes, pretty sure the sweet woman wouldn't last another week. This burst of energy was either a positive sign . . . or the final effort.

Vera pulled her hands away and smiled apologetically. "I'm sorry. It's so beautiful, I just couldn't help myself."

Anna studied her a moment, then nodded. "Don't touch it again, please. It's too valuable."

Vera nodded her understanding, but she couldn't stop thinking about it. Later, while eating lunch, she turned on the television in the kitchen to watch the news, and her jaw dropped. Had she just found the answer to all her financial prayers? Neuhansberg's royal family had offered an incredible reward for the return of the painting.

She tiptoed out of the kitchen and to the doorway of Anna's room. Once she confirmed Anna was fast asleep, she took her cell phone out of her uniform pocket and snapped several pictures.

Her hands shook as she swiped the photos to enlarge them, trying to decide what to do. She would hate for Anna to lose the painting, but if her husband had stolen it . . . ?

Her course was clear. She picked up the phone and dialed.

VENICE, ITALY

"I think we lost him," Willa said. She had piloted them up one narrow canal and down another for the past twenty minutes, wending their way around the city.

"Head back to the Grand Canal."

"I think we have more options—"

"I need to buy a painting." Sophie pointed to the street artists who'd set up shop along both sides of the busy waterway. "Let me out here. I'll be right back."

"More bait?" Willa pulled alongside the seawall.

Sophie looked over her shoulder as she stepped out. "You have a better idea?"

"Nope. I'll be here."

Sophie slowed her pace as though she had all the time in the world. Some of the artists were quite good, and she smiled as she studied their work. Others were clearly amateurs, so she offered praise and encouragement and smiled even wider. Everyone started somewhere. And everyone had to make a living.

She kept walking until she spotted a booth displaying the right-sized canvases. She wouldn't get to keep the painting, but she chose a nicely executed night scene depicting moonlight over the love locks fastened to the Rialto Bridge. She haggled a bit, then handed over the money and asked the smiling artist to wrap it for her.

As he worked, she glanced toward Willa, who made a "hurry-up" motion and nodded toward the alley.

She interrupted the chattering artist with a smile. "I'm in a bit of a hurry."

"Of course, signorina." He quickly tied off the last knot holding the brown paper in place.

With a murmured, "Thank you and good luck," she snatched the painting and headed for the dinghy at a fast clip.

Sophie handed Willa the painting and hopped aboard, gripping the sides as the other woman hit the throttle, and they took off in a spray of water.

As they sped down the canal, she looked back just as Mac rounded the corner from a side street.

When he spotted them, he took off running, weaving through the tourists that crowded the street, trying to keep pace.

Sophie kept her eyes on him, but then movement behind him caught her eye. "We've got two out of three behind us. Hoodie Guy is a few paces behind Mac."

Willa muttered a curse and sped up. "Lucky for us, they're on foot."

34

"Nothing stands out? No distinguishing marks, anything that could help us identify the men?" Camille shook out her last blanket and wrapped it around the woman's thin shoulders. Outside, snow from an unexpected storm was falling faster and thicker with every passing hour.

The young mother, who looked to be in her early twenties, shook her head, clutching her baby more tightly. "They all wore masks. I am sorry. I wish I could help you." She tugged the blanket from her shoulders and wrapped it securely around her child instead. "But I thank you for the blanket."

Frustration twisted Camille's insides. Mothers and babies should not be outside in weather like this. Certainly not in this small tent, cobbled together from leaky tarps and bits of rotted rope. She gave the woman her last pair of mittens before she stepped out into the falling snow, spoke into her earpiece. "Hank, I need more blankets."

"Last batch. I'm headed your way. She know anything?"

"No. Same story as everywhere else. No one noticed a thing beyond the masks."

They'd been out here for hours but had no new information.

"I'm back," Mercy said. "Sorry, my meeting at the clinic ran long and it took forever to get here. Visibility is bad. Where are you guys?"

"Hold on. White van. Incoming," Hank said.

"Now?" Mercy asked. "They always show up at night."

"They just pulled up near the camp." Hank's muttered curses filled their earpieces.

Camille sprinted back the way she'd come. "I'll see if I can get pics." She attached the telephoto lens to her cell phone while she told the young mother what she needed.

"I'm almost back at the bike. I'll follow them." They could hear Mercy breathing hard as she ran.

Camille peeked through a slit in the tent opening. "I should be on the motorcycle and you should be here," she whispered.

"Your two long legs can outrun my prosthetic one every day of the week. Besides, who suspects a nun?"

Camille knew she was right. "I worry."

"Oh ye of little faith," Mercy said. "You're not fooling anyone with that tough girl act, you know."

"Neither are you," Camille shot back.

"Are you two going to hold hands and break into 'Kumbaya' next?" Hank growled into her earpiece. "They're getting closer."

Camille sobered instantly. She heard them now, too, boots crunching in the snow.

"Can't believe they sent us out here now. What's the hurry? These girls aren't going anywhere," one of the men grumbled.

"They're not paying me enough for this," another groused.

Earlier, Amalia had told them to expect four masked men. She was right. Picasso claimed she could—probably—identify the men, masked or not. It was worth a try.

"Let's go. Everybody out," the tall guy who seemed to be in charge shouted, moving toward the handful of makeshift shelters.

Camille snapped photo after photo through the slit in the front of the tent as the two men herded the women in a line toward the other two, who studied the younger women in a way that made Camille nauseous.

All around, the men shouted orders, throwing the encampment into chaos as mothers tried to soothe frightened children and fussy infants.

"They just grabbed a young woman," Camille whispered furiously, filming. He'd grabbed her by the arm and dragged her out of sight behind the van.

Who were these monsters?

She aimed at their faces, shutter clicking fast and furiously as they moved ever closer to her tent. While the thug was busy rousting the young mother next door, Camille tucked the phone inside her jacket, slipped out of the tent, and headed toward the trees.

She'd taken two steps when a hand grabbed her arm and yanked her back.

"Where do you think you're going?" He spun her around.

Camille didn't hesitate. She brought her leg up and used her momentum to land a solid knee to his crotch. He let out a groan and collapsed in a heap.

She darted into the trees. "One down, one behind me." She heard a second thug shout for her to stop, then chased after her, huffing and puffing as he crashed through the forested area.

"Lose him," Hank said.

"That's the plan," Camille said, picking up speed.

"Go left, over the footbridge. I've got you in my sights."

She made the turn, then stopped, looked around at the thick foliage. "There's no bridge here."

"The other left," Hank grumbled.

"Right. Sorry." She retraced her steps, made the turn, and ran over the footbridge, embarrassment heating her cheeks. Her dyslexia was always worse when she was under stress.

"Make another left, take the right fork in the path."

"This one?" She hated asking but wouldn't risk getting caught due to her stubborn pride.

"You're good. Keep coming toward me."

Feeling more confident, she found her usual running rhythm and grinned as the thug's footsteps receded in the distance. To buy time, Camille made an extra loop before she exited the park several blocks away. The falling snow would hide her tracks.

She opened the passenger door of a small car and hopped in.

Hank shoved it into gear and took off just as the second thug burst out onto the street. "You cut that close."

"Despite the little detour, I still got it done." Adrenaline made her feel invincible. She wouldn't let Hank spoil her sense of accomplishment. "We need to stop these low-life scumbags."

"Agreed. You did good, Eagle Eye." Hank's teeth gleamed white in the dimness.

"Van loaded and taking off," Mercy said.

"Keep your distance," Hank said. "Don't let them see you."

"Not my first op, Hank."

"Just don't do anything stupid."

"That's *not* part of the plan."

Camille's heart pounded as Hank took them farther and farther from the van. She gripped the armrests, trying to quiet her nagging worry. Mercy hadn't worked with them that long.

"She'll be fine," Hank said. "I hope."

Just as Camille's heart rate returned to something approaching normal, they heard the squeal of brakes. Then Mercy muttered, "Oh, sweet Mary, mother of God."

"Mercy? What's going on? Mercy!" Camille shouted.

They waited but heard nothing but silence.

Camille and Hank exchanged quick looks as Hank spun the car around, tires squealing, and they raced back the way they'd come.

VENICE, ITALY

Sophie didn't loosen her grip on the sides of the dinghy until she was sure they'd left both men behind. Willa slowed down and finally turned onto one of Venice's smaller canals.

"We still have three places on our list," Willa said. "Should we keep going?"

"Absolutely. The next shop isn't far from here, right?"

"Just ahead." As at previous stops, Willa pulled up slightly ahead of the building so they could make a quick exit.

Sophie went inside and came back with another excellent treat but no sign of the missing painting.

When she offered Willa the cream puff, the other woman shook her head. "This one's all you."

Sophie grinned and took a huge bite. "Happy to suffer for the cause."

Several minutes later, they were back in the Grand Canal, Willa dodging and weaving around the ever-present water taxis, which were the size of city buses. With so many boats speeding along in both directions, it looked like a highway during rush hour, only with no lanes, speed limits, or brake lights.

As they passed under the famous Ponte di Rialto, Sophie turned back to gawk. The oldest bridge in Venice, its white stone arches were instantly recognizable. Despite the endless steps, tourists crowded both outer walkways, while others browsed the small shops that lined the covered interior section. She shaded her hand against the afternoon sun. Unfortunately, the glare kept her from seeing the man before he leaped off the bridge.

He dropped right into the dinghy, almost landing in Sophie's lap.

Because the craft was inflatable, he bounced right back out and landed in the water beside them. Sophie squeaked in surprise as she and the painting were bounced out the opposite side.

The murky water closed over her head, and she sank down, down, much farther than she'd expected, before she got her bearings and started swimming for the surface.

As her head popped up, Willa angled the boat sideways, desperate to keep boat traffic from running over her. Sophie spun in a circle. Where was the Blond Guy?

She spotted him about ten yards away, the soggy paper-wrapped painting clutched in his hand as he swam toward the banks. A water bus barreled toward him. At the last second he dove, releasing his hold on the painting.

It bobbed on the surface for several seconds before it started sinking. Blond Guy popped up and darted toward it, barely yanking it and himself out of the way of the next boat.

Sophie wasn't a strong swimmer, but she gave it everything she had, determined to get back to Willa. The wash from passing boats sloshed over her head, and she spit out dirty water, trying to stay afloat. She heard Willa shouting but couldn't figure out what she was saying.

Another small boat raced toward her. Before she could duck to keep from getting run over, a hand reached down and a voice yelled, "Get in."

She looked up to see Mac at the helm, hand outstretched. He glanced over his shoulder. "Hurry up. There's another water bus coming."

Sophie didn't have time to think it through. She grabbed his hand and he hauled her into the boat like she weighed nothing. She landed in a heap at his feet and simply held on as he bounced over the waves and skirted the water bus, the boat's horn and the captain's angry shouts echoing behind them.

She scrambled onto the wooden seat and looked behind her. Willa had been neatly trapped by several of the water buses and was weaving and dodging toward the banks, trying to get around them. Blond Guy and the painting had disappeared.

Mac glanced her way as she coughed up the last of the water she'd swallowed. "Are you all right?"

"I will be."

"Hang on," he warned, two seconds before they hit the wake of a luxury yacht. If he hadn't said anything, she'd have been bounced right out of this boat too. She came down hard on the wooden bench and groaned.

They heard several popping sounds, and Sophie looked back again. Her heart stuttered. Hoodie Guy from St. Agnes was also in a small boat and he was gaining on Willa. He pulled a gun and aimed it at the little inflatable. One shot. Two. Three.

Why would he shoot the dinghy? He must not have seen Blond Guy grab the painting and take off.

The dinghy started to sink.

"No!" Sophie gripped Mac's arm. "We have to save Willa. Go back!"

He glanced over his shoulder. "Can't. He's gaining on us." He swerved toward shore to avoid another large boat.

Sophie's heart pounded as she scanned the churning water. Where was Willa?

Hoodie Guy fired several more shots at the sinking inflatable. Willa's head popped up, then disappeared under the water again.

"You have to go back."

When Mac shook his head again, Sophie scanned the area once more, desperate to locate Willa. When she still couldn't find her, Sophie scrambled onto the wooden seat and jumped into the water before he could stop her.

35

Mercy followed the van out of the city, keeping a nice safe distance so they wouldn't see her. She rounded a blind corner and almost ran headlong into a police van that was parked crosswise, blocking the road. She slammed on the brakes and fought to maintain control of the motorcycle, desperate not to get tossed over the handlebars.

It took everything she had, but it still wasn't enough on the slick roadway. She went into a skid and had to lay the bike down. Luckily, she was able to do that in snow-covered grass, not gravel, but still, it was not a happy landing.

She skidded to a stop and lay there for a moment, heart pounding, all the air knocked out of her. When she could breathe again, she took a few seconds to assess the damage, testing her arms and legs before she tried to climb out from under the bike.

When she looked up, a uniformed Polizei officer stood over her. Where had he and his van come from? Instead of offering her a hand up, he had a gun aimed at her.

"What are you doing? Put that away and help me," she ordered.

He studied her for a long moment, then shouted to someone she couldn't see from this angle. Another cop appeared and they moved the heavy bike off her. She slowly sat up, wincing. She accepted his help to get to her feet, making sure her prosthesis would support her weight.

The first officer said, "Hands where I can see them."

Mercy turned to him, wiped snowflakes off her headscarf, and pulled out the cross she'd tucked inside her habit while she rode.

"Do you always point weapons at Sisters of Mercy?" She rubbed a hand over her aching hip.

His eyes widened as her habit registered. He made the sign of the cross, then slowly lowered the weapon. "Sorry, Sister."

"Get that out of my sight. And kindly explain to me why your vehicle is blocking the road. If I hadn't stopped in time, I would have run right into it. The next person might not be so lucky."

He looked away, then back. "We, ah, got an anonymous tip. We thought you were someone else."

She just bet they did. "Move that vehicle, now, before someone really does gets hurt."

He exchanged glances with the other cop, then nodded in that direction. While the other officer moved the van, the first speared her with a look. "Where are you going in this weather, Sister?"

Mercy raised an eyebrow. "I was offering aid to a poor, lost soul. But I didn't expect to be questioned about it."

"No offense, Sister. I had to ask."

"May I go now?"

"Yes, of course." He motioned to the other officer. "Is it safe to ride?" When the man nodded, he waved a hand in that direction. "Go with God, Sister."

She clasped her hands in front of her and nodded regally. "I shall pray for your souls."

Her steps were measured and slow as she took hold of the bike and climbed aboard. As soon as the cops returned to their vehicle and started it up, she ducked her head and whispered, "They're leaving. Stay behind me."

She got no response. A quick check confirmed her earpiece was gone. It must have fallen out when she crashed.

Which meant she was on her own.

Instead of heading back the way they'd come, the police van turned around and pulled up beside her.

The cop rolled down the window. "We don't want to leave you alone out here, Sister. We'll follow you wherever you need to go."

"Thank you, but that isn't necessary."

"I insist."

With no other options, Mercy started the bike and headed down the road, scrambling for a reasonable destination a nun would go to in the middle of a snowstorm.

VENICE, ITALY

Sophie went into the water again, but this time she sucked in a breath before she went under. She pushed up to the surface as quickly as possible, desperate to get to Willa. She spun around, trying to find the other woman, but she didn't see her.

"Get down!"

The shouted command had Sophie diving again, just as more bullets hit the water. She swam toward what she hoped was the bank of the canal, but she couldn't be sure. She popped up again and was rewarded with more bullets hitting the water near her head.

He wasn't giving up. But her body was about to. Her legs weren't propelling her as fast as before, which meant her burst of adrenaline was wearing off. She had to reach land. By the time she breached the surface again, her lungs felt like they would burst.

"Finally. Get over here," a voice growled.

Sophie spun, ready to fight, then sagged in relief when Willa swam over and wrapped an arm around her neck to keep her head above water.

"We need to get out of here. That is one determined son of a gun."

Gasping, Sophie swam with all her remaining strength. "Where did he go?"

"He's trapped behind a water bus. This is our best shot at getting away. Come on."

Sophie almost cried with relief when they reached the slippery seawall. Willa hopped out of the water and slid onto the pavement like a sea lion at SeaWorld. She scanned the canal, spun around, and reached a hand down.

"He's coming back. Hurry."

Though she did her best to imitate Willa's smooth move, Sophie flopped onto the seawall with all the grace of a beached whale. She rolled to her hands and knees, panting, then looked up and stumbled to her feet. Willa was already in a full-on sprint.

Several bullets hit the concrete beside her, and Sophie zigzagged around a group of tourists, apologizing to the flustered tour guide as she barreled through the crowd.

Willa darted around a corner and Sophie careened after her, sliding in her wet shoes. They ran several more blocks before Willa slowed to a walk. Sophie caught up to her and huffed and puffed for another block before she was able to catch her breath, hand clasped over the dull ache in her arm. They trudged along, squishing in their shoes.

"My phone fell out of my pocket. Any chance you still have yours?" Willa glanced at her, then stopped dead on the sidewalk. "What happened to your arm?"

Sophie looked down, surprised to see blood oozing between her fingers. She turned her head and took a few shallow breaths, willing the annoying queasiness away. "I don't . . . He must have shot me." It was at that moment her brain decided to register the pain. A sharp sting, followed by a slow throb.

"Let me see." Willa pulled her out of the traffic pattern and against the side of a building to examine the wound. "Thankfully it's just a flesh wound, as Monty Python would say." She offered a wry smile. "But we need to clean it up a bit." They ducked into an alley and rinsed off the blood at an outdoor spigot.

"You okay?"

Sophie grinned. "As long as I don't look at it." Distraction also helped, so she pulled out her burner phone, checked it. "To answer your earlier question, my phone's dead. But maybe we can sweet-talk a shopkeeper into letting us use theirs."

Willa pointed to another chocolatier. "That's what I'm thinking."

"Two birds. One stone. I like it."

They walked into the shop and Sophie winced as her shoes squeaked on the stone floor. "My apologies," she murmured to the scowling shopkeeper.

While Willa tried to explain away their appearance and asked about using the phone, Sophie glanced out the window in time to see several policemen speed by on scooters. She hoped they caught the shooter, but she wasn't holding her breath. Hoodie Guy seemed not only determined but quick on his feet.

She turned from the window and her eyes landed on a poster beside the door, advertising an art show. To be held in the salon upstairs. Tonight.

Sophie sighed at the words *by invitation only*. If she were here on vacation, she'd absolutely wrangle an invite somehow. An intimate showing of works by Italian artists, in Venice? Yes, please.

Willa's sudden laugh at something the shopkeeper said momentarily drew Sophie's attention. But something about the poster nagged at her. She turned back and leaned closer for a better look, hiding a smile as recognition sizzled along her nerve endings. The bucolic landscape advertising the art show obviously wasn't one of the royal portraits.

But the frame definitely was.

It was identical to the others.

Which meant the portrait had to be hidden behind it.

All she had to do now was figure out how to get it.

219

36

By the time Sophie and Willa wound their way around what seemed like half of Venice to get to the marina, Sophie was completely miserable, despite the excitement of her discovery. Her teeth chattered, her lips were blue, and her arm ached. December was no time for a dip in the canals. Thankfully, Scoop was waiting at the helm, and Willa cast off as soon as they boarded.

"There should be dry clothes belowdecks and enough hot water for a shower. You ladies need to get warmed up."

Sophie nodded her thanks and stumbled down the stairs and into the shower on shaky legs, sighing as the hot water hit her chilled skin. Afterward, she examined her arm, relieved the bullet had, in fact, merely grazed her and she was no longer bleeding. She'd had worse aches and pains after fencing matches. When she returned to the salon, Willa was already there, also fresh from a shower and wearing identical sweats.

"You guys keep these in stock?" Sophie indicated her outfit.

Willa looked up from her laptop. "We've learned that warm clothes and water usually go together."

"You didn't have a chance to upload any of those photos before the camera went for a swim, did you?"

"Sadly, no."

Willa's laptop started chirping and Picasso's face appeared. "Hello, Willa. Is Sophie there with you too?"

Willa angled the screen so she and Sophie could both see. "Hi, Picasso. What do you have for us? And why aren't you sleeping?"

The other woman grinned, and Sophie caught a glimpse of puckered scar tissue underneath the ball cap.

"You can't have it both ways. I can't get eight hours of beauty sleep and ferret out information at the same time. I got you information. Let me share my screen." Data scrolled by as Picasso's fingers flew. "When I kept hitting brick walls, I ran a search on Neuhansberg's royal family. A bit more digging and I learned that they used to own property in Venice."

"Excellent. Will you send me—?"

"I know where it is," Sophie blurted out.

Both women looked at her.

"The chocolatier we were in a little while ago. I was about to tell you. That's where the painting is."

"How do you know?" Willa asked.

"Did you happen to notice the flyer by the door about an art exhibit in the upstairs salon tonight?"

Willa shook her head.

"The poster advertises a landscape painting—" When Willa started to speak, Sophie held up a hand. "The frame is identical to the other two."

A beat of silence ensued.

"Are you sure the painting is behind it?" Picasso asked.

"As sure as I can be without taking it off the wall. Which, by the way, I plan to do. Tonight. I'll be there to look around, mingle, and then liberate the painting while everyone is otherwise occupied."

"How do you plan to pull that off?" Willa asked.

Before Sophie finished outlining her plan, Willa was shaking her head. "It's bold and audacious and could go utterly wrong. And you still haven't said how you plan to get in without an invitation, which I assume is required."

Sophie shrugged. "I haven't figured out that detail yet. But I will."

"Lucky for you, you won't have to. We'll handle the invite."

Sophie gazed at her. "More Speranza connections?"

"Exactly. And you won't be flying solo this time either. We're both going."

Sophie opened her mouth to argue, then closed it again. As they fine-tuned the details, she decided maybe there was something to this teamwork thing after all.

SOMEWHERE OUTSIDE MUNICH

Nadine gnawed on the stale bread and hunk of cheese, then washed it all down with water. The events of the night caught up with her, and she was surprised to wake sometime later, disoriented, not sure how much time had passed. She returned to the front of her cell and whispered, "Girls! Is everyone all right? Get close to the bars. Maybe we can see each other."

She heard rustling and pressed her forehead against the iron bars, desperate to see them in the flickering lantern light.

Finally, she could make out all four girls, each in a separate cell, all with tear-streaked faces. They were so young, not one more than seventeen, and all incredibly beautiful, with dark eyes and long, flowing hair. They could have been sisters. Which meant someone was seeking a very specific type of girl. Her mind shied away from the horrible images it concocted, and she gripped the bars until her knuckles turned white.

She had to get them out of here.

"Why have they taken us?" one of the girls asked, eyes wide and panicked. "What do they want?"

"The important thing is to figure out how to get out of here," Nadine said.

"How?" another girl asked. "Look at this place. It's like something out of a horror movie."

"Actually, I think we're underneath a castle," Nadine admitted.

"That doesn't help at all," another girl said. She appeared to be the oldest of the four.

Out of the corner of her eye, Nadine saw the girl in the cell diagonally across from her sway on her feet. She was probably the youngest. "Are you all right?"

The girl shook her head slowly, deliberately. "I think my blood sugar is low. It happens sometimes."

"Did you eat?" The food they'd been given earlier hadn't been much, but it would keep them alive.

"I was asleep. I didn't hear them bring it."

If she called for the guards, who knew what would happen if they decided the girl was a liability. But she was clearly in trouble. "When was your last meal?"

"I–I don't know."

Sadly, not unusual for those who lived on the streets. Nadine patted her pockets, found the roll of hard candy she always carried. "Try to catch this." She put her arm through the bars and threw the candy with all her might. The roll hit the cell bars, bounced off, and rolled partway into the hallway. She muttered under her breath. "Can you reach it?"

"No." The girl reached through the bars, her fingers inches away, straining. She finally lay on her stomach, which gave her the extra inch she needed to scoop it up.

Nadine let out a relieved breath. "Suck on them; don't chew. And sit down, okay?"

"How are we going to get out of here?" the oldest of the girls asked again.

"I'm working on it." Nadine narrowed her eyes and studied every inch of her cell again, searching for anything that could be used as a weapon, but there was nothing. She studied the hallway. Could she overpower one of the masked men when they brought them food later?

Maybe. She paced, one eye on the girl, who no longer looked like she was about to collapse. The candy would buy a little time, but not much.

Suddenly, her eyes widened and she ran to the bars and plucked at the rusty chain holding the door closed. But it wasn't the chain that mattered. It was the obviously modern padlock that held it closed.

"Thank You, God." She plucked half a dozen sturdy hairpins out of her bun. Thanks to curiosity and a love of YouTube instructional videos, she had the lock open in about three minutes.

She positioned the lock so the guard couldn't tell it was open, then pocketed the rest of the hairpins. She couldn't risk throwing them to the other girls. Her aim wasn't that good. She'd have to get herself out and then set them free.

Somehow.

Voices sounded from the tunnel. The guards were coming back. It was now or never. "Okay, girls. Follow my lead and get ready to run."

"What are you going to do?" the oldest girl demanded.

The iron door swung open and the same guards appeared, masks in place. One pushed a cart with a wobbly wheel that clattered over the stone floor.

Nadine's heart raced. She'd have to get the weakest girl out first, carry her if necessary.

The two men worked their way down the line of cells, handing out trays, not saying a word.

When the stockier of the two reached her, Nadine was at the bars, wearing her most annoyed expression. "We need more supplies."

"What supplies? You've got food. What more do you want?"

Nadine met his gaze, lowered her voice so he had to get closer to hear her. "Female supplies."

It took him a second to catch her meaning, then he barked with laughter. "You don't need no supplies."

"No, but *she* does." Nadine hitched her chin toward the other cell.

He hadn't locked the pass-through yet, or realized the cell itself wasn't locked. As he turned his head to glance over his shoulder, Nadine snatched the chain and wrapped it around his throat, yanking him tight against the bars to cut off his air.

He clawed at his neck and tried to break free, but she gritted her teeth and held tight, praying Mean Eyes was out of sight.

When the guard slumped, unconscious, Nadine let him slide to the floor and slipped out of the cell. She darted across to the weakest girl and had the lock almost open when an arm came around her neck.

"I knew you would be trouble. Just like the other one."

Other one? Did that mean Lise *was* here?

He released his arm and poked a gun in her back, marching her in front of him, past the other cells.

"Stay strong, girls. This is not over yet," Nadine said.

"For you it is," Mean Eyes said, and Nadine tried not to flinch.

The tunnel was long and dank and equally dim. Eventually, they turned down another corridor that opened into a large cavern that had been used as a storeroom, filled with shelving and barrels and whatnot stored there through the centuries.

As he shoved her farther into the large expanse, a familiar voice rang out. "Leave her alone. She's just a child. If you want a plaything, you can take me!"

Goose bumps popped out on Nadine's skin as a loud crash and a scream echoed through the cavern. She spun toward the sound just as Mean Eyes grabbed her by the arm and hauled her in that direction. "It's time you learned what happens to troublemakers."

He hustled Nadine into another section of the cavern, where wooden shipping crates were being readied for transport.

Lise stood in the open area in the middle, face bruised, hands bound behind her back, eyes blazing with fury. A young girl was held upright between two guards, tears streaming down her cheeks, terror in her eyes.

"What kind of man are you to assault a child?" Lise spat out.

The guard beside her balled his fist, and the force of the blow sent Lise to her knees.

"No!" Nadine tried to break free, but Mean Eyes simply tightened his hold.

From where she lay on the ground, Lise turned her head and their eyes met, held. The acceptance in her friend's eyes made Nadine see red. She couldn't let her give up. There had to be a way to save her and the girl. But how?

The guard hauled Lise to her feet, then stepped out of reach. She swayed slightly, then straightened her spine. "Let go of her!" Then she shot Nadine a glance that clearly said, *"Save the girl."*

Heart breaking, Nadine nodded that she understood. Lise was right. She couldn't save them both.

As the guard beside Lise raised his weapon, Nadine did the only thing she could think of. She lunged backward. The motion startled Mean Eyes enough to momentarily loosen his grip, so she scrambled away and leaped across the space, tackling the girl and sending them both to the ground in a tangle of arms and legs.

Before the guards could react, she rolled them out of reach and whispered, "Run. Hide!"

As the girl took off, Nadine turned to rush back toward Lise just as the guard raised his weapon once more.

Without stopping, Nadine lunged toward her friend, desperate to get between her and the bullet.

She almost made it.

The gunshot reverberated through the cavern.

37

Sophie wasn't entirely happy with her disguise, but at least it covered the bandage on her upper arm. Willa had made a few calls and they'd gone to a dress shop in Venice, where the proprietress kissed both their cheeks and led them to the back room, the Speranza emblem flashing on her ring as she waved a hand and told them to take whatever they needed.

When Sophie requested quilt batting, the proprietress hadn't blinked. She simply dispatched a young shopgirl while Willa and Sophie tried on dresses and chose accessories. Afterward, they'd stepped outside, where another smiling young woman waited aboard a small bowrider. She welcomed them, then handed Willa a black-and-white catering crew uniform.

"I am Juliana, and I will be your driver for the evening. Where shall I take you?"

"Thank you, Juliana. Back to the marina, please," Willa said.

"Certainamente."

Sophie still worried about the number of people involved in

their scheme, but she couldn't dwell on it. They had a tight schedule. An hour later, Sophie stepped in front of a mirror and nodded. She'd added lines and crow's feet with makeup, used the quilt batting to fill out the body shaper she'd purchased, and powdered the blonde wig to give it a grayish cast. She fastened on a gaudy necklace and slipped several rings on her fingers.

When she emerged in a deep-blue floor-length gown, Willa's eyes widened. "Wow. I'd heard you were good at disguises, but I didn't realize you were that good."

Sophie smiled and bowed slightly. "Tools of the trade."

Willa's phone rang. "Yes, I have it, along with a backup lighter. I've got this, Camille, but thank you for checking." She disconnected and glanced at Sophie, amusement in her eyes. "Normally, anything related to pyrotechnics or smoke bombs is Camille's baby. She's making sure I know what I'm doing."

Interesting. Before Sophie could ask more questions, Scoop entered the room in an immaculately tailored black tuxedo, and she almost swallowed her tongue. The man looked amazing, in a James Bond kind of way. She glanced at Willa and hid her smile. The other woman wore that same dazed look but was trying desperately not to show it.

Scoop reached Sophie and held out his arm. "Shall we, darling?" He leaned closer and whispered, "By the way, you look ravishing tonight."

Sophie batted her lashes at him. "You do marvelous things for my ego, you know. It's why I keep you around."

"That's not the only reason," he teased and waggled his eyebrows.

Sophie snorted, ignoring the blush racing over her cheeks.

"Enough or we'll be late," Willa grumbled from behind them.

Sophie's grin got wider. "Don't worry, you can have him when I'm done with him."

If looks could kill, she would have died right there from the daggers Willa's eyes aimed her way. Scoop's laugh didn't help, but a little levity wasn't a bad thing.

They climbed into Juliana's boat, and she expertly guided them back to the chocolatier. Scoop stepped out and offered a hand to Sophie, who grinned when he kissed her knuckles. This could be fun, after all the times she'd gone in alone.

Juliana eased away from the seawall and ducked down a side canal to drop Willa off.

They walked toward the door, where a security guard in a well-cut suit was checking invitations. Scoop slipped a white vellum card from his pocket and handed it over. The man checked it against his list and waved them in without so much as a glance at their faces. Perfect.

Sophie glanced around as though admiring the view and murmured, "Security camera next door aimed this way."

"Got it," Picasso responded through her earpiece. "I'll be sure it malfunctions at just the right time."

They entered the tiny foyer, bypassing the door into the chocolatier to head upstairs where classical music floated down, mingling with the scent of hot hors d'oeuvres.

Sophie reminded herself not to gawk when they reached the living room of the luxury apartment. She'd never seen quite so much gilt outside a museum. The furnishings consisted of exquisitely polished antiques that looked decidedly uncomfortable. But the paintings drew her like a magnet.

As though her feet had a mind of their own, she started toward the far corner, dragging Scoop in her wake.

"Slow down, darling, we have all evening."

Sophie caught his warning and slowed her pace, then stopped in front of a glorious landscape. "Sorry, love. I was just excited. This is a DeMitri."

He chuckled indulgently. "Why don't you explore to your heart's content while I fetch us something from the bar."

"Wonderful." She patted his cheek, then slid her finger down to tap his chin. "You are too good to me."

He winked, then disappeared into the crowd.

She turned back to the painting.

"Why, Mrs. Bauernstein. What a surprise to see you here."

Sophie froze, schooling her features before she turned to see Mac grinning at her, looking as devastatingly handsome as he had the first time they met, the rat.

"I'm sorry," she said in Italian. "You must have me confused with someone else."

He leaned closer. "I'd know those beautiful green eyes anywhere, disguise or no disguise."

Scoop returned and neatly stepped between them. "Here you are, darling. A little champagne for the occasion."

"What occasion is that?" Mac asked.

Scoop turned as though seeing him for the first time. "And who might you be?"

Mac stuck out his hand. "Mac McKenzie, an old friend of your, ah, companion."

Scoop eyed the outstretched hand and tucked Sophie up against his side. "Really?" He gazed down at her with narrowed eyes, every bit the jealous lover. "Darling, you've never mentioned him before."

Sophie cupped his cheek with her free hand. "Because our relationship was so inconsequential it was hardly worth mentioning."

Mac put both hands over his heart. "You wound me, dear lady." He bowed. "But alas, I will leave you to your companion. Enjoy your evening."

As soon as he was out of earshot, Scoop growled, "Who the heck was that?"

Before Sophie could respond, Picasso answered. "High-dollar private investigator, specializes in artwork."

Scoop frowned. "Just what we need."

"He's been on my tail every step of the way."

Sophie heard Picasso's keyboard clicking from half a world away. "I'll see if I can figure out who he's working for."

"I think Prince Benedikt, but he won't confirm or deny," Sophie murmured.

"Have you located the painting yet, Sophie?" Willa asked.

"Working on it." She tucked her hand in the crook of Scoop's arm, and they resumed their circuit of the room.

The crowd was expensively dressed, and from what she could see, all the jewels on display around necks and on fingers were the real deal. The artwork on the walls represented a staggering amount of money.

Which made the painting by an unknown artist even more conspicuous.

She let out a sigh of relief when she spotted it. She walked over and studied it, trying to decide how it came to be part of tonight's event. Did someone already know what was behind it?

An older woman stepped up beside her. "I don't believe we've met before."

"Signora Donatelli," Picasso murmured in Sophie's ear. "The hostess."

Sophie held out a hand. "Signora Donatelli. Thank you for adding us to the guest list at the last minute. We were traveling through town and were delighted when we heard about this show."

"We are happy to include fellow art lovers." She glanced at Scoop, but Sophie made no move to introduce him.

"Tell me, signora, what is the story of this painting? It's lovely, but I'm afraid I don't know the artist."

The woman beamed. "That is because he isn't well known. Yet. But I am hoping to change that." She leaned closer and her heavy perfume tickled Sophie's nostrils. "He is my grandson."

"Crud," Willa muttered in her earpiece.

Sophie smiled widely. "It's lovely, so I'm sure it's only a matter of time. And with your patronage, he'll be a household name before you know it."

"Thank you. If you'd like to purchase any of the artwork, please let me or—" she pointed across the room—"my assistant know."

Sophie wanted to howl in frustration. As soon as the woman moved out of earshot, she leaned closer to the painting and whispered, "The assistant is Interpol agent Eloise Cuvier."

"Wonderful," Scoop muttered around a sip of champagne.

"Are you in place, Willa?" Sophie asked.

"I just told Mrs. Donatelli about the bananas Foster dessert cart. Five minutes."

Sophie and Scoop made their way around the room, keeping Mac and Eloise in sight.

One minute before showtime, they were back in front of the painting.

"Ladies and gentlemen, may I have your attention." The conversations in the room tapered off, and the music faded to nothing as Signora Donatelli began speaking. "Thank you all for coming and celebrating art and the various artists whose work is on display tonight. It is a privilege to offer it to you from our private collection. Art should be shared, and before my husband passed on, God rest his soul, he and I decided it was time to allow some of our most treasured pieces to travel to new homes."

A smattering of applause followed, and she waited until it stopped before she said, "Our caterer has prepared a special dessert, my late husband's favorite, so please gather around and enjoy."

On cue, Willa wheeled the tea cart into the center of the room. The lights went out, producing a collective gasp from the guests. She flicked on her lighter and lit the alcohol on the dessert. As the crowd oohed and aahed, she reached under the white tablecloth.

Within seconds, smoke billowed and filled the room.

Sophie and Scoop leaped into action.

She grabbed the painting off the wall while he faced the room and ran interference. When Mac raced toward them, Scoop spun and whipped Mac's legs out from under him. He landed in a heap but was back on his feet in seconds. When he lunged toward Sophie, Scoop stopped him with a sharp jab to the midsection.

Painting tucked under her arm, Sophie darted for the circular staircase. She was halfway up when she glanced back. Eloise was gaining on her. "Interpol on my six," she muttered and ran faster.

"On it," Willa said.

Seconds later, Sophie heard a splat and Eloise muttered, "What the heck? Did she just throw cake at me?"

Sophie used the extra moment to slip into the back bedroom and silently close and lock the door.

She reached under the bed and yanked out the duffel Willa had placed there earlier. Once she tugged on the leather gloves, she clipped the rope around her waist, opened the window, and secured the grappling hook to the window ledge.

She had one foot over the sill and was reaching for the painting with her free hand when the door burst open.

Eloise lunged toward her, weapon aimed in her direction. "Don't move."

"Sorry. No can do." With the rope in one hand and the painting in the other, Sophie jumped.

38

Mercy gripped the handlebars of the motorcycle and kept one eye on the police van behind her as she headed back toward the heart of Munich. She hoped Hank and Camille were somewhere behind the van, ready to scoop her up, but there were no guarantees. She was, for all intents and purposes, on her own.

Never completely alone, she amended.

She led them directly toward the Frauenkirche, the Cathedral of our Great Lady, then drove around the block to the Pension Dom, a guesthouse she'd stayed in once before. She hated to barge in on the sister in charge without warning, but it couldn't be helped.

She dropped the kickstand, then slowly climbed off the bike, her hip aching. She straightened her robes and habit before she walked up to the front door, limping slightly, and rang the bell. She could hear the police van idling behind her.

There was no answer, so she knocked again. A light flicked on in the hallway.

Finally, someone peered through the peephole and then opened the door.

"Guten Tag, Sister. I am Sister Mercy and I apologize for disturbing you, but I wondered if you could give me a room."

The older woman studied Mercy for a moment, then glanced at the policeman leaning against the van, arms crossed over his chest. "We do not want trouble with the authorities."

"I apologize for bringing them here, even briefly. It won't be for long."

The cop suddenly stepped up behind Mercy and she jolted, appalled that she hadn't heard him approach. He nodded to the elderly sister. "Sister. Is this woman one of yours?"

The sister drew back, affronted. "We are all children of God and serve Him as best we can."

"Does she have a room here?" the cop asked.

The sister's chin came up. "She does. But what concern is that of yours?"

"Just making sure." He touched the brim of his cap. "Be careful in this weather."

Neither of the women moved until the van pulled away from the curb. Then the sister motioned Mercy inside and crossed her arms over her habit in a pose much like the cop's. "Now, what is this all about?"

Employing a hunch, Mercy made to straighten the cross she wore and pulled out her Speranza medallion as well.

The sister's eyes caught the motion and she stilled, then nodded. "Come with me and I'll show you to your room."

"Thank you, Sister." Mercy followed her down a narrow hallway and into a simply furnished room at the back of the guesthouse. Perfect.

"I trust this will meet your needs?"

"It will. Thank you."

She waited until she heard the sister's footsteps recede down the hallway before she peeked through the sheers but didn't see Hank and Camille.

After thirty minutes, the guesthouse had settled back into silence. Mercy left payment on the dresser and tiptoed down the hall to the rear door, praying there wasn't an alarm system. Since she hadn't seen one on the front door, she hoped there wasn't one on the back either.

She eased the door open and let out a breath when nothing happened. She quietly closed the door, then hurried down one of the snow-covered paths that led through the garden. At the back gate, she glanced both ways before she slipped out onto the sidewalk, easing the door shut behind her.

Headlights flashed on and blinded her as an engine sprang to life. She spun and took off in the opposite direction.

As she rounded the next corner, she risked a glance over her shoulder. The streetlights had come on early due to the storm and she made out the police van. Why were they following her? It made no sense unless they were in cahoots with the lowlifes raiding the camps. Which meant she couldn't get caught.

She picked up her pace, but she wouldn't be able to keep running for long. Her prosthetic leg was good for many things. Endurance running—through snow—had never been one of them.

She rushed past a narrow alley, then doubled back and shot down it, knowing the van couldn't get through.

As she got closer, she spotted a group of men standing around a burning trash barrel. They turned to stare at her, and she ignored the knives that suddenly appeared in too many hands.

"Please help me," she said as she hurried past them. "I'm being chased by a police van. Please don't let them find me."

"Don't worry, Sister, we've got your back."

The men fanned out behind her, blocking the width of the alley.

"God bless you," she called over her shoulder as she reached the next corner.

As she slipped out of sight, she heard shouts behind her. The cops had followed on foot.

How far would the men go to stop them? Maybe she should have been more specific about what she wanted.

She debated going back, then darted onto the street and took off running again, her pace much slower than before. But she couldn't stop.

She had her head down, trying not to draw attention to herself and also to make sure she didn't trip over her feet, when a car jumped the curb and screeched to a stop in front of her.

The passenger door swung open. "Get in."

VENICE, ITALY

Sophie was grinning as she slid down the back side of the building. It was probably wrong of her, but she loved the thrill of outsmarting the police and escaping right under people's noses.

The second her toes touched down, she unclipped the rope and shifted the painting to her other hand.

As she spun on the balls of her feet, she collided with a hard chest.

"There you are, darling," Mac said and pulled her close.

Her pulse jolted. A quick peek over his shoulder confirmed a dozen partygoers wandering the water's edge, laughing and joking. He turned them so his body shielded her, which put her back against the wall, with no way out. She shoved against his chest.

He didn't budge, simply murmured, "Play along," as his lips descended toward hers.

Sophie was still breathing hard from the adrenaline rush. When she opened her mouth to suck in air, he swooped in with a kiss that stole whatever scraps of breath she had left.

She wanted to protest, should protest, but for one suspended moment, she sank into the kiss, into the feel of his strong arms around her, the oh-so-tempting combination of passion and playfulness evident in the touch of his lips and the way his hands cupped her cheeks.

He slid his lips along the side of her neck and whispered, "Sophie."

Her brain snapped back online and she looked over his shoulder, spotted a working barge approaching in the canal behind them.

She ducked under his arm and ran down the street beside the barge, gauging the distance. A low bridge was mere seconds away. Painting in one hand, she grabbed the hem of her dress in the other and leaped aboard, then zigzagged around crates of produce toward the front of the craft, ignoring the indignant shouts of the pilot.

Mac was no more than a dozen paces behind her. He leaped aboard at the stern, eliciting more shouting from the barge's pilot.

Sophie looked ahead and dropped flat on the deck just in time to avoid being swept off the boat by the low bridge.

She glanced back as Mac and the pilot ducked as well.

"Sophie!"

She snapped her head around. Willa and Scoop were heading toward her from the opposite direction, Scoop at the tiller of a tiny boat.

Willa motioned for her to jump. Sophie's gut clenched. Jumping onto a flat-bottomed barge was one thing. But that little boat looked like an overgrown canoe with a motor. She'd been bounced into the water once already. She couldn't lose the painting.

She swiveled her head back again. Mac would reach her in three strides.

Willa and Scoop pulled even with the barge.

"Toss me the painting," Willa shouted, arms outstretched.

Sophie hesitated for a fraction of a second, then slung the painting like a giant Frisbee. Willa grabbed it, thank goodness, but the impact knocked her back on the seat. The tiny craft rocked precariously as Scoop fought to keep them from tipping over.

"Jump!" he shouted.

Sophie judged the distance. She couldn't make it. But she had no choice.

She leaped out just as Mac grabbed for her.

He caught her foot and her high-heeled pump slid off in his hand. Arms flailing, Sophie landed in the water with a mighty splash.

As Scoop tried to turn the little boat toward her, she heard another splash behind her.

Mac was swimming toward her with strong strokes.

"Take the helm," Scoop shouted and he and Willa traded places.

He knelt in the bow and held out a hand toward Sophie. "Get over here. Now."

As if she wasn't already swimming with all her strength.

Sophie put on a burst of speed as she heard sirens. Another boat raced in their direction. The moment her fingers touched Scoop's, he hauled her up and into the boat as though she weighed nothing.

She landed in a puddle of water, gasping for air and gripping the sides of the boat as it rocked. This was becoming all too familiar. Willa opened up the throttle and they sped away.

Sophie looked back as Mac climbed onto the seawall, then darted between buildings moments before Eloise burst out the back door and a police boat arrived on the scene.

It was wrong, but Sophie couldn't help giving them a little smile and a wave as their boat disappeared from sight.

39

Mercy scrambled into the backseat, and Hank hit the gas before she'd pulled the door closed behind her.

Hank glanced in the rearview mirror. "You okay?"

Mercy took a deep breath, tried to settle her racing heart. "I am now, though I hated taking advantage of the kind sister's offer of refuge."

"Desperate times and all that." Hank slowed their speed to avoid attracting attention as she threaded her way around the quiet city.

Camille peered over at her from the passenger seat. "We were worried when you lost your earpiece."

Mercy smiled. "Me too. I like having that safety net."

"Go ahead, Picasso," Hank said into her earpiece. "On it." She made a U-turn and headed in the opposite direction. "Picasso found what she thinks might be our white van."

"What about the cops?" Camille asked.

"She says she found them on the traffic cams. They went right back to the police station."

Camille flopped back in her seat. "So that's a dead end."

"Not necessarily. She'll use security footage to run background checks on them. See if they're legit, or somehow involved in this."

Mercy felt disconnected, sitting in the backseat without being able to hear what Picasso was saying. They relayed information, but it wasn't much. Unfortunately, that left her imagination free to conjure up horrific scenarios. "We still don't know why someone's snatching young girls."

Hank met her eyes in the rearview mirror. "It's probably not to be part of a sewing circle."

Mercy's stomach churned and she automatically crossed herself. As a Sister of Mercy, she'd seen far too much of man's inhumanity against man. The sense that all their efforts were futile washed over her, like they were tossing starfish back into the ocean, only to have them wash back with the next tide. She was officially on sabbatical from her order, and while she loved being part of Speranza's work, sometimes she longed for the quiet, safe, structured days she'd spent in the convent years ago.

But hiding safely behind those walls didn't get justice done. She rubbed her aching hip, then straightened her spine. They had work to do.

VENICE, ITALY

Willa sped down the narrow canal and steered them back into the main channel, weaving around other boats. Sophie was surprised at the amount of traffic this late at night. But when water served as the main highway, it made sense.

"Here's good," Scoop shouted, and Willa darted down another side canal and pulled up to the seawall. He hopped out and looked at his watch. "Meet me at the mouth of the river in thirty minutes."

"Be careful," Willa said.

He winked. "That's my line. Stay safe."

He disappeared and Willa spun the boat in a wide arc. "Keep your eyes open."

Shivering, Sophie shifted into Scoop's seat in the bow. She was tired of getting soaked and then riding around in open boats, freezing. She squeezed her palms against the soggy batting under her gown and water poured out. The only saving grace was that same padding kept the wind off her.

She glanced down one of the canals. "Police boat, heading this way." She gripped the sides as Willa picked up speed and the little outboard canoe bounced over the wake from passing boats.

She was tired of being chased too.

MUNICH, GERMANY

With Picasso giving directions into Hank's earpiece, they were soon on a highway headed out of Munich. Before long, the buildings thinned out, replaced by cattle pastures on both sides of the autobahn.

"If they were trying to get their prisoners out of the city, wouldn't they head for an airport or train station?" Camille asked.

"Maybe they're going to hold them somewhere for transport later."

Both options increased the churning in Mercy's stomach.

They'd been traveling for thirty minutes and Picasso hadn't reported any sightings since they left the city.

"Is there any place along this route where they could stash the trucks?" Hank asked.

Camille snorted. "You mean besides barns and woods and fields?" She indicated the area around them.

Hank cocked her head, listening. "Picasso says she'll keep checking and let us know."

But as the silence lengthened, it became obvious she had nothing else to tell them.

Hank finally pulled off the road, cussing a blue streak, and smacked a hand on the steering wheel. "We've lost them. If they turned off the road somewhere, we'll never find it in the dark. We'll need to come back in the morning."

Even though they'd all realized the same thing, hearing her voice it aloud was hard. They were quiet as they headed back toward the city.

———

VENICE, ITALY

By the time Willa guided them to the mouth of the river thirty minutes later, Sophie's teeth were chattering like a pair of castanets.

"Keep an eye out for the *Nodo D'amore.*" Willa slowed their speed.

Sophie squinted into the darkness, searching for the boat's familiar silhouette through the fog that had begun to settle over the city. Streetlights gave off a ghostly glow, and buildings had begun to disappear as the fog deepened. An eerie sense of anticipation raised more gooseflesh on her arms. "I can't see a thing."

"Keep looking."

They passed under a streetlight and back into darkness.

"There." Sophie pointed at the red light facing them, near the seawall. The boat was completely dark except for the navigation lights. The white stern light wasn't lit, so she couldn't make out the name of the boat either. She supposed that was the point.

Willa eased up to the stern. "Go on. Get up there."

"You're sure this is the right boat?"

"Pretty sure."

As reassurances went, it needed work, but Sophie reached back as Willa handed up the painting.

"Don't wait for me. I'll be right behind you."

Sophie climbed aboard, both relieved and alarmed when Scoop's brisk voice sounded from somewhere above. "Pick up the pace, ladies. We've got company."

"Working on it." Willa turned off the motor, climbed aboard the larger vessel, then used both feet to push the dinghy toward the seawall. "I'm in. Go!"

They hurried into the salon as Scoop eased the boat into the Grand Canal. Sophie looked out the glass doors and spotted a police boat racing toward them, lights flashing but no sirens at this late hour, dodging boat traffic.

Scoop kept heading west, maintaining a steady pace.

Sophie let out a sigh as the police boat sped past them. "Where are we going?"

"A friend is helping us. Get out of those wet clothes before you freeze."

Sophie wanted to demand more information, but her teeth wouldn't stop chattering, so she simply nodded. Another hot shower, another set of sweats, and she was back in the salon twenty minutes later. Willa, also in dry clothes, handed her a mug of hot chocolate.

"Heading in." Scoop's voice drifted down from the helm.

"I'll go say hello." Willa stepped through the sliding door.

"I'll come with you."

Sophie held on to the railing as they walked to the bow of the boat. They were heading toward one of the mansions along the Grand Canal, but this one had no boat dock. Willa pulled out a flashlight and flicked it on once, twice, then off again.

From shore, an answering beam did the same.

A large garage-style door slid open and Sophie gaped at the huge boathouse. Scoop eased them into the open slip beside another boat, and the giant door immediately closed behind them.

Overhead lights clicked on and the space turned bright as day.

Willa hopped off the boat and secured the lines, while Scoop powered down the engines.

A woman approached from the opposite side. "Welcome." She motioned them to disembark. Sophie guessed her to be in her forties, tall, with dark hair and beautiful dark eyes, a warm smile.

Sophie glanced toward Willa, whispered, "Do I bring the painting?"

Willa gave a sharp shake of her head. Then she turned to the other woman, hand extended. "Signora Faggini. Thank you for offering us your hospitality for the night."

The woman bypassed the handshake and kissed both of Willa's cheeks, then Sophie's, then Scoop's. "Any friend of Speranza is a friend of mine. Come. I had my cook prepare a little pasta. You must be hungry."

They followed her through a doorway and into a mansion so opulent, Sophie couldn't help gawking. The place looked like a museum, with gilt and paintings and sculptures everywhere. The artwork was staggering, created by household names in the art world.

Signora Faggini shepherded them into a large kitchen and indicated a table that overlooked the water. The shutters were closed against the night, but red police lights flashed between the slats.

They pretended not to notice. Conversation flowed while their hostess poured wine and the housekeeper served a wonderful lasagna with fresh bread and a salad.

For tonight, they were safe.

40

The sun hadn't yet cleared the horizon when Hank nudged Camille's foot with her booted one, then did the same for Mercy. "Up. We're burning daylight."

When they'd gotten back to their Airbnb the night before, Hank had sent them to bed, then gone back outside and fiddled with the engine on the nondescript sedan Mercy had rented. Nobody would rent Hank a car because of the minor detail of a suspended license, which annoyed her almost as much as the relentless itch for a drink. The car was a piece of junk, which further fueled her indignation, so she spent a few hours making adjustments, coaxing the machine to run more efficiently. As a side benefit, removing critical parts kept her from cruising into town to find an open bar while she waited for the craving to subside. She'd finally collapsed on the couch around 4:00 a.m. and now, with dawn imminent, it was time to get moving.

"Let's go. Rise and shine, people. This is not a vacation."

"It's still dark out, you sadist." Camille rolled over and threw her pillow at Hank.

Hank deftly caught it and winged it back, where it bounced off Camille's head.

"Hey. Geez."

But she was awake. Which was all Hank cared about.

Mercy sat up without a word and fastened her prosthesis, slid her feet into fuzzy slippers and made the bed with military precision before she padded off to the bathroom.

Hank shook her head. They were a motley crew, but they were *her* crew, which, given her background, was a reality that still boggled her mind.

With her riding herd on everyone, they were out the door within the hour, which Sister Mercy would no doubt consider a minor miracle. Camille rode shotgun, grumbling as she used the visor mirror to put on makeup. The snow had stopped around 10:00 p.m. the night before and the temps had gone up, creating a slushy, nasty mess on the roads.

Mercy had said little since she got up. "Where are we going, Hank? Back to the homeless encampment?"

"Yes. We need to keep talking to people, see if anyone saw anything yesterday that can help us." She glanced over at Camille, who was dressed in jeans and running shoes, scrolling through pictures on the camera around her neck. "You posing as a photojournalist today?"

Camille looked at her, raised an eyebrow. "Picasso sent a few pictures of the masked men from yesterday, which I loaded onto the camera. I want to see if they're the same guys."

"Smart."

"Do you think they'll be back tonight?" Mercy asked.

"No idea. That's why we need gear." Hank turned off the highway and wound her way through a residential neighborhood. She pulled up to the curb and then walked along the side of the house. When she returned, she had a long canvas duffel with her.

She stowed it in the trunk, then turned the car back toward the highway.

Camille sent her a sideways look. "You going to tell us what that was all about?"

"Picasso sent the address. Said to go grab a tent from the side of the house. This came with it." She pulled a note from her pocket, held it up for both women to see. The Speranza emblem was scrawled on it.

Even Camille fell silent, which Hank appreciated. Dawn was just breaking when they made it back to the camp.

Or what was left of it.

Hank stopped the car and they all climbed out.

"Oh, dear Lord, have mercy," Camille whispered as she looked around.

"There's nothing left." Fury hummed under Mercy's words. The small camp had been utterly obliterated. The few tents and makeshift shelters were gone, along with any trace of bedding. The handful of personal belongings left behind had been scattered everywhere, soaked and muddy in the melted snow.

Several raccoons busily raided whatever food scraps they could find.

"We need to find something that'll help us figure this out." When Mercy turned to head in the opposite direction, Hank said, "We stay together." Something about this whole setup raised her hackles. They exchanged uneasy glances, and Mercy rubbed her arms as though chilled.

They walked three abreast, working their way through the encampment, sifting through personal belongings, trying to find a clue of some kind. Camille picked up a ratty teddy bear and tucked it under her arm. Hank pretended not to see Camille's tears and ignored Mercy's murmured prayers. She had no patience for emotions.

When they stepped into the shadows under the bridge, all of Hank's senses went on high alert. She'd caught a faint whiff of something, and memories she'd spent years burying tried to rush back full force.

She put a hand out to stop them, then turned in a circle, making sure they were truly alone. "Something bad happened here."

"What do you mean?" Mercy asked.

"Do you smell that?"

Both women shook their heads.

"Stay behind me." Hank hoped she was wrong. Prayed she was wrong, but her gut said she wasn't wrong.

The smell got worse.

"Is that a dead animal?" Camille asked.

"Hopefully." Hank followed the stench, even though her work boots felt like they were filled with lead.

They slowly walked the entire area under the bridge, trudging through the knee-high weeds, but didn't find anything.

"Now what?" Camille asked.

Mercy's attention was caught by something at the corner of the bridge. "Oh, please, no." She took off running.

Hank and Camille sprinted after her.

They arrived just in time to hear Mercy say, "Lise. Oh no. Lise." She turned her head and retched.

For a moment Hank froze, trapped in the past. The stench of gunpowder filled the air, the noise of machine-gun fire not quite enough to drown out men's screams. Her hands tightened as though she were back in a helo cockpit, desperate to get her men to safety.

Someone touched her shoulder and she spun, hooked an arm around their neck.

"Easy, Hank. It's Camille."

It took a moment for the words to penetrate and the past to recede. Hank blinked, dropped her arm, and stepped back. "Sorry."

"I'm good." Camille coughed, rubbing her neck, and tried to smile.

Hank shook her head to clear it, then marched over to where Mercy sat beside the body, gripping her cross and murmuring prayers.

Hands on her hips, Hank shoved the past back into the box she kept it in. She refused to look at Mercy. Instead, she focused on doing her job. She studied the dead woman dispassionately. She had short blonde hair, like the missing Lise Fortier, though decomp and the area wildlife had obliterated her facial features. But her coat fit the description Willa had given them. Even more telling, the Neue Anfänge logo on the breast pocket was still visible through the blood that covered the coat and matted her hair.

Mercy's body was rigid, her hands clenched into fists. "I can't help her."

Hank knew exactly how she felt. Mercy was an RN and trained in wilderness first aid. "We can't bring her back, but we *will not* stop until we track down whoever did this to her."

Camille pulled Mercy to her feet, then tried to pull the tiny woman into a hug.

Mercy stepped away, palms up, eyes flashing with fury even as a tear slid down her cheek. "I know she's with God but no one should go like this, left out here alone like so much trash."

On that they all agreed.

Camille straightened. "Let me get my camera. We need to collect all the evidence we can before we call the police. Just in case."

Hank pulled out her phone. "I'll call Willa."

Mercy scanned the area. "I'll fan out, see what I can find." She set her jaw. "If we're lucky, maybe we'll find a murder weapon."

Hank's surprise must have shown on her face.

Mercy propped her hands on her hips. "Not all of God's work gets done in a pretty church or big city hospital. I've spent time in some very rough places."

Mercy's grief had hardened into a tough determination Hank understood and respected. She nodded. "Then let's get to work."

They fanned out from the body, searching the high grass, Camille taking pictures of anything that might help. There was no sign of a murder weapon or any obvious clues.

Hank made an anonymous phone call to the local police, and an hour later they were back in the rental, parked just far enough away to stay under the official radar. Camille had her camera out, zooming in on the faces of the law enforcement officers and officials milling around the scene, snapping pictures.

"Oh, hello." She scrolled through her photos. Stopped. Scrolled again. "The two cops who followed Mercy last night are here again."

"Because it's their job," Hank said.

Camille scowled. "Maybe, but they're standing off to the side, just watching, not doing anything."

"Then let's find out if they're involved." Hank reached under the seat and passed two small disks to Camille. "You'd better go out there, since they've seen Mercy."

Mercy took off her headpiece and handed it to Camille, then passed her cross over.

"Will anyone question the partial, ah, uniform?" Hank asked as Camille checked her face in the makeup mirror.

"No. It should be fine," Mercy said.

"You ready?"

Camille nodded and climbed out of the car. They kept watch as she approached the official vehicles, then skirted around them to speak to the officers. Hank had the windows down, but they couldn't hear what was being said.

Camille stood by as the medical examiner loaded Lise's body into the back of the van. She continued speaking to the cops until the ones they were after got back in their vehicles and drove away. The crime scene techs continued their work, paying her no mind.

Fifteen minutes later, she climbed into the passenger seat. "Done. One on each car."

Hank opened the app on her cell phone and set the phone in the cup holder so she could keep an eye on the GPS signal. She cranked the engine and followed the little red dot. "Let's hope they don't go back to the station and switch to their personal cars."

"Sophie is going to be crushed." Camille stared out the window.

"Take me back to the shelter," Mercy suddenly said.

Hank glanced into the mirror. "Now?"

"Right now. I want to talk with the women there, see if anyone knows something. Maybe something they don't even know they know." She shrugged. "People talk to nuns even when they won't talk to others."

Camille pulled off the head covering and cross and passed them back to Mercy.

Hank made a U-turn. "It's as good an idea as any."

VENICE, ITALY

Sophie woke from a deep sleep to Willa shaking her shoulder and bolted into a sitting position. "What's wrong?" She shoved the hair out of her eyes and tried to focus. Where was she? Her gaze darted around the room. Right. Venice. Mansion. Last night, she'd slipped down to the boat to confirm the portrait of the princess was behind the landscape. Then she'd spent several hours studying the back of the new painting. But the so-called clue on the back hadn't offered up any answers.

Willa sank down on the side of the bed, and Sophie finally zeroed in on her face. A chill slid down her spine.

"Tell me," she whispered.

Willa gripped her hand and Sophie's heart pounded. "I just heard from Hank, Camille, and Mercy." She looked away, cleared her throat. "There's no easy way to say this, Sophie." She pulled in a deep breath. "They, uh, they found Lise's body near one of the encampments a little while ago."

Sophie blinked, trying to process the words in a way that made sense. But they didn't, and her mind straight up rejected them. She leaped from the bed. "It's not true. It can't be." She paced the room, turned back. "Are they absolutely sure it's her?"

Pity and sorrow filled Willa's expression. "They're not 100 percent sure, no. But the, ah, victim has short blonde hair and is wearing Lise's coat. Height and weight match. I'm sure the police will make a positive ID before any official announcements are made."

"I need to get back to Munich. I need to find her. I should have been there all along. She needs me." Sophie grabbed her tote bag and started shoving things inside it, thoughts slamming around inside her head like it was a pinball machine.

Lise couldn't be dead, she couldn't.

"Even if it isn't Lise, the team is convinced her death wasn't an accident."

Sophie swiped at the tears blurring her vision. "How do they know?" She spun, jabbed a finger in Willa's direction. "And don't spare the details."

"Hank thinks she was shot." She paused. "In the back."

Sophie sank onto the edge of the bed. *Please, God, no. Not Lise. Not like that.*

After a minute or two ticked by, Willa spoke. "The coronation is tomorrow. Are you still convinced Lise's, ah . . . disappearance is connected to the paintings? What if it's been about the missing women all along?"

Sophie tried to wrap her mind around what Willa was asking, but her head felt like it was going to explode from the emotions pushing in from every direction. She took a deep breath and rubbed the hollow ache in her stomach, willing her brain cells to kick in.

She stood and forced the emotions into a locked box so she could function. Then she paced while she examined various theories. She sifted fact from fiction, then lined up speculation for a closer look. After she'd turned all the pieces around in her mind, the picture that emerged was staggering in its implications.

"It's possible that whoever was killed, either Lise or someone else—" though her mind utterly rejected the idea that her friend was dead—"was simply at the wrong place at the wrong time when the women were taken." Sophie paused. "It's the timing that bothers me, with the coronation coming up. If this is about the paintings, and I think it is, then someone besides us knows Lise's identity and wants her out of the picture before the coronation."

Willa opened her mouth to respond just as a quick knock sounded on the door, and Scoop stuck his head in. "You might want to turn on the news."

41

Willa aimed the remote at the television inside a carved mahogany cabinet. She found a news channel, and both women sat on the bed as a photo of the first painting of Princess Johanna and her children filled the screen.

"The official investigation into the missing portrait of Neuhansberg's beloved Princess Johanna and the death of Henri Marchant, an employee at the Fortier Gallery where the painting recently appeared, has taken an unexpected turn."

Henri's face filled the frame, and Sophie's breath hitched. She remembered his excitement about art, his love of parties, and how giddy he got every time they prepped for debut artist events. *Oh, Henri. You shouldn't have died. Especially not for stealing a copy.*

"Earlier, a source inside the police department told us that an anonymous tip from someone calling themselves 'a friend' led them to the residence of Herr Heiko Jung, a local official overseeing the homeless crisis, where investigators found the missing painting of Princess Johanna and her family on display. Sources close to the investigation claim that Frau Jung, who is confined to her bed, is a cousin of Princess Johanna and claims no knowledge of where the painting came from, only that it was a gift from her husband." Heiko's face filled the screen.

Sophie gasped. "That's the blond guy who has been chasing us."

Willa nodded her agreement but said nothing as the story continued.

"Police have been unable to locate Herr Jung, so they are asking for help from the public. If you have any knowledge of Heiko Jung's whereabouts, please contact local police immediately. In the meantime, sources say officials have reached out to Bernadette Rainier, the reclusive American artist who originally painted the portraits, for help in authenticating the painting. All of this comes just one day before Hereditary Prince Felix is scheduled to take over as the next ruler of Neuhansberg, one of the richest countries in the world."

The anchor moved on to another story, but Sophie's mind was spinning. She met Willa's eyes. "Should we let Interpol know where to find him?"

The other woman cocked her head. "Doesn't your friend Mac have ties to Eloise Cuvier with Interpol?"

Irritation spiked at the mention of Mac's name. "I wouldn't call him a friend, but yes, he talked to her in Cologne, outside the cathedral."

"Since he was dogging us today, too, I assume Mac knows Jung is here."

What if Heiko killed Henri? Was he hoping to find all three paintings for his wife?

Her gut clenched as another realization hit home. What would happen when Ms. Rainier confirmed the painting was a forgery? Or, more accurately, a copy?

"I need to get back to Munich."

In a small boutique hotel in Venice, Mac was also watching the news. The suspicions that had been growing suddenly took shape and fit into a larger picture.

Since he thought best on paper, he muted the television and took the little pad of hotel stationery. He jotted down all the random and seemingly unrelated facts of this case and drew a circle around each one. He eyed the bits and pieces, then started drawing lines between the people and places that intersected in some way.

Always, still, Sophie and the paintings were the link that connected everything.

But there was also another link. Had anyone else spotted it yet?

Another face flashed on the screen, and he grabbed the remote and turned the volume up.

"More controversy surrounds the homeless encampments popping up along the banks of the Isar River after police found the body of a woman under the bridge early this morning. Sources close to the investigation tell us that several women have reportedly disappeared from the makeshift camps over the past few weeks. From what we've learned, police have not made an identification yet, but residents at a shelter associated with the encampments worry that the deceased could be Lise Fortier, one of the employees of Neue Anfänge, a charity that helps the homeless. Ms. Fortier also owns the Fortier Gallery in Munich, where the missing painting of Neuhansberg's Princess Johanna and her family first appeared."

Mac added more information to his sketch and the picture got even clearer.

Sophie was in more danger than she'd ever been.

And he was almost out of time.

42

VENICE, ITALY

Willa set down the remote. "I'll meet you downstairs in ten minutes."

Sophie barely heard her. She walked into the luxurious bathroom, pulled on her red wig, then shoved her toiletries into her tote along with the rest of her belongings.

Once downstairs, she, Willa, and Scoop exchanged cheek kisses with their hostess and lavished her with effusive thanks before hurrying aboard the boat. Sophie confirmed the painting was still where she'd left it while Scoop backed out of the garage and headed straight toward the marina.

Willa found her studying the painting. "Why not cut it out of the frame? It'd sure be easier to hide. And transport."

That exact question was what had kept Sophie awake most of the night. "I know, but I think it needs to stay in the frame. That's where the clues are written." She met Willa's gaze. "I can't explain it, but my gut says it has to stay intact."

Willa simply nodded.

Once Scoop dropped them off, Sophie tucked the painting

under her arm and she and Willa set off on foot. They ducked into a boutique and purchased oversize sunglasses and colorful scarves, which they tied under their chins.

"We need two more decoy paintings." Sophie scanned the artists' booths as they walked along the Grand Canal. She didn't want to visit the same artist, so she nodded at a display near the end of the row. "You buy the large canal scene—" she hitched her chin toward another booth—"and I'll get the bridge painting. Make sure you get it wrapped."

Several minutes later, they ducked into the alley behind a small café. Willa stood guard, her new painting in hand, tapping a foot as though waiting for someone. Behind her, just out of view, Sophie untied the string and used her knife to remove the frame. She cut the new canvas from its stretcher and carefully fitted it over the princess's portrait, concealing it from view. Once it was secured in the original frame, she rewrapped everything, then tossed pieces of the cheap frame in various trash receptacles as they walked by.

They split up, each carrying a wrapped painting. Willa caught a water bus to the main train terminal, while Sophie walked, both watching the policemen standing on the wide stone steps. One of them asked Willa to unwrap her painting, studied her face, and then waved her into the building.

Sophie waited several minutes before she started up the steps.

"Excuse me, signorina." The officer stepped in her path. "I need to see your painting, please."

Sophie cocked her head and responded in stilted German. *"Ich verstehe nicht. Varum müssen sie mein Geshchenk sehen?"* I don't understand. Why do you need to see my gift?

He instructed her to unwrap the painting, but movement in her peripheral vision caught her attention. A small boat pulled to the cement seawall and Mac stepped out, casually scanning the crowd. Sophie took a half step to her right so she was hidden behind the cop. The loudspeaker announced the outbound train would depart in three minutes. *"Das ist mein Zug."* That's my train.

He turned down a corner of the brown paper, shrugged, then eyed her for a moment and wished her a nice day.

Sophie gripped the painting and hustled into the terminal. Willa stood on the other side of the turnstile, Sophie's ticket in hand. Willa rushed toward the front of the train bound for Verona, Italy, and boarded the third car. Sophie scanned her ticket and hurried in the opposite direction, leaping aboard one of the last cars of the same train, skidding in just before the doors closed.

She glanced over her shoulder as the train pulled away, and a feeling of déjà vu swept over her. As he had in Munich, Mac stood on the platform, hands on his hips, shaking his head in obvious frustration as several cops piled up behind him.

Their eyes met, and she hitched her chin in the air, refusing to look away.

———

Sophie kept the painting tucked next to the window during the seven-hour train ride to Munich. Shortly after they left Venice behind, she and Willa searched the train but found no sign of their usual tails. When the train pulled into the main station in Verona, Italy, and later Innsbruck, Austria, they found no sign of Mac, Interpol, Heiko, or Hoodie Guy there either. Their relative safety, at least for the moment, had Sophie's head bobbing like a dashboard dog as the train sped through the mountains toward Munich. Her mind raced, while her body fought for rest, leaving her disoriented.

Later that afternoon, driving in the rental car, Willa said, "Hank, Camille, and Mercy should be here within the hour."

Sophie sat up straight as Willa turned the car off the highway and onto a narrow country road south of the city, pulling up beside a tidy stone cottage surrounded by fields and rolling hills.

Sophie tried to focus on what she was saying, her mind still numb. She couldn't accept that Lise was dead. Her mind categorically refused to believe it. "Where are we?"

"Little town called Grünwald, about twelve kilometers south of

Munich. The house is ours for the next few days." They stepped out and Sophie took a deep breath. It was peaceful here. Quiet.

Willa's phone buzzed with a text. "Scoop says the police questioned him when he docked in Venice. They let him go after they searched the boat. He's boarding a flight from Milan to London." She checked the time. "I need to hit the road too. My flight also leaves in a couple of hours."

"You're leaving? Now?"

"We got another call for help. You're in good hands here." She motioned toward the painting Sophie had taken out of the trunk. "Let Picasso help you decipher the code. She's standing by."

Sophie nodded automatically, her mind already back on Lise.

"Don't go haring off without the rest of the team. They'll be here in a bit."

Willa's words penetrated and Sophie raised a brow. Hadn't Nadine said almost the same thing? "You know I've been handling things on my own for a long time, right?"

"So you've said. But you also know there's strength in being part of a team. Don't go Lone Ranger now, Sophie."

She nodded and accepted a set of house keys and the other woman's hug.

The moment Willa's taillights disappeared, Sophie went to work. She agreed with most of what Willa had said. She was learning to appreciate the camaraderie and sense of belonging, the confidence that someone always had her back in a tight spot.

But this was different. Some things, like what she had to do tonight, had to be done alone.

43

Sophie walked down the quiet road to the neighboring farm. It took less than ten minutes of looking helpless and desperate—and a significant bit of cash—to convince the older couple to let her borrow their car for a few hours. Once she explained why she needed it, they were extremely sympathetic, and the wife quickly drew Sophie a map to the city morgue where her family member would have been taken.

Back at the cottage, Sophie did a quick search of her temporary home. A climb up the rickety ladder into the attic netted exactly what she needed. She hid the painting behind several others that leaned against the sloped ceiling, then rooted around an old trunk for a suitable disguise. She found several faded dresses. Perfect. She chose one, then tucked a soft feather pillow under her long workout tank. It rounded out her figure nicely.

Ball cap and sunglasses in place, she climbed into the borrowed car. The city morgue wasn't too far from the farm, so that helped with timing. Her plan was to get in and out before the others arrived at the farmhouse and tried to talk her out of it.

She had to see Lise.

Thankfully, the morgue was in the basement of the large hospital, and since people generally didn't want to go there, security was pretty lax. Still, the smell of death overlaid with antiseptic almost knocked her off her feet. She leaned against the dimly lit hallway and willed herself not to throw up.

She could not accept that Lise was dead. The Bible story she learned as a child about Doubting Thomas, the disciple who said he wouldn't believe Jesus had risen from the dead until he touched the scars in His hands and feet, suddenly made sense. She wouldn't believe Lise was dead without proof either.

Breathing through her mouth, she walked down the long corridor, grateful she hadn't passed another person since she'd slipped off the elevator. As she neared the corner, she heard the pneumatic doors to the morgue swish open and people talking as they exited. She ducked into a supply closet and waited, counting off seconds in her mind.

Once they passed, she slipped out of the closet and through the doors just as they swung closed, keeping her face averted from the security camera above the door.

Inside, she stopped short in front of a long wall of refrigerated drawers that bore an eerie resemblance to a giant filing cabinet. How would she find Lise? She wouldn't have time to check all of them before she was discovered.

She walked closer and pulled gloves from her dress pockets as she studied the labels, which indicated gender, age, and name— when known—and date of death.

That made it easier. She hurried down the row. The most recent arrivals were along the far right. Her heart pounded in her chest as she scanned labels. Several females had arrived today.

Her hand trembled as she slid out the most recent drawer. This woman was barely out of her teens, rail thin, with Asian features. Sophie whispered a prayer for her family and moved on to the next drawer, which held a plump, gray-haired grandma with laugh lines etched in her wrinkled cheeks.

She opened the next one and all the breath whooshed from her lungs. *Dear God, no.*

A blonde cap of hair. Lise.

You can do this. Make sure.

It took every ounce of her courage to pull the drawer all the way open. She lifted the sheet and studied the face more closely, forcing back the bile as she took in the damage wrought by decomposition, the elements, and the wildlife. The face was unrecognizable. Sophie wanted to run, to scream and rage at the injustice of all of it. But she did none of those things. She stroked her friend's hair and let the tears flow. She owed Lise this much and so much more.

But was this Lise? The coat was clearly hers. Sophie didn't recognize the clothes, but her friend dressed to blend in when she went to the encampments. No fancy charity dinner suits in the field.

Sophie pulled the sheet all the way down so she could examine Lise's legs and feet. Was the birthmark still visible? There was so much damage, she couldn't tell. She pulled out her phone and snapped pictures from every angle, then pulled up the picture from the New Year's Eve party that she'd shown to Camille and Mercy. She held it next to Lise's body and finally shook her head in defeat.

There was no way to be absolutely certain. She wanted to howl in frustration.

Tears blurred her vision and she swiped them angrily away. They helped nothing. She reached out and touched Lise's damaged face with the back of her gloved fingers, stroked her cheek, then pulled up the sheet and swallowed hard. *God, no. Please, no.*

She'd just slid the drawer shut when voices sounded in the hallway. She spun and scanned the room, looking for a place to hide. There weren't a lot of options besides the metal drawers, and Sophie couldn't bring herself to hide in one of those. She raced across the room and flattened herself against the wall beside the doors, seconds before a man and a woman in scrubs entered. They were deep in conversation, so she slipped out the door before it closed behind them.

The man glanced over his shoulder, spotted her, and shouted for her to stop.

Sophie took off running. The few seconds it would take for him to reopen the pneumatic doors bought her time to bolt into the stairwell. She took the stairs two at a time and burst out through the emergency exit.

The alarm screeched as she raced around the side of the building. She ducked into some bushes next to a dumpster, pulled the dress over her head, and yanked the pillow out of her tank top, tossing both into the trash. She spun her ball cap backward and kept running.

Finally, she slowed to a stop on the sidewalk in front of the hospital, hands on her knees, breath heaving, just another jogger taking a break.

Security guards raced past her as she strolled to her borrowed car, rubbing the stitch in her side.

She reached her vehicle and stopped short at the figure leaning back against it, arms crossed.

"What do you think you're doing, Sophie?"

44

Sophie nudged Hank out of the way and unlocked the door. "If you want to lecture, get in."

Hank propped her hands on her hips and scowled. "This was stupid."

"It was necessary." Sophie slid into the car and slammed the door. As she pulled out of the parking lot, Hank climbed into another nondescript sedan and followed. No doubt Camille and Mercy were with her, all of them tsking and shaking their heads.

Whatever. She didn't have the patience for any of that. She wound her way out of the city and back toward the cottage, more frustrated than she'd been before.

She still didn't know for sure if that was Lise's body. The not knowing made her stomach clench and her hands tremble.

Logic said it was Lise. But in her heart, Sophie wasn't convinced. Maybe she was living in fantasyland, but until fingerprints or dental records proved it, she was going with the assumption that this was some poor soul who Lise had given her coat to and that Lise was still out there somewhere, depending on Sophie to find her.

That was where Sophie hit a mental wall, and her confidence wavered like an unsteady first brushstroke. She slumped in her seat and gripped the wheel. After all this time, all her searching, she didn't know where to look next, still had no idea how to find her friend.

Sophie was out of time and out of options. There were no leads left to follow.

Her head felt stuffed with cotton and her brain hurt from trying to make sense of everything. She was tempted to climb into bed and pull the covers over her head, pretend this was all a bad dream.

Instead, she drove past the cottage and pulled into the neighbor's long driveway. She returned the keys and thanked them again for their help.

"Did you identify your sister?" The woman gripped her hands together.

Sophie shrugged, making no effort to hide her sadness. "I'm still not 100 percent sure it's her. I'll have to wait for an official identification."

The woman nodded, sympathy shining in her eyes. "Waiting is very hard. I am sorry."

"Thank you. I appreciate your concern." Sophie thanked them again and then started walking back to the stone cottage. She took her time, not in a hurry for a lecture from anyone in Speranza.

A lovely stretch of woods was located between the two farms, and Sophie breathed deeply as she left the pavement and strolled under the big trees. She'd missed this. Being out in the forest, listening to the birds. She usually didn't mind the city, but getting out in nature had always reset her spirit in ways she couldn't explain. She hadn't realized how much she needed it.

She meandered through the thick stretch of forest, gazing up at the trees, inhaling the loamy smell, trying to think. *Where are you, Lise?*

A ray of sunshine slipped through the trees, and Sophie stared skyward. *God, a little help here would be good.*

Suddenly, the birds went silent. She stopped.

There.

A rustling sound. Did bears roam in this part of Germany?

She slipped behind the trunk of a tree and waited, listening.

The rustling grew louder.

She changed her stance, braced to run if necessary.

The rustling morphed into footsteps, jogging through the forest. Animals did not sound like that when they ran.

Sure enough, a man rushed past the tree she hid behind.

She would have stayed quiet.

Except he had the painting gripped in his hands.

"Hey!" She took off after him. "Give that back!"

He glanced over his shoulder and Sophie recognized Hoodie Guy, the same one from St. Agnes in Cologne and from Venice. Geez, he just wouldn't give up.

He pulled out a gun and a bullet pinged off a nearby tree, sending bark flying. Sophie ducked into a crouch and ran from tree to tree, keeping him in sight. Gun or no gun, he was not getting away with that painting, not after she'd rappelled down a building and ended up in a Venice canal—twice—to get it.

He was pulling farther ahead, angled toward the road. She hadn't seen a car parked there, so where was he going?

She picked up her pace, but that wouldn't be enough to stop him. She needed a weapon.

Without breaking stride, she glanced around for a sturdy branch and scooped one up as she ran by. It was about the length of a fencing sword and looked strong enough to do the job. She stripped off the leaves as she chased after him.

He was nearing the edge of the woods.

Timing would be critical.

She spotted a stump and raced toward it. She stepped up onto it, then leaped into the air and landed right behind him. She shoved him up against a tree and poked the branch into his back.

"Move and I'll run you through," she warned. "Drop the gun."

He didn't respond. She leaned forward and pressed harder. "Don't make me repeat myself."

The gun slid from his grasp.

"Nicely done, Soph." Camille emerged from behind the man, breathing hard, clutching a carving knife.

Mercy emerged from the other side and pulled off her braided belt. "Hands behind your back," she commanded.

Sophie stepped sideways, the stick still holding Hoodie Guy in place, while Mercy neatly tied his hands.

Hank stepped around the tree and took possession of the painting. She handed it to Mercy, then said to the man, "Move. That way." She pointed toward the cottage.

"Please, you have to let me go. I need that painting."

Sophie blocked his path. "Why do you need that painting?"

"Let's ask that again when we're inside, yeah?" Camille tilted her head to the side, and Sophie spotted the farmer and his wife watching from the trees, him holding a pitchfork, her holding a rifle over her shoulder.

Sophie smiled. "Everything is fine. Thank you."

The silence stretched. Nobody moved.

Finally, the couple nodded once and then turned back toward their own homestead.

"Please. Don't do this," Hoodie Guy said.

They ignored him and marched him back to the cottage. Once inside, Mercy tied him to a chair.

Sophie sat at the table across from him. He was much younger than she had first thought. "Tell me why you need the painting."

He swallowed audibly and looked from Sophie to Hank, who leaned against the sink, scowling, to Camille and Mercy, who occupied the other chairs at the table. "He'll kill my family if I don't bring him all the paintings by tomorrow."

"Who?"

He shook his head.

"We can't help you if you don't tell us," Mercy added.

He froze, then studied each of them in turn, eyes wide with the faintest glimmer of hope. "Why would you help me?"

"We'll help each other," Sophie said.

Hank straightened away from the sink. "Mercy, will you get him a drink of water?"

Mercy locked eyes with Hank, then stood. Smiled. "Certainly."

Hank motioned the others toward the living room. "We'll be right back."

Sophie followed Camille and Hank into the other room, closing the kitchen door behind her. "What's going on?"

"Nothing. We just need to give Mercy a bit of time."

Sophie glanced from one to the other. "You think she can get him to talk?"

Camille grinned. "Mercy can get anyone to talk. It's a gift."

Suddenly, all three of their cell phones buzzed with an incoming text from Picasso: **Breaking news. Now.**

They glanced around the room. No television.

Camille held her phone in front of her mouth. "Siri, find breaking news."

They crowded around as she scrolled through various headlines.

Princess Johanna Portrait Declared a Forgery by the Artist

Sophie hissed out a breath as the princess's face filled the screen. Camille enlarged the photo and then started reading the article aloud. "'Earlier this week, authorities followed up on an anonymous tip and discovered the portrait of Princess Johanna that went missing Saturday evening hanging on the wall in the home of Heiko Jung. Police are still searching for Jung in connection with the murder of Henri Marchant, a gallery employee, who was found dead that same night. A source close to the investigation says authorities reached out to Bernadette Rainier, the reclusive artist who originally painted the three portraits, to verify the painting's authenticity. Ms. Rainier studied a series of photographs of the portrait and declared that it was an exceptionally good forgery, but a forgery nonetheless.'"

Sophie wrapped her arms around her middle as the same photo of Lise and her, the one from the New Year's Eve party that had been posted on the gallery's social media page, appeared on the screen.

Camille kept reading. "'At this time, authorities are searching for these women in connection to the investigation: Lise Fortier, owner of Fortier Art Gallery, who received the painting Friday night, and American Sophie Williams, who manages the gallery. If you have any information . . . ,' blah, blah, blah," Camille finished.

Sophie looked up and found both women studying her, eyes narrowed.

"You copied the portrait?" Hank asked.

Sophie nodded. "As a precaution. Lise asked me to, the night she first got it."

"Where's the original?" Camille demanded.

"Somewhere safe."

Camille crossed her arms over her chest. "You still don't trust us."

"It's not about trust." Well, not entirely. "The less you know, the less you'll ever have to deny. That's always been Lise's and my philosophy."

"You can't protect a dead woman," Hank said.

"Hank!" Camille sent her a what-the-heck look.

"Well, you can't. I know it sucks that she's dead, but there it is."

In that moment, Hank's bluntness cut through all the noise swirling in Sophie's mind, all the second-guessing and self-doubt as the truth became clear. "I don't think she's dead."

Mercy slipped through the kitchen door just in time to hear the last bit. The three women exchanged glances.

"What makes you think that?" Mercy asked.

Sophie held out her hand to Camille for her phone. She enlarged the party photo of her and Lise and turned it to face them. "I can't say for sure if the birthmark is there."

At their dubious looks, Sophie reached for her cell phone and pulled up the photos she'd taken in the morgue. She held it out. Camille took a quick look and turned away, but Hank enlarged one of the photos and spent several minutes comparing the two.

"There's not enough there to prove it one way or the other," Hank finally conceded.

"Her nail polish is the wrong color," Sophie said, the realization slamming into her.

"What does that have to do with anything?" Mercy asked.

Sophie pulled up another photo of the body. "Lise has never worn blue nail polish in her life. She thinks it's a ridiculous color. She wears pinks and reds, especially bright red, which is what she was wearing when she went missing. I can't for the life of me believe she changed her polish to something she hated the night she disappeared. That makes no sense."

The silence lengthened as Sophie studied their faces. One by one, they set aside pity and sorted through the facts, same as she had done.

She repeated what she'd told Willa. "I think someone else knows Lise is really Katharina, namely someone in the royal family, especially Felix's people, and they want to be sure she can't interfere with the coronation tomorrow."

"If we suppose it's not her in the morgue, then why not grab her and kill her outright the night she disappeared?" Hank asked. "Problem solved. No offense," she added when both Mercy and Camille glared at her.

"None taken. I don't think whoever it is has been able to find her. Which tells me she's hiding somewhere. I need to find her before they do."

"If she was hiding, wouldn't she have tried to contact you?" Mercy asked.

"She absolutely would have, if she could."

Camille studied Sophie closely. "What's your plan, girl?"

"I'm going to keep doing what I've been doing. I believe the paintings are the clues I need. I'll figure out where this painting leads. If I'm right, I'll find Lise when I get there."

"That's not a lot to go on," Hank said.

"Nobody is asking you to go along," Sophie snapped. She looked at all of them. "I will find her and I won't stop searching until there is absolute proof that . . ." Sophie swallowed. "That she's been found."

Mercy glanced at Sophie, shook her head. "You still don't get it, do you? We're not leaving you to do this alone. We want all the info we can get so we can devise a plan to help you."

"I'll get my laptop and get a Zoom call going," Camille said.

"I'll call Willa," Hank said.

"Before you do that," Mercy said, halting them in their tracks. "Hoodie Guy—whose name is Laszlo, by the way—had quite a bit to say once I got him talking." She met Sophie's gaze. "You were right about this having to do with the coronation. He was supposed to get the paintings or his family would be killed, starting with his son. But then the plan changed." She filled them in on the details.

"Interesting," Hank said afterward, eyes narrowed. "This opens up all kinds of possibilities."

45

Using phones, a secure mobile hotspot, and Camille's laptop, they started hammering out a plan, ignoring the gradfather clock in the corner that ticked off every passing minute.

"There were only three portraits of Princess Johanna, right?" Mercy asked.

"According to Bernadette Rainier, yes."

"We have all three, right?" Mercy asked.

Sophie nodded. "Yes. One is hidden in Munich. Willa has the second one secured in Cologne, yes?"

"Absolutely," Hank said.

"And we have the third one here. So we're not looking for another painting." Mercy drummed her fingers on the table.

Sophie had set the portrait on the kitchen table, face down, so they could study the inscription on the back. "Not unless there's a fourth one Ms. Rainier forgot about, given the article about her declining mental health. But I don't believe that. All three portraits were displayed for the public to see."

Camille read the inscription out loud. "'Though knights confer and jesters prance, the rose of silence tells no tales.'" She shrugged. "I got nothing."

"Knights and jesters say 'castle' to me," Hank said. "But given how many of those are littering the continent, that doesn't help."

"What about castles connected to Prince Felix?" Camille asked. "I'll ask Picasso to check." She sent a text.

Sophie started typing. "Let's see what 'rose of silence' gets us." She started scrolling. "Wait. Check this out." She turned her phone so they could see as she read from the Burg Eltz website. "'The rose of silence in the Knight's Hall was a promise that the spoken word wouldn't leave the room.'"

"But that castle doesn't have anything to do with Felix's family, does it?" Mercy asked.

Camille checked her phone. "Nothing yet from Picasso, but I'll ask her to check that specifically."

The doorbell rang and all Sophie's instincts went on high alert until she saw who it was. "Simone, thanks for coming."

The young woman with blue hair, large gauges in her ears, and black lipstick worked as a makeup artist and costume designer for one of the local theatres in Munich. Sophie had met her during a production of *Hamlet* several years ago, when Sophie volunteered as her assistant.

Simone turned her ankle and showed off the Speranza tattoo above her combat boot. "I hear you girls need to stage a murder." She eyed Sophie. "You part of the group too?"

"I guess I am." Sophie let the knowledge settle, all the way down to her bones. "Appreciate you coming."

Simone held up a gallon jug filled with red liquid. "Hope I brought enough blood."

When Camille and Sophie paled, Simone chuckled. "Relax, ladies. It's corn syrup and food coloring."

"Good to know," Camille said.

"Our victim is in here," Sophie said and led her into the kitchen, where Hank and Laszlo were playing poker.

Several hours later, Sophie, Hank, and Mercy crowded around Camille's laptop, watching her photoshop the images with lightning speed.

"Oh, that looks scary real," Sophie said. "Nice job, Camille."

"All we have to do now is set the trap and hope we catch the right rat," Hank said.

Hank, Mercy, and Camille's cell phones all buzzed with an incoming text.

Hank scanned it, then said, "Picasso has been tracking the cop cars we tagged. They stopped and now she's picked up the white van on traffic cams, heading toward one of the encampments. So those two are involved."

"We need to go, now." Mercy headed for the stairs to get her gear. "This is our chance to figure out where they're taking their captives."

"I'll stay here with Sophie. I need to finish this," Camille said.

"You're with us," Hank countered. "We need your skills with a camera." She nodded to Sophie. "Can you e-mail the pics to Picasso and keep an eye on our bait?"

"I may not be quite as skilled as you, but yeah, I think I can handle it." She rolled her eyes.

"All this and sarcasm too."

"No need to be condescending."

"But you're so easy."

Hank grinned, and Sophie realized she'd been had. She laughed. "Go. Geez."

After the three of them piled into Hank's rental, Sophie sent the photos to Picasso, then roamed the farmhouse, trying to decide what to do with herself. She'd never been good at waiting. But she wasn't dumb enough to go out when her picture was plastered all over the news either.

She checked on Laszlo, who'd wolfed down the sandwiches they'd offered like he hadn't eaten in a week and was now snoring on Hank's single bed down the hall.

She texted Picasso: **Anything on the list of castles connected to Prince Felix?**

Picasso texted back: **I'll get to that as soon as I get the photos sent. Stand by.**

Thanks, Sophie sent back, duly chastised. Admittedly, her mind had glazed over earlier during Picasso's exposition on the technical magic involved in locating Laszlo's blackmailer—and his family, to get them out of harm's way.

She poked around in the refrigerator, made herself a sandwich, then went back to studying the portrait. She turned it face up. This third portrait depicted only Johanna and Katharina, both of them wearing the ducal hats and smiling, heads close together. Had either Prince Benedikt or Princess Johanna realized the firestorm these portraits—and his plan to change the laws of succession—would cause?

A few minutes later, the laptop pinged with an e-mail from Picasso, confirming she'd found where Laszlo's mother and son were being held and Scoop was on his way to free them, as soon as his plane from London landed. Then she'd sent the doctored pics, ostensibly from Laszlo's cell phone, along with some kind of techno-genius, untraceable, tracking thingamajig attached, embedded or whatever.

A car turned into the gravel driveway. Sophie grabbed her cell phone and a kitchen knife and sprinted into the living room. She peeked through the white sheers and spotted three police cars. She muttered a curse as one of the local cops Camille had photographed at the encampment climbed out of his car. He marched toward the door, Eloise Cuvier beside him, both with their weapons drawn.

What was Interpol doing here? Was Eloise working with these cops?

The other officers climbed out of their vehicles and stood behind their open car doors, weapons trained on the cottage.

Sophie grabbed the painting and raced to the rear bedroom and shook Laszlo's shoulder. "Wake up. Now. We've got company." He snapped awake and shot up from the bed, then jammed his feet into his shoes. At least he didn't ask questions before jumping into action.

She poked her head out the kitchen door, looked in both directions. "Stay behind me." She leaped down the three steps and raced across the lawn and into the cornfield, the back of the painting facing out so it wouldn't get scratched.

Lazlo stayed right behind her as she zigzagged down the rows. She tried to memorize their route but quickly got disoriented. She hoped the way back would become clear later. For now, she just wanted to put as much distance between them and law enforcement as she could. They needed Laszlo for their plan to work.

A figure stepped out of the tall stalks and Sophie stopped short at the shotgun aimed at her middle. Laszlo slammed into her from behind, grunting in surprise.

The woman narrowed her eyes and held a finger to her lips in a "quiet" motion.

Sophie froze, her mind scrambling for a way out.

46

Laszlo's eyes were wide as they met hers. Sophie eased the painting under one arm and shifted her weight, ready to kick the shotgun away.

"Stay behind me unless you want the police swarming you like fleas on a dog," the farmer's wife barked. She lowered her weapon, turned, and marched back the way she'd come.

Sophie gripped the painting in both hands as they hurried after the woman.

Several minutes later, they emerged in a clearing. Sophie recognized the outbuildings of the neighboring farm.

The sturdy woman looked both ways before she crossed the open area and led them around the back of the largest barn. Double wooden doors that reminded Sophie of a storm cellar were built into the ground and secured with a rusty padlock.

The woman pulled a key from her pocket, opened the lock, and wrestled the heavy doors open. Concrete steps disappeared into the cellar below. She jerked her head, indicating they should climb in.

Was this a trap?

"Why are you doing this?" Sophie asked.

The sounds of men shouting as they searched the woods were getting closer.

The woman's eyes narrowed. "You want help or not?"

When you put it like that . . . Sophie nodded her thanks and indicated Laszlo go first. The woman handed Sophie a flashlight, and she followed Laszlo into the pitch blackness inside.

"I'll come back and get you after they're gone."

Flashlight held in her teeth so she could protect the painting, Sophie descended into the root cellar, shining her light around the eight-foot room.

The dirt walls were braced with wooden shelves filled with dusty canned goods. She stepped closer. Some of the dates were twenty years old.

Above them, the door closed with a thud. Sophie's heart skipped a beat as the lock clicked shut. She set the painting down, then turned off the light, Laszlo's panting loud in the silence.

"Are you okay?"

He cleared his throat. "I have never been a big fan of enclosed spaces."

"You're not going to freak out and start screaming, are you?"

"No." He paced the small area. "But I hope we won't be here long."

Sophie rubbed her arms to combat the chill in the damp air. "Me too."

The silence grew heavy, except for Laszlo's shallow breathing. She needed to distract him. "How did you get sucked into all this, anyway?"

He didn't answer for a long moment, pacing and panting. "I am a history professor, from Hungary. I also wrote articles for a website that wasn't always, how do you say it, complimentary of the government. They told me to stop, but . . ." He pulled in a deep breath. "One night I came home and our building was on fire. Someone had set a bomb in our apartment. My wife died trying to save our son." She heard him pace some more. "It wasn't safe there anymore, so I took my son and my widowed mother and used my contacts to get us into Germany."

Sophie sensed anger, frustration, and grief churning behind the matter-of-fact words. The silence lengthened again and she waited, curious if he'd tell her the rest. At least he'd stopped gasping for air.

"I'd found work washing dishes in a restaurant, and we were living in a small hostel while I searched for better work. I saw an ad for someone with a history degree to research artwork for a prominent family, with room and board provided. It sounded like the perfect opportunity. When I called, I was told to bring my family to the interview, to see if we were a good fit." Bitterness coated his tone.

"Next thing I knew, I'd been told to get the paintings—no matter what—or my family would die." He swallowed hard. "Based on what they did to the man who had the job before me, they will do exactly what they said." She heard him step closer, felt the desperation pouring off him in waves. "I don't know what I'll do if they kill my son."

"We'll make sure that doesn't happen." Sophie meant those words with every fiber of her being. She just prayed she could make good on them.

"White van on the move," Picasso said into their comms. "Get back on Grünwalder Strasse and you can tuck in behind them."

"Do you never sleep, woman?" Hank asked.

"I'll sleep when this mission is over. Unless you don't want my help?"

"Yes, we want your help," Camille said. "Don't listen to Hank. She woke up on the wrong side of the world a decade or so ago."

"Shows what you know. It was fifteen years."

Hank maneuvered into position, several car lengths behind.

"If you don't hang back farther, they'll spot us," Camille grumbled, snapping pictures of the license plate.

Hank glanced her way. "You do your job and let me do mine, okay?"

"I'm just saying."

"Stop saying."

"Ladies. They're turning," Mercy said from the backseat.

They were in a different car, but they weren't taking any chances on being recognized. Camille tied a colorful scarf over her hair and added big dangling earrings, while Mercy pulled on a ball cap, as did Hank, to go with their ratty band T-shirts and jeans.

Instead of heading toward the encampments, the van sped away from the city. Mercy leaned forward between the front seats to help scan the area. Where were they going?

After thirty minutes, traffic had essentially trickled to nothing, and Hank had to hang back even farther to avoid being spotted. Then the road started curving into the mountains, and within minutes the rolling hills turned into narrow switchbacks.

"This is fun." Mercy gripped the door handle as Hank attacked another sharp curve. "Not."

Hank glanced at her. "You gotta puke? Out the window, or you're cleaning it up."

"You mean you don't want it down your neck?" Mercy raised a brow, smirked.

"Eww. Stop, you two." Camille groaned.

They came around another sharp bend and Hank muttered a low curse.

"What?" Camille straightened, peering ahead.

"I lost them again."

"Are you sure?" Mercy asked.

"Yes, I'm sure." Hank checked her phone. "I can't find the GPS tracker we planted. Picasso? Can you track them?"

A pause, then, "Negative. I've got nothing. Don't know if they found it or it malfunctioned."

"There are no lights ahead so they must have turned off somewhere. I'm going back." Hank spun the car in a tight U-turn.

47

Sophie made small talk, trying to keep Laszlo engaged, but as the minutes dragged by, his rapid breathing got worse again.

"Take some deep breaths, okay? If you hyperventilate and pass out, I'm going to leave you here in the dark."

She felt him stiffen. "You wouldn't."

"Wouldn't I?"

"You talk tough, but you wouldn't."

She shrugged. "Maybe. But don't push me. You need to chill."

"Will she come back?"

Sophie tried not to think about the click of the padlock as the woman closed it before she left. "I hope so. Preferably alone too."

"As encouragement goes, that isn't helping very much."

Sophie chuckled. "I suppose it isn't."

"Who are you people? You don't strike me as cops."

"We're not."

"What then?"

Sophie thought about Speranza and their long and secret history. "We're just trying to help a friend, that's all."

"You have a tech wizard helping you."

"Nothing wrong with having crazy-smart, talented friends, is there?"

Laszlo's pocket lit up and a buzzing sound filled the cellar. She'd returned his phone to him, and as he pulled it from his pocket, his eyes widened at the text. "You sent him the pics while I was sleeping? What about my family?"

Sophie held out her phone. Showed him the message from Picasso. "They're safe."

He reached for the phone with shaking hands, studied the text, then slowly exhaled. "You're sure? You're absolutely sure they're both safe?"

"Yes, I'm absolutely sure." She pocketed her phone. "And yes, we sent the pics. You looked very dead, by the way. What did he say?"

He cleared his throat, then read the text aloud. "'You, whoever you are, are already dead, you just don't know it yet. Nobody double-crosses me.'" Laszlo grinned. "He also said three million was the most he was willing to pay for the paintings and that was final."

Sophie smiled. "Perfect. Did he suggest a meeting place?"

Laszlo nodded and held out his phone so she could read the message.

"Let's let him stew a bit before we send him *our* choice of meeting place."

"Is that a good idea?"

"We want to make him nervous, let him worry that maybe he doesn't hold all the cards."

More panting. "Where are we going to tell him to meet?"

Sophie had no idea. Yet. But she—and Speranza—would figure it out.

Camille gasped and grabbed for the dashboard as gravel spit under the tires, mere inches from the steep drop-off.

"Jesus, take the wheel," Mercy muttered, crossing herself.

"You'd better hope I've got it too," Hank muttered, yanking the car back onto the road. "See if you can find where they turned off."

They went silent, focused on the dense forest surrounding the car.

"There. Maybe." Mercy pointed.

Hank backed up on the deserted road and studied the dirt track that led off the straightaway and disappeared into the forest. She turned onto it and stopped. They climbed out, studied the ground.

"I think this is it. Those tire tracks are from a heavy vehicle. Let's go."

Hank followed the tracks, driving partially off the road whenever possible to avoid the soft areas.

After several hundred yards, she turned off the headlights, and Camille held a flashlight out the window. It still made them visible, but not quite as much.

The dirt track eased off to the right and dead-ended abruptly in front of a rock face.

"Now what?" Mercy asked.

Hank turned off the engine and grabbed her own flashlight. "Let's check it out. Keep the beams hidden as much as possible."

They walked toward the rocks, following the tire tracks, using their hands to shield most of the light.

When they reached the rock wall, they stopped abruptly.

"This makes no sense. Where did they go?" Mercy asked.

Hank stepped up to the wall. "See if you can find a seam in the rock." She aimed her light to the left, checking the area in a sweeping motion.

"You think this is some kind of tunnel?" Camille shone her light on the right side.

Mercy spun in a circle, checking the surrounding trees. "Uh-oh. Hey, guys?" She aimed her light into the trees, right at a security camera facing the rock wall.

A rumbling noise started deep in the mountain.

"We need to go. Now!" Hank spun for the car, Camille and Mercy hot on her heels.

48

Sophie couldn't wait any longer. Laszlo was roughly 2.5 minutes from a full-blown claustrophobic meltdown, and she didn't have the energy to keep calming him down. Besides, her own panic was rising. Was the farmer's wife really trying to help them? Or would she open the door and hand them—and the painting—over to the cops and Interpol?

While Laszlo paced, she ran her hands along the cellar doors. They reminded her of the storm cellar in *The Wizard of Oz*. She turned the flashlight on under the hem of her dark T-shirt and used the meager light to search the cellar. She spotted a couple of three-foot-long metal stakes, probably used for vegetables or something, and slid one between the doors, trying to wedge it open. The angle wasn't right and she couldn't exert much force with the rod over her head.

"Stop pacing and help me."

He hurried over.

"Grab two more of those stakes."

He nudged her aside and shoved all three into the narrow slit and then put his entire body weight on the rods. The double doors heaved upward several inches, but the padlock held. He tried again. And again, his arms bulging from the effort.

"Take a break," Sophie said, and he dropped the rods, breath heaving.

She used her covered flashlight to judge their progress, but not only was the lock holding, neither of the wooden doors showed any signs of giving way.

Wait. What about the hinges? Sophie looked closer. "Yes!" She worked one of the rods under the edge of the hinge until she created a small gap. "Give me a hand here."

Laszlo instantly understood. Together they pried the hinges off one side of the door.

It took both of them to slide the heavy door to one side without making a racket. Sophie squeezed through the opening and motioned Laszlo to hand her the painting and follow her out. They slid the door back into position and hurried around the side of the barn.

Sophie stopped short when she heard the farmer's wife speaking to someone. Laszlo was still panting, but he worked hard to quiet his breathing. She peeked around the corner of the building and spotted the woman talking on a cell phone.

"Ja, I found the Fräulein I saw on the television. The art forger. She had one of the paintings. For the reward money, I will tell you where they are."

Sophie nodded to Laszlo, and they hurried back the way they'd come and then sprinted into the woods and disappeared into the cover of the trees. Behind them, they heard more shouts as the woman flagged down the officials. It was only a matter of time before they started searching the woods.

Heart pounding, Sophie led them deeper and deeper into the trees, then sent a quick text to Picasso, asking her to call in another tip and send the police on a wild-goose chase somewhere else.

Minutes dragged by as they waited, poised to run, but finally— finally—they heard sirens and squealing tires as the police took off. *Thank you, Picasso.*

Sophie waited another ten minutes before she led them to the cottage by a circuitous route. As they reached the back door, Sophie whispered, "Don't turn on any lights."

She told a sweat-drenched, exhausted Laszlo to get some sleep, then she pulled on another disguise and settled into a chair by the window to wait for the team to return.

Hank, Camille, and Mercy took off running as the rock wall shook and a portion of the rock face began to open, revealing a dark pit like the mouth into hell.

They ran back to their car, and Hank spun it in a tight circle before Mercy got her door completely closed. It swung open again from the force of the motion, and Mercy almost slid out with it. Camille reached over the seat and grabbed her arm with one hand and the door handle with the other, pulling both to safety a split second before Hank stomped on the accelerator and they raced back to the highway.

"White van, coming in hot," Hank muttered, glancing in the rearview mirror.

"Can you lose them?" Camille asked.

"Have to. Unless you have a better idea?"

"Actually, I might." Camille rooted around in her tote, pulled out a lighter and what looked like a fistful of paper. She rolled her window down. "Keep driving at the same speed, but be prepared for some noise." Two at a time, she lit fuses and tossed firecrackers out the window.

The van's brakes screeched as it swerved to avoid them.

Hank's grip tightened on the wheel with every bang. Camille kept lighting and tossing, lighting and tossing, until the headlights fell farther and farther behind.

Mercy leaned over the front seat as the speedometer climbed steadily. She looked back. "What did you do to this car?"

Hank shrugged, loosened her death grip on the wheel. "Made a couple necessary adjustments."

Camille snorted, then shook her head as she rolled up the window. "Of course you did. And we love you for it." She checked the side mirror. "They can't keep up."

Hank nodded and kept her foot steady on the accelerator. She drove all the way into Munich, then doubled back and headed south, toward the cottage.

The night was quiet as they headed for the front door.

"Nice driving, Hank." When Mercy touched her arm, Hank spun away but stopped before reflex kicked in and she grabbed Mercy's throat. Mercy nodded and Hank shrugged. It was progress. Sort of.

Inside, they found Laszlo asleep on the couch, snoring softly. Sophie sat in the armchair opposite, head propped on her fist, also asleep.

Camille poked her in the shoulder. "Wake up, Sophie. No time to sleep."

Her eyes flew open and she popped out of the chair, blinking rapidly, trying to get her bearings. "You guys okay?"

"Yeah. Now." Hank filled her in, then hitched her chin toward Laszlo. "We had a little more excitement than you two, apparently."

Sophie propped her hands on her hips. "I wouldn't say that, exactly." She told them about the police and Interpol's visit, the mad dash through the cornfield, and getting locked in the neighbor's cellar.

By the time she got to the part about the farmer's wife calling in Sophie's description, Mercy's eyes were wide and Hank shook her head.

Camille scowled, then glanced at her watch. "That means we don't have much time to plan. Where are we meeting this scumbag?"

"We need to figure a way inside the cave to rescue the women too," Mercy said.

An hour later, they crashed for a few hours of shut-eye, the bare bones of a plan to do both in place.

49

Just before nine the next morning, Sophie crossed the drawbridge over the swampy-looking moat surrounding Burg Rosen. Not as touristy as Burg Eltz or some of the other nearby castles, this one nevertheless offered guided tours with costumed docents and had volunteers strategically placed within the giant stone fortress.

She mentally reviewed the castle layout the team had pored over just before dawn, reconciling the map with the reality. Adrenaline hummed through her body, as it always did before a "performance," but she plastered a bored expression on her face and merged into the crowd of costumed reenactors converging on the courtyard before breaking off to their various duty stations. There were servants and lords and ladies, musicians and entertainers like herself.

Her sword clanked against her leg as she walked, the court jester's hat in place, white paint covering her face. She had a colorful drawstring bag slung over her shoulder, filled with everything she might need.

Hopefully, it was enough. "Heading in," she murmured.

"Right behind you," Camille answered. "Heading for my lady's chambers."

"I'm in the chapel," Mercy answered, "headed for the main house."

Sophie heard the clank of metal on cobblestones before Hank said, "Got my cart and potions to sell set up in the courtyard."

They'd had to wake Simone, Sophie's costume designer friend, in the middle of the night to score the costumes they needed, but Willa's generous donation to the theater's next play had assuaged Sophie's guilt.

Now all they had to do was hope Picasso's research had sent them to the right castle.

And hope Sophie could find whatever it was the clue pointed to.

And hope that led to Lise.

And that she was still alive and they could rescue her in time. *Please, God.*

And that they found the missing women too.

Easy-peasy.

"Though knights confer and jesters prance, the rose of silence tells no tales." She mentally repeated the clue as she crossed the courtyard and started up the stairs to the Knights' Hall on the second floor.

Under whitewashed plaster framed in dark timbers, the slate floor of the large, high-ceilinged room would be slicker than ice if it got wet. Which was why straw was strewn here and there. Personally, she'd have put down more area rugs, but she wasn't in charge of that.

Draped above a fireplace so large she could easily stand inside, a huge banner with a coat of arms embroidered on it stretched halfway across the room, complete with crossed swords above it.

The banquet table was oval. Not quite the knights of the Round Table, but close. Twelve heavy, dark wooden chairs with faded crimson velvet seats ringed the massive table.

She turned in a slow circle and spotted what she'd been looking for.

There, above the door, were two symbols: the red rose of silence and the jester's pointy, colorful hat.

Back when the knights met here, those symbols represented pretty radical ideas, but ones they took seriously, from what she'd learned. The rose of silence was the medieval equivalent of "What happens in Vegas, stays in Vegas." The knights vowed anything discussed under that symbol was confidential. No exceptions. No mercy.

The other symbol, though, was fairly rare. Jesters weren't among the upper class and were often considered stupid. But this symbol meant that in this room, any and all opinions were not only welcomed, but they carried equal weight. No dumb ideas. No class discrimination.

The concept definitely appealed to Sophie.

"Anything?" Willa asked in her earpiece, and Sophie pulled herself sharply back to the task at hand.

"Working on it," she murmured. No one was in the room yet, so she peeked behind the coat-of-arms banner. She hadn't thought it would be that easy. Or that obvious.

She worked her way around the room, checking under each chair and the table, then under the uncomfortable-looking sofa in front of the fireplace, then between and under the matching chairs. Nothing.

A massive desk stood in one corner, but all the drawers were empty. A quick check underneath and behind every drawer didn't yield any hidden compartments either.

Voices sounded in the hallway, which meant the tourists would arrive soon. She was running out of time.

Where would someone hide something in this room? She sighed. This would be so much easier if she knew what she was looking for. Another painting? She checked behind each one, not surprised that nothing was here but what was expected. They looked like cheap reprints you could buy online, and after a closer examination, she confirmed that's all they were.

Now what?

The rose and jester symbols were along the ceiling above the fireplace and over the entrance to the room. They were painted on the wall, so there couldn't be anything behind them.

She studied the room again, then pulled open the door to the original "water closet" and grinned. Talk about a risky proposition. The small alcove was suspended out from the castle wall. There were two holes cut into the board as seats, one larger than the other, depending on the person's size. You did your thing and it dropped down the side of the exterior wall. Just make sure you chose the right size hole so you didn't fall through yourself. Yikes.

Sophie shut the door and moved to the long buffet against one wall. It, too, was empty, but there was a niche carved into the wall above it, containing a bronze vase. On the curved wall inside the niche, the rose and jester symbols were also painted on the plaster. They were so small she hadn't seen them at first. She reached in to move the vase, but nothing happened. She tugged harder. She studied it a moment, then pushed it farther into the niche, instead of trying to pull it out.

It slid free of the notch holding it in place.

Sophie lifted the vase out and gaped at the square opening beneath it.

Footsteps sounded in the hallway outside.

She stuck her hand into the fairly large hole and pulled out a wooden box. Excitement hummed along her nerve endings as she pulled a bobby pin from her hat and made short work of the small lock, then flipped the lid open. Her anticipation dimmed when she riffled through a rather innocuous stack of papers. Just to be sure, she unfolded the first, then the second. Her heart picked up speed as she realized what she was holding. Underneath was a cloth bag. A quick peek inside and she sucked in a breath.

It wasn't what she'd expected at all, but it was exactly what she needed. She reached for her bag to secure the box just as a male voice said, "I'll take that, if you please."

The barrel of a gun poked her in the back.

Camille hurried downstairs and into the kitchens on the lower level, a small cloth bag with her supplies over one shoulder. She was dressed like a lady-in-waiting, which meant she would have had access to most of the house. She attended her mistress in the family chambers, but also personally saw to her mistress's needs. It provided the perfect cover.

"Where are you going?" an older woman demanded, setting out the bread and rolls she'd be showing the guests.

Camille kept her back turned, hand on the door. "Going down to the storage area. They told me there's a candelabra I'm supposed to bring to the third floor."

"You have a flashlight? They didn't bother with electricity down there."

Since a portion of the castle was still occasionally occupied by descendants of the original owners, certain sections had electricity. Others, not so much.

Camille shivered and pulled the flashlight from her skirt pocket. "Got it, thanks."

According to Picasso's research, the kitchen level, which would normally be a basement, had another level or two below it, set deep into the hillside. From what they could tell, some of it was used for storage, while the deeper levels had probably been either hidey-holes or led to tunnels or passageways to escape invaders. And let's not forget the dungeons to torture your enemies.

Important advantages during the whole medieval fighting-over-land thing.

She flicked on her light, then shut the door behind her and suppressed a shiver. It was cold and damp and the circular stone steps reminded her of the haunted houses she'd run screaming from as a child. There was no handrail, and the steps were wicked slippery, so she held the light in her left hand and ran her right along the wall as she wound down into the belly of the castle.

"Mercy, where are you?" They were supposed to go down together.

Silence.

"Can anyone hear me?"

Still nothing.

"Probably the thick stone is blocking the signal or whatever," she muttered.

There was no sound but her footsteps, and the stairs felt like they went on forever. She'd gone much deeper than just another level down. Had she missed a doorway or something?

No. She hadn't missed anything. *Trust your instincts. Even in a creepy castle.*

Where was Mercy? Had something happened to her?

When the stairs finally ended, Camille's legs were shaking, but she'd made it. Good thing she'd worn hiking boots under her costume.

"I'm at the bottom." Even if she couldn't hear them, hopefully the team could hear her.

She reached a wooden door just like the one up top and eased it open and peeked around the corner. It led into a narrow stone corridor, lit with caged lights along a low ceiling, like they used in mines. She paused, hearing what sounded like hammering.

She turned left, toward the sounds of activity.

50

Sophie tried to ignore the gun barrel pressed against her spine as she glanced over her shoulder. "Hello, Heiko," she said calmly, so the team would know what she was dealing with. "Fancy meeting you here."

Blond, sixtyish, and paunchy around the middle, the last time she'd seen him he leaped off a bridge in Venice, trying to steal the painting. He must have followed them somehow. His kind, grandfatherly face seemed at odds with the weapon jammed against her kidneys.

"How do you know my name?"

"Oh, everyone knows your name by now. Didn't you know? You've been all over the news. They discovered the stolen portrait of Princess Johanna hanging on the wall in your home."

He poked the gun into her back again, harder. "It wasn't even the real thing. It was a forgery, completely worthless," he spat. "I risked—" He cut off the rest of what he'd been about to say.

Sophie kept her tone conversational. "You did see the news, then. Yeah, that's so unfortunate. They want to talk to you about

Henri's murder, too, by the way." Fury surged at that, but she wouldn't let him see it. "You might want to lie low for a while, you know? Give everything time to blow over."

"Hand over the box." He jabbed the gun into her back again.

While they'd talked, she'd transferred the box to her left hand. In one fluid move, she dropped to the floor and set the box down, then sprang up and rammed her elbow into Heiko's throat.

He stumbled backward and fell, the gun clattering to the stone floor while she spun out of reach. She drew her sword, glad she'd added it to her costume.

He scrabbled toward the gun, but she used the tip of her sword to slide it out of reach, then was caught off guard when he leaped up in a fighting stance. She sidestepped to avoid his fist, but the blow glanced off her cheek and pain radiated across her face.

As she struggled to regain her balance, he slammed into her, almost knocking the weapon from her grip.

She tried to spin away, but he grabbed her foot and she winced as she hit the slate floor. Feet sliding on the slippery stone, she reached him just before he scooped up the gun.

She had to remember this was not the regulated battle of her fencing studio. This guy was a street fighter. She leaped onto his back, stretching past him for the gun, but he bucked her off and she immediately rolled to her feet.

Before she could get her bearings, he'd ducked his head and rammed her midsection, forcing all the air from her lungs. Her sword slipped from her fingers as she dropped to the floor again, gasping for air.

She had to get that gun. She lunged forward and tackled him around the knees. Cursing, panting, they rolled across the floor, fighting for control of the weapon. Sophie straddled him and finally wrestled it from his grasp.

Before she could get away, he flipped her over, pinned her down, and pounded her hand against the floor, pain radiating up her arm.

Desperate, she groped around with her free hand and almost sighed with gratitude when her fingers touched her sword. Her hand closed over the hilt just as he wrested the gun from her and leaped up.

She rolled to her feet and lunged toward him, determined to put an end to this. Voices, young and old, rang out in the hallway. Tours were starting.

He grabbed the blade of her sword and shoved her backward with it, propelling her into the heavy sideboard. Pain shot through her hip, but she ignored it as she reached for the box.

Bellowing with rage, Heiko knocked her aside with his shoulder, grabbed the box, and ran out the door. She rushed after him, one hand on her sore hip.

A group of elementary-age children swarmed into the room, blocking her exit. They saw her sword and froze. One of the boys said, "Oooh. Are you going to fight the other man?"

Sophie stopped and grinned lazily, despite her panting. "I am. Cool, right? You guys have fun." She ran out the door and scanned the hallway in both directions but didn't see him. "Heiko's got the box and is heading out of the knights' dining room," she muttered into her comm device. No response.

Left or right? She followed her gut and went left.

Mercy arrived at the kitchens, frantic and out of breath. She'd heard Camille say she was heading down, but she got caught by a family of Czech tourists and had finally managed to break free of their questions. The heavyset woman setting up the cooking display scowled.

"Another one? What do *you* want from the storeroom?"

Mercy shrugged and wouldn't meet her eyes. "I'm looking for a prayer book they said is supposed to be in the chapel."

The woman's kerchief quivered as she shook her head and planted her hands on her ample hips. "You have a flashlight?"

Mercy blanched as she checked her pockets. "I did."

Muttering unflattering German words about foolish people, the older woman pulled a small flashlight from her skirt pocket and tossed it across the room. Mercy leaped forward and grabbed it before it hit the floor.

"Be careful," the woman warned, then turned away as several people entered the room. "Welcome to the castle kitchens."

Mercy switched on the light and stepped through the doorway. When it closed behind her with a solid thump, she automatically crossed herself. Her childhood had taught her to hate dark, enclosed spaces. She took a deep breath for courage. "I'm heading down. Can you hear me, Camille?"

No response.

"Can anyone hear me?" She waited.

"Okay, then. I'm on my own." She started down the circular stairway and immediately lost her footing on the mildewed steps. Arms flailing, she managed to stay on her feet, but she had to slow her pace significantly.

Her prosthetic-wearing leg was not happy by the time she reached the bottom. She rubbed her hip as she eased the door open and peeked up and down what looked like a narrow mine shaft. Another shiver passed over her skin. Which way had Camille gone?

As she debated, a faint banging sound reached her. She tucked the flashlight into her pocket and set off in that direction.

"Camille? Can you hear me?"

Still no response.

She hadn't gone far before a figure slipped out of a side tunnel and blocked her path.

Sophie slipped around the gaping children and their annoyed teacher and ran down the hallway. At the next corner, she glanced right and left. Tourists clogged the corridor, but she spotted Heiko's blond head not far down the hall and sprinted after him.

"Excuse me, pardon me, so sorry," she murmured, weaving around the guests.

"Well, hello, jester," a balding, fiftyish American drawled, gripping her arm to stop her progress.

Sophie spun out of reach, then placed the tip of her sword right under his neck. "Don't."

The people with him laughed.

His hands flew up, palms out. "Sorry, just kidding. Geez."

"Never funny to grab a woman." She slid her sword back into its sheath and kept going.

"What's your name, honey?" he called after her.

If she had time, she'd stop to wash off the man's slimy implications, but she had more important things to do. She raced down the hallway, glancing into each room, trying to figure out where Heiko had gone.

As she ran past the largest bedchamber, she peeked inside. Movement in the corner caught her eye and she reversed direction, peering around the door. Sure enough, Heiko stood in front of the open doors of a gigantic wardrobe, one that would have done C. S. Lewis's Narnia stories proud. Unless she missed her guess, he'd just put the box into one of the drawers.

She drew her sword again, tiptoed up behind him, and poked him with her blade. "I'll take that back, thanks."

This time, when he spun and tried to knock her sword away, she was ready. She leaped out of reach, then leaned forward and knocked the gun out of his hand before holding the tip of her blade against his neck. "I wouldn't move if I were you." She shrugged. "Just a suggestion."

"You can't kill me."

She raised a brow. "Can't I?" She pressed the blade forward, just a smidge. A trickle of red slid down his throat.

"You cut me, you worthless—"

"*Tut, tut.* Not nice to call me names."

He scowled but didn't say anything else.

"Slide the weapon toward me with your foot, slowly, or things will get worse, fast."

They faced off for a minute before he ever so slowly complied.

She trapped the gun under her boot. "Now turn around, hands behind your back."

Sophie kept the sword at his back with one hand while she rooted around in her colorful jester-appropriate bag for the zip ties. She retrieved the gun before she sheathed her sword. "Unless you want to be shot with your own weapon, you'll hold still."

She used her body weight to keep him pinned against the wardrobe while she secured his hands, then she swiped his feet out from under him and bound them before he could react.

The unmistakable sounds of the children's group chattering and laughing as they headed their way sounded from outside the room. She reached into her pack again and tied a bandana around his mouth, then stood him up in the wardrobe and secured his bound wrists above his head.

"In case you were thinking about screaming at this point, I wouldn't if I were you." Two quick tugs and his pants and boxers pooled around his ankles.

He tried to shout behind the gag, but she simply raised an eyebrow and closed the wardrobe doors, making sure they were securely latched. Then she added a zip tie for good measure.

Ten more seconds and the kids would be in the room.

Sophie grabbed the box and ran, hiding in the only other spot available. The "comfort room."

Inside, she made sure the covers over the holes were in place before she stepped onto the board they were cut into. She tucked the box into her pack, pulled out her rope and grappling hook, and secured the line around her waist with a carabiner.

The sound of excited young voices got louder.

She opened the largest seat cover, secured the grappling hook, and then wiggled through the opening, squirming a bit to get the backpack through.

With the speed of long practice, she let out the rope and rappelled down the side of the castle.

Halfway to the ground, she heard, "Whoa. The poop just falls right through the hole."

She glanced up and waved at two young boys peering through the openings like a pair of raccoons, grinning with delight.

A finger to her lips, she grinned widely, then picked up speed and slid the rest of the way to the grassy area below the castle wall. She unhooked the rope, glanced back up with another wave, and took off running.

51

Hank stepped from the shadows and scowled at Mercy. "You look like you're gonna puke. What happened?"

"Nothing. It's just a long way down." She rubbed a hand down her thigh, trying to ease her cramped muscles.

Hank's eyes narrowed. "Your leg okay?"

"I'm fine. Let's go."

As they walked down the narrow tunnel, following the banging noises, Mercy asked, "Do we know what's going on down here?"

Hank shrugged. "Not yet, but whatever it is, someone has gone to a lot of trouble to keep it secret. Picasso's still digging."

Mercy rubbed her arms over her habit against the chill. "Have you seen Camille? The earbuds don't work down here."

"We'll find her."

Mercy eyed the other woman. "Is there ever a time you're not utterly confident? Never the teeniest bit worried about anything?"

Hank stopped, shot her a cheeky grin. "Fake it till you make it, baby."

"It's really starting to tick me off."

Hank grinned and said, "Deal with it, Sister," as she kept walking. "Let's find Camille before she stumbles into a mess."

"Have you known—?"

Hank yanked her into a side tunnel and clapped a hand over her mouth just as two men in black walked by, carrying rifles.

They waited in silence for several minutes before Hank whispered, "Let's go," and they set off again.

———

Last night, Mac had followed the police to the cottage, surprised to see Eloise with them. Had she figured out Robin Hood's identity? Why else would she be there? He had pulled up in the wooded area nearby and settled in to wait. It wasn't long after Eloise and the police left in a flurry of slammed doors and frustrated muttering that the little sedan returned, with three women inside. Sophie wasn't one of them.

When they went inside, he slipped up next to the house. He peeked between the window frame and the old-fashioned roller shade and spotted Sophie with the other women. But that wasn't what surprised him. The young guy who'd been chasing the paintings was there, too, as they sat around with laptops and maps. Were they working together now?

Despite his desperate need for sleep, Mac went back to his car and kept watch the rest of the night. He wouldn't risk them leaving without him.

Though he had his own agenda for coronation day, he felt compelled to keep an eye on Sophie. Whether she realized it yet or not, she was an integral part of all of this. Which put her directly in the line of fire.

He was scrubbing a hand over his face the next morning, desperate for coffee and frustrated that he'd dozed off, when the four women left the cottage. He followed them, surprised when they got out of the car at Burg Rosen, all dressed like medieval reenactors.

Why this particular castle and not one of the many others in the area?

Without a costume, he had to wait outside the gate until it opened for business.

Once it did, he made his way to the ramparts and the walkway around the top of the castle wall, wandering among the tourists, constantly scanning the courtyard below. With that ridiculous jester's hat, Sophie should have been easy to spot.

Except he couldn't find her.

The moat only went partway around the castle, ending at a gravel road that led into the hillside behind it. He'd read that the castle inhabitants had shot burning arrows onto their enemies from this vantage point. As a means of defense, he figured it was pretty effective.

A flash of color caught his attention. He glanced down and spotted Sophie running across the grassy area directly below the wall, heading toward the castle's back entrance.

But that wasn't what stopped his heart.

It was the gun in the hand of the man chasing her.

The man raised his arm and fired.

Sophie stumbled but kept going.

Mac spun around and raced toward the stairs.

When a bullet whizzed by her ear, Sophie was so surprised she almost fell flat on her face. How had Heiko gotten free? And where had he gotten another gun? She had his tucked in the small of her back.

She scooped up her hat and glanced over her shoulder as she ran. Who the heck was that? It wasn't Heiko. And they'd left Laszlo safely hidden at the cottage.

Another shot spit grass and dirt in front of her feet. She picked up her pace. "Got a shooter on my tail, guys. Little help?"

No response.

Finally, Picasso's voice. "Copy that. The comms must not work in the tunnels. The others haven't been answering."

"Good to know," Sophie said, panting. "But not what I wanted to hear."

She sprinted around the corner of the wall and up the stairs that led to the back entrance of the castle. A group of men were unloading wooden tables and dozens of elegant carved chairs from the open back of a delivery van. No doubt there was a wedding or some other fancy-schmancy event on today's schedule.

She stepped around them and slipped back inside the castle. "Picasso, you said they went down through the kitchen?"

"Yes. Be careful."

"Always." She put her hat back on and hurried down more steps, dodging tourists.

A young girl asked for a selfie and Sophie fidgeted impatiently when her mother insisted on endless retakes because "the lighting is terrible in here."

"Sorry, ma'am. Gotta go," Sophie said after the sixth "last one."

In the kitchens, she skidded to a stop behind a group of Canadian tourists who were snapping pictures of the cook and the items displayed in front of her, politely asking questions about her history lesson.

Sophie hurried to the stairwell door and eased it open. "Can you lock this behind me?" she asked the woman, leaning around the gathered crowd.

The cook marched over and looked her up and down. "What's *your* excuse for going down there?"

"Pardon me?"

The woman crossed her arms. "The other two both gave me some namby-pamby, made-up reason."

Relieved to know the others were in place, Sophie played a hunch. "I'm with them." She met the woman's eyes. "And I'm being chased."

The woman studied her a long moment, then tugged up the

sleeve of her blouse, exposing the Speranza medallion on her brace-let. She waited.

Sophie met her eyes, shrugged. "I'm new."

Another pause. "I'll make sure no one follows you."

"Thank you."

"Ma'am? You were saying?" one of the tourists asked.

"Hold your horses," the woman barked over her shoulder.

As Sophie headed into the darkness beyond the door, the woman handed her a flashlight. "That's my last one. Go."

After last night, Sophie was loath to trust the woman's un-expected help, but she was out of options. She had to trust the emblem. She thanked her and ducked into the stairwell. Absolute darkness surrounded her, and she fumbled to turn on the flashlight.

Outside the door, she heard a cultured male voice demand, "Open this door. Right now. Do you know who I am?"

Sophie pressed her ear against the wood, but she couldn't hear the woman's answer. It didn't matter anyway. She had to find the team.

And then they had a coronation to stop at a nearby castle.

She glanced at her watch as she hurried down the stairs.

They were almost out of time.

52

Hank and Mercy slowed their pace as the banging grew louder and a bright glow indicated they were nearing the end of the tunnel. They pressed their backs against the stone as they inched along, keeping to the shadows.

"Let go of me!" someone shouted. "What do you think you're doing?"

"Found her," Hank muttered.

They peeked around the corner. Two camouflaged guys had a tight grip on Camille, who was tugging and squirming and trying to wrench free.

That wasn't good, but it wasn't what made Hank's blood turn to ice.

Beside her, Mercy peered into the storeroom and made the sign of the cross. Twice.

The missing women were lined up against the storeroom's outer wall, on their knees, hands behind their backs, guarded by two men Hank recognized from the encampments.

Several feet away, two more men were assembling large wooden shipping crates that looked too much like coffins for Hank's peace

307

of mind. The fact they weren't wearing masks added another layer of worry.

"I'm going to check it out," she whispered to Mercy and slipped into the storeroom in a crouch.

Mac hurried down several staircases, desperate to find either Sophie or the man chasing her. He stopped to listen every few yards but couldn't make out any running feet below the hum of excited children and tourists.

He rounded another corner of the basement level, peeking in doorways as he passed.

"Do you know who I am?"

Mac grimaced. He'd found one of them, at least.

He entered the kitchen. "Prince Moritz. What brings you here?"

The group of tourists perked up at the word *Prince* and cell phones and fancy cameras started whirring and clicking.

Moritz whirled on them. "Put those away," he snapped and most of them hurried to obey.

"I thought you'd be at the royal residence, getting ready for your son's coronation." Mac glanced at the blue blazer over the prince's casual slacks and collared shirt. The gun tucked at his back was obvious under the jacket.

"I had some business to attend to first. What are you doing here?"

Mac smiled cordially. "Playing tourist, actually. I've never been here, but the online reviews are excellent. Since I'm already here, I'm happy to help, if you'll tell me what you're after. Extra hands and all that." He glanced around the kitchens. "I'm sure you don't want to be late for the coronation."

Moritz's smile was strained. "It's really nothing to worry about. I have it well in hand."

Mac inclined his head. "As you wish. I'll see you at the coronation." He walked out the kitchen door and then stood in the hall to listen.

"Open this door," the prince barked at the cook.

"I'm sorry, sir, but that area isn't open to the public. It leads to a storage area."

"I am not the public. Open. The. Door."

"I would be happy to help you, sir, but I don't have a key to it. I just work here."

A long, strained silence followed.

"You will regret this," Moritz growled, his heels beating a sharp staccato on the stone floor.

Mac slipped down the corridor and hid in a small alcove. Once the prince marched past his hiding place, he returned to the kitchen.

The ample woman was well into her spiel again, displaying cooking tools. She scowled as Mac approached. "What now?"

He kept his back to the tourists and whispered, "Did you let a blonde woman dressed as a court jester through?"

The woman's eyes flickered, then her chin came up. "There's nothing but a storage area down there."

"Please. I'm trying to help her."

She propped her hands on her hips and studied him. It was the same look his mother had used when he was a child. "What's the snooty guy that was just here after?"

"He's who I'm trying to protect her from." Mac paused. "Is there another way to reach the storage area besides this staircase?"

"At least two others. But this one is faster."

"Will you help me? It's urgent."

After another stare down, the woman slipped a key from her apron pocket and opened the door. "I don't have any more flashlights, so you're on your own. Hurry up. And don't let me live to regret this."

Mac thanked her as the door closed and locked behind him. The darkness was absolute. He fumbled for his cell phone flashlight and started running, sliding on the slippery stone.

Moritz's presence confirmed his involvement in the cover-up, and if Mac's hunch was correct, his son, Felix, wasn't far behind.

Mac had to find Sophie. Fast.

53

When Sophie reached the bottom of the stairs, she forced herself to stop and think before she raced out the door. She had to be smart or she wouldn't be any good to anyone. Especially Lise.

The moment she spotted Prince Moritz chasing her with a gun in his hand, she'd known without a doubt that Lise was still alive. Otherwise, what would he be doing here on the day his son was to be crowned the new prince of Neuhansberg?

Lise was a loose end he wanted tied up. Permanently.

Sophie tightened her grip on the sword at her side. They'd have to go through her first.

She eased the door open and peered up and down the dimly lit tunnel. She heard banging and started in that direction, hoping the team was already there. If not, she'd do this alone.

When a side tunnel appeared, she ducked inside, shone her light around. It dead-ended about twenty feet in, a pile of rubble indicating a previous cave-in. Perfect. She pulled off her backpack and hid the box under a pile of loose rocks.

She hurried back into the main tunnel, keeping to the shadows as she moved closer, one hand on the hilt of her sword. The gun was tucked into the waistband of her pants, though she hoped she wouldn't have to use it. She was an excellent shot, but she hated guns. Go figure.

When she reached the end of the tunnel, she peered into the large storeroom and let out a huge breath. The missing women were alive. They were being held at gunpoint, but they were alive. She'd be back to free them in just a little while.

She had to find Lise before Felix's coronation.

She heard a female shout and hurried into the cavernous room, then crouched behind rows of what appeared to be whiskey barrels. From there she ducked behind the waist-high metalwork counter that ran the width of the room.

"Let. Them. Go!"

Sophie briefly closed her eyes in relief when she heard Lise's voice. *Thank You, God.* Not only was her friend alive, she was shouting like Charlton Heston raging at Pharaoh in the old *Ten Commandments* movie.

A man laughed in response, and the hair on Sophie's neck stood up.

"A truly inspiring performance but, in the end, worthless." A brief pause, then, "Stop that racket!"

Sudden silence filled the room. Sophie inched her way to the end of the counter and risked a quick peek around the corner, getting her first up-close view of the speaker. It was none other than Prince Moritz, Prince Benedikt's brother and father to Felix, the son slated to be crowned prince of Neuhansberg in just over two hours. But not if Speranza could help it.

Moritz propped his hands on his hips, annoyance dripping from every pore of his body. Sophie scanned his crisp blazer, noting the gun hidden at his waist.

"You have caused me no end of trouble."

Lise and Nadine stood side by side, each with a black-clad guy behind them, rifles aimed at their backs. Sophie stifled a low growl at the bruises on Lise's face, the bandage soaked in dried blood wrapped around her shoulder. The growl deepened. Nadine had also been beaten, badly.

Several feet away, two other guys had a grip on Camille, who kicked and struggled, eyes scanning the storeroom. When they made eye contact, Camille flicked her glance to the side. Sophie couldn't see Hank and Mercy but took that to mean they were nearby.

Felix hadn't arrived yet, but Sophie expected him anytime.

Better act now. She stood and raised her voice to be sure everyone heard. "Too bad the guy you sent to kill Lise was such a failure." She stepped closer so they were face-to-face, hands rock-steady on the gun aimed at the prince's torso. She tsked. "All this could have been avoided."

Moritz calmly turned in her direction, yanking his own gun out, cold indifference in his eyes. "You're the one who killed that worthless excuse for a man?"

She kept her eyes on Moritz, shrugged. "Someone had to. I was tired of him chasing me around Europe while I was trying to find my friend." She cocked her head. "I'm curious, though. Why do you want the portraits? You don't strike me as the sentimental type."

"Drop your weapon."

"You drop yours." She smiled sweetly as she said it, trying to buy time for Hank and Mercy to do . . . something.

Without warning, Moritz spun around and grabbed Lise. Before Sophie could blink, he held her in front of him like a shield, gun pressed to her temple. "I don't like repeating myself," he warned.

Sophie held her arms out, weapon pointed toward the ceiling. "How about a trade? You let my friends here go, and you can have me. Seems like a good deal. I'm younger and a whole lot prettier." She raised an eyebrow and winked.

Sparks flew from Lise's eyes. She tried to shake her head but couldn't manage it with the gun pressed to her temple. Sophie got the message. She ignored it.

When Moritz looked between the women, Sophie kept talking. She wanted his attention on her. "Where's my money, Prince? We made a deal. Three million for the portraits."

There was a pause and a speculative light came into his eyes. "You're not here for your friends. Or the money. You found the treasure," he growled, eyes alight with certainty. "Hand it over. All of it, or she dies!" he roared.

Sophie figured he planned for Lise to die regardless, so she kept her eyes focused on his, voice deliberately calm, almost indifferent. "Not until you let my friends go."

"I want the portraits too."

"You can have them. Once I get my money. Now let them go."

"Father!" a man shouted from the opposite side of the room. "What are you doing here?"

All eyes turned in that direction, including Moritz's, as almost-Prince Felix hurried toward them.

Sophie lunged toward Lise, but Moritz yanked her out of reach, tightening his grip.

"You should be at the palace. Why are these women here?" Moritz's fury rose with every word. "What have you done?"

"I could ask you the same thing." Felix pointed at Lise.

"I've been trying to protect your birthright," Moritz shouted. "While you've been dragging the royal house of Neuhansberg into the gutter."

Felix paled slightly, then his jaw firmed. "Don't go all high and mighty on me, Father. This is just business. Doesn't look like your hands are clean either."

While they squabbled, Sophie met Lise's eyes and nodded. Lise let her body go limp and dropped to the floor, the sudden shift forcing Moritz to loosen his grip or be pulled down with her.

Nadine dropped as well, while Camille kicked one guard in the groin and another square in the chest, sending him careening into the wall of shelves behind them.

She disappeared. Within seconds there was a hissing sound and smoke started billowing in front of the counter.

Thank you, Camille.

Several women screamed.

"Run!" Sophie shouted, positioning herself between Moritz and Lise and Nadine. "Everybody hide!"

Felix took advantage of her momentary inattention and leaped forward, knocking her gun from her hand. It slid across the counter and vanished into the smoke.

"You won't get away with this." He reached for her with one hand, raising his firearm with the other.

"With what? Freeing the women you kidnapped?" She spun and hopped up onto the long metal counter, slid her sword from its scabbard, and lunged toward him, knocking his weapon aside. It, too, disappeared in the smoke.

His hands clenched as he leaped onto the counter, searching the smoky room for his minions. "I'll see you in chains before the day is over. Don't you know who I am?" His voice rose with every word.

From the corner of her eye, she saw Camille hustle the women out of sight, into the smoke. Several loud thumps accompanied by male cussing told her Hank and Mercy were busy too.

Eyes steady on Felix, she used her blade to force him back one step at a time, ever closer to the edge of the counter. "I think you're a bully and a coward, and the only thing you're going to do today is get yourself arrested. I've heard kidnapping is a major no-no with law enforcement types."

Felix propped his hands on his hips and laughed. "You have no idea what you're talking about. I had nothing to do with this. And while your antics have been amusing, I'm tired of the game." He checked his watch. "I have things to do."

In a lightning-quick move, he slid a knife from his sleeve and lunged toward her. Sophie leaped out of reach, jumped onto a whiskey barrel, and spun out, kicking him square in the chest.

He grunted as the force knocked him backward, arms pinwheeling as he fell off the counter.

Sophie launched herself on top of him and landed on his chest, knocking the breath out of him a second time. While he was wheezing and gasping, she rolled him over, grabbed two zip ties from the stash in her bag, and secured his hands and feet.

She leaned over and whispered in his ear, "Looks like you won't be crowned today after all."

"You won't get away with this," he gasped.

"Oh, I'm pretty sure I just did." She patted his shoulder and stood. The smoke cleared enough for her to make out Moritz aiming his weapon at Lise's back.

"Lise! Look out!" Sophie leaped across the two steps that separated them and used her sword to knock the gun from his grip. She moved closer, waving her blade sharply back and forth as he tried to grab it.

A knife suddenly appeared in his free hand, and he sliced upward with the blade, nearly knocking her weapon from her hands. What was it with these guys and knives? The clang of metal on metal vibrated up her arm as they fought. For a puny guy nearing seventy, he was a lot stronger than he looked. He lunged; she parried. She spun, lunged again.

He tried to stab the knife into her neck.

"I can't believe you caused your sister-in-law's death all those years ago," Sophie taunted.

There was a split second of hesitation before he lunged again. "I did no such thing."

Back and forth they went, neither giving an inch.

"The fact you're here says otherwise."

"No one will prevent Felix from becoming prince. I've been protecting my son's birthright."

"By trying to have the real heir killed?" she scoffed. "I'm pretty sure every law enforcement agency on the planet will take exception to that. And to your son kidnapping women for some nefarious purpose."

"You have much to learn about how the world works, little girl."

Sweat dripped into her eyes and mixed with the smoke, temporarily blinding her. As she swiped her eyes with her arm, pain slammed into her upper thigh. He'd cut her.

"Right back at you, Your Highness." She whipped her sword up, and the tip sliced through his shirt and across his chest.

He sucked in a gasp of pain as he looked down at the streaks of red. The fury when he met her gaze warned her a split second before he lunged with the knife again. She tried to spin out of reach, but she wasn't quite quick enough. The blade sliced her left side in a wide arc.

The sudden rumble of an engine reached her just before a four-wheeler raced into the room and slid to a halt between her and the prince, Hank at the wheel.

Hank rammed the vehicle back and forth, but the prince managed to duck around it and head toward Sophie again.

When he raised the knife and lunged, Sophie tightened her grip on her sword and stepped into position, ready to attack. The crack of Mercy's whip exploded through the air, and the knife was snatched from Prince Moritz's grasp. He screamed and dove after it.

Sophie leaped forward and caught him before he could get to his feet. She tucked her sword under his chin, pressed the blade just far enough to draw blood. "You tried to kill my friend."

Fury darkened his eyes. "She should have died years ago. My son is the rightful heir."

Sophie applied a bit more pressure. He deserved to die for what he'd done.

"Don't, Soph. Please," Lise said, from somewhere behind her. "He's not worth it."

Sophie saw the moment Moritz decided to act. His fingers tightened around his knife and his arm stiffened in preparation.

"Do it and I'll run you through."

Before he could throw the knife at Lise, Sophie jabbed the tip of her sword through his forearm, pinning him to the stone floor. He howled in agony, struggling to escape, but she kept the pressure on.

Mac stepped up beside her, his gun aimed at Moritz. "You can let go, Sophie. He's not going anywhere."

She narrowed her eyes, then withdrew her weapon. Mac pulled a bandana from the pocket of his pants and crouched next to Moritz, but Mercy took it from him and nudged him aside. She tied it around the wound, looked over her shoulder at Sophie. "Nice work."

Moritz stopped sputtering and cursing long enough to say, "You're a nun. You're supposed to be nonviolent."

Mercy merely raised a brow. "Didn't Jesus clear the trouble-makers from the Temple with a whip?"

Once Mercy got the bleeding under control, Mac looked over his shoulder at Sophie. "You okay?"

She nodded, her heart still racing from the adrenaline. She checked her thigh, annoyed at the blood, pulled a scarf from her bag, and tied it tight. *Good gravy, that hurt.* Her side was bleeding, too, but didn't throb nearly as bad. "I'll be fine."

"What are you doing here?" she asked.

He stood. "Saving your butt. What do you think I'm doing?"

"I had it under control." She scanned the room. Hank climbed down from the four-wheeler as Mercy coiled her whip and Camille gave orders. "Actually, we all did."

"Yeah, you did." He looked around. "Where's your friend?"

Sophie turned and spotted Lise through the last of the curling smoke, her injured shoulder in a makeshift sling while she spoke to the group of women, who huddled against the far wall, safely out of the line of fire.

"I'm so glad you're alive," Sophie murmured as she reached Lise, wrapping her in a careful hug.

"Thanks for coming to get me." Lise pulled back to meet her eyes. "They told me you wouldn't believe I was dead." She nodded to where Nadine stood next to Camille and Mercy.

Behind them, the rest of Felix's men had been disarmed and secured with more zip ties. Hank stood over them, a weapon in each hand.

"I knew you weren't. I would have felt it." She glanced down at Lise's dirty bare feet, the red polish chipped and ragged. She grinned. "And because you absolutely hate blue nail polish."

At Lise's quizzical expression, Sophie decided she'd tell her about the innocent homeless woman who'd been killed later. No doubt also at Moritz's command.

First, they had to worry about the living. She glanced at the beautiful young women, nausea churning at their physical similarity to each other. "Do you know what this was all about, besides the obvious?"

"Felix was obviously involved since he showed up here, but I never heard his name mentioned. Only that their 'benefactor' had provided a storage location for the 'product,' before delivery." Lise's eyes flashed with fury.

Sophie looked past her to where a glaring Prince Moritz was secured to a support pole, makeshift bandage around his forearm.

"What did any of this have to do with the paintings?" Lise glanced from Moritz to Felix and back.

Sophie led her friend to a crate, sat down opposite, and chose her words with care. "Did you read your mother's letter?"

Lise shook her head. "I haven't been able to, not yet."

"I understand, but I think you'll want to. Eventually. For now, brace yourself." Lise looked wary and Sophie took a deep breath. "I have proof that your mother was actually Princess Johanna's personal secretary. Johanna was still alive when your mother arrived at the crash site, and Johanna asked her to take care of you, to save you. Werner was already dead. You are Katharina, the real heir to the throne of Neuhansberg."

Lise's eyes widened in disbelief and she sagged and nearly slid off the crate. Sophie motioned to Nadine, who sat on Lise's other side.

"That can't be true," Lise whispered.

"It is. The woman who raised you—your mother, whose real name was Ilse Krause, by the way—came up with the clues and then hid the paintings, planning to retrieve them later. But then she got sick and couldn't go back to get them. The clues were her backup plan, so you'd be able to find them if something happened to her. I think she contacted you when she heard that Prince Benedikt planned to pass the crown to Felix. She wanted to tell you."

Lise covered her mouth with her hand. "Only I didn't go, so she tried to come to me and died on the way."

Sophie pulled her in close while silent tears slid down Lise's cheeks. "You didn't cause the heart attack, Lise. And your mother had no way of knowing what kind of chaos the paintings would create. I think Prince Moritz figured out you were Katharina—you do look a lot like Princess Johanna when she was younger—and wanted you out of the way to be sure Felix became the ruling prince of Neuhansberg."

"I believe Princess Johanna's car accident was orchestrated by Moritz," Mac added, joining them.

Lise gasped and Mercy crossed herself as Nadine, Hank, and Camille came over and stood beside them.

"I know it wasn't an accident," Sophie said. "The box I found today includes proof. There are photos of the vehicle. Um, after. I'm guessing Ilse had brought a camera with her that day, probably to take pictures of Johanna and the children."

Lise still looked shell-shocked. "The princess was my mother?" Tears filled her eyes, but then she swiped them away. "I'm not royalty. I–I can't be. I have more important things to do than go to balls and teas."

"Not something you need to think about right now, certainly. The coronation obviously won't happen today," Nadine said.

Lise suddenly stood, swiped the tears from her cheeks. "We need to get these girls out of here. Immediately."

Mac stepped forward, pulled out his phone. "No signal down here. I'll head up and call the police."

Sophie waited until he was out of earshot, then looked at the team. "I need to grab something, then we'll head out."

She hurried back into the tunnel and went straight to the side shaft. She dug through the rubble and pulled out the box, then turned around and froze.

Mac stood in the opening, blocking her exit. "I'm afraid I'll need that box."

Sophie tightened her grip on it. "No. This belongs to Lise."

"You said it contains proof of the accident. That's what Prince Benedikt hired me to find, along with the paintings."

"I figured that's who you were working for." She'd known he

was after the paintings, but accepting he'd simply been using her still stung.

"He deserves to know the truth about what happened to his wife and son."

She couldn't argue with that. "And he will, eventually. The police will sort it out."

Mac held out a hand. "I need the box now, Sophie. Before the police get here. Don't make this harder than it needs to be."

Her chin came up and everything inside her stilled as his expression hardened. "Or what?"

"Or I tell Interpol where to find Robin Hood."

Sophie refused to so much as blink as she felt a chasm open beneath her feet.

Their eyes locked as they stared each other down.

One minute. Two.

Finally, he huffed out a breath, rammed a hand through his hair. "Look, if I deliver the paintings and the proof to the prince today, before the coronation, the money he's promised will pay for my mother's cancer treatments."

Of all the things she'd expected him to say, that wasn't one of them. She studied his face, searching for a telltale flicker or sign of deception. "How do I know you're not lying to me?"

"You don't." One side of his mouth kicked up in a roguish grin. "But why would I make something like that up?"

She thought about Lise, about the additional proof contained in the box, about Lise's true identity. She had to protect her friend.

Sophie sorted through her options, eyes steady on his. Finally she said, "There's only one way this can work for both of us. We schedule a meeting with the police, Prince Benedikt, Lise, and Lise's lawyer, and we show them all three paintings and what's in the box so everyone sees it at once. That way, you get the money for your mother, the police and the prince get the proof they need about the crash, and everyone sees the proof of Lise's identity, which will help protect her."

Mac looked at his watch. "The coronation deadline is in less than an hour."

"I'll need more than that to get the paintings. We'll meet at the gallery in four hours. You call Prince Benedikt and tell him you need more time. I'll call Detective von Binden." She paused. "There is one more thing. Any mention of Robin Hood to Interpol or any other police agency and the deal's off."

"Who's Robin Hood?" he quipped, then he sobered. "You have my word." One corner of his mouth curled up. "Besides, we make a good team. I'd hate to mess that up."

Sophie rolled her eyes as she hurried back the way she'd come, the box tucked in her jester's bag.

Mac returned to the storeroom several minutes later. "The police will be here shortly, along with medical and counseling professionals."

"We need to go," Sophie said to Lise. "I'll see you at the gallery later."

"I don't understand. The police will want to talk to you, all of you."

Sophie met Nadine's eyes, then smiled at her friend. "I'll explain later." She glanced at Mac, who'd taken over guard duty from Hank. "See you in a couple hours."

He winked. "Wouldn't miss it."

She started walking, then turned back and glanced over her shoulder. "One more thing. Be sure the police check the wardrobe in the Knights' Hall." She pulled the key from her pocket and tossed it to him.

At Mac's puzzled look, Sophie laughed, then turned and followed Camille, Hank, and Mercy. They climbed the endless stairs, relieved when the cook answered their knock. She slapped them all on the back, grinning as though she'd personally orchestrated the whole rescue.

Several minutes later, Team Speranza slipped out the back of the castle just as the police and paramedic units pulled up in front.

EPILOGUE

"You don't need me here," Sophie said for the umpteenth time. She stood in Lise's office and peeked through the doorway to where far too many people were studying Sophie's paintings like it was their job. Any minute now, someone would call her bluff and state the obvious, that the paintings were terrible. It was the story of the emperor's new clothes all over again. Only this time, she was living it.

"I'm going to throw up," she muttered, snatching a glass of water from Lise's desk and gulping it down.

Lise took the glass and turned Sophie to face her. "No, you're not. Not with that killer dress. Take a breath, Soph. You faced down armed men without blinking. Why is this freaking you out?"

Sophie started pacing. "That was different. That was for you. For Nadine. For the missing women. It wasn't about me. But this . . ." She waved a hand. "I don't do spotlights." She shuddered. "Certainly not without a disguise."

Lise turned Sophie back toward the open doorway, where people were smiling as they pointed and little SOLD signs were starting to appear at the bottom of her paintings. "Your talent is amazing, Sophie, and not just for copying artwork, although that is nothing short of incredible. Let me celebrate you tonight. If you need a reason, do it for me. Let me thank you for everything you did, for never giving up."

"You could have just bought me a cake."

Lise shook her head and grinned. "There are some people here to see you. Time to stop hiding and get out there."

Sophie rubbed a hand over her galloping heart, told herself not to hyperventilate.

"Will you relax? It's not a firing squad."

Feeling like her shoes were encased in cement, Sophie followed Lise into the gallery, which was more crowded than before. What were all these people doing here, for crying out loud?

She snagged a glass of white wine from the refreshment table and turned. "You clean up nice, Hank."

The other woman snorted and tugged at the lapels of her fitted jacket before she helped herself to cheese and crackers. Sophie hid a smile when she spotted the combat boots under the navy slacks.

"These paintings aren't bad," Hank muttered around a mouthful of food. "Who knew you could do more than dress up and wave a sword around?"

"That's high praise coming from Hank," Camille said, joining them. She looked like a runway model in mile-high heels and a formfitting white dress that showed off her olive skin to perfection. She kissed both of Sophie's cheeks. "Girl, this show is amazing. I love the bold colors in your paintings, especially the landscapes." She pointed behind her. "Though the city scenes are a wow too." She sighed. "I can't decide which one I want. Every single one draws me in, makes me feel like I'm right there, standing inside the painting. You have an incredible gift."

"That's what I just said," Hank grumbled.

Sophie glanced past them and swallowed hard. Willa and Scoop had flown in from New York and were talking with Lise, who had just attached a SOLD sign to the Rialto Bridge love locks painting they were standing in front of. Even with Lise's hounding, it had taken Sophie weeks to decide which paintings to display. She felt like a parent with a favorite child but had to admit her Venice collection held a special place in her heart.

Mercy stepped up beside Sophie, wearing a prim collared dress and sensible pumps. "I'm so freaking proud of you, Sophie. I'd love to have even a thimbleful of your ability. Add the fact you're giving all the proceeds to Neue Anfänge, and I like you even more."

Sophie ignored the heat rushing over her face. "It's for a good cause. Excuse me." She hurried toward Amalia and Nadine, who held Sam in her arms, smiling widely as Sophie crossed the room and hugged them both.

She turned, surprised to see Laszlo crouched down beside his son, gesturing toward one of the paintings, his mother standing beside them, the boy's hand in hers. Sophie patted Laszlo's shoulder as she walked by and sent him a quick smile.

She rejoined Hank, Camille, and Mercy just as Willa, Scoop, and Lise joined them. Willa gave her a hug, then held out a small wrapped present. "We wanted to give you this."

Sophie looked from one to the other as she opened it, seeing the smiles on all their faces. Inside was a Speranza medallion on a sterling silver chain.

"Will you officially join us, Sophie?" Willa asked. "Help us right wrongs against women and children?"

She swallowed an unexpected knot of emotion. "I'd be honored. Thank you." She took the medallion and turned to Lise, who fastened the chain around her neck. "To be part of this is—"

"Enough with the gushing," Hank muttered. "Hottie. Incoming."

Their laughter faded into the background as Sophie looked over her shoulder. Her heart stuttered as Mac approached, looking better than any man should in an immaculately tailored black suit and crisp white shirt.

"Hi."

"Hi, yourself." The group drifted away, and she found herself standing alone with him. "Didn't expect to see you here tonight."

"Didn't you?" He glanced around the room. "Your work is impressive, Sophie. It utterly captivates." He sent her a teasing grin. "And since I make a good bit of my living evaluating art, I should know."

She nodded, unsure how to respond.

"How are the girls doing?" he asked as the silence lengthened.

"Good. Lise and Nadine have been working nonstop to help them get on their feet, build a future."

"Those ladies do good work."

Sophie smiled. "Yes, they do. I heard the crooked cops were blackmailed into helping, so their sentences will be lighter."

He nodded at her necklace. "Is that new? Looks familiar somehow."

She tucked it inside her neckline. "It was a gift." Speranza didn't need an investigator doing any unauthorized wondering. "How is your mother?"

"She's started the treatments, and so far the side effects aren't too bad. Appreciate you asking." He paused. "Are you free for dinner tomorrow night?"

"Oh. Ah." Her heart pounded. "I don't know."

He raised an eyebrow. "It's dinner. Not a lifetime commitment. Say yes."

She paused, then sent him a flirty grin. "Maybe. I'll let you know." She looked over his shoulder. "Excuse me."

Prince Benedikt came into the gallery, the two men behind him obviously bodyguards. He stopped just inside the door and studied the paintings, then came directly to Sophie and kissed both her cheeks. "It will be an honor to have some of your work hanging in my home. I cannot thank you enough for all you did to secure the paintings and give me the greatest gift of my life." He looked at Lise for a moment, then cleared his throat. "You gave me back my daughter, and I will be forever grateful."

Sophie smiled. "It was my pleasure. Lise, I mean Katharina, is worth everything to me."

The prince's eyes glowed as Lise approached and kissed his

cheek. Since they'd been reunited, he stood straighter and his overall health had definitely improved.

He nodded at the stunning emerald choker and matching earrings Lise was wearing and smiled. "Does the fact you're wearing your mother's jewelry mean you're ready to give me an answer?"

He wanted Lise to step into his place and let him retire, but she'd told Sophie she wasn't ready for that.

Lise smiled, patted the choker. "My answer is still the same. Not yet." The choker was just one part of the treasure everyone had tried to get their hands on. Lise's mother, Irmgard, had hidden the priceless collection of Princess Johanna's family jewelry in the bottom of the wooden box, along with the proof of Lise's identity, which the princess had begged her to do before she died.

Sophie wandered away to let them talk, astonished to see yet more SOLD signs on her paintings.

Gripping her medallion, she munched on a cracker and returned to the security of the Speranza Team, who stood together in one corner of the room.

It took a moment to recognize the woman from the castle kitchens, but when she did, Sophie laughed and hugged her.

She was proud to be part of this network of women who helped other women. Who righted wrongs and got things done. Things that really mattered.

Robin Hood had found her very own band of merry men—or rather, women.

Much later, after the party ended, Sophie returned to her apartment feeling a wee bit flushed with success—or maybe that was the champagne Lise had opened at the end.

Sophie studied the painting she'd finished just that morning and nodded, satisfied. It would fit perfectly next to the portrait of her family. The spires of the majestic Cologne Cathedral reached for the heavens, each detail of the iconic church exquisitely rendered. In the expanse of blue sky between the towers, she'd painted:

I believe in God, even when He is silent.

She'd never have all the answers to her parents' deaths, but this motto was enough. She smiled, then slipped into black jeans, a black shirt and jacket, and pulled a watch cap over her head. On her way out the door, she pressed a kiss to the painting of her parents.

Robin Hood had one more thing to do tonight.

Rain beat on her hooded jacket as she wound her way around the city and let herself into Heiko's house. He'd been arrested for Henri's murder and would spend the rest of his life in jail. But Sophie had read an article that outlined why he'd been after the paintings. His wife, who was indeed Princess Johanna's cousin, was dying and desperately wanted one of the paintings.

The original portraits had all been returned to Prince Benedikt, of course, who'd promptly given the third painting, titled *The Future* and depicting Lise and Princess Johanna, to his daughter.

Tonight, though, Sophie tiptoed down the hall and peeked in at Heiko's sleeping wife before she returned to the living room. She unwrapped the copy of *Today* she'd painted and took a moment to study Lise and the smiling faces of the rest of the royal family, forever frozen in time. It seemed appropriate to leave a copy of the portrait that had started it all. She hung it on the wall, made sure it was straight, and then let herself out.

As she reached the street, she caught movement in a doorway across the way. Mac stepped from the shadows and shot her a grin and the now-familiar two-fingered salute before he turned and walked away.

Sophie hid a smile as she turned in the opposite direction, fingering the medallion around her neck.

Halfway home, her phone buzzed with a text from Hank:

Camille's got trouble. Team Zoom call in an hour.

Sophie picked up her pace, adrenaline shooting through her.

She was officially part of Team Speranza—and she couldn't wait to see what came next.

A Note from the Author

I love adventure stories, especially those involving treasure hunts and secret societies. Add in a castle or two, and I'm hooked. But a few years ago, I realized that too often, women were mainly supporting cast. They weren't the ones saving the day and changing the world. So I started dreaming and imagining. What if there was a team of strong, flawed, compassionate, determined women who make a difference in this world, especially by helping other women? What if they were part of a centuries-old, women-only secret society whose symbol and name meant *hope*? All those what-ifs became *The Crown Conspiracy* and the Speranza Team.

During my research, I came across the phrase *"I believe in God even when He is silent"* and it grabbed me by the heart. In my own life, I've had to wrestle down those silences. Believing He is always there is the foundation of my hope, my anchor. I tried to find the author and discovered the phrase is part of a longer poem, with different variations. It's also a choral arrangement. Most believe it was written during WW2, but where and by whom isn't clear, with attributions ranging from the wall of a concentration camp, a tunnel in Cologne, a Warsaw ghetto, to a basement wall of Cologne Cathedral by a child hiding from the Nazis. I've fictionalized that last theory for the purposes of this story.

While the Speranza Team is fictional, I believe it exists in spirit. Women have always banded together around common causes and used their gifts and talents to help other women and make a difference in this world. These informal teams have always been about hope, shining light in the darkness. Keep linking arms, ladies, wherever you are in the world. What you do matters, in big and small ways. And if you're not part of a Speranza Team, I encourage you to take the risk and either join one or build your own. It's totally worth it.

Until next time . . . *Speranza*.
Connie Mann

Acknowledgments

Authors may work in isolation, but it takes a whole team to get a book out into the world. I am so thankful for every single person who helped me turn this idea into a published book.

My thanks to Leslie Santamaria, my amazing friend and longtime critique and brainstorming partner. She's the woman who walks me off ledges and always knows what I meant to say—and then helps me say it much better.

Thanks to my agent, Ali Herring, who championed this story from the moment she read it. Thank you, Ali, for everything.

Many thanks to the entire team at Tyndale House Fiction, especially Acquisitions Director Stephanie J. Broene, who fell in love with this story and the characters the same way I did. Thank you for taking a chance on me and this story and making the publishing process go so smoothly. Thanks to Elizabeth Jackson, line editor Julee Schwarzburg, and the eagle-eyed copyeditors for all the spot-on input that made this story better. Huge thanks to Sarah Susan Richardson for designing the amazing cover. Also, heartfelt thanks

Andrea Martin, Wendie Connors, and every single person at
Tyndale who has worked so hard on my behalf.

Thanks to my writer friends Lena Diaz, Jan Jackson, Caro
Carson, Susan Meier, and Jenna Kernan who've offered endless
encouragement along the way.

Thanks and love to my fabulous hubby, aka my biggest cheer-
leader, who keeps the household running when I'm in writer mode.

My heartfelt thanks to you, dear readers, for joining me on
another adventure. I couldn't do what I do without you. Thanks
for purchasing and recommending my books and spending time in
the worlds I've created.

And last but never least, bottomless thanks to the Great Creator
Himself, who gives the gift of stories and invites us to share them
with the world.

Discussion Questions

1. Do you see yourself in any of the Speranza Team members? Which one's flaws or strengths do you most relate to? Do you have a favorite character?

2. Does Sophie's epiphany surrounding the words *"I believe in God even when He is silent"* resonate with you? How do you cope with God's apparent silence at times in our lives?

3. Making friends and becoming part of a team requires risk and putting yourself out there. Have you taken the risk and had it work out great? What about when it didn't?

4. Once you get past the awkward making-friends stage, what's the best part of having friends and being part of a team? How do you keep your friendships alive and thriving?

5. Sophie is passionate about righting wrongs and returning stolen artwork to its rightful owners as Robin Hood. Do you agree with her thinking? Why or why not?

6. Sadly, women getting kidnapped, trafficked, or sold into slavery isn't a new problem. Have you considered what you can do in your corner of the world to help keep women safe?

7. "Trust, but verify" is one of Sophie's mottos. She's surprised to learn the Speranza Team follows it as well. How do you balance this idea in your own life? Do you trust easily? How do you verify if someone is trustworthy? Have you ever been wrong?

8. When have you banded together with other women to make a difference, maybe through your church or a local or international organization? If you aren't part of a team now, where could you start looking for one?

About the Author

Connie Mann loves taking readers on heart-pounding, suspense-filled adventures featuring strong, determined women who fight for what they believe—and for those they love. When those stories take place in exciting locales and include a tempting hero, so much the better. She is the author of *The Crown Conspiracy*, an adrenaline-fueled adventure where an expert art forger must team up with a mysterious women-only secret society in order to rescue her best friend—and save a country. Connie's other titles include the Florida Wildlife Warriors series, the Safe Harbor series, *Angel Falls*, and *Trapped*. She has won several writing awards, and Amazon declared *Beyond Risk* an Editor's Pick.

Connie is also a USCG-licensed boat captain, and when she's not writing, "Captain Connie" gets to introduce Florida visitors and students to dolphins, manatees, and other coastal creatures, which is as much fun as it sounds like. She is also passionate about helping women and children in developing countries break the poverty cycle and build a better future for themselves and their families.

She and her husband love spending time with family and friends and heading off to explore new places, especially those involving water and boats. Visit Connie online at conniemann.com and sign up for her newsletter for all the latest news.

CONNECT WITH CONNIE ONLINE AT

conniemann.com

Ahoy and Welcome!

Thanks so much for stopping by! I hope you'll come back often and sign up for my newsletter (form below), so you'll never miss the latest book news and giveaway opportunities.

Like most of you, I wear many hats. Besides being a romantic suspense author, I'm also a USCG-licensed boat captain and an advocate for women and children in developing countries. I'm a wife, mom, traveler, nature lover, believer, and hit-or-miss fisherman. (Hubby says we're great at fishing, but lousy at catching.)

I've wanted to write books since I penned an epic story about my hamster in the third grade. I'm the kid whose mother took my books away on vacation so I would actually spend time with my family.

My current Florida-set romantic suspense series centers around the Tanners—a family of tough Florida law enforcement officers. Book 1, **BEYOND RISK**, is sister Charlee's story. Publisher's Weekly called **BEYOND RISK**, "...charming, exciting, and thoughtful...the strong sense of place and exciting action make this worth picking up."

Book 2, **BEYOND POWER** is brother Josh's story and is available now. Book 3 is in the works, so stay tuned. Or read the fun novella in the **TURN THE TIDE** Anthology.

I also had a blast writing the **SAFE HARBOR** books, a Florida-set romantic suspense series featuring three foster sisters. Book 1, **TANGLED LIES**, introduces boat captain Sasha and book 2, **HIDDEN THREAT** tells environmentalist sister Eve's story. Mysterious and shadowy sister Cat's story, **DEADLY MELODY**, wraps up this fun, heart-pounding series. I'd love to hear what you think of the Martinelli sisters.

After 24 years near Ocala, Florida, hubby and I recently relocated to the Atlantic coast. I loved showing students and guests from around the world the beautiful Silver River. Now I'm captaining for the Marine Discovery Center and having a blast showing guests this lovely area and its amazing dolphins and other

OR FOLLOW HER ON

@ConnieMannAuthor

@captconniemann

@Connie_Mann

CP1966